THE CHAIN GARDEN

The chain garden: linked circular beds bright with summer colour present a charming picture unless you understand the coded language of flowers...

Guilt-ridden at the number of men dying in her father's tin mine, Grace Damerel works hard to help the village's bereaved families while caring for her frail mother and preparing for her brother's homecoming. The arrival in Treworthal of Edwin Philpotts, a former missionary, ignites a dramatic sequence of events that brings to light long-buried secrets, but what is the reason for Edwin's return to Cornwall and how will Grace respond to his shocking confession?

THE CHAIN GARDEN

THE CHAIN GARDEN

by

Jane Jackson

Magna Large Print Books
Long Preston, North Yorkshire,
BD23 4ND, England.

British Library Cataloguing in Publication Data.

Jackson, Jane
    The chain garden.

    A catalogue record of this book is
    available from the British Library

    ISBN   978-0-7505-2785-9

First published in Great Britain in 2006 by Robert Hale Limited

Cover illustration © Ben Turner by arrangement with
P.W.A. International Ltd.

Published in Large Print 2007 by arrangement with
Robert Hale Ltd.

Magna Large Print is an imprint of Library Magna Books Ltd.

Printed and bound in Great Britain by
T.J. (International) Ltd., Cornwall, PL28 8RW

This book is dedicated to Daphne,
with gratitude.

Acknowledgements

To Mike, as always. And to three Janets,
without whom...

Chapter One

Grace flicked hopefully through the envelopes arranged on a silver tray. Glimpsing foreign stamps and her brother's familiar scrawl her heart leapt as she seized it. *Thank God.* She sped up the wide staircase and along the galleried landing to her mother's room.

Propped against lace-edged pillows fragrant with lavender, Louise Damerel, lily-pale in frilled peach gauze, was sipping tea.

Grace held up the envelope. 'At last, Mama. A letter from Bryce.'

Thrusting the cup at her daughter Louise held out a fragile hand. 'Quick, give it to me. Dear Lord, I've been so worried.'

Moving a water glass and three enamelled pillboxes Grace set the cup on the bedside cabinet, then sat at the foot of the big bed and smoothed faint creases from her long skirt.

'They did warn us about the primitive postal system,' she reminded gently.

'Yes, but it's been five months. *Five months.* I know they're grown men and very busy, but they are still my sons. If you had children you would understand.'

9

Grace looked down at the tight cuffs of her cotton blouse pretending to refasten a pearly button. *If you had children.* Oh how she wished... But she was three years short of thirty and didn't even have a gentleman caller.

Zoe attracted admirers like jam attracts wasps. Seven years older and lacking her sister's beauty and sparkling talent, Grace did not. But resenting Zoe would have been as foolish as resenting a comet.

For a while she had cherished hope. Occasionally she had been sought out, her heart opening like a flower in sunshine when her callers brought flowers and accepted with gratifying enthusiasm her shyly offered invitations to tea. The painful and mortifying realization that she was no more than a route to Zoe had eroded, then finally demolished, her self-esteem.

Granny Hester had shown neither surprise nor sympathy. 'Look at you. Men like to see a young woman in pretty dresses that show off her figure, not plain skirts and mannish blouses. Fair hair and grey eyes are no help either, unless you *want* to be invisible. You should learn from your sister, make a bit of effort. Zoe knows how to flatter men and make them laugh. No wonder everyone loves her.' Shaking her head in disgust at Grace's lack of such basic accomplishments she had retired upstairs to her sitting-room.

Patting her hand, her mother had confessed relief. 'Darling, I'm so sorry you've been hurt. I know it's dreadfully selfish of me but I'd hate to lose you. I don't know how I would manage. You take such wonderful care of me.'

After the last time three years ago, to spare herself further pain Grace had buried her dreams of a husband and children of her own. Instead, burdened with guilt because her difficult birth was the cause of her mother's fragility, she had channelled all her energy into running the house and taking care of her mother, helping at the school and chapel and doing charity work in the village. In this busy demanding life she had rediscovered a sense of worth.

Then Reverend Peters died. A few weeks later, after consultations between the chapel elders and the circuit superintendent, a new minister was appointed. Within days the whole village buzzed with the news that the Reverend Edwin Philpotts had left mission work in India to return to his native Cornwall.

He had been standing in the vestibule with Mrs Nancholas, the chapel organist, when Grace arrived for her turn on the cleaning rota. Tall and thin, with straight brown hair that flopped over his forehead, he had a sallow complexion and dark shadows of strain

11

beneath his eyes. Deep creases bracketed his mouth.

'Ah, Reverend,' Mrs Nancholas beamed. 'This 'ere's Grace. Miss Damerel, I should say. I dunno what we'd do without 'er and that's a fact.'

He turned. As the soft brown gaze met hers, Grace's heart leapt into her throat and she averted her eyes. But courtesy demanded she offer her hand. His grip was warm and firm, and her entire body tingled.

'It's a pleasure to meet you, Miss Damerel.'

'How do you do. Will you excuse me?' Hot from her toes to the roots of her hair Grace had fled down the aisle to the back room where she leaned against the door, breathless and trembling.

She watched her mother fumble with the envelope. Edwin Philpotts had been in the village three months one week and five days. Every time Grace saw him she was torn between hope and terror. His duties and her voluntary work brought them together often enough for her to recognize his innate kindness. So even if he guessed her feelings he would not mock or patronize. But the thought that he might pity her: that she could not bear.

Her gaze shifted to the pale walls, the subtly shaded Chinese carpet and elegant French-style furniture. This had been the Damerel family home since her great-grandfather inherited it from a distant relative who had been the last of his line. And this pretty *feminine* room perfectly reflected her mother's taste: from gathered voile that could be released from silk tassels to filter strong summer sunlight behind drapes of rose brocade, to the quilted satin bedcover.

Zoe's had the same air of femininity. On her rare visits home the frilled counterpane was swiftly hidden beneath carelessly tossed silk gowns and lace-trimmed petticoats. The walnut dressing-table was strewn with combs, brushes, little pots of cream, perfume bottles and scattered jewellery.

If bedrooms reflected their occupants' personalities hers said *neat* and *dull*. If she left things lying about it wouldn't look feminine, merely untidy. Besides, her nature craved order. Anyway, except to sleep and change her clothes she spent very little time there. It was different for her mother.

The room's subtle fragrance reminded her of summer tasks to come: making up tiny bags of fresh lavender for the linen cupboard and stripping pounds of the tiny flower heads from their stalks. These would be distilled with quarts of water over a slow fire to make the lavender water her mother depended on to soothe her nerves and help her sleep.

Unfolding the letter, Louise scanned the contents. One delicate hand flew to her

13

throat as joy lit her face. 'Oh my goodness.'

'What is it, Mama?'

'They are on their way home. Grace, they're coming home!'

'Do they say when they expect to arrive?' Louise frowned. 'May the fourteenth.'

Grace caught her breath. 'What? That's today. Are you sure?'

Louise thrust the letter at her. 'See for yourself.'

Grace scanned the bold black writing, wishing she could linger over descriptions of mountain and jungle scenery, illness made light of, plant specimens discovered and seeds so carefully collected. There it was, 14 May. Her gaze flew to the date at the top: 5 March 1902.

'Bryce wrote this nine weeks ago. He probably thought he was giving us plenty of warning.'

'Oh, good lord.' Louise started to push the bedclothes aside. 'I must–'

'You must stay exactly where you are,' Grace said gently, pulling the covers up again. 'You haven't finished your tea.'

'Where's your father? Has he gone?'

Grace stood up. 'I think so. He mentioned an important meeting at the mine, so–' Her mother wasn't listening.

'My tea, Grace.' She took the cup Grace offered. 'I can't wait to see my dear boys again. When do you think they'll arrive?'

'Not before late afternoon. It will depend on the times of the trains from London. Then they still have to make the carriage drive from Truro station.'

'But that only gives you a few hours–'

'Don't worry, Mama. We'll manage.' Grace mentally crossed her fingers.

'I can't possibly lie here when there's so much to do,' Louise fretted. 'Oh, I do wish Zoe could be here. It's so long since we were all together.'

'Perhaps she'll come later in the year. Once she knows the twins are home she's sure to want to see them.'

'You're right. It's just ... time is passing so quickly. Sometimes I worry that–'

'No, Mama. No more worrying.' Grace was quiet but firm. 'The twins will want to hear all the news. So you just relax and try to remember everything that's happened since you last wrote to them. While Violet runs your bath Kate can air their bedrooms.'

She hurried along the open landing and down the stairs reaching the hall as her father was about to leave. Through the open front door Grace glimpsed Will, the groom, turning the gig on the drive while Patrick, who combined the roles of butler and valet, handed her father his bowler hat.

'Papa, Mother's had a letter from Bryce. They are on their way home.' Pleasure and anticipation bubbled inside her. 'All being well they should be here later this after-noon.' Surely this would cheer him up? His moods these past few months had set the entire household on edge.

'Are they now?' His florid face had been shaved shiny except for the bushy silver-streaked moustache obscuring his upper lip. Only the top button of his dark suit was fastened, the lower ones open to reveal the gold watch chain inherited from his father looped across his waistcoat. His bull-like neck was confined in a stiff wing collar and maroon tie.

'That will certainly please your mother. But you'll have to watch her or she'll get herself into a state long before they arrive.'

'It's all right, Papa. I've persuaded her to stay in bed a while longer. Kate can start on the bedrooms and if she needs help Violet will lend a hand.'

'Has your grandmother been told?'

Grace shook her head. 'Not yet.' Her fingers tightened on the polished banister rail. 'It won't be easy for her. She's grown used to there being only four of us.'

'Well, she'll just have to make the best of it.' He was curt. 'Don't let her upset your mother.'

Grace bit her lip. That was more easily said than done. 'Mary Prideaux is coming over after lunch. Mama always enjoys her company.'

16

Henry Damerel set the bowler hat on his close-cropped silver head. 'You'll see to everything?'

Don't I always? The words remained unspoken. 'Of course.' She smiled hopefully. 'Might you get home before they arrive?'

Her father's heavy features darkened. 'For God's sake, Grace, what does it matter? Why should they care? Most sons would have wanted to follow in their father's footsteps and build their future on the successes of the past. But mine preferred to be gardeners.'

'Oh, hardly, Papa.'

'What else would you call it then?' Thrusting his chin forward he fingered his tie. 'I daresay I'll see them at dinner. I must go. Some of us have work to do.'

After three years he was still angry. But beneath the anger Grace recognized his deep hurt at the twins' rejection of everything he held dear.

The news that Master Bryce and Master Richard were coming home spread swiftly through the servants' quarters to the gardens and stables.

Despite Grace's reassurance, the short notice caused uproar. Yet she could not regret the letter's delay. Had it arrived a week ago her mother would be prostrate with nervous exhaustion by now.

As shutters were unlocked and windows

17

opened, Grace gave thanks for the glorious weather. It had rained almost every day from November until mid-April. During those long wet months the view from the house had been one of bare boughs and sepia tones. But at long last the clouds had parted, the sun's warmth worked its magic, and in the space of a few brief weeks spring had painted the Cornish countryside with vibrant colour.

Fetching sheets from the linen cupboard, and lifting from the chest blankets faintly perfumed with the cedar balls that kept moths away, Grace paused to look out of Richard's bedroom window.

Beside the front lawn emerald with new growth, a flowering cherry was heavy with dense clusters of pale pink blossom. What beauty to welcome the twins home. She loved spring even though it made her heart ache. Everything was so bright and new and full of promise.

While Kate swept, dusted and polished, Grace walked down the lower drive beneath the pale-green shade of tall beech trees to consult head gardener, Jack Hooper.

Tall double doors painted dark green were set in the high brick wall between the boiler house and the open-fronted pot shed where the apprentice stood at a trough washing pots and stacking them on the shelves in rows according to size.

'Good morning, Billy.'

'Morning, miss.' The boy raised a dripping hand, wrinkling his freckled nose as water splashed his face. Like all the garden staff he wore thick trousers, a waistcoat over his shirt and tie, and heavy boots. But instead of the flat cap worn by Jack, Ben and Arthur, Billy had a shapeless brown felt hat with a narrow, drooping and very grubby brim.

Grace walked through the open doors into the fertile warmth and colour of the kitchen garden. The south-facing border between wall and path was sown with early dwarf peas and beans, beetroot, endive, chicory and radishes. Behind them, trained against the warm red brick, were apple and peach trees and a bushy tomato plant.

On the lower side of the path stood the glass house. Ahead of her ran a gravel walkway wide enough for a horse and cart, spanned at each end by iron arches. The nearest supported a riot of purple clematis and winter jasmine. At the far end the other arch was hidden beneath pale pink clematis entwined with a blood-red rambling rose.

A small lavender hedge separated bushes of red and white currants and gooseberries from the rows of vegetable crops. Beyond the vegetables was a six-foot-wide border of flowers. Behind patches of red and white double-daisies, yellow pansies and cushions of anthemis nestling in silvery green foliage were banks of scarlet, cream and yellow tulips and stands of purple bearded irises that would fill vases in the dining- and drawing-rooms.

There was, Grace knew, an even wider selection of colours and blooms in the chain garden at the back of the house. But the chain garden was her mother's domain and she guarded it jealously, refusing to relinquish a single flower. Jack and Ben had quickly learned that, despite their mistress's sweet smile and gentle voice, on this matter she was adamant.

Hearing the clop of hoofs and the crunch of wooden wheels on the gravel, she glanced round. Ben, Jack's 26-year-old son, came through the arch leading a brown cob hauling a cartload of manure.

'Morning, miss.' Ben knuckled his forehead. Quiet and serious, he lived with his parents in the head gardener's house built into the west wall. But not for much longer. At Christmas a blushing Kate had confided that she and Ben were courting and hoped to marry in late summer. Grace had wished Kate happiness, congratulated Ben on his good fortune, and wondered if she would ever meet someone who might love her the way Ben loved Kate.

'Father's in the boiler'ouse. Want me to fetch'n, do ee?'

'No, Ben, don't trouble. Just tell him that

my brothers will be home today.'

'Today is it?' Ben sucked air through his teeth.

Grace smiled. 'Rose is cooking a celebration dinner, so if Jack has got anything special it would be greatly appreciated.'

'Doan' you fret, miss. You'll 'ave the best of all that's ready. Want me to bring it up, do ee?'

'No, I'll come down. You have enough to do.' *And I'll be glad of a few minutes to myself.*

As soon as news of the twins' return had reached the kitchen, Rose Trott, familiar with their appetites, had immediately begun baking and the house was fragrant with the results of her labour.

'Of course you'll be glad to have them home, Louise,' Hester Chenoweth sniffed as she sat down at the dining-table. 'I only hope all the upheaval doesn't make you ill again.'

'There won't be any upheaval, Granny,' Grace said quickly. 'I know this morning was a bit–'

'It certainly was. Everyone rushing about and banging doors. You'd think King Edward himself was coming.'

'Oh, Mother,' Louise laughed, pressing slender fingers to her bosom. 'The King is a great traveller and a most sociable gentleman, but I doubt he's even heard of Cornwall.'

'Anyway, Granny, everything is finished upstairs,' Grace soothed. 'So you won't be disturbed if you want to have a rest.' With several hours still to go, it was vital that nothing should upset her mother.

'No, I shall do my embroidery. You may read to me.'

Dressed in the habitual black of a dedicated widow, her only jewellery a thin gold wedding band and a rope of pearls she wore pinned to her bodice, Hester Chenoweth resembled an elderly jackdaw. Her hair was arranged in a roll over her forehead with the rest drawn back into a small hard bun. Her narrowed eyes and down-turned mouth reflected a lifetime of expecting the worst.

'I'm sorry, Granny, I can't. Not this afternoon. I still have—'

'I thought you said everything was ready.'

'It is *upstairs*. But there are still—'

'Oh well, if you're too busy.'

'Only today. But I'll read to you tomorrow if you—'

'I may not feel like it tomorrow,' Hester snapped. 'Where's Patrick? I want my lunch. It's too bad, all this fuss and bother.'

She's jealous, Grace realized. Settling her mother she hurried to the sideboard. 'I told Patrick we would manage on our own.' She picked up the ladle and removed the lid of the tureen. 'It's only for this meal, Granny. Tonight everything will be back to normal.'

Catching her mother's eye she smiled. 'No, it will be better than that. It will be wonderful.'

Mentally blessing Rose who knew her grandmother's preferences and had somehow found time to prepare chicken broth, fresh sweet rolls, slices of cheese and cherry tartlets, Grace was careful to serve her mother small portions. Given a full plate, Louise invariably pushed it away untouched.

Seated once more, she racked her brain for snippets of gossip picked up in the village. Absorbed in the conversation Louise ate enough to allay her daughter's anxiety and Hester was distracted from voicing every complaint as it occurred to her.

After an hour she could ill afford, Grace dropped her crumpled napkin beside her plate. 'Will you excuse me?'

'Where are you off to now?' Hester demanded.

'Not far, Granny. Just to the kitchen garden to fetch the vegetables.'

'Why can't one of the gardeners bring them up? That's a job for the boy. No doubt he's hidden himself away somewhere to avoid doing any work.'

During the winter Grace had often seen Billy alone in the pot shed, shaking with cold, his blue hands barely able to hold the flowerpots he was washing in the icy water. She knew how seriously he took his job. But contradicting her grandmother would only invite trouble. As Louise pushed back her chair Grace went to help her.

'They are really busy just now, Granny. There's an awful lot of work for just the four of them.'

'A place this size needs a proper staff to run it,' Hester stated. 'Where's the money going? That's what I'd like to know.'

Louise sighed. 'Mother, you know as well as I do it's going to the mine. But Henry says it's only a temporary measure.'

'He said that a year ago.'

'True, but with the boys abroad and Zoe in London we haven't really needed more indoor servants. As for the gardens, Henry didn't dismiss the journeymen. He just didn't replace them when they moved on.'

'I don't know,' Hester sniffed. 'There's no loyalty these days.'

'Granny,' Grace said, 'would you like me to call Violet for you?'

'Good heavens, girl, whatever for? I'm perfectly able to cross the hall by myself.'

Leaning on a silver-topped cane with Grace on her other side, Louise whispered, 'It's not easy for her, darling. Granny really misses Zoe. They were very close.'

Grace's memory threw up vivid images: Granny Hester cuddling Zoe, telling her how pretty she was, how gifted, how special. Tears of adoring pride trickling down Granny's

24

face in chapel while Zoe sang her solos. Zoe brought downstairs to sing for guests.

Grace recalled standing at the side of the room as they listened, their eyes wide with amazement. When Zoe curtsied she saw them turn to each other as they clapped, saying what a remarkable voice it was, and how like an angel Zoe looked with her golden hair and sapphire eyes.

Told to make herself useful while Zoe was admired, Grace carried cups of tea and offered plates of sandwiches or cake to the guests. Smiling, always smiling, in case they thanked her. Occasionally someone would notice her and smile back. When they asked *Aren't you proud of your little sister?* She said yes, because she was.

Now Zoe was in London fulfilling her dream. Now her audiences weren't just friends and family but a whole theatreful of strangers who also adored her. Her infrequent letters were most often addressed to her grandmother who would read aloud from them but refused to let them out of her hands.

Scribbled between rehearsals and performances or while she was dressing for yet another supper party, Zoe's notes were as frothy as the lace on her lingerie. She wrote of her current play, her new gowns, and boasted of the titles of her most ardent admirers.

'We've lived so quietly since the boys left.' Her mother's voice brought Grace back with a start. 'You can understand Granny being nervous that Bryce and Richard's return will change things.'

'Mama, this is their home. Granny knew they weren't going forever. In any case, and I mean no disrespect, she spends so much time upstairs in her sitting-room she might as well have remained at Trenarren.'

'It's not quite as simple as that, darling. After your grandfather died she didn't want to stay there on her own.' She paused. 'Granny is a wealthy woman and your father needed money for the mine.'

'Oh.' Grace had always assumed it was her mother's wish to have Granny live with them. But if it were not, if her presence were instead a business arrangement, that might explain the tension Grace sensed between the three of them. Her father's attitude to his in-law was civil but had never been warm.

'Off you go.' She waved Grace away.

'What will you do, Mama?'

'It's such a lovely afternoon I shall take a turn in my garden.'

Chapter Two

Carrying two shallow baskets laden with asparagus, new potatoes and a variety of fresh vegetables and salads, Grace entered the big kitchen. Maggie, the scullery maid, was standing at the deep stone sink up to her elbows in suds as she worked her way through a small mountain of used mixing bowls, pans and dishes.

At one end of the huge scrubbed table two loaves, four fruit pies, two trays of sausage rolls and a Dundee cake were cooling. At the other end, Rose Trott, her sleeves rolled up, cap askew, scattered flour on the marble slab and tipped a large lump of pastry from a bowl. The once pristine white apron covering her long blue cotton dress was marked with fruit-juice stains and smears of cake mixture where she had hurriedly wiped her hands.

Grace gasped. 'Rose, there's enough here to feed an army.'

Her plump face scarlet, Rose wiped her perspiring forehead with the back of her wrist leaving a trace of flour. She clicked her tongue. 'I know they two. Make short work of this they will. 'Specially after all that foreign food. You jest put the baskets down over there, my handsome.' She nodded towards another table under the window.

Grace did as she was told. The wide shelf normally stacked with baking dishes and mixing bowls stood almost empty and there were several gaps along the row of gleaming copper pans.

Copper, Grace thought. Copper had built this house and almost destroyed it. Tin had made it live again. But what if–? She blocked the thought. This was a time for rejoicing. The twins were coming home.

'Jack will bring the melons and strawberries himself,' she said. 'He gave me his word you'll have them by five.'

'The dear of 'n. A weight off my mind that is. Mistress all right, is she?'

Grace held up crossed fingers. 'So far. And Miss Prideaux should be here shortly.'

'Good job too. Best if mistress have company. The last few hours is always the hardest when you're waiting for something.' Rose turned the pastry. 'Master be home to greet them, will he? He been working some hard lately.'

They both knew what Rose really meant. Her father was rarely at home.

'These are difficult times, Rose.'

'Could be worse though. At least the mine's still working and Treworthal men still got jobs.'

'True.' *But for how long?* Grace pictured her father's face: the permanent frown, his air of distraction. Pain darted beneath her breastbone and she pressed her fingers against it.

'What's up with you then, my bird?'

'Nothing, Rose. Well, perhaps a touch of indigestion. It's been a busy morning,' she added wryly. 'And – well, never mind.'

'I daresay Mrs Chenoweth don't like all the upheaval. She's not one for change,' Rose nodded sagely.

'Mizz Trott,' Maggie hissed. 'You was s'posed to say about Becky.'

'Dear life. I'd ferget my head if it wasn't screwed on.' Straightening up, Rose blew sideways at a stray wisp of hair. 'You know Becky Collins? Live down Miner's Row? Ernie Treneer who live next door caught Maggie on her way up this morning. He says he haven't seen Becky fer days. She won't come to her door. He's worried about her.'

Oh no. Not today. Grace looked down, heat prickling her skin with shame as she imagined the minister's response to such an uncharitable thought.

'What's wrong? Has something happened to her?'

Rose's mouth pursed. 'Nobody knows. That's the trouble. Ernie don't know what to do.'

'Waiting for me he was, miss,' the kitchen maid said over her shoulder. 'Said I was to

29

ask Mizz Trott to tell you. He said you'd know what to do.'

'He's sure Becky's at home?' Grace said. 'I mean she hasn't gone to stay with her sister or something?'

'No, she's there. He've heard her.' Rose turned the pastry, the short sharp strokes of her rolling pin reflecting her irritation. 'I dunno why he bother with her. She never got a good word for'n.'

Grace sighed. 'I'd better go down.'

'What *now?*' Rose was startled.

'There's nothing more I can do here for the moment.' Grace thought for a moment. 'If Becky hasn't been out she probably won't have any food in the house.'

Rose's eyes rolled. Wiping her hands on her apron she waddled around the table. 'Hold on a minute,' she sighed. 'I'll put a few bits together for you to take down.'

'Rose, you're a gem,' Grace smiled.

'I don't know about that,' Rose sniffed. 'What I do know is you got too much to do without taking on more.'

Privately Grace agreed. But Becky lived alone, no one had seen her and Ernie was worried. How could she *not* go?

Seated at the head of the table, Henry Damerel gazed at the other four men seated two on either side. A sudden surge of anger set his heart pounding. He slapped both

30

hands down on the reports and papers strewn over the table in front of him.

'What's the matter with you?' he roared. 'We've faced depressions before. They happened in my father's time as well. They're nothing new. The mine survived then and it will now. Remember '94 when the price of tin went down? Remember how many mines closed? But we hung on and came through.'

When the price of tin had begun climbing, just as he had said it would, the increase had given him the leverage he needed. He had been able to introduce machine drills powered by compressed air. The benefits were immediately apparent as the amount of unpayable ground extracted by each core of tutworkers doubled. The adventurers were delighted. For though the tributers still worked the stopes with hammer and boryer to extract the tin, the ore was reaching the main shaft much faster.

But it hadn't taken long for the true and terrible cost of machine-drilling dry holes to become clear.

Henry caught himself. He couldn't afford distractions. In any case, all underground work carried risks. He shuffled through the papers, extracted two, scanned them briefly then looked up.

'I haven't come this far to give up now. We'll get through this slump just like we've got through the others. But we'll have to cut costs.' At these words all four men around the table shifted on their chairs. 'I know,' he said, before anyone could speak. 'We're pared down to the bone already. So at the next setting day I shall take the mine off tribute.' He brandished the papers. 'These reports say the lode is good in both shafts. Putting the men on contract and paying them weekly wages will save a substantial amount of money.'

The purser immediately began jotting figures and making calculations. The two mine captains exchanged a glance.

'Tidn' right nor fair,' Joe Gainey muttered. Both men had worked in the mine since childhood, starting underground when they were ten years old. Their first job had been to operate fans at the entrance to unventilated ends. Big and strong for his age, Joe had soon moved to rolling barrows of spoil in places where there was no tram-road. Before long both were working alongside their fathers, developing skill, judgement and a comprehensive knowledge of the lode.

Their role as mine captains was to supervise the underground work and act as agents between the miners and the adventurers whose investment paid the men's wages.

'No, it isn't fair,' Henry agreed. He knew they hated what he was proposing, not least because it was they and not he who would have to break the news to the miners. But he also knew they would accept it. The alternative was closure.

'What else can I do?' he challenged. 'If any of you have a better idea I'd like to hear it.' He waited a moment but none of them would meet his eye. 'Things are bad. But they will improve. They always have in the past. The price is bound to start climbing again. We just have to hold on.'

Leaving the kitchen Grace went to find her mother. The house was designed in the Palladian style: a central block flanked by two wings, built of mellow stone with granite quoins and lintels. Midway along the back of the house a wide recess, two storeys high, echoed the four-columned portico at the front. In the centre of this recess, with a long window on each side and three more above, was a black-painted door. This was known to all as the garden entrance.

A paved area outside the door led to a short flight of wide shallow steps. Opposite these, through an arched iron trellis foaming with pale pink clematis was a gravelled walk bordered by rhododendron bushes, their trumpet-like blooms scarlet, crimson and purple against dark green glossy leaves. Down the centre of the walk a series of linked circular beds were vibrant with spring colour.

This was the chain garden. It was her mother's creation, begun shortly after her paternal grandparents died in the influenza epidemic and her father inherited the house and estate.

When her health and strength permitted, Louise Damerel spent every spare moment in the chain garden. As a child, Grace had helped her, digging holes for each new plant, then helping firm earth around the roots. But as the years passed there was less and less time. Busy with schoolwork and then with running the house she had become a visitor rather than a participant.

And by then, after reading that book, she was seeing the chain garden through different eyes. What she saw she didn't understand. But she couldn't ask. Though her mother needed her, depended on her, they had never shared thoughts or confidences. In any case, Grace wasn't sure she wanted the truth. Knowledge conferred additional responsibility and she hadn't the strength to take on any more.

She looked along the row of beds. There were nine links in the chain. Which had always seemed strange until it occurred to her that perhaps one was for Grandfather Chenoweth, her mother's father. She had been only eight when he died. That had been a terrible year. A month after his death, her sister Charlotte and brother Michael, who were three and two, had caught scarlet fever. They had both died. But they were still remembered.

Earlier this year their beds had been dense cushions of snowdrops surrounded by crocuses that symbolized the joys of youth. According to the book, snowdrops signified hope. Yet the children were dead. But perhaps if you lost a child you had to hope that they were safe and happy, somewhere.

Each link in the chain was neatly edged with box. All were bright with colour. As children they had raced up and down the walk and played in the garden. The twins, their cousins Neil and Catherine Ainsley, Zoe and her: each of them so different in personality yet recognizably family. Now Neil was a doctor in London, Catherine secretary to an MP at Westminster, Zoe a star in musical theatre. The twins were coming home after three years on the other side of the world, and she – Grace didn't want to think about her life. She needed to find her mother then get down to the village.

At the far end of the chain garden stood a small folly. Built of the same mellow stone as the house, it had two tall arched windows and a semicircular one above the solid oak door. Bone-dry, with an open fireplace and carpet on the wooden floor, it was her mother's refuge when the sun grew too hot or the wind too keen.

Furnished with two deep armchairs it also contained several shelves stacked with gardening books, and a short-legged table of polished oak planks big enough to hold a tea tray without the need to remove the large planting diaries. There were no curtains and the windows at the back commanded a panoramic view of the deer park, the valley and the wooded hills beyond.

Opening the door, Grace saw her mother sitting in one of the armchairs. She was hatless, her head against the high back, one hand on her lap, the other resting on the arm as she gazed out of the window.

Below the sloping park, oaks, sycamores and the occasional copper beech hid the road and the upper reaches of the river. Across the valley, partly screened by more trees, were the mine workings. The two engine houses with their tall chimneys and surrounding sprawl of wooden sheds stood on scarred earth tinged red as a wound by tin ore that turned the river to blood.

Grace was relieved to see the jacket covering her mother's high-necked lace-trimmed gown. Hip length with wide lapels, the dark blue silk-lined velvet had huge puff sleeves that narrowed from elbow to wrist. The fact that she had chosen this in preference to the elderly green tweed she usually wore if she planned to do a little gentle hoeing was a clear indication of her fragility today.

Louise glanced round and before Grace could speak, smiled, holding out her hand.

'Won't it be wonderful to have them back?

What stories they will have to tell us. It doesn't seem so long ago they were falling out of trees and bringing frogs to the kitchen to terrify Rose. We must have a party. I'm sure they'd enjoy that. What do you think?'

Grace took her mother's slender hand between her own, anxiety flaring at the hectic colour along her mother's cheekbones. But long familiarity with signs of impending trouble reassured her that the brightness in the violet eyes had not escalated into fever. *Yet.*

'It's a lovely idea. But perhaps we had better let them get settled first. It's a long way from India. They'll probably be tired after so much travelling, don't you think?' Grace dropped her gaze from the fading smile, the shadow of disappointment.

Why did she always seem to be saying no, blighting her mother's happiness? Yet what choice did she have? She had tried the alternative. But agreeing to her mother's ideas and spontaneous schemes had brought a nervous collapse in their wake. Not only had her father been furious, calling her foolhardy and thoughtless, she had also incurred the wrath of her Uncle John, who was Neil and Catherine's father and a widower since the death of his wife who was her mother's sister. He was also the family physician.

'I suppose you're right.' Louise forced a smile. 'I just thought – but never mind. As

37

you say, there'll be plenty of time.' Patting her daughter's hand she withdrew her own. 'When Mary arrives, ask her to join me here, will you?'

'I have to go down to the village, but I'll tell Violet. No, she's up with Granny. I'll tell Kate and Patrick. In any case, I'm sure she'll know where to find you.' She bent to kiss her mother's cheek. The fine skin looked like crumpled tissue paper.

'Grace, I've just thought of something. We didn't know the boys would be home in time for your birthday. Why don't we make it a proper celebration? What would you say to a dance? I'm sure there are any number of people we could invite.'

Why do you do this? Why do you make me feel so ungrateful? Grace straightened up. 'Oh no. It's sweet of you, Mama, but, really, I'd rather not. I'm hopeless at dancing. Besides, you've only been out of bed just over a week. You ought not to overdo things.'

Louise sighed deeply. 'Oh well, if you say so, darling. It's your day so it must be just the way you want. Dinner, then. A special dinner for family and close friends.'

Grace forced a smile. 'That will be lovely.'

'You are my dearest girl. I rely on you utterly. You know that, don't you?'

Grace kissed her mother again, noting the grape-coloured shadows under her eyes. *Please, no more illness for a while. There was so much to do and never enough time.*

'I'd better go. You're sure you're warm enough?' She could remember as a child seeing her mother's hair tumbling almost to her waist, thick and shining like spun gold. Now it was the dull silver of smelted tin.

'Darling, it's delightfully cosy in here. I can enjoy all the afternoon sun and be safe from the wind.' She turned her head once more to the window. 'This is such a beautiful view. Now the trees have their lovely new leaves you can hardly see the mine at all.' She waved her daughter away. 'Off you go then. I'm sure you have lots more important things to do than fuss over me.'

As Grace climbed the steps to the garden entrance, the door opened.

'Mary! I'm so glad to see you.'

Mary was short, rounded, unmarried and in her late thirties. Her friendship with Louise had begun at a garden party ten years previously when they fell into conversation beside a plant stall and discovered a shared passion for gardening. It had flourished despite the fifteen-year age gap and difference in family circumstances.

Because Mary favoured muted colours she was often overlooked in company: except by those who knew that her self-effacing manner allowed her to observe without attracting attention.

'Grace, my dear.' Mary grasped the outstretched hands. Her voice was low-pitched and musical. Today it held a hint of laughter and her hazel eyes danced. 'I can imagine how it has been since the letter arrived.'

Grace made a wry face. 'Everyone is thrilled and excited. We knew they were coming back sometime this month, but to hear this morning that they would actually be home today was rather a shock.'

'How is your mother?'

'She's ... exactly as you might expect.' Grace's glance swept from the straw boater sitting squarely on neatly coiled brown hair, the fitted jacket and long skirt of smoke-grey gabardine over a pin-tucked white blouse with a lilac bow, to polished black boots. When she really looked she could see the beautiful cut and elegant line of Mary's clothes. Though if more than four people were present Mary seemed to become invisible. Yet she possessed great charm and a wicked sense of humour.

'Mama's so looking forward to seeing you. She's in the folly. I have to go to the village but I shouldn't be long. Will you stay?'

'Until you get back? With pleasure.'

'No, I meant will you have dinner with us. Stay and welcome the boys home. I know Mama would be delighted.'

'It's sweet of you, Grace, but I think not.'

Though not surprised at the refusal, Grace fought down disappointment.

'Tonight will be a family occasion,' Mary smiled.

Grace knew that only too well. Family occasions always tied her nerves in knots. It was why she'd wanted Mary to dine with them.

'But I certainly hope to see them soon. At your birthday dinner perhaps? You are having one, I hope?'

'It seems so. But that's not for another week. You must come before then.'

'I probably will. Talking of your birthday dinner' – she dropped her voice to a conspiratorial whisper – 'no doubt Louise will seat me next to John Ainsley?'

Grace's ever-present anxiety immediately increased. 'Would you prefer she didn't? I thought you got on well with him.'

'My dear Grace, don't worry so.' Mary gave her hand a reassuring pat. 'John and I are the greatest of friends. He has no wish to marry again and knows I have no desire to change his mind. But your dear mother continues to harbour hopes. Heaven knows why. Do you think she will prevail upon the new minister to come? I understand she's taken quite a shine to him. He does seem a very pleasant young man. A little withdrawn perhaps. But I expect he's still settling in. I'm sure he will have found you an enormous help.'

'Yes. I-I hope so. I'm sorry. I really must go. Will you excuse me?' Her face on fire, Grace bolted into the house.

Chapter Three

Seated at her easel in her favourite spot in the garden, a paint-smeared smock buttoned loosely over her muslin blouse and blue calico skirt, Dorcas Renowden slowly straightened on her stool.

As she drew back, the detail over which she had taken such care blurred into patches of colour without shape or definition.

She released a slow sigh determinedly ignoring momentary panic. She would go and see John Ainsley. No doubt he would scold her for not coming sooner. But he would understand why she had delayed, how desperately she had hoped it might be merely a matter of strain, of working too many hours at a stretch on the fine detail that made her work so sought after.

Rinsing her brush in the jar of cloudy water she wiped it on a rag. Behind her bees droned in a lilac bush heavy with purple blossom. The sun was warm on her back, the air heavy with the lilac's sweet scent and the dark loamy smell of moist earth.

For months she had been telling herself it would pass and everything would be normal again. When she had begun tripping over things and misjudging distance she had attributed it to carelessness, or age. But she was only 56. She did not *feel* old.

The cottage stood alone on the edge of the Damerel estate, about half a mile from the village. It had been her home for twenty-eight years. Hal had been born here. She had not wanted to come but had been in no state to fight. Now she could not imagine living anywhere else. She relished the solitude and the privacy that allowed her to live as she pleased and paint for hours if she chose.

It had been a rewarding life if not an easy one. Nor was it over. She had much to be grateful for. Hal was doing well in South America, his clear firm handwriting easy to read as he described progress and setbacks in developing the new pump.

Loath to see him go she had understood why he could not stay. His quarrel with Henry had been too deep, too bitter: one bound by tradition, the other impatient for change: neither prepared to give an inch. Age and youth, past and future. It was inevitable they should clash. Loving them both, it had crucified her to see them at each other's throats.

Closing her eyes she lifted her face to the sun. She would say nothing until she had consulted John.

Her basket slung over the handlebar of her bicycle, Grace pedalled hard. The breeze caught the wide brim of her straw hat and would have blown it off but for the ribbons tied beneath her chin. On either side of the road the hedgerows were lush with new growth. Bluebells, red campion and the white flowers of wild garlic splashed the grass with bright colour.

Blowing from the north-east, the wind carried the faint unceasing roar of the stamps. Day and night they worked, some driven by waterwheel, others by the huge beam engine, crushing the tin ore to powder. A century ago rich veins of copper had made Cornwall one of the wealthiest places on earth. More than 600 beam engines had worked on mines whose names were legendary for the quality and amount of ore they produced.

But the discovery of vast deposits in South Australia, Canada and Chile at the same time as the lodes in Cornwall were pinching out had signalled catastrophe. Villages were abandoned as mines shut down, and many miners risked long dangerous weeks at sea to seek work abroad. Those who remained had found work in the tin mines. But tin lay much deeper. In mines without gigs or cages the only way down was by ladder. The climb back up after an eight-hour shift proved too much for some. Nearly every week another woman mourned a husband or son who had fallen to his death.

Reaching the top of the hill that sloped gently down to the village Grace was glad to stop pedalling. In the dappled shade of tall sycamores the breeze still had a bite and she shivered inside the bronze wool jacket she had buttoned over her cream high-necked blouse. Her long skirt of bottle-green serge had seen better days but there hadn't been time to change it. Once she had made sure Becky was all right she would still have time to bathe and put on something more appropriate before the twins arrived.

Approaching the chapel she felt her heartbeat quicken. Heat climbed her throat to her cheeks and even her ears burned. Drawing level with the big square two-storey building she couldn't resist a sidelong glance. One of the blue-painted double doors stood open. But because of the frosted glass screen at the back of the pews to protect the congregation from draughts she couldn't see who was inside. Then she heard the triumphant blare of the organ as Mrs Nancholas practised the hymns for Sunday's service.

The village's main street was busy. Women chatting by the village pump as they waited their turn to fill large stoneware pitchers glanced up as Grace braked and dismounted. 'Afternoon, Miss Damerel,' they chorused.

'Good afternoon,' Grace smiled back,

aware that every detail of her appearance would be noted and commented on as soon as she was out of earshot. Aware too that while they appreciated her visits to the sick and elderly – though being Henry Damerel's eldest daughter it was expected – they positively doted on Zoe. From the age of five Zoe had entranced the chapel congregation singing solos. She always wore impractical gowns of silk and lace quite unsuitable for sick visiting, only ever drove through the village on her way to somewhere else, and never put herself out for anyone. Long before she had gone to London Zoe had behaved like a star and the village had loved her for it.

Grace steered past the butcher's van gleaming with a fresh coat of daffodil-yellow paint. The huge grey mare harnessed to the shafts waited patiently while the butcher leaned out over the open half door at the back of the enclosed van with a parcel of bones.

'There you are, Lizzie. Make some lovely broth they will. Afternoon, Miss Damerel, 'andsome day.'

'It certainly is, Mr Rawling.'

The butcher gave a brief whistle and while he chopped meat the grey mare walked on to the next group of cottages.

Stale beer and old tobacco wafted out of the Red Lion, and the powerful smell of fermenting malt, hops and yeast issuing from the adjoining brew house caught in Grace's throat as she turned into Back Lane.

Propping her bicycle against the hedge she lifted her basket off the handlebars. Known in the village as Miner's Row, the small cottages were built of whitewashed cob and had tiled roofs that shed slates in every gale. Those that faced south opened on to a small patch of garden with a brick privy. They caught the sun. But the north-facing ones were always dark and needed a fire burning all year round to keep out the damp. Their gardens and privies were on the other side of the cobbled lane.

Lifting her skirt, Grace stepped across the brick-lined gutter into a small yard where a lean-to housed a copper with a firebox underneath, an iron mangle with thick wooden rollers, and a tin bath hanging from a six-inch nail hammered into the wall. A small outward-opening window covered with a scrap of lace curtain faced the yard. This was separated from its neighbour by a four-foot wall. The brown paint on the wooden front door was dull, cracked and curling.

Grace knocked then pressed the tongue to lift the rusty iron latch. The door was bolted. She leaned close.

'Becky, it's Grace.' She heard muffled coughing then silence. 'Becky, I know you're in there.'

'I don't want no callers today, miss,' a

voice quavered.

Grace leaned forward again. 'Let me in, Becky. I've got some news.' Still nothing happened. Grace played her trump card. 'I expect Ernie will be out in a minute to see what's going on.'

Through the door she heard the old woman shuffle closer, coughing. Then the bolt was drawn back, the latch rattled up and the door opened a few inches.

Red-rimmed watery eyes in a lined grey-yellow face peered out. Beneath a grubby woollen shawl clutched around thin shoulders Grace glimpsed a stained nightgown.

'You didn't ought to 'ave come.' Each breath was a struggle not to cough. 'I don't want to see no one.'

Grace pushed gently, opening the door wider. The smell was appalling. But years of visiting similar cottages had taught her to breathe shallowly and not think about it. 'Rose was worried about you.'

'Better if she minded her own business.'

'If you let me in I can close the door. Before Ernie comes out.'

'Nosy old sod,' Becky said, with a flash of her old spirit. 'You can't fart without him peering over the wall.'

'Becky!' Grace bit her lip so as not to laugh.

'Beg pardon, miss, I'm sure. But it do get on your nerves.'

'He's only trying to help.'

'I don't want no 'elp from 'e.' Becky shuffled painfully across a once-spotless kitchen now squalid from neglect. 'He isn't putting one foot over my step.'

'Well, if that's the way you feel there's nothing more to be said. But it does seem a shame. At least he would be company–'

'Company, is it? And what would we talk about? The grandchild he's going to have? While *my* boy, who Betty Lawry was promised to, lies in the ground alongside of his father. Both of 'em gone afore their time. Twenty-five Jimmy would have been. 'Tis no age to go, not like that, all skin and bone and spitting up blood. As for that Betty: didn't take she long, did it? Jimmy was hardly cold in his grave afore she took up with Will Treneer.' Her bitter outburst was cut short by a paroxysm of coughing that shook her frail body like a terrier shaking a rat.

Having heard it all before Grace said nothing. What comfort could she possibly offer? There were more widows and bereaved parents in these cottages than any other street in the village.

More men worked at the mine than in the boatyards or surrounding farms. Proud of the skills that placed them high above mere labourers and were reflected in their earning power, the miners paid dearly, sacrificing

49

their health and too often their lives in the narrow shafts deep underground.

With an arm around heaving shoulders as fragile as a bird's, Grace guided the sick woman to the wooden rocking chair beside the range. With the only bedroom in the cottage occupied by his parents, Jimmy, like so many others along the row, had slept on a narrow bedstead against the back wall of the kitchen. Rumpled blankets and a flattened pillow showed that Becky had been sleeping in it, perhaps for warmth, but more likely because climbing the ladder-like stairs required more strength than she possessed.

Seizing a scrap of rag from the debris on the wooden table Grace passed it over, looking away as Becky spat into it then sank into the chair and lay back, exhausted.

'What's this here news, then?' she muttered without opening her eyes.

Not yet 50, Becky Collins looked twenty years older. The bronchitis that affected many of the villagers, especially those living in this lane, was exacerbated by the mild wet winter and a spring that had seen more wet days than dry.

'The twins are coming home today. We had a letter this morning.'

'They are?' Interest flared briefly in the watery eyes. 'Yer ma'll be glad to see 'em back safe.'

Grace scanned the cluttered table. As well

as a teapot with a knitted cosy, a breadboard on which lay the stale curled crust of a loaf, a jug covered with a beaded circle of cheese-cloth and some knitting, the table held a large enamel basin. Bits floated, soggy and unrecognizable, on grey scummy water that half covered plates, bowls and cups. In this basin, Grace knew, Becky washed her face and her dishes and prepared her vegetables. The cottage had no sink.

A big dresser filled most of the wall inside the door. China plates stood upright at the back of the shelves. Cups hung from hooks along the front. The lower shelf was crammed with sepia-toned photographs in painted wooden frames. Several were of stern-faced elderly couples in stiff poses. Others showed a younger Becky with a baby; a little boy on a beach, barefoot and laughing as he held up a streamer of kelp, a youth in shirtsleeves and long trousers, and a young man with an arm over his father's shoulders, both of them smiling.

Though she had seen them many times Grace's throat tightened. She turned to the range. About to reach for the blackened kettle she noticed the sodden foetid pile of rags inside the fender and swallowed hard.

Hooking the cover off the top of the stove she poked the ash, relieved to see a few red embers as Cornish ranges could be very temperamental. A few sticks on top of the coal in the scuttle indicated Becky's intention to rebuild the fire. But she had lacked the strength.

Unfastening the string, Grace separated one of the newspapers from the bundle she always brought to villagers she visited. The papers were rarely read. Each page was neatly folded several times then cut or torn into squares, threaded onto a length of string and hung in the privy.

Quickly crumpling and twisting several sheets she poked them down among the embers. Dropping the sticks in on top she replaced the cover and, crouching, rammed the long poker in between the bars to let air in as she pulled the knob to riddle ash into the box below. A tongue of flame licked around the paper. A few moments later the sticks began to crackle. Once they were well alight she hooked the cover off again and with a small black shovel dropped coal on top of the burning wood.

'I think you need a nice cup of tea.' She reached for the pitcher to fill the kettle. Both were empty. 'Becky, when did you last have a hot drink?'

'I don't know. I can't remember. What do it matter anyhow?'

'I'm just going to fetch some water. I won't be long.'

Becky closed her eyes trying not to cough. As Grace went out, the door in the adjoining yard opened to reveal a short barrel-shaped man wearing a waistcoat over a collarless shirt soft and faded from innumerable washings. A broad leather belt that curved under his belly held up shapeless trousers. Between the old flat cap that shaded his eyes and the bushy grey moustache masking his upper lip his ruddy cheeks shone. He nodded towards the pitcher in Grace's hand.

'Daft old besom. I'd have got it for her. But she wouldn't even open the bleddy door. Here, you have mine while I go and fill that.'

'It's very good of you, Ernie.'

'No such thing. 'Tisn't right her being on her own, not while she's so bad. Where's that sister of hers I'd like to know.' Grace had been wondering the same thing. 'I'll give her the edge of my tongue next time she show her face, just see if I don't.' He clicked his tongue. 'Hark at me going on and you there waiting for that water.' He turned away, emerging a few seconds later with a full pitcher. 'Manage all right, can you?'

'Yes. You're very kind.'

'You wouldn't think so,' he muttered gloomily. 'Not to hear she talk. I dunnaw, bleddy women. More trouble than they're worth sometimes.' He trudged away down the lane.

Grace went back inside, the full pitcher heavy and awkward.

'You was quick.' Becky's face puckered in

53

a frown.

Grace hid a sigh. 'Ernie let me have his pitcher while he fills yours.'

'I don't want him doing nothing for me.'

'I can't imagine why,' Grace replied calmly. 'But actually he's doing it for me. He was kind enough to offer and it would have been rude to refuse.'

The fire was burning nicely now, filling the cheerless room with warmth. Hooking the cover off the stove again, Grace held her breath as she shovelled up the disgusting mess of rags and dropped them on to the flames. She filled the kettle and pulled it over the opening.

Rolling up her sleeves she took an apron from the hook on the back of the door and tied it over her skirt then carried the enamel basin out into the yard. Stacking the dishes carefully on the wall she emptied the basin into the gutter. She had just rinsed and wiped it clean when Ernie returned with the water.

Setting the pitcher down he went into his own yard and reached for the dirty dishes on the wall. 'Don't you say nothing,' he warned. 'If she don't know she can't fuss. I'll put 'em back here when they're done. You'd best get on in, else she'll be wondering what you're at.'

'Thanks, Ernie.' Closing the door, Grace put the basin on the table and poured in clean water. From her basket she took a small package of tea and one of sugar, a lidded enamel can of milk, a jar filled with pale gold jelly and a fresh loaf. Pulling the beaded cloth from the jug she recoiled. The milk was solid.

'Come on,' she coaxed a few minutes later, holding the steaming cup until she was sure Becky could manage without help. 'You'll feel better for a cup of tea and a bite to eat.'

'I don't want food.' Becky moved her head weakly. 'Couldn't stomach it.'

Grace felt queasy herself. But before she could open the window and let in some fresh air the room had to be warm. 'That's a pity. I've brought a jar of my quince jelly for you to try. You gave me the recipe after Harvest Festival last year, remember? Just try a taste. I'm going to change your bed then I'll help you wash.'

'You can't do that, miss.' Becky's eyes widened. 'Whatever would people say?'

'Well, I wasn't planning to shout it down the street. So who is to know?'

'It's kind of you, miss. But 'tis never proper for you to be doing such things. Sister will give me a hand when she come over.'

Grace didn't argue. She finished making the sandwich, slid it on to a clean plate and cut it into quarters. 'Ernie was just saying he hasn't seen Vera lately.'

'Yes, well, Vera got troubles of her own.' Becky sipped the hot sweet tea and allowed

Grace to tuck the blanket around her. 'That girl of hers.' She shook her head. 'Be the death of Vera she will. I tell you, Miss Grace, and I wouldn't say this to another living soul, but that Ruby do spend more time on her back than she do on her feet.' The flash of anger triggered another coughing spell. More sips of hot tea soothed her and Grace appeared not to notice when Becky reached for the triangle of soft bread. 'You didn't ought to be doing this,' she repeated. But it lacked the conviction of her earlier protests.

Opening the window, Grace inhaled deeply, steeling herself to deal with the slop bucket in the corner. Judging from the smell Becky had not been able to get up the garden to the privy for several days. Grateful it had a lid she picked up the stinking pail.

By the time Grace reached the privy her arm felt as if it was being torn from its socket and her chest hurt. Lifting the rusty-hinged wooden seat she turned her face away, almost gagging at the stench. She hoisted the pail up onto the brick edge, all the muscles in her lower back straining as she tried to avoid any spills on her skirt or shoes, and tipped the contents into the cesspit.

After shovelling ashes down the hole from a battered bucket kept in the corner she replaced the wooden seat. Outside in the sweet spring air she breathed deeply, ladled rainwater from the old butt beneath the sagging gutter, and rinsed the pail several times.

Back in the cottage she took a bar of scented soap from her basket, washed her hands thoroughly, then refilled the basin with hot water.

An hour later bathed and wearing a clean nightgown, her hair brushed and braided, Becky was back in the rocking chair with a blanket shielding her from draughts.

After building up the fire and making a fresh pot of tea Grace picked up the empty pitcher.

'Where you going with that?' Becky demanded.

'You'll need more water.'

Becky's expression was scandalized. 'You can't go up the pump.'

Grace peered through the window. 'Of course I can, and I will if I have to.' She dropped her voice to a whisper. 'But as Ernie is across in his garden I daresay he'll offer, and I shall accept with gratitude.' She glanced over her shoulder. 'I think he's lonely, Becky. It's – what – five years since his wife died? His son is married. Ernie's all by himself with all that kindness to give and no one to give it to.' She shook her head. 'It seems such a waste.'

'I s'pose you think I should jest forget what happened and be friends with'n.'

'You always used to be friends. I remember when your Tom and his wife Molly were alive–'

'Yes, well, they aren't no more.'

'I know. And it must be hard for you seeing Betty with Will.'

Becky's eyes filled. ''Tisn't that so much, though I still say 'twasn't decent how quick she took up with'n. And now she's in the family way.' She shook her head.

'Then what is it, Becky?'

'Can't you see?' Becky's face reflected her despair. 'My man have gone. I only had the one boy and I've lost he. I won't never have grandchildren. So what's the point?'

Chapter Four

As the train puffed its way slowly over the Tamar Bridge Bryce looked across at his brother. They both grinned. There was no need for words. Even though it was still sixty miles to Truro they were back in Cornwall. They were home.

Staring out of the train window at rolling hills, small fields edged with wild parsley and speedwells, pastures dotted with daisies and buttercups, grazing cattle, bluebells spilling down wooded banks and pastures bobbled with sheep, Bryce felt the weight of black misery begin to lift. *I will conquer this. I will.*

Bryce hefted his bag on to the coverlet. Crossing to the window he looked over the park and wooded valley that hid the road to distant hills now hazy in the sinking sun. The river was a ribbon of gold twisting between grassy banks strewn with cushions of pink thrift. Everything was so clean and quiet but for the distant thud of the stamps.

The humid heat, brilliant colours and seething crush of Calcutta had stunned after the soaring silent mountains of Tibet.

Despite their permits and passes it had taken two weeks of hard bargaining in the raucous squalor of Kidderpore Docks to obtain passage on a steamship carrying tea to London.

Turning from the window he looked from the empty grate with its green and white tile surround to the vase of cream and yellow tulips on the chest of drawers. The large wardrobe in the alcove, his bookshelves and bureau were instantly familiar. Yet they belonged to another person, another life.

The floorboards gleamed and the air was scented with lavender and beeswax. *The house in Zayul had smelled of pine resin and smoke, of oil paint and turpentine, of sweat and wet leather and Pinzo's mutton stew.*

He could hear his twin across the passage laughing with Patrick who had helped Thomas Coachman carry up the luggage. Opening his battered leather bag, Bryce pulled out a toilet bag, a grubby towel, his writing case and, finally, wrapped in a length of hand-woven white cloth, two thick leather-bound albums. Closing his eyes he held them to his face, inhaling the faint fragrance of spices. Anguish stopped his breath.

Moving the oil lamp with its fat pearl-glass bowl to one side, he laid the albums on his bedside table, unlocked his trunk and threw back the lid. But as he lifted out clothes and boots a waft of wood smoke and curry triggered a torrent of memories. Limpid agate eyes, curling blue-black hair, warm skin as dark as liquid honey, and a smile that had made the delays, frustrations, hardships and disasters bearable.

He closed his eyes visualizing the supple body and slender unexpectedly strong fingers that had worked magic whether massaging the ache from strained muscles or giving pleasure so exquisite that he had wept, his teeth clenched so as not to cry out.

Pierced by overwhelming loss he gripped the edge of the trunk as he fought for control. Nothing here had changed. But he had. He was not the man the family thought him. Not the man he had tried so hard to be. Even if he wanted to – and God knew his life would be easier – he could not undo what he had done, could not unlearn or forget what he now knew. As he took out the wooden box containing the rest of the photographs his chest felt as if it might burst with grief he could not share and must never betray.

Hearing Patrick's measured tread outside in the passage, he blinked quickly to dispel shaming tears and drew a ragged breath. Then down the hall Grace's voice, breathless, asked if they had arrived. Bryce listened as his brother strode across the landing and called down to her.

'We certainly have. Where were you? Too busy to welcome us?'

Dropping the box on the bed he went out to join his brother as Grace raced up the stairs towards them.

'I'm so sorry. I thought I'd be back long before you got home. I know I look a mess. Don't ask what I've been doing, you wouldn't want to hear. Oh, it's wonderful to see you both again.' She flung her arms around Richard who lifted her off her feet and kissed her soundly. Freeing herself she turned to Bryce. 'I've missed you so much.'

As they hugged each other Bryce was startled to feel the sharpness of her shoulder blades and the knobs of bone down her spine. Releasing him she linked an arm through each of theirs.

'Richard, I'm dying to see your sketches and paintings.' She turned to Bryce. 'And your photographs.' She squeezed his arm. 'You must have seen some amazing places.'

'We certainly did,' Bryce smiled, noting the shadows under her eyes.

'We'll tell you all about it later.' Richard extricated himself. 'Better finish unpacking first.'

Peering at the chaos of crumpled clothing, boxes, packing cases and half-emptied trunk, Grace wrinkled her nose. 'I'll send Kate up with a laundry hamper. Though she might need help to carry it down.'

'Well, what do you expect after three years away?' Richard demanded.

She gaped. 'You can't mean–'

'He's teasing you,' Bryce said.

Richard grinned. 'She was ready to believe it though.'

'Oh, you,' Grace laughed. As Richard vanished into his room she followed Bryce. 'Not *quite* as bad.'

'I've only just started.' As her smile faded he saw how tired she looked. 'You all right, Gracie?'

'I'm fine. It's just–' She clasped her hands together. 'Mama's health isn't good. It seems the slightest thing is enough to trigger one of her attacks.'

'And Granny?'

'Oh, she's fine. Since you went I don't think she's had so much as a cold.' Grace pulled a wry face. 'She says she can't afford to with Mama ill so often. "There's only room in a house for one invalid",' she mimicked wearily but without malice.

'I don't suppose she'll be overjoyed to see us back.'

'Oh, Bryce, of course she–' At his ironic expression she stopped. 'Well, you know how it is. She's grown used to having Mama all to herself.' As his brows climbed she brushed her hands down her skirt. 'We see little of Papa. There are problems at the mine. He spends most of his time there.

Goodness, listen to me. I didn't mean to–
I'd far rather hear your news.' She studied
him. 'Is anything wrong? You look–'

'Terrible. I know.' He forced a grin. 'But
we've been travelling for weeks. You didn't
let Mother plan anything for this evening,
did you?'

'Your letter only arrived this morning.
Which was all for the best as she didn't have
time to get into a state. I told her you would
need a few days to recover. You've been
living such a different life.'

Bryce hugged her to hide his face.
'Thanks.'

'There'll be no guests until next week. I'm
so glad you're home for my birthday
dinner.'

'You're a treasure, Grace. I can't imagine
why you're still here.'

She leaned back, bewildered. 'Where else
would I be?'

'In a home of your own with a decent man
who had the luck and good sense to marry
you.'

He felt her tense. She looked away and he
saw colour flood her face.

'Grace? Is there–? There is! Well, it's about
time.' He was pleased for her. Though only
five years older Grace had been far more
than just a sister when they were growing
up. Their mother's frequent ill health meant
it was to Grace that he and Richard had run

when grazed knees required a bandage or splinters needed removing. Grace had helped them build a tree house. She had given him a whole pound towards dry plates for his camera. *He longed to tell her. But how could he expect her to understand?*

'I hope he has more about him than those idiots who used to moon after Zoe. But if he loves you he's bound to be a good sort. So, when's the wedding?' He winced inwardly. He was trying too hard.

'Don't.' She pulled free.

He was instantly contrite. 'I'm sorry. What is it, Gracie? The parents don't like him?'

'No, it's not – goodness, look at the time. I must go and change.' Forcing a smile that made him ache in sympathy, she went to the door. 'I hope you're both hungry. Rose has been cooking all day.' He heard her run down the passage, then the distant slam of her bedroom door.

John Ainsley was seated at his desk writing when his housekeeper knocked lightly on the door of his book-lined consulting-room.

'Come in,' he called. Mrs Tallack entered, neat in a brown skirt and striped blouse, a cameo at her throat.

''Tis Mrs Renowden, Doctor. She wondered if you got a minute. But she'll come back another time if you're busy.'

John raised his head. 'No, I'll see her. Show

her in, will you?' Setting down his pen he closed the folder containing his partly written report. At last Parliament had called for an investigation into the sudden increase in deaths from lung disease among men working in Cornish tin mines. Rubbing tired eyes he adjusted his spectacles, swivelled his chair and rose to his feet as the door opened once more.

'Mrs Renowden, Doctor.' Mrs Tallack withdrew and the door clicked shut behind her.

'This is very good of you, John.' Dorcas came forward. She looked cool in blue and white cotton voile, a deep pointed frill of white lace over her full bosom. Her thick hair was piled up under a soft straw hat trimmed with matching ribbon. 'I hope I'm not interrupting?'

'Not at all.' He clasped her extended hand. 'It's always a pleasure to see you. The occasions are all too rare.'

He saw her mouth quirk. 'You know you are welcome to call whenever you pass the cottage. If you wait for me to be ill, heaven knows when our paths will cross again.'

He laughed. 'How I wish I could bottle your constitution and prescribe it to some of my more *loyal* female patients. Come and sit down.' He indicated a chair and waited while she settled herself, dipping her head so the brim of her hat hid her face. Years of experience had made him expert at deciphering silences. This one rang a faint alarm bell.

He had always admired her directness. She had no time for false modesty, nor for the arch simpering affected by so many of her sex when consulting him about intimate female problems. Perhaps being an artist afforded her a different perspective and greater detachment. What quality in Henry Damerel had attracted and held this remarkable woman? He tried to make it easier for her.

'So you're not ill. But you want my professional opinion?'

She raised her head. Her eyes narrowed and the furrow between her brows deepened. 'I'm looking at you, John. But I can't see you clearly.'

'Ah.' Turning to his desk he reached across books and papers for the velvet-lined wooden case containing his ophthalmoscope. 'How long?'

'A few weeks. I should have come sooner. But I hoped – I thought perhaps eyestrain, or tiredness.' He saw her take a deep breath. 'That's only partly true. I put off coming because I'm afraid.'

'Well, let's have a look.'

After a few moments he pushed his chair away and swivelled once more to his desk to make brief notes. Fitting a heavy frame over her nose he slotted in lenses and asked her to read different lines on a chart at the far side of the room. After she had done this several times he removed the frame and picked up his pen.

'I want the truth, John,' she said, as he finished making more notes. 'It's obvious from my difficulties with the chart that something is wrong.'

'Dorcas, I advise you to seek a second opinion.'

'Oh dear.' She tried to laugh. 'That sounds ominous.'

John surprised them both by taking one of her hands. Her fingers closed tightly on his as she leaned forward to see him clearly. 'I can prescribe glasses. They will make a considerable difference...' He forced himself to go on, to say what had to be said. 'For a while.'

'What exactly is wrong with my eyes?'

'A condition called malignant myopia.'

'And?'

'It's progressive and irreversible.'

Her gaze didn't waver. 'I'll go blind?'

'In the sense that you will lose acuity, yes. But you will still be aware of light and shade, and you will still see colour.'

He waited for the question he could not answer: *How long?* But it never came. 'I meant what I said, Dorcas. You really should get a second opinion.'

'Do you think you could be mistaken? Or you may have overlooked something?'

'No.'

'Then what purpose would it serve? John, in all the years we've known each other you have never given me reason to doubt you. Why should I start now?' Withdrawing her hand she began to rise.

He could not let her go so soon after such news. 'Will you join me for some tea? I usually have a cup about now and would enjoy it much more with company.'

She relaxed. 'Thank you. That would be most welcome.'

'I won't be a moment.' As he opened the door his housekeeper emerged from the kitchen carrying a tray.

'I put an extra cup on, Doctor. You and Mrs Renowden being friends and all.'

As John poured the tea Dorcas removed her hat and dropped it on the floor beside her chair. 'Does it take long to make spectacles?'

Handing her a cup and saucer he picked up his own. 'It depends. I'm going into Truro tomorrow. I'll take your prescription with me. You should certainly have them within ten days.'

'You'll send me an account?'

He nodded as she sipped tea. Then she lowered her cup, placing it carefully on the saucer.

'I shan't stop painting. Obviously I won't be able to continue in my present style. But

I won't give up.'

'Of course not.' His tone implied he had never doubted it. But until this moment he hadn't been certain she had understood the full import of his diagnosis. Though her courage would be tested to its limit, the fact that she was already contemplating life *after* was a good sign. 'But there will be difficulties. Have you heard from Hal lately?'

'I had a letter a fortnight ago. Why?'

'He's happy? Doing well?'

'Both, thank you. Speak plainly, John. What are you getting at?'

'I wondered if he ever mentioned returning to Cornwall, that's all.'

'No. You know why he left. There's nothing here to bring him back.'

'Except you. So don't you think–?'

'I should tell him? No, I don't. What could he possibly do in South America except worry? Hal has his life: I have mine. It would be wicked to burden him with knowledge he can do nothing about.'

He nodded. He had expected as much. 'And Henry?'

'Henry has enough to cope with right now. If I choose to tell him, it will be–'

'*When*, Dorcas, not if. Dear God, don't you think he would *want* to know?'

'Perhaps. But not yet, not until there's no alternative. And *I* will decide when that is.'

'Then there's nothing more to be said.' He

smiled. 'More tea?'

She touched his hand. 'You're a dear. Most men in your position couldn't have resisted criticizing Henry and condemning me. You never have.'

He shrugged. 'Henry should never have married Louise. But he did, and has done his best by her, which he could not have done without your love and support. But you, why–?' He shook his head. 'Forgive me. I've no right.'

'Why Henry? Because I love him, and because he needs me.'

'Have you never wanted to remarry?'

'Henry isn't free. Besides, I prefer things the way they are. I was perfectly happy being Zander's mistress. Marriage was his idea, to give me legal protection. Wise and unconventional though he was Zander treated me differently afterwards. I was a *wife.*' Bending to pick up her hat she slanted a smile at him. 'I'm independent and enjoy my solitude. Why change something that has worked so well for so long?'

'Why indeed?' Returning her smile he stood as she rose to her feet. But change was coming and it was beyond her control.

Laughing over her shoulder at Bryce, Grace urged the cob into a faster trot. Determined to master her bicycle he was wobbling all over the road. Beside her in the trap Richard rested one arm along the back of the wooden seat.

It was cooler today and the fresh breeze had persuaded Grace to wear a short jacket over her navy skirt and pale-blue shirt-blouse. Towering white clouds fringed the horizon, piled up like scoops of ice-cream. But over-head the sky was vivid blue and in the shelter of the high hedges the sun's warmth held a promise of summer.

'Hey.' Richard clung to the side with his free hand. 'What's the hurry?'

Her smile teased. 'I had this notion that you would be anxious to get to Polwellan as quickly as possible.'

He grimaced. 'I'd rather arrive in one piece. Do you always drive this fast?'

She raised her brows at him, laughter lurking at the corners of her mouth. 'Whatever happened to the intrepid adventurer? This isn't *fast*. At least, Sophie has never objected.'

He reddened slightly as he shook his head. 'She must have nerves of steel.' There was a short pause. Grace hid a smile and waited. She knew what he was about to say, knew it had been on his mind ever since he and Bryce arrived home.

'I don't suppose – would you happen to know...? I certainly wouldn't blame her if – I mean, three years is a long time, and the mail – well, it just wasn't possible to–'

'For goodness' sake, Richard!' Grace burst out laughing. 'How am I supposed to make sense of that? And how can I answer if you never finish what you're trying to say?'

He rubbed a thumb across his forehead beneath the rim of his flat tweed cap. Both he and Bryce were wearing tweed suits. Bryce had teamed his with a checked shirt with a soft turned-down collar and long tie. But Richard had opted for a slightly more formal look with a white shirt and a stiff collar. Grace bit the inside of her lip, amused and touched by his visible nervousness.

'I couldn't say anything to her before we went. It wouldn't have been fair. She was barely sixteen.'

'Ah,' Grace said softly. 'So it's Sophie you want to know about?'

'Of course it's Sophie! Who else?'

'Alice?' Grace suggested.

Richard shook his head. 'No. It was always Sophie. I know she's three years younger than Alice. Too young: that's what the colonel would have said. Too young to know her own mind; too young to consider herself bound to someone going abroad for three years. He'd have called me selfish, and he'd have been right. So I had to hold my tongue. But no one knows– Grace, I've thought about her so much. You would know, is she – has she...?'

'While you were away I've seen quite a lot

of Sophie. Each time we've met the first thing she does is enquire after Mama's health. She really does have beautiful manners, Richard. Her second question was always the same. Had we received a letter from you? She was thrilled with those you sent her.' Grace darted a sidelong glance. 'She rereads them every night. In fact they have been unfolded and refolded so often they are beginning to fall apart. Don't tell her I told you. She didn't say it was a secret, but I wouldn't want to embarrass her.'

'I won't say a word. She really said that? About my letters?' He beamed with delight and relief. 'It was so difficult. I mean, I didn't know if she would be interested in what we were doing. Yet there wasn't much else I could write about.'

'Not–? How on earth could you imagine she wouldn't be interested? She has grown up with her father's passion for rhodo-dendrons. She has lived her entire life aware of his determination to amass the largest collection of specimens and hybrids in the British Isles. She couldn't help but know how much your travels from north India to Tibet would mean to him. Of course she was interested. On his account as well as her own.'

'So she's not walking out with anyone, then?'

'She has had several serious suitors.'

He jerked round, his smile wiped away by frowning anxiety. 'Who? No, don't tell me. Yes, you must. I have to know what competition–'

'*Richard!* Before you get yourself all knotted up, let me finish. Apparently – and this is what she told me herself – she thanked them for their interest, told them that she was very flattered, but that it would not be fair or kind to encourage an interest she could not return.'

For the second time relief spread in a slow relaxing smile across his face. 'She did? Sophie said that?'

Grace nodded, envy and longing tugging at her heart. *If only.*

'She's a sweet girl, Richard.' He nodded. 'There's just one– Look, please don't think I want to spoil things for either of you, but–' She stopped, uncertain how to continue.

'What? It's all right, Grace, just tell me.' It was his gentleness that gave her the courage to voice her worry.

'It's just ... three years is a long time to be apart. It's obvious your feelings for Sophie haven't altered, nor have hers for you. That's wonderful. But you have lived very different lives during this separation. And you will both have changed – especially Sophie. As you said, she was barely sixteen when you left. What I'm trying to say is that the image you have of each other – it's out of date.'

Lifting his arm from the back of the seat, Richard put it around her shoulders and squeezed. 'You're a dear. And you needn't worry. I had realized that.'

She slowed the dogcart and they turned in through the open wrought-iron gates set on tall granite posts that marked the entrance to the Polwellan estate. On one side, behind a post and rail fence a herd of black and white dairy cattle grazed on lush grass. On the other an ocean of bluebells lapped the bases of trees that followed the gentle curve of the hillside down towards the house.

Withdrawing his arm Richard sat up straighter. Grace glanced at him, sympathetic, *envious*. 'Nervous?'

'Me? Nervous?' He laughed, his voice cracking. 'Whatever for?' He pulled a face. 'Last year in a forest near one of the villages in Tibet I came face to face with a Himalayan black bear. I'd been painting and was on my way back to camp. I hadn't taken a gun. I don't know which of us was more startled. Anyway, we stared at each other for a moment then he spun around and loped away. It happened so quickly. It wasn't until I told the others that I realized the danger I'd been in. Then I started shaking.' He held out his hand, palm down.

'Look at that.' He mocked the tremor. 'Ridiculous, isn't it?'

'No, it isn't.' She could imagine only too

well what he was feeling right now. 'But you'll be fine. Don't forget, Richard, Sophie will be just as uncertain, just as nervous.' She glanced over her shoulder as Bryce drew up alongside the dogcart.

He blew a soundless whistle. 'This is a lot harder than it looks.'

'Try not to run over the colonel,' Grace warned, straight-faced, as she followed the drive between tall rhododendron bushes vivid with pink and purple blooms, that screened the house from the prevailing westerly wind. She drew the cob to a halt on the gravelled circle in front of the house. Bryce skidded to an undignified stop, muttering under his breath.

Chapter Five

Built in the Georgian style with an additional wing set back from the main block, Polwellan had two long windows on either side of a pillared porch. The narrow flower-bed between house and drive contained dwarf rhododendrons with shiny dark leaves and bell-shaped flowers that shaded from marble-white through pale pink to cerise. Behind them the granite stonework glittered as the sun struck tiny quartz crystals.

'Richard, look!' Bryce was pointing at the bushes as Richard jumped down.

'They look like *arboreum*,' Richard frowned. 'But they can't be. The young plants don't produce flowers.'

The front door opened and a tall thin figure emerged. Hatless, his greying hair trimmed short, he wore a dark double-breasted suit of superb cut. A thick beard almost obscured his stiff collar and silk tie.

'My dear boys, what a pleasure to see you both again.' He gave each a hearty hand-shake. 'Welcome home. Good morning, Grace.'

'Good morning, Colonel Hawkins. Isn't it a lovely day?'

'It is indeed. All the better for seeing these two.' A broad smile deepened the creases around his eyes. As word of their arrival reached the servants' quarters a boy ran round the side of the house.

'Morning, Miss Damerel.' Knuckling his forehead he grasped the cob's bridle.

'Good morning, Ned.' Dropping the reins Grace climbed down and walked towards the open front door.

'Colonel' – Bryce indicated the bushes beside the porch – 'are these *arboreum?*'

'They are. I told Percy you'd spot them. Don't they look well? We want to breed both the palest and the deepest of the colours.'

Grace reached the porch as Sophie and Alice came flying down the elegant staircase. Though Alice was the elder by three years, both wore identical day dresses of white muslin trimmed with lace and satin ribbon.

Cream kid shoes with low curved heels peeped from beneath the frilled skirts. Glimpsing white silk stockings and light petticoats of finest silk edged with cobweb lace Grace was acutely aware that her triple-flounced petticoat of navy glacé silk – recommended for its durability – was definitely out of date. Worse, it rustled. This, according to her mother's copy of *The Lady,* was totally unacceptable to ladies of quality.

Grace's inward sigh gave way to a smile as Sophie and Alice slowed in their headlong dash to welcome the travellers.

'Grace, how lovely to see you.' Taking Grace's hands, Alice leaned forward to kiss her cheek. Then Sophie took her elder sister's place.

'Oh Grace, I'm so glad you came too.' Sophie's complexion was pink and her eyes shone with nervous anticipation. 'Do I look well?'

Grace pressed the quivering fingers. 'You look absolutely beautiful as always. Richard talked of you all the way here. He's been looking forward so much to seeing you again.'

'Really?' Sophie's transparent joy wrenched Grace's heart. 'Oh Grace, he's been away such a long time. I was so afraid he might have met someone else.'

'In the jungle? Up a mountain?' As Sophie's eyes widened in confusion Grace squeezed her hands again. 'I'm sorry. I shouldn't tease. The truth is Richard has been equally afraid that *you* might have.'

'Oh surely not? How could he even imagine I would.'

'You were only just sixteen when he left, Sophie. And three years is a long time.'

Looking past her, Sophie gave a tiny start. Her blush deepened. 'Yes,' she whispered. 'Yes, it is. Oh dear. I feel–'

'Nervous?' Grace whispered back. 'No more than he, I promise you.' Turning, she saw Alice staring at Bryce who was talking to the colonel. Though Richard appeared to be listening his eyes constantly flickered towards the doorway.

'Oh Grace,' Alice breathed. 'Bryce is so *brown*. I swear he's taller.'

Grace looked at her brother. 'No, but it might appear so because he's lost weight.'

'It really suits him.' Alice clasped her hands to her bosom, her expression dreamy as she watched Bryce. 'He's very handsome.'

Grace hid her surprise. She could not recall Alice ever indicating a particular interest in Bryce. But they had all changed during the past three years.

'Do you think so? Richard has always been considered the better looking,' Grace confided. 'He favours our mother. Bryce is more like Papa.'

'Come, girls,' Colonel Hawkins turned suddenly. 'Come and welcome these brave young men.'

Watching Richard clasp both Sophie's hands Grace wished with all her heart that Edwin Philpotts might hold her so, and look into her face with such warmth, such *hunger*.

'Sophie, it's good to be back.'

'It's wonderful to see you again,' Sophie blurted, her cheeks now deep rose. Impulsively Richard leaned forward and brushed her cheek with his lips. Though her lashes dropped shyly her smile was radiant.

As Sophie turned to welcome Bryce, Richard was beaming. Turning from Richard to Bryce, Alice held out both hands. 'We've really missed you.'

A hunted expression flashed across Bryce's face. Then because she clearly expected it and good manners forbade him denying her, Bryce took Alice's hands and kissed her upturned cheek. But it was obvious from the speed with which he stepped back and the distance he established between them that whatever hopes Alice harboured, he did not share them.

As Bryce crossed to the dogcart and Alice struggled to mask disappointment, Grace ached in sympathy. She knew how it felt to yearn for someone who saw you only as a friendly acquaintance, a useful pair of hands.

There was no doubt Edwin valued what she did. If it was her week for the flowers he never failed to compliment her arrangement. When she was cleaned the chapel or it was her turn to make teas for the Ladies' Bright Hour, he thanked her for being so generous with her time.

Unable to meet his eye, her burning skin dewed with nervous perspiration, she would murmur incoherently then rush away. How she longed for him to like her for who she was, not just for what she did.

But were it not for her jobs she would be simply one more vaguely familiar face among the three villages on his circuit. At least he knew her name. And it was nice to be thanked. Old Mr Peters hadn't believed in gratitude. In his view work done for the Lord was its own reward. Grace's breath caught on a sigh and she wrenched her thoughts back to her surroundings.

Reaching beneath the seat, Bryce pulled out a wooden box. He had shown her its contents the previous evening: dozens of small paper packets of seed, all carefully marked.

Reluctantly Richard tore himself away from Sophie and turned to her father. 'We sent back five–'

'Six,' Bryce corrected.

'Yes, you're right. Six parcels of seeds and specimens.'

Colonel Hawkins nodded. 'We received them all. Percy Tresidder is not a demonstrative man. But each time one of your parcels arrived he was like a dog with two tails. How did you do it?'

'It wasn't easy,' Richard admitted. 'After we left Sadiyya the only way we could send mail was by entrusting it to the Digaru.'

'What's a Digaru?' Sophie asked shyly.

Richard smiled at her. 'One of the two Mishmi clans who live in the valley and are always fighting each other. In return for keeping the jungle track to Rima open, the Digaru are excused paying taxes and are allowed to carry firearms. Most important for us, they guarantee the safety of travellers passing through their country.'

'We recruited fifty of them to carry all our baggage and rations,' Bryce added. 'But once we reached Rima they refused to march more than ten miles from their village, which meant that every ten miles we had to recruit new coolies.'

'Our letters and packages probably passed through twenty different hands before they reached Sadiyya,' Richard said. 'If one man had decided to hide them or throw them away there was nothing we could have done.'

'No doubt you want to see what Percy has been up to during your absence?' Colonel Hawkins's eyes twinkled. 'The nurseries cover twenty-five acres now.'

'Twenty-five?' the twins repeated in unison.

Their patron's grin was proud as he nodded towards the box in Bryce's arms. 'The other half?'

Bryce fell into step beside him. 'I saw some amazing specimens in the alpine region near a glacier. The strangest were two growing on wet scree. One looked as if it was creeping across the cold stones. It had scarlet trumpets that always pointed down the slope. The other had matted stems and such a dense spread of magenta flowers you couldn't see a single leaf.'

'You have photographs?' the colonel demanded.

'Of course, sir. They clearly show the habit.'

'But not the colours.' Colonel Hawkins sighed.

'That will come, sir. You mark my words.'

The colonel glanced back. 'Will you excuse us, Grace? Girls, take Grace in to see your mother.'

As the three men strode towards the walled garden and nurseries, Sophie tucked her arm through Grace's.

'Did Richard do lots of paintings while he was away?' she asked as the three of them moved towards the house. 'Have you seen them yet? Are they wonderful?'

'Yes, yes and yes,' Grace laughed. 'You will see them for yourself when you come to my birthday dinner next week. There are so many it would take days to look at them all properly.'

'I cannot imagine a more delightful pastime,' Sophie beamed.

'I can't wait to see Bryce's photographs,' Alice said. 'When I look at them I shall imagine what it was like to be in the jungle and the mountains. I daresay it was interesting to see such places, but I'm sure they must be glad to be home.'

Grace smiled but said nothing. Of Richard's feelings there could be no doubt. About Bryce she wasn't so sure. He had warned her he was very tired. But something about him worried her: an air of strain which, the instant he knew himself observed, was instantly masked with jokes and questions that distracted her. She wanted to help. But at the moment he was keeping what troubled him to himself.

Home to each new Methodist minister, the manse was an early Victorian house set a few feet back from the road and sufficiently spacious to accommodate a large family and several servants. A wooden gate set in the low stone wall stood permanently open.

To the left of a paved path leading to a granite front step, tiny white bells of lily-of-the-valley sheltered beneath a myrtle bush. To the right, hydrangeas were unfurling fresh green leaves. An oblong of plain glass above the front door allowed light into a hallway that would otherwise have been dark and gloomy.

In the small back bedroom he had chosen for its view over fields to the river, Edwin Philpotts tied the tapes of his black vest behind his back. Securing the stiff white band with a flat stud he eased it away from his neck, the edge as sharp as a blade against his finger. Buttoning his waistcoat he shrugged into the old-fashioned black frock coat that proclaimed his calling as clearly as his dog collar.

From the mirror standing on the chest of

drawers a sombre face frowned back at him. Pastoral visits were one thing: this was different. Nor was it wise. He could have declined. The invitation had been written, not verbal.

Flora Bowden, the housekeeper inherited from his elderly predecessor, had brought the sealed envelope to his study and handed it to him with a loud sniff, a signal that something had upset her. The first time he heard that sniff had been the day he met Grace Damerel. Introduced by Mrs Nancholas, his encounter with Grace had been fleeting. No sooner had they shaken hands than she had rushed away.

Tall, slim, fair was all he had registered of her general appearance. But wide grey eyes and fiery colour staining creamy skin were images that had remained with him for the rest of the day and long into a sleepless night.

He had had to force his attention back to Mrs Nancholas who was telling him how helpful he would find Miss Damerel. It was then that Miss Bowden, carrying a dustpan, had passed them with a sidelong glance and a loud sniff. Guessing a response was expected he had asked Miss Bowden politely if she too was succumbing to the head cold going round the village. The words were out before he caught Mrs Nancholas's warning look.

Miss Bowden, her pigeon chest swelling with indignation, had responded that she enjoyed excellent health thank-you-very-much. Not like some she could mention who took to their beds every time the wind changed.

Aware of undercurrents best ignored, he replied he was delighted to hear it and, turning back to Mrs Nancholas, asked about hymns for the following Sunday.

Laying the letter aside while Miss Bowden fussed about putting more coal on the fire he resumed work on his sermon. Not until several moments after her reluctant departure had he laid down his pen and picked up the envelope. He recognized the writing from various lists pinned to the chapel notice board.

He should have declined. He had quickly grown used to hearing her name mentioned by the sick and elderly he visited. He couldn't think of any village organization to which she didn't contribute in some way. Even those embittered by loss and hardship softened when they spoke of her.

His parents claimed no church could function, much less flourish, without women. He had seen that truth for himself. Ministers and missionaries might draw in converts. But it was women who cleaned and polished, arranged hospitality for visiting clergy, ran all the support groups, organized activities for raising funds, and comprised more than half the congregation.

But such observations found little sympathy with his superiors who warned him that while an occasional word of appreciation was permissible it must be general. He must at all costs avoid singling out any one person for praise. Doing so risked fomenting jealousy and ill feeling. It was a well-known fact that women, especially single women, were prone to developing emotional attachments to doctors or clergymen. This applied particularly to women of a certain age whose balance of mind was in any case precarious. As his circuit covered three villages containing a number of such creatures, it behoved him, a younger man and unmarried, to be doubly careful.

Exhausted, still traumatized, and grateful to be allowed to continue in his vocation, he promised circumspection. A missionary since his ordination he had no experience of life as a circuit minister. It required, he was discovering, boundless tact and diplomacy. Praise given to one group had to be matched by gratitude to another. Yet it cost little. Their initial shock informed him their efforts had never been considered worthy of mention, let alone deserving of thanks. And they showed their appreciation by working even harder.

He heaved a deep shuddering sigh. He

should have declined. He could have found a legitimate excuse. She would have accepted it: believed it. But he didn't want to lie to her, even though she would not know it was a lie. *You'll tell her the truth then? You'll tell her the real reason you were sent back to England?*

The image in the glass gazed back at him, hollow-eyed, anguished. He had not known her long. But three and a half months was more than sufficient to recognize that her kindness to the poor of the village went far beyond what might be expected from local gentry. Long enough to sense hurts bravely covered. Long enough to realize the true depth of his feelings for her. Feelings he could never admit.

He knew she was not indifferent to him. When they met in the village, in the chapel, after Sunday school, she always smiled when she returned his greeting. Though she never initiated conversation, never tried to detain him as others did, she would willingly discuss chapel matters provided he took care to look at her only when her own gaze was lowered. For if he caught her eye her colour rose and she shied away like a startled gazelle.

He should have sent his regrets. But he had not. He would go. He would be polite and pleasant to her parents and the other guests: do and say all that was proper. For a little while he would be near her. And perhaps she might look on him as a friend.

In her bedroom Grace frowned at her reflection in the long glass. She had planned to wear the pretty cameo her parents had given her for her twenty-first birthday. But her hands were shaking so much she couldn't get the pin level. Her skin prickling with nervous perspiration she dropped the brooch on her dressing-table and snatched up a crumpled handkerchief soaked in lavender water.

Pressing it to her upper lip then her forehead and temples she drew deep breaths and mentally repeated the greeting she had been rehearsing all afternoon. *Good evening, Mr Philpotts.* The villagers called him Reverend. But that term was properly used only in writing. *Good evening, Mr Philpotts. How kind of you to come.* That would be polite and welcoming without being effusive.

Why was she so flushed? Her bath had been deliberately tepid. Staring into the glass she pressed her fingers to hot cheeks. A lady's hands were supposed to be cool. Hers were cold. But the rest of her was far too warm. Perhaps if she held her wrists under the cold tap – no, that would mean unbuttoning her cuffs. If fastening one brooch was beyond her she couldn't possibly manage twelve tiny buttons.

Her mother had wanted her to have a dress

specially made for this evening. But she had refused. How could she justify an unnecessary luxury when her father was beset by financial problems? Besides, she had worn her blue so seldom it was virtually new.

In her heart of hearts she did not feel she had anything to celebrate. What was different from last year? Or the year before?

Tonight Edwin Philpotts was coming to dinner. As her heartbeat quickened she refocused on her reflection. At least the high close-fitting collar hid the hollows at the base of her throat. The dress was white figured net over blue silk, the bodice drawn in by a broad sash of blue satin that emphasized the slenderness of her waist. Full sleeves of pleated chiffon were gathered into deep tight cuffs, and the hem of the deeply gored skirt was edged with a narrow frill that brushed her white kid slippers. Violet had gathered up her hair into a loose topknot of curls.

She glanced at the clock. It was time to go. Her gaze fell on the brooch. She reached out a hand, observed its tremor and left the cameo on her dressing-table.

Descending the staircase ahead of her, her father was immaculate in a single-buttoned dinner jacket with silk facings. Against the dense black his stiff collar was starkly white, his face the colour of raw beef beneath close-cropped pewter hair. A gold link gleamed in his pristine cuff.

Elegant lavender silk flattered her mother's pale complexion. Her hair appeared thicker than usual, and was dressed in a becoming style enhanced by two silk flowers that matched her dress. Realizing that Violet had used pads of false hair to create the fullness, Grace was touched that her mother should think the occasion worth such effort.

Following them downstairs and across the hall to the drawing-room, Grace drew another tremulous breath.

Louise took a small glass of dry sherry from the tray Patrick offered and smiled at Grace. 'Darling, you look lovely. Doesn't she, Henry?'

'Indeed she does.' Lifting a crystal tumbler containing an inch of whisky he raised it in salute. 'Happy birthday, lass.'

Grace's heart swelled. 'Thank you, Papa.'

Louise extended her free hand to her elder daughter. 'I want this to be a special evening, my darling. I do wish you had agreed to a dance. I would so like to see you have *fun*. You work so hard.'

'Wow!'

She turned to see Bryce studying her in open astonishment.

'You look really nice.'

'There's no need to sound *quite* so surprised,' she teased.

'Really, Bryce,' Louise scolded.

'No, I didn't mean–' He pulled a face.

'Sorry. Out of practice, I'm afraid. Evening, Father. How did the meeting go?'

As her father remained silent Grace held her breath.

'Perhaps this isn't the right time to ask,' Bryce said. 'I just– I was interested that's all.' As his father's eyebrows lifted, Bryce continued quietly, 'I couldn't do what you do, Father. And God knows you wouldn't want my life.' There was a painful edge to his voice that startled Grace. 'But that doesn't mean I'm not concerned when I read about mines all over the county closing down. It can't be easy for you or any mine owner at the moment.'

'It's not.' Henry cleared his throat. 'I'm much obliged to you.' He drained his glass and turned away looking for Patrick.

'Here's Granny,' Grace murmured.

'Good God,' Bryce whispered. '*Still* in mourning?'

In unrelieved black except for her customary pearls, Hester stood in the doorway waiting for someone to escort her to a chair. Spotting Grace she beckoned.

'No.' Bryce restrained her. 'Richard and I will take care of Granny this evening. A couple of glasses of sherry should loosen her up.'

Grace caught his arm, her voice low. 'Bryce, be careful. We don't want–'

'We don't want to see you running about

94

after Granny. This is your party and your guests will be arriving at any moment. There's the doorbell.' He patted her hand. 'Here they come. Enjoy yourself.'

Grace's heart had leapt into her throat. She clasped her hands tightly hoping to stop their renewed trembling as the door opened to admit John Ainsley.

'Happy birthday, Grace.' John kissed his niece's cheek and handed her a package. 'I hope you'll find this useful.'

She undid the wrappings and found a writing case of tooled leather and an elegant fountain pen. 'Oh, how wonderful! Thank you, Uncle John. How very kind.'

'It was my pleasure.' Smiling, John Ainsley took a glass of sherry. As he moved away the door opened again to admit Mary Prideaux with Alice Hawkins close behind. Richard turned expectantly towards the door.

'Happy birthday, my dear.' Mary kissed Grace. 'I came via Polwellan and collected Alice. Poor Sophie sends her apologies.' Her words stopped Richard in his tracks. 'She's developed a streaming cold and is confined to bed. Mrs Hawkins asked me to tell you how desperately disappointed she is. She was so looking forward to coming.'

'I'm so sorry she's not well.' Seeing Richard's expression Grace knew Sophie's disappointment could not be deeper than his.

'Happy birthday, Grace.' Alice pressed

two flat packages tied with red ribbon into Grace's hand. These were opened to reveal some embroidered handkerchiefs and a handmade bookmark.

'That's so kind of you, Alice. Please tell Sophie I'll write to her.'

'Yes. Will you excuse me?'

'Oh dear,' Mary said softly beside Grace as they watched Alice approach Bryce with fluttering lashes. Turning to Grace she smiled. 'I have a feeling the coming year is going to be a very special one for you.' She pressed a package into Grace's hand. 'A small token of my affection and regard.'

Opening the little box Grace gasped. Nestling in midnight-blue velvet was a dainty gold ring set with a turquoise surrounded by seed pearls.

'Oh, Mary! It's beautiful.'

'Here, let me hold the box.' Mary took it as Grace extracted the ring and slipped it onto the third finger of her right hand.

'It's just perfect. I-I don't know what to say. Except thank you,' she added quickly. 'It's– I'm–' Shaking her head she gazed at the ring.

Mary squeezed her arm. 'Happy birthday, my dear. Your mother's calling me. And you have another guest.'

Chapter Six

Grace looked up as Edwin walked in. A head taller than Richard whose hand he was shaking, he looked thin and pale in his black frock coat and clerical collar. Brown hair, silky as a spaniel's, flopped over his forehead. Her heartbeat thundered, drowning the babble of conversation. Her mouth was suddenly dry. Aware of telltale heat climbing her throat she bent her head. She had been so afraid he wouldn't come. *Go and welcome him.* She forced herself forward, saw him excuse himself to Richard. She swallowed.

'Good evening, Mr Philpotts. How kind of you to come.' Hearing her own voice sounding perfectly calm lifted a great weight from her shoulders. Shyly she offered her hand. As he took it she was astonished to feel his fingers as cold as her own.

'Good evening, Miss Damerel. It was generous of you to invite me.'

Though brief his clasp was firm. Suddenly she felt immeasurably better.

He cleared his throat. 'Given our short acquaintance I cannot presume to call myself a friend.'

Yes you can. I wish you would. Acutely conscious of an audience she felt her face burning.

'However, in honour of your birthday I hope you will accept this small gift with all – with my best wishes.'

Raising her eyes she glimpsed agony in his brown gaze. Seeing beads of perspiration on his upper lip her heart went out to him. For an instant she was reminded of Bryce. At village fêtes he would address the crowd with confidence. Yet on a personal level he was quiet and reserved. It had never occurred to her that a minister might be shy.

'Th-thank you.' Grace knew everyone was watching. It must be difficult for Edwin Philpotts, still very much a newcomer, to join a family party. *He had known that and still come.* The villagers were used to having a new minister every three years. That was the way it had always been. Old, young, with or without family, a minister stayed three years then moved on to a new circuit.

The Cornish were wary of outsiders. Because of their calling ministers met with less suspicion than most. Even so it could take several months to be accepted as part of the community. Then all too soon it was time to move on and face the same situation all over again. The demands on a shy man would be immense.

She fumbled with the wrapping, her

fingers clumsy. She looked up, speechless, then dropped her gaze to the slim volume.

Edwin cleared his throat. 'Being so busy you probably don't have much spare time in which to read. But these poems are quite short.'

She couldn't resist opening the cover to see if he had written anything inside. *To Miss Grace Damerel,* she read, *on the occasion of her birthday, with kind regards, Edwin Philpotts.*

'Thank you,' she repeated, the words hopelessly inadequate. *Kind regards.* But he had given her poetry.

'Ladies and gentlemen.' Bryce nodded at his brother and everyone drew back so Grace could see.

Richard was holding a framed painting, sixteen inches by twelve, of a pale-cream rhododendron with dark green glossy leaves.

'This is one of several previously unknown species we discovered in Tibet,' he explained.

'Richard, it's beautiful,' Grace exclaimed in delight. 'Whenever did you find time to do it? Thank you so much. I shall hang it on my bedroom wall.'

'That's not all.' Richard looked at Bryce who held out a rolled parchment tied with red ribbon.

'Percy has germinated the seeds,' Bryce announced. 'At this moment twenty young plants are thriving in the nursery at Polwellan.' As everyone clapped and called out congratulations Bryce raised his hand for silence. 'It has a sweet fragrance. Because it was a new discovery we had the privilege of naming it. We have called it *Grace*.'

'Oh!' Grace's eyes filled and she threw herself into Bryce's arms. 'Oh, what a wonderful – but you shouldn't – I don't deserve–'

Laying a finger on her lips he muttered hoarsely as he hugged her, 'No one deserves it more, Gracie.'

Wiping away tears with her fingertips Grace smiled, her vision misted and her heart full as Patrick announced that dinner was served.

Taking his place at the head of the table, Henry Damerel fought impatience. Ignoring Grace's quiet prompting Hester Chenoweth was peering at each place card, obstructing everyone as they tried to take their seats.

Looking away – Grace would deal with it – he took a large mouthful of his second whisky. The neat spirit burned its way down his throat as he surveyed the dining-room. Elegant, tasteful, stylish, it was the result of his efforts. Rebuilt, restored and redecorated thanks to *him*. *His* vision and *his* hard work had hauled the estate back from the brink of ruin.

He looked along the mahogany table, past gleaming crystal, polished silverware, crisp white napery and bowls of cream and yellow roses. He was a man of substance. Reassured, he drained his glass, feeling the tension ease in his neck and shoulders as the fear that threatened to engulf him retreated.

His gaze fell on his wife seated at the foot of the table talking to her mother. She enjoyed company and certainly looked cheerful enough. No doubt tomorrow she would be confined to her bed, prostrate with exhaustion. Louise's pleasure carried a heavy price. *Thirty-one years.* It seemed like forever.

On his left Mary and John were laughing together while Alice Hawkins simpered at Bryce. On his right Grace was scarlet as she replied to some remark of the minister's. She was a good lass: ran the house like clockwork; took care of her mother. But blushing at her age? She had never been easy in company. Not like Zoe who had been born knowing how to charm. Zoe was a minx: stubborn and infuriating. But she defied anyone not to adore her.

His gaze slid back to Mary. A strange woman: could make herself invisible, yet not in the least shy. Assured: that's what she was. Why wouldn't she be? She was gentry and had money: a combination that bred confidence.

As she laughed she looked up, meeting his gaze. A brief yet unmistakable *frisson* startled him. He'd never thought of her in that way. Yet there was definitely more to her than the subdued clothes and quiet manner suggested. He let his gaze drift.

It still rankled that the twins had preferred to go chasing off around the world gathering plants instead of following in his footsteps, as he had followed in his father's. But he had to admit the experience had matured them, particularly Bryce. He'd always been boisterous, hurling himself into any challenge, forever in trouble and usually sporting at least one bandage.

In the past Bryce had provided entertainment, both at dinner and afterward, reducing the family and any guests to helpless laughter with tales of disaster. Tonight he was virtually silent. But after a long and tiring journey home, not to mention three years of travelling, they would need time to recover.

He'd always had a soft spot for Bryce. A fine shot and a bruising rider, Bryce reminded him of himself: a man's man. Whereas Richard... Henry frowned. Richard had talent. Dorcas had left him in no doubt of that. But painting was hardly a *manly* occupation. Photography was different. Involving science and technology it was far more acceptable.

After melon came asparagus soup, then salmon cutlets. The main course of roast lamb was accompanied by dishes of new potatoes, spinach, peas and baby carrots. Draining his glass Henry motioned to Patrick for more wine. Down the table Alice Hawkins was trying to hold Bryce's attention by asking what part of India he had found most interesting.

Watching Bryce divert her questions to Richard, Henry experienced a pang of envy. Not for the travelling: the thought of the noise, heat, filth, and slow swaying trains packed with people made him shudder. What he envied, *resented*, was their freedom. No business worries denied them sleep. Neither of them had a wife who had ailed nearly the whole of her marriage, nor a mother-in-law who had bought her way into the house and would never leave.

Plates were removed and Kate brought in Charlotte Russe, strawberry cheesecakes, cherry tarts and dishes of clotted cream.

Ignoring Louise's reproachful glance Henry called for more wine.

Oaks and sycamores cast dappled shadows across the road as Dr John Ainsley, his leather bag beside him on the wooden seat, clicked his tongue and urged the pony into a trot. To his right, flat and glassy in the sun, the river stretched from just beyond the hedge to the overhanging trees on the far side a hundred yards away.

The high tide had totally submerged the

twisting channels and grassy banks. Swallows skimmed and swooped over the water's surface feeding off spiralling clouds of insects. The clop of hoofs and creak of the trap's wheels disturbed a heron and it took off with heavy flapping wings.

In his capacity as the mine's medical officer appointed by the adventurers, John made this journey every month so that any mine employee with a medical problem could see him without having to take time off work and so lose pay. These regular visits had given him chilling insight into the repercussions of dry drilling.

Crossing the bridge he turned left off the main road then took a right-hand fork. As he reached the top of the hill the thunder of the stamps grew louder. Ahead of him trees gave way to a wasteland of red-tinged rubble and spoil heaps, piles of wood for props and shuttering, and discarded pieces of rusting machinery.

Guiding the pony through the open gate at the entrance, John drove down to the count house. A skinny boy, his clothes covered in thick red dust, was kneeling on the ground, coughing and gasping. John halted the pony.

'Are you all right, lad?'

Trying to heave air into his lungs, the boy looked up and nodded, tears streaking his grimy cheeks. He scrambled to his feet. 'Yes, sur.'

His jacket and trousers had been cut down but were still too big for him, as were his boots.

John looked harder. 'You're Annie Banks's son, aren't you? Luke, isn't it?'

'Yes, sur,' the boy repeated, touching his cap again. He turned his head, covering his mouth with a filthy hand as another bout of coughing shook him.

'Don't you usually drive one of the ore carts for the small stamp mill?' John nodded towards the waterwheel. 'What were you doing underground?'

'Kenny's home sick, sur, and they didn't have no one to work the air pump while they was drilling.' His lower lip quivered. 'I stuck it so long as I could, sur, honest. But I aren't used to it, see?' He coughed again, wheezing as he dragged air into his lungs.

John tried to imagine the ninety-degree heat in the lower levels, the noise of the drills in the confined space, the candles dimmed by dense swirling red dust that filled eyes, nose and mouth. Familiar impotent anger swelled inside him. That was no place for a child.

'I'm sure you did your best.' Stepping down from the trap he lifted his bag from the seat. 'Take Clover to the shed for me. Then I want you to stand where you can feel the breeze and brush that dust off your clothes. When you've finished, take ten deep breaths and blow the air out as hard as you can. All right?'

The boy lifted one shoulder. 'If you say so, sur.'

John could see from his expression that while he understood the instructions he didn't see the point of them.

Touching his cap the boy reached for the bridle to lead the pony to an open-sided shed where hay and water waited.

John turned away, hesitating as memory stirred. 'How is your mother? Is she still brewing her nettle and herb beer?'

The boy nodded. 'Yes, and she've started selling chips, dinner times and evenings.'

'Has she indeed? How very enterprising.' Seeing the boy's uncertainty John winked at him. 'That means she's brave and clever. Tell her I said so.'

The boy's teeth flashed white in his grubby face. 'I will too, sur.' He led the pony away.

John watched them go. Annie Banks lived in Miner's Row in a cottage the sun never penetrated. In the past ten years she had lost a 5-year-old son to post-measles enceph-alitis and her longed-for baby daughter to pneumonia. Her 38-year-old husband was bedridden and in the final stages of tuber-culosis. With medicines to buy and Luke's wage as a pump boy only a pittance, Annie had turned brewing skills learned from her mother into a thriving business. But Annie was exceptional.

A short queue had already formed outside the count house. Many years ago, when the mine was thriving, the room where now he held his surgery had been an additional office. At that time the purser had required an assistant and a clerk. It was large enough for two straight-backed chairs and the table on which he wrote up his notes. But once he had erected the folding trestle table that, when padded with a pair of blankets covered by an old clean sheet, served as an examination couch, the room was very cramped. However, it possessed two useful advantages. The west-facing window let in plenty of light. And it adjoined the lavatory containing a wash-hand basin fed with hot water piped from the boiler house.

During the next two hours John checked the progress of several crushed fingers, a badly gashed leg and a powder burn. Because it was necessary to clean these wounds thoroughly of any purulent discharge and the inevitable gritty dust before applying fresh bandages, his hands reeked of carbolic.

Five years ago almost all the injuries he dealt with were the inevitable by-product of physical labour in cramped conditions: cuts, bruises, sprains, burns, crushed fingers and toes, and the occasional broken limb. Now, though these still made up a good proportion of cases, many more men came to him with breathing difficulties, bronchitis and wet, rattling coughs. These were men in their twenties and thirties. Men whose corded muscles and strong-looking bodies disguised lungs already damaged beyond repair. As he examined them, looking and listening for the inevitable signs of TB, he found it hard to contain his anger.

These men worked in hellish conditions to give their families a decent standard of living. They were proud to be miners for it gave them status no other manual work could match. They were in the prime of life, possessing skills and knowledge the mine could ill-afford to lose. But they were dying like flies, leaving widows and young children in desperate straits. Something had to be done.

When he visited as a physician and not a shareholder he ignored lunch, fuelled instead by cups of tea and coffee. During the quiet spell after two o'clock, when the afternoon shift had started down and the early shift were still on their way up to grass, he used the time to file away each man's record card. These were kept in an oblong tin box to which only he had a key. After that he worked on notes to add to the report he intended sending to Parliament. But to ensure it was read and acted upon with the urgency it deserved, he would have to bypass the barrier of civil servants and government minions, and place it directly into the hands of someone with the authority to do something. Perhaps his daughter Catherine might be able to help him.

He became aware of shouting followed by the approaching thud of heavy boots, running. The door burst open to reveal a dust-caked miner still wearing his hardened felt hat; its stub of candle attached to the front with a lump of sticky clay. His jacket, shirt and trousers of coarse sun-bleached drill were tattered and stained reddish-brown by the tin ore. But the wet splash across his thighs was scarlet.

'Doctor, come quick. 'Tis Paul Moyle. Started coughing on the ladder he did. We got'n up to grass but he've collapsed. Bleeding something awful he is.' The miner clattered out with John close behind him.

Paul Moyle lay on his side, eyes closed, knees drawn up, blood dribbling from the side of his mouth to pool, obscenely bright and frothy, on the bare ground. Someone had removed his hard hat and skullcap, and sweat-darkened hair clung damply to his scalp and forehead. Around him his workmates crouched or stood silent and frowning. John sensed their unease and growing anger. Similar scenes were becoming all too frequent.

'Fainted, have he?' a miner enquired with

a trace of anxiety.

'Best thing if he have,' another grunted. 'Poor bugger couldn't get no breath. Choking he was.'

John crouched beside the young man whose face beneath its dark-brown coating of sweat-smeared dust was pale and waxy. At least he was still alive. But a lung haemorrhage at his age did not bode well.

'How are us going to get'n home?' someone demanded.

'I'll take him,' John said. 'Did any of you want to see me? If there's anything urgent–'

'Nothing that can't wait,' a miner said.

'Don't you mind about we. 'Tis Paul who need you now, Doc.' A rumble of agreement greeted this statement.

'Thank you. Will someone–?' But they had already anticipated him and two men at the rear were already striding towards the shed.

By the time they returned with the pony and trap, Paul had opened his eyes, but, clearly in shock, he seemed barely aware of his surroundings. As another miner fetched one of the blankets that had covered the wooden table, two more helped the young man up and John wrapped the blanket around him. He was lifted gently into the trap where he hunched against the wooden seat, ashen-faced and shaking.

'You'll be all right, boy,' one of his workmates said gruffly. 'Coughed too hard you did. Prob'ly strained something. We've all done it.'

But his was the only attempt at encouragement. The others hadn't the heart. They didn't need John to tell them that there was very little chance Paul would ever return to the mine.

With the young man slumped against his shoulder, John guided the trap into Miner's Row, scattering the playing children. They stood in the gutter, pressed against grubby cob walls, watching in silence as he passed, except for one grave-faced little girl in a calico dress and grubby pinafore. No more than six years old, she was clasping the hand of an even grubbier toddler.

'Hey, that's my da!' Her tone was accusing. Her expression reflected bewilderment and fear.

John leaned down keeping his voice low. 'Run and tell your mother that Daddy's not very well and the doctor is bringing him home.'

The little girl whirled round, dragging her brother who pulled against her, squealing in protest. She yanked his arm and his head jerked backward, his wail choked off by a gasp. Jumping over the gutter she dived into a small yard, hauling her brother after her.

'Ma! Nan! Come quick!'

John could hear a baby crying inside the cottage.

'Fer God's sakes, Polly, what's wrong now?' A thin careworn young woman emerged from the back door wiping her hands on a rag, her faded blouse and skirt covered by a piece of sacking that served as an apron. 'I told you–' She stopped. John saw the blood drain from her face. 'Oh no, no, no. Jesus, no.' Dropping the rag, she started forward, but after two uncertain steps she stopped, clinging to the wooden gatepost as she swayed.

Her cries brought out an older woman. John recognized her. Martha Tamblin had been widowed a year ago when her miner husband died aged 44, another victim of lung disease. As she realized what she was seeing she froze, her jaw dropping in dismay.

John's heartbeat quickened as he wondered how he would cope with the young miner and two hysterical women. But after her momentary horror Martha straightened up, sucked in a deep breath, and took charge.

'Come on, Ellie.' She gripped her daughter's shoulder. 'Go on in and get the bed ready. I'll help Doctor with Paul. Polly? Listen, my bird, run next door and ask Mrs Kessell if she'll mind Mark and Meggy for half an hour. Tell her your da have been took bad.'

John's admiration was tinged with relief as they half-carried the young man into the dark and cluttered cottage. At least Ellie Moyle was blessed with a capable mother. But with a sick husband and four young children, how would she manage financially? He steered his thoughts on to the immediate medical problems. *The rest was not his concern.*

Chapter Seven

As the gate hinges squeaked, Dorcas sat back from her painting. Rinsing her brush she picked up a rag and wiped the fine bristles, waiting for her visitor to follow the path round the side of the cottage. It was too early to be Henry. But those who knew her well enough to call without an invitation also knew where to find her on sunny days.

The back garden covered nearly half an acre. Will Treneer came once a month to do any heavy work. The rest she managed by herself. The noisy hinges offended Will, but she refused to let him oil them. The squeak acted as a warning. If she felt like being sociable she remained outside. If not, the few moments' notice allowed her – and Henry if he were with her – time to retreat into the cottage. But the situation at the mine meant his daytime visits had grown increasingly rare.

Today she remained where she was. Alongside her easel a small folding table held the paraphernalia of her painting. On a tray at her feet two tumblers flanked a glass jug covered by a circle of bead-edged muslin. Though she missed his company his absence relieved her of the need to tell him about her failing sight. He would have to know eventually. But with so many demands on him already she was reluctant to add another worry, especially one he could do nothing about.

Removing her glasses Dorcas rubbed the bridge of her nose where they had rested. It wasn't until she took them off that she realized how heavy they were. Her vision blurred uncomfortably so she quickly replaced them, flexing shoulders stiff from concentrated effort. Her gaze roamed over the garden committing the shapes and colours to memory. Last month misty with bluebells, the grass in the orchard was now bright with buttercups.

A slender figure appeared hesitantly around the side of the cottage.

'Grace! How lovely to see you.' Henry's elder daughter was one of the few people whose company Dorcas welcomed. She had watched Grace grow from a self-effacing child into a sweet-natured hard-working young woman taken for granted by her family.

She knew Grace always had, and probably always would, consider herself her sister's inferior. No one would argue that Zoe was the more beautiful, or that her voice was remarkable for its sweetness and purity, but Zoe was as cunning as she was gifted, using her undeniable charm to acquire whatever her selfish little heart craved. In contrast Grace was kind, willing and helpful to everyone. It irritated Henry.

'Why?' he had demanded of Dorcas, as he shook his head in bewilderment. 'I accept it's our Christian duty to look after those less fortunate. Though some of them might not be quite so unfortunate if they got off their backsides and made a bit of effort. Nor do I begrudge any of the vegetables or fruit she takes to retired staff or the sick and elderly in the village. But why is she forever visiting those flea-ridden hovels behind the forge or down by the quay? When she isn't there she's in Miner's Row cleaning up after some sour old widow who won't see Christmas. Why?'

'Have you asked her?'

'Of course. She says it gives her a sense of purpose. I think she's wasting her time. She'll never change them. Do you know what she said? *We have so much and they have so little.* I told her straight, we've got what we've got because *I've* worked for it, and damned hard too, just like my father did, and his father.'

Understanding that his anger sprang from fear, frustration, and the crushing weight of his responsibilities, Dorcas did not argue. Instead she soothed him and with long-perfected skill diverted his attention to other things. But she could see what Henry could not: that in trying to help wherever she perceived a need, Grace was trying to expiate guilt at being the cause of her mother's ill health. It was not her fault and she should never have been allowed to believe that it was. But Dorcas could say nothing to Grace. To do so would admit knowledge she should not have, and provoke questions the answers to which would cause untold damage to people she had no wish to harm.

'Am I disturbing you? Please say if it's not convenient. I can always come back another time.'

'I wouldn't hear of it.' Dorcas smiled up. 'Come and sit down. Will you have some lemonade?' She reached down for the jug by her stool. Filling a glass she offered it to Grace who hesitated.

'What about you?'

'I have another glass here.' Realizing Grace would assume a guest was expected and that she was intruding, Dorcas quickly thought up an explanation as she poured the cloudy liquid containing fine curls of lemon peel. 'I can guarantee a wasp or fly will try to drown itself so I always bring out a spare.'

'Thank you.' Leaning back on the rustic seat Grace drank deeply. 'Oh, that's delicious. If I'd known today was going to turn out quite so warm I'd have worn something lighter.' She stretched out neatly shod feet revealing fine wool stockings below a long skirt of navy serge, then hooked one finger into the collar of her high-necked blouse.

'My dear girl, undo a button or two before you suffocate. There's no one to see you. Even if there were you would not get a second glance. Not while I sit here with bare feet and no corset.'

Visibly relaxing, Grace unfastened two buttons and pulled the fabric away from her skin. She rolled the glass against her perspiring forehead. 'Oh, that's lovely. It was so kind of you to say you were glad to see me. But I've interrupted your painting.'

'Not at all. I had stopped for a rest. Besides, you can't leave without telling me why you came.'

'I want to ask you a favour. I'll understand if you can't, but I was wondering if you might be willing to contribute to the summer fair?'

'In what way? Money?'

'No, no. And not on a stall,' Grace added quickly. 'The same ladies have been looking after the same stalls for years, and, well' – she gave a wry shrug – 'you know how it is.'

'I do indeed.'

'So what I thought – I know it's a lot to ask – but–' She took a deep breath and her next words tumbled out in a rush. 'Would you be willing to give one of your paintings for the raffle? It's for a really good cause. All the money raised is going to the poor of the village.'

'Grace, forgive me for asking, but who exactly are these *poor* people?' She had listened to Henry's baffled complaints. Now she wanted to hear Grace's explanation.

'There are a few elderly farm workers, and old folks who don't have children to look after them. But mostly it's the families of miners who are too sick to work, and women whose husbands have died in accidents or of lung disease.'

'I see.' Dorcas thought for a moment. 'I'll give you a painting if you want. But I have a better idea. Can you organize an awning for me? Or an open-sided tent? And two chairs?'

'Yes, I'm sure I can. Why?'

'What if I were to draw portraits? Just a pencil sketch, each taking ten minutes? We could charge – I don't know – how about sixpence? That's more than people would pay for a raffle ticket, yet it's affordable to everyone. I'll supply the paper. And all the money will go to your charity.' Astonishment, delight and gratitude chased across Grace's features.

Her eyes glistened as she shook her head. 'I-I never expected– What a wonderful idea. It's so kind of you.'

'My dear, it's little enough compared to what you are doing every day.'

Grace blushed. 'That's different. I mean,

I'm not like you. I don't have your wonderful gift.' Setting down the empty glass she jumped to her feet and refastened her blouse. 'I must go. I've taken up far too much of your time.' She paused, glancing round, and yearning shadowed her face. 'It's so peaceful here.' Then the smile was back. 'Thank you so much. I can't tell you how grateful–'

'Enough,' Dorcas interrupted smiling, and waved her away. She heard the hinges squeak and the gate bang shut. *No gift?* 'Oh my dear,' she murmured, 'if only you knew what a rarity you are.' With a deep sigh Dorcas gazed at the garden she had first seen almost thirty years ago. It had looked very different then: overgrown and neglected.

She hadn't wanted to come here. But an apparent conspiracy of events had forced her to leave her waterfront cottage in Falmouth.

The only child of feckless artists, she had been left at home the day they joined friends for a boat party. Too much wine and insufficient care had piled the boat on to rocks drowning everyone on board. She was fifteen, penniless and alone in the world when Zander took her in.

To help her come to terms with her loss he had allowed her a corner of his studio and told her to paint her memories. The results, revealing unexpected talent, had astonished him. And he, who had always refused to teach, began to instruct her in technique.

Spending all their time together they had quickly grown close. Despite her youth, her careless upbringing had made her self-sufficient. She brought him an eagerness to learn, honesty, and a passionate nature. She was his muse, model, pupil and soon his mistress. He gave her a home, his adoration and, when she was eighteen, he married her. Loved, protected and fulfilled as an artist she accepted childlessness with equanimity.

His sudden death when she was twenty-five had been a far greater blow than losing her parents. Not long afterward she fled from St Ives, sickened by propositions from men who, blind to her annihilating grief and judging her solely on her unconventional appearance and lifestyle, considered her fair game. Women who had admired her devotion to Zander now turned their backs. She was alone and therefore a threat.

Zander left her all his paintings. But his house and studio had to be sold and the proceeds split between a son and daughter of whom she'd been unaware. They arrived for the funeral accompanied by a solicitor, all three tight-lipped with disapproval.

Selling all but two of his paintings she had moved to a rented cottage just above the Town Quay in Falmouth. There she had nursed her grief, painting delicate water-colour land and seascapes, and occasional studies of local faces rich in character. Signing her work with a simple DR she had sold it through a small gallery in Arwenack Street.

Two years later she had met Henry. In Falmouth on business he had also been looking for a birthday present for Louise. Dorcas had arrived at the gallery with a batch of paintings when he walked in. The attraction was instant and mutual. He had asked if she had any other work he might see and she had invited him back to her cottage. She was twenty-seven, he was twenty-four and the first man she had allowed across the threshold.

Theirs was a fiery relationship, their most frequent clashes over his insistence that she needed protection, which she interpreted as jealousy. She laughed at his fear that she might find someone free to marry her. She had been married. What she had shared with Zander could not be repeated. Nor did she wish to try. She enjoyed her independence.

Her pregnancy came as a shock to them both. Fearful for her wellbeing after an outbreak of enteric fever from contaminated well water, Henry wanted her to move. Though touched by his concern she preferred to remain where she was. But once her pregnancy began to show, people's attitudes to her changed. Once more she was made uncomfortably aware of the price of her freedom.

A fire at the gallery destroyed several of her paintings. Days later she received an eviction notice from solicitors representing the owner of her cottage. Exhausted and at her wits' end she turned to Henry. Within a week he had brought her here, explaining her presence by letting it be known she was newly widowed: her late husband his closest school friend. All she needed to do to forestall possible questions was to change the spelling of her name from Renaudin – which might be recognized – to Renowden.

Henry had been with her the night Hal was born. He had brought his doctor, who was also his brother-in-law, to assist her. Since that night John Ainsley had become her trusted friend and confidante. Grateful for her adored son Dorcas had ensured there were no more children. Part of her grieved that it was necessary for Hal to believe his father dead. But that was the price of avoiding a scandal that would hurt too many people.

The gate hinges squeaked again, rousing her from her memories. Hearing heavy footsteps she smiled. Settling her glasses more comfortably she rose from the garden seat and went to meet her lover.

'What a day!' Henry blew out a long

breath. Lifting her hand he pressed it against his cheek.

'I'm covered in paint,' she warned.

'I don't care.' As he drew her hand down his face so he could kiss her palm she felt the roughness of beard stubble. 'Just touching you makes me feel better.' He let her hand fall but kept hold of it as he studied her. 'You're wearing glasses. When did you get those?'

'Last week.' Pulling them off she rested her head against his. *Not now. Not yet.* 'I need a little help for close work. It's one of the hazards of growing older.'

Henry's arms enfolded her, pulling her against him. His body, strong and stocky, was as familiar to her as her own. 'You'll never be old. You're still as beautiful as the day I first saw you.' He buried his face in her hair. 'I don't know what I'd do if I didn't have you to give me strength.'

'You'll always have me, Henry.'

'Let's go inside.' He kissed her temple. 'I want to hear what you've been doing.'

She thought of the letter from Hal. Maybe she would show him later. 'Grace came by. I'm going to help at the fair.'

Holding hands they crossed the grass to the door. 'You're never going to run a stall? That would put the old biddies in a flutter.'

'Not a stall, no. I had a better idea.' She led the way into the living-room and he closed the door behind them.

As he entered the long greenhouse and inhaled the smell of warm moist earth and vegetation, Bryce was bombarded with memories. Richard and Percy were in the top section of the main shrubbery checking the formation of roots on plants they wanted to propagate by layering. He should have been with them, but hadn't the strength or the will to resume the role he had played in the past: the cheerful joker, always ready with a quip. Soon they would ask what was wrong. *How could he tell them?* He couldn't tell anyone. To put off the moment he had volunteered to remain behind and pot up cuttings.

While he worked he searched desperately for a way out of the prison to which he had returned.

What if he hadn't fallen ill with fever while he and Tarun were on a week-long trip to the edge of the glacier? What if – within arm's reach of death – he hadn't experienced a man's tenderness and physical affection for the first time? Tarun's touch had been sweet water to the arid desert of his soul. Would life have been easier if none of it had happened?

He would not now ache and grieve. But nor would he have known a love that had brought him incomparable joy. Though others might call it depraved, for the first time in his life he had felt at peace with himself. Doubt, shame, the fear that he alone in the world was out of step, had dissolved like mist in the clean mountain air.

Until Tarun he had never known gentleness from anyone except Grace. His mother's ill health had forced her children to keep their distance. The closest his father had ever come to demonstrating physical affection was a firm handshake.

For as long as he could remember *manliness* had been held up as the ultimate goal, the achievement for which a boy should strive. Terrified that he was different, not normal, he had hurled himself into activities that would prove to himself and his father that he was indeed a real man.

It was a bitter irony that he had succeeded so well. He could hunt, shoot, fish and wrestle with the best. But the greater his father's pride, the greater his fear of being found out. Since his return the strain – worse now because he had lived a different life, had loved and been loved – had grown so bad he had even begun to wonder if living with the truth might not be easier.

Easier for whom? His father? Whose cherished illusions and pride in his son would explode in his face? Who would be mocked and pitied, gossip-fodder for people not fit to lick his boots? What of the effect on his mother's already precarious health: the future prospects of Richard, Grace and Zoe? Which family would want to marry into the Damerels once their son's depravity became known? What if the taint could be inherited? Who would want to risk having such children?

How he envied his twin. Richard knew who he was. Despite their father's irritation and mild embarrassment at his artistic talent Richard was totally secure in himself. Adoring Sophie who loved him in return, he could openly talk of her, go about with her, start building a lifetime of shared memories.

He could do none of that. To protect his family, to avoid shame and imprisonment, he must deny Tarun's love, deny his own true nature, live a lie. As he contemplated a bleak future of intolerable loneliness, he set each cutting carefully, firming it in with hands that trembled.

The door at the far end of the glasshouse opened. Bryce swallowed hard and the lump in his throat moved down to lie heavy in his chest. Expecting Richard or Percy, when Alice called his name his heart sank.

'I was just wondering which plants Sophie and I could take to sell at the summer fair.'

Her voice had a nervous brightness that set his teeth on edge. He continued to set the cuttings. 'You'd better ask Percy.'

'I would, but he's so possessive.' She pouted. 'He never wants to part with any of them. I'm sure you must know which varieties there are plenty of. We only want half a dozen.' She stood beside him, fiddling with a wooden spill on which Bryce had pencilled the name of the species.

Dusting soil off his hands he gently took the spill from her fingers and stuck it in the tray of cuttings. 'I'm sorry, Alice, but it really would be better if you ask Percy. He's at the top end of the shrubbery.' Avoiding her eyes, willing her to leave, he put the tray on the broad shelf just above the pipes. Reaching for another empty tray he moved towards the huge wooden bins to fill it with a mixture of sand and peat. Alice followed.

'Bryce?'

'Yes?' Straightening, he carried the tray back to the rest of the cuttings lying on the bench. *Don't say it, whatever it is.*

'Are you quite well?'

'Yes.' He made an effort. 'Still rather tired though.'

'Only – I – have I offended you in some way?'

At this he looked up. Her cheeks were crimson, her eyes brimming. Pity and anger churned in him.

'Come on, Alice. You could never offend me. Haven't we been friends for years? I'm just tired that's all.'

Her mouth widened in a tremulous smile. 'Friends. Yes, we are, aren't we?'

Despite her visible relief he knew this wasn't what she wanted. But it was all he could give.

The day of the summer fair dawned dull and overcast. But by mid-morning the grey blanket had dissolved and the sun shone in a sky the colour of forget-me-nots.

In a field bordering the river, Edwin watched groups of villagers set up stalls with displays of plants, toys, books, china and glassware and homemade fancy-goods. A vast brown canvas tent had been pitched at the far end of the field. It was here, with the cake stall alongside, that teas were served. The committee had deliberately chosen this site, reasoning that few villagers would be able to walk the length of the field without being persuaded to buy something. And by the time they had visited most of the stalls they would be ready for a cup of tea and a plateful of home cooking.

Opposite the stalls various games and amusements were being organized. Farm labourers were erecting two tall posts with a movable crossbar. During the afternoon each would demonstrate his strength and skill at tossing a sheaf of straw over the bar which would then be raised. With a barrel of beer for the winner competition would be fierce.

There was a coconut shy and a pitch for

tossing horseshoes marked out with tape and an iron peg. With the village band providing music, the children would show off the country-dances they had been practising in school.

As Edwin moved slowly down the field stopping to lend a hand or offer a word of encouragement and appreciation, his gaze continually strayed to Grace Damerel. No sooner had she finished assisting with preparations at one stall than she was busy at another. Most of the girls and women worked in pairs or groups. Grace remained alone, separate. Though clearly popular and welcome she was still the mine-owner's daughter.

His heart went out to her for he knew what it was like always to be slightly apart. The day they were introduced he had felt a tug of awareness, of recognition. Since that day he had been waging a continuous battle.

Being pleasant and courteous to ladies involved in the various chapel activities presented no problems whatever. Only with Grace Damerel did his tongue tie itself in knots. He found himself looking forward to her turn for a particular duty. As a newcomer he had plenty of reasons to ask her advice or seek her opinion. Experienced in the way things were done and the foibles of the other ladies, her suggestions invariably smoothed his path. But she would not meet his eye. When she had answered his questions and he was racking his brain for a remark that wouldn't sound inane or patronizing, she would excuse herself and hurry away leaving him angry and frustrated at his awkwardness.

She had moved away from the stalls and was hammering pegs into the grass to secure a small blue and white awning. Reaching for one of two easels clearly borrowed from the school she opened it and set it at an angle under the awning. Watching as she placed a chair in front of the easel a wave of grief engulfed him. She was kind and generous, and to see her laugh was like watching the sunrise.

This morning she had come dressed for work in a plain dark skirt, a simple white blouse and black lace-up shoes. Her thick hair was tucked up beneath a wide straw hat. She was everything he could desire in a wife. But all the regrets in the world could not change the past. He might watch Grace Damerel and yearn. But there could never be more, not for him.

Chapter Eight

Moving the chair back under the awning and out of the sun, Grace opened the second easel. Turning it to face the field she looked round. Had someone called her?

Her gaze ranged over the stalls where women were pinning decorative ribbons and coloured paper streamers to the front of long trestle tables. At one side of the raised platform from which the fair would be declared open, members of the ladies' circle were laying small boughs of greenery around the edge. This was considered a wise precaution after Mrs Williams had taken a nasty fall six years ago. As the platform was barely three feet above the grass the only injury Mrs Williams had suffered was to her dignity. Being a good-natured soul she had laughed it off. But as Mr Williams owned and loaned the field, as well as supplying a sheep for the ram roast, it was imperative such a thing never happened again.

Her glance fell on Edwin Philpotts who was looking directly at her. Heat rushed to her face as she tensed, smoothing her skirt with unsteady hands. How long had he been watching her? Would he come over? She must not appear forward. Her heart was beating so fast it made her feel dizzy.

The chairman of the parish council hurried through the gate clutching a wad of printed programmes. Spotting the minister he called out and waved. As Edwin turned away Grace swallowed her disappointment and tucked a loose strand of hair up under her hat. She unwrapped the notice Richard had painted for her on a two-feet-square piece of white board. Vivid crimson lettering invited one and all to have their likeness sketched by a well-known local artist. Setting the board on the smaller easel Grace took a few steps back to observe the effect.

'What a splendid idea.'

She jumped, her heart leaping into her throat.

'I'm sorry,' Edwin said quickly. 'I didn't mean to startle you.'

'It's all right.' Grace could feel her face burning. 'I didn't realize – I didn't hear.' She bit her lip to stop herself babbling.

'Did you make the notice?'

She shook her head, staring blindly at the bright lettering. 'My brother Richard did.' She pressed folded arms against her stomach. She could feel herself trembling and hoped fervently that he wouldn't notice.

'It's exactly what's needed to attract people's attention, Will he be our artist in residence for the afternoon?'

'No. He doesn't do portraits. But I did persuade him to donate one of his flower paintings for the raffle.'

He smiled. 'It would take a hard heart to refuse you anything, Miss Damerel. So if not your brother, who?'

'Mrs Renowden.' Grace moistened dry lips with the tip of her tongue. The drum-beat of her pulse was deafening. 'She's quite famous. Perhaps you've heard of her? Dorcas Renowden?' At his rueful shrug she hurried on, 'You've not been here long. And she doesn't come to chapel.'

'Then it's most generous of her to volunteer her time and her talent.'

'It is a good cause,' Grace reminded him quickly. 'The village has lost a lot of good men. Their widows and children need all the help we can give.' The strand of hair had come loose again and was tickling her hot cheek. As she pushed it back she looked up at him. 'This is the least I can do.'

His fleeting frown was replaced by a smile. 'You were telling me about Mrs Renowden?'

Relief loosened Grace's tongue. 'She usually paints land and seascapes. I've seen her pictures and they are beautiful. But she thought people might prefer to have a likeness of themselves.'

'I'm sure she's right. Your brother's notice will certainly attract attention. But you'll need a volunteer to be the first. So people

134

will know what they have to do and can see what they are getting.'

Grace's hand flew to her mouth. 'I hadn't thought – you're right, of course. It's very good of you to offer. I'm sure–'

'Not me. I'm part of the platform party. Which I'm told means I have to accompany Mrs Williams on a tour of the stalls. In any case, while people might be amused to watch me having my likeness drawn, the result is not likely to encourage anyone else. No, I think the villagers would much prefer to see you, Miss Damerel.'

Grace shook her head. 'I couldn't.'

'If you won't, how will we persuade anyone else? We cannot allow poor Mrs Renowden to sit idle all afternoon. Besides, I thought the purpose of her coming was to raise money?'

'It is. But–'

'Then let us make a pact.' He coughed and Grace noticed a flush along his cheekbones. 'If you will sit for Mrs Renowden, I will start the collection with two shillings.'

Grace gasped. 'Two? You can't. I mean–'

'Indeed I can, especially for such a worthwhile cause. Do we have an agreement?'

Flustered, Grace nodded. 'You're too generous.' She glanced at the watch pinned to her blouse. 'Goodness, I had no idea. The time–' She backed away. 'Please excuse me.' Turning she hurried towards the gate where her bicycle leaned against the hedge.

It was almost two o'clock, time for the official opening. Grateful for the awning's shade, Dorcas untied the thin ribbons that held closed a large folder. Lifting out a sheet of heavy creamy paper she pinned it to the smooth board resting on the easel pegs. Opening a rectangular wooden box she took out several pencils with thick soft leads and placed them on the narrow shelf. She was ready.

Making herself comfortable on the chair she looked towards the gate. People were streaming on to the field like a tide. Many of the women carrying baskets or cloth-covered trays headed straight for the tea tent.

From experience of past fairs Dorcas knew that long tables spread with crisp white cloths would soon be covered with plates of sandwiches and sausage rolls, trays of pasties, sponge cakes, saffron buns, yeast buns, *hevva* cake and fruit pies. Pairs of women would take turns to split dozens of freshly baked scones, spread them with jam, and top them with a spoonful of thick clotted cream.

Scores of thick white china cups and saucers would be set out together with a basin of sugar and a bowl containing tin spoons. Five large brown enamel teapots awaited water now boiling in the copper.

An hour earlier she had stood in front of

her open closet wondering what to wear. She was attending as an artist and the villagers would expect her to dress like one. With a smile she had selected a white muslin gypsy blouse with full sleeves and a deeply frilled neckline, a maroon taffeta skirt with a broad flounce around the bottom and, a paisley shawl patterned in maroon, emerald and gold. A wide-brimmed straw hat adorned with crimson and emerald ribbons completed her ensemble.

When Grace arrived to collect her in a brougham driven by Will Treneer, Dorcas knew she had never seen Henry's daughter look so pretty. It wasn't just her clothes. Though high-necked white lace over apple-green tulle looked cool and elegant. Silk stockings, white kid shoes with a bar and button fastening and a low curved heel and a hat of white straw trimmed with holly green ribbon and white flowers completed her outfit. Beneath the brim Grace's normally pale face was rose pink.

'My dear, you look absolutely charming.'

'Do I?' Grace's colour deepened. 'Th-thank you.'

Will halted the carriage beside the field entrance. Grace alighted first and took the folder and box of pencils while Dorcas stepped down. Shaking out her skirts Dorcas smiled to herself, aware she was being scrutinizd by Cyril Dunstan and his

40-year-old bachelor son, Horace.

Side by side on wooden chairs in the shade of an oak tree they were collecting the entrance money. In front of them a green baize card table held a stack of programmes, books of pink, blue, white and green raffle tickets and an enamel plate on which a few silver sixpences glittered among the pennies. Despite the June warmth both wore their Sunday-best black suits with waistcoats and stiff white collars. They were freshly shaved and had slicked their hair down with water.

'Aft'noon, Mizz Renowden.' Horace's polite grin revealed blackened broken teeth. His father, clutching a gnarled pipe in a weathered arthritic hand, simply nodded. Cyril's brown, seamed face, eyes like blackcurrants and a scrawny neck around which his collar hung loose all reminded Dorcas of an elderly tortoise.

She smiled. 'Good afternoon.'

'Will this be all right for you?' Grace asked anxiously, as they reached the awning.

At a right-angle to the platform it was set back slightly from the stalls that ran the full length of the field.

'It's perfect,' Dorcas assured her.

'You won't be bored?'

'My dear Grace.' Dorcas touched her hand lightly. 'Don't worry so. I find watching people fascinating. This is a rare opportunity for me.'

'Thank heaven for the glorious weather.' Grace clasped her hands. 'Everyone has worked so hard. I've never seen the stalls so full.'

'It must be almost time for the official opening,' Dorcas reminded gently. 'You'd better go and take your seat.'

'If you're sure there's nothing–'

'I'm positive. Go on, now. I think your mother is wondering where you are.'

Chairs had been set out below the platform and Dorcas watched the Damerel family take their places at the front. Colonel Hawkins was performing the opening ceremony and was already on the platform. Next to him Mrs Hawkins was resplendent in jonquil and cream lace, and a hat trimmed with matching ostrich plumes. On her other side sat the chairman of the parish council and next to him the Reverend Barton Penwarne whose parish encompassed three villages.

As Edwin Philpotts escorted Mrs Williams on to the platform Dorcas saw Louise Damerel murmur to Grace whose hat hid her face.

The vicar, a plump unctuous man, intoned a prayer. The chairman thanked Mr Williams for the loan of his field then introduced Colonel Hawkins. Mercifully brief, the colonel thanked everyone for their hard work, reminded them of the worthiness of the cause, told everyone to enjoy themselves and declared the fair open. During the applause Mrs Hawkins and Mrs Williams were presented with bouquets. Formalities complete, the crowd scattered across the field.

As Dorcas pinned the first sheet of paper to the board she looked up to see the minister with Mrs Williams on one side of him and Grace on the other.

'Mrs Renowden' – Grace was blushing furiously – 'may I introduce Mrs Williams?'

'How do you do?' Dorcas extended her hand.

'I've heard of you,' Mrs Williams nodded, her fingers limp. 'I used to dabble a bit myself. It's such a relaxing hobby. But once grandchildren come along it's so hard to find the time.'

'Indeed,' Dorcas murmured politely. She switched her gaze enquiringly to the tall figure in dark suit and clerical collar.

Grace cleared her throat. 'This is our new minister, Mr Philpotts.'

Dorcas offered her hand again. 'Good afternoon, Mr Philpotts.' His handshake was brief but firm. She observed dark-brown eyes, fair straight brows, and sallow skin that hinted at illness or severe strain.

'Miss Damerel has volunteered to be your first sitter, Mrs Renowden.'

Dorcas glanced in surprise from the minister, whose face was now slightly flushed, to

Grace. 'That's splendid.' Henry always spoke of Grace as shy.

'I didn't vol– I mean it wasn't exactly my idea,' Grace stammered, her colour darkening. 'But we thought it would be dreadful if you were sitting here with no one to draw. Mr Philpotts said that if I would go first so people could see how it was done, he would put two shillings in the dish.' She glanced down at the bare grass. 'Oh my goodness, I forgot, I'd better go and–'

'No, Miss Damerel.' Edwin Philpotts's voice echoed the firmness of his handshake. 'We have an agreement, remember? I will go and borrow a saucer from the tea tent.'

'Now, Reverend,' Mrs Williams smiled archly, 'I hope you haven't forgotten you're supposed to be taking me round the stalls. I'm sure Mrs Renowden and Grace would like it better if we was to leave them be. I know I could never abide anyone watching me when I was drawing or painting. Much better to see it when it's finished. Any'ow, seeing you've paid for it you'll have plenty of time to look at it later. Don't worry,' she said over her shoulder. 'We'll send someone back with a dish.'

As the minister was borne away Dorcas turned to Grace. 'Do sit down, my dear.' She waited, reminded of a butterfly alighting briefly on blossom. 'Would you humour me and remove your hat? It's very pretty, but if I am to draw your likeness I do need to see your face.'

'Oh.' Grace bit her lip.

'I know. You feel horribly self-conscious. Turn your chair away a little. Now forget about me. Watch the crowd. People are so interesting, especially when they don't realize they are being observed. I expect you've been rushing about all morning so think of this as a well-earned rest.'

While she was speaking Dorcas had begun to draw. Her pencil strokes quickly captured the shy tilt of Grace's head, the softness of her mouth. As she brought the curves and hollows of Grace's face alive on the paper a couple stopped to watch. They were joined by several more. Some moved to look over Dorcas's shoulder and watch the portrait take shape. But mostly they stood silent as if afraid to disturb either artist or sitter. When Dorcas sat back there was a collective sigh.

'Dear life, that's 'andsome,' announced Mrs Rawling, the butcher's wife, her hands folded under her pillowy bosom. 'How much are you charging?'

A boy clutching a china plate wriggled through the watchers. 'Minister said I was to give you this.' As Grace took the plate he opened his other hand and dropped three silver sixpences and six pennies into it. Errand discharged he turned and ran.

Dorcas saw Grace's blush as she set the

plate on the grass, picked up her hat, and rose to her feet.

'Mrs Renowden is only charging sixpence.' Above the rustle of whispers she continued, 'This is a rare opportunity, and for such a good cause.'

Dorcas unpinned the portrait and handed it to Grace whose face registered shock, then pleasure and uncertainty.

'Oh, it's ... it's...'

'It's you,' Dorcas said simply.

'It's wonderful,' Grace breathed. 'I had no idea I looked–'

'Caught you just right she did,' Mrs Rawling said, with the confidence of a connoisseur. 'I'm next.' She settled herself on the chair. 'Better than any photograph this is. But I aren't taking me 'at off if it's all the same to you. I'll never get'n on straight again, not without a looking-glass. Don't mind, do you?'

'Not at all,' Dorcas smiled, swiftly pinning another sheet of paper to the board. 'It's a most charming hat. And it suits you so well.'

Mrs Rawling's imposing chest swelled with pride, and pleasure lit her face.

Dorcas's pencil flew over the paper. 'Grace?' she murmured without looking up. 'Would you be kind enough to fetch me a cup of tea?'

'Of course. I should have – I'll go right away.'

An hour and five portraits later people had drifted away to look at other stalls. Glad of the respite Dorcas stretched, wondering what had become of her promised cup of tea. Reluctant to move while waiting for Grace she turned the board on its side, pinned on a fresh sheet and began an impressionistic sketch of the scene.

Zander had always insisted that raw talent was useless without draughtsmanship to contain and guide it. He had taught her how to draw, how to use perspective, and how to alter her focus so she would see objects in terms of the space around them. During the few short years they had shared she had evolved from child to woman, from chrysalis to butterfly.

Zander had been her father's friend. Her mother hadn't liked him though she would never say why. He had declined the trip because he was busy with a painting. When news of the tragedy arrived it was to Zander she had run, meeting him on the road for he had been on his way to her.

She had soaked up like a sponge everything he could teach her. Understanding his need for solitude she would often take her drawing board into the garden and leave him alone in his studio. It was there that he died one summer afternoon, lying on the couch where she had so often posed while

144

he painted her, and where they had first made love.

His head was turned away and at first she thought he had simply fallen asleep. The day was hot and he had been working since early morning. She had laughed, calling his name, ready to tease. But he hadn't stirred and something about his stillness had tightened her skin.

Kneeling beside him, her heart refusing to accept what her head recognized, she had gently turned his face toward her. His skin was cool, his brows drawn together in a slight frown, as if death were an irritating interruption.

Sitting on the floor she had rested her face against his, holding him while the sun went down and his body grew cold. She had wept for all the years they would not have and for a future without him. Yet in the midst of her shock and grief she was glad his passing had been so swift, that it had occurred in his studio where he had created such wonderful work and they had spent so many happy fulfilling hours.

Grace was nearing the front of the long line in the tea tent. No one would have objected if she'd gone straight to the head of the queue. But everyone here had worked equally hard: she would wait her turn. It was a relief to be free of demands for a moment, pleasant to pass the time of day with people around her.

Hearing her name called she glanced towards the entrance. Violet was standing on tiptoe, her normally stolid countenance creased with anxiety as she craned her neck.

'Miss Grace?'

Immediately abandoning the queue Grace eased through the crush. 'Violet? What's the matter?'

'Thank God I've found you, miss. You'd better come quick. Mistress is in some state.'

Taking the maid's arm Grace gently pushed her out of the tent away from curious stares. 'What's happened?'

''Tis Martha Tamblin. I never hear the like. I know she've had some bad time of it. But going at Master like that.' Violet shook her head. 'Raving she is.' Violet pointed to a knot of people clustered near the platform.

Fear gripped Grace. Her mother was already tired. What would this do to her? 'Go and find Will. Tell him to bring the brougham round to the gate at once.' She hurried closer.

'Don't you bleddy *dare* tell me to be quiet, *Mister* Damerel!' Beneath her battered straw hat Martha Tamblin's face was white with fury. ''Tis time somebody faced up to you. These 'ere' – she flung out an arm, encompassing the watching crowd – 'they might be scared of you but I aren't. My man died because of you. Now my Ellie's husband is going the same way. Twenty-four he is, and his lungs in shreds. All because of your bleddy drills. Do you know how many men in this village are sick and dying because of you? Do you know how many have died in the past ten years? My girl will be a widow soon, and she's twenty-three. How can you sleep nights? Haven't you got no conscience?'

Pushing her way through, hearing the low murmuring, Grace saw her father standing in front of her seated mother who, pale and wide-eyed, pressed one thin hand to her bosom. Mary held the other, talking quietly.

Anxiety and embarrassment made Henry Damerel brusque. 'Mrs Tamblin, this is hardly the time or the place–' Grace closed her eyes. Oh, *Papa*.

'So when *is* the right time?' Martha demanded. 'There isn't no right time. Not for you. How many more men got to die before you'll listen?'

Grace saw her father dart a glance at the watching faces, visibly fighting anger at being made a public spectacle. 'Mrs Tamblin, you have my sympathy. But with tin prices so low we have to get the ore out faster. We can't do that without the drills.' Another murmur greeted his words, this time of reluctant agreement.

'Who's this *we*, then?' Martha shouted.

147

''Tisn't you down there breathing all that dust and muck. 'Tisn't you coughing till you spit blood.'

The rumble from families with sick miners grew louder.

'No, it isn't. But those drills are necessary if Wheal Providence is to remain open,' Henry blazed at her. 'I employ more than half the men in this village. What will they do if the mine closes? Where will they find work then?' As he turned away, offering his arm to his wife, Grace saw his hand was shaking.

Faced with the stark reality his words had spelled out, the watching crowd began to melt away. At the far end of the field the band struck up a jaunty march. Alone and defiant, Martha Tamblin glared around her with contempt.

Grace hesitated. Supported by her father on one side and Mary on the other, her mother was led towards a beckoning Violet. Across the field, Edwin Philpotts was by the blue and white awning talking to Dorcas. Her parents didn't need her, and she couldn't intrude on the minister and Dorcas. She turned.

'Mrs Tamblin? This must be a really difficult time for you. May I walk you home?'

As the woman swung round, Grace flinched at the bitterness in her expression but didn't move. Martha Tamblin's shoulders sagged and tears trickled down her lined cheeks.

'Want to get rid of me, do you?'

Taking Martha's arm, Grace drew it gently through hers. 'It must be a dreadful worry for you.'

Martha shook her head. 'You don't know the half of it.'

'What does the doctor say?' Grace asked, as they left the field and walked up the street.

'About Paul?' Martha shrugged wearily. 'Nothing he can do. 'Tis only a matter of time.' She glanced across to the workshop of Wesley Grummet, a carpenter who was also the local undertaker. 'Wesley have took on two new apprentices since Christmas. 'Tis all the coffins.' Martha heaved a shuddering sigh. 'Still, that's two lads who won't have to go down the mine.'

'How is Ellie?'

'How d'you think? She got four kiddies and her man too sick to work. Nor she haven't been right since the babby was born.'

Grace's throat tightened. 'I'm so sorry.'

'Yes, well.' Martha patted Grace's hand wearily. ''Tisn't your fault.'

With all the children down at the fair Miner's Row was oddly quiet.

'May I have a quick word with her?' Grace asked, as they reached the cottage.

'You can try.' Opening the door Martha

led the way in.

Ellie was sitting in an old wooden rocking chair feeding the baby. The sound of her husband's coughing could be clearly heard from the room above. Martha picked up a filthy toddler from the floor and wrinkled her nose.

'Dear life, boy. Need changing you do.' She looked at her daughter. 'Want me to do it?'

Ellie didn't react. Despite her youth and bearing four children in six years Grace knew she'd always been a caring mother.

While Martha filled a basin with hot water from the kettle on the stove Grace crouched by the rocking chair.

'Ellie, is there anything you need for Paul or the children? Anything at all?'

Leaning her head back Ellie closed her eyes as someone knocked on the door. Tucking the squirming toddler under her arm Martha opened it.

'What do you want?'

Grace glanced round, catching her breath at the sight of Edwin Philpotts on the threshold.

'To help if I can,' he said quietly.

Martha snorted. 'Help, is it? Well, you listen here. I don't need no minister telling me 'tis God's will my girl's going to lose her husband, and four dear children won't have no father to care for them.'

'Of course you don't. Nor would I be so cruel.'

'Want to talk to the minister, Ellie?'

Eyes still closed Ellie shook her head.

'Then I won't intrude. But if you change your mind just send for me and I'll come. Day or night. Will you remember that, Mrs Moyle?'

Tears slid between Ellie's closed lids and down her cheeks. She turned her head away.

'Best if you go too, Miss Grace,' Martha said. 'There isn't nothing you can do right now.'

Grace straightened up. 'Mrs Tamblin, I know how proud miners are, and how they hate the thought of accepting charity. But the money made from the fair isn't charity. It's the village helping its own. Paul was born and brought up here, just like Ellie. They've both helped at fairs in the past. Their efforts helped other families facing difficulties. So please, make a list of whatever you and Ellie need and I'll see that you get it.'

Martha nodded. ''Tis good of you, Miss Grace. Listen, what I said earlier – don't pay no mind–'

Grace waved her to silence. 'It's already forgotten.'

She walked in silence beside Edwin down the cobbled road.

'Is something troubling you?' he asked quietly.

'It's Ellie.' Grace shook her head. 'Martha's worried about her.'

'You've offered every help possible. Miss Damerel, the last thing I want to do is offend you, but why do you take so much responsibility for so many people?'

Turning to face him Grace felt telltale heat climb her face. 'Who will if I don't? My father owns the mine that is killing these men.'

'Your father, Miss Damerel. Not you.'

'You don't understand. I have to – it was my fault that my m–' She clamped her mouth shut, stopping just in time, and stared blindly at the cobbles willing him to excuse himself and go. The silence stretched.

He cleared his throat. 'May I escort you back to the fair? The children would be so disappointed if you were to miss their dancing. Is it true that your brother Bryce is an expert sheaf pitcher?'

Relief and gratitude were like warm honey in her veins. She glanced up, saw kindness in his eyes, and felt her mouth tremble into a smile. 'Oh no, not an expert. But he has come third a couple of times.'

Chapter Nine

The camera club met once a fortnight at a harbour-side hotel in Falmouth. Bryce was looking forward to renewing old acquaintanceships and catching up with developments in the photographic world. But both would have to wait until after his talk.

Dry-mouthed, he made his way to the table on which stood the epidiascope he would use to project his photographs on to the large screen. Unfastening his case he opened the folder and removed the prints. The crowded room felt claustrophobic. Suddenly he wished he had declined the invitation to speak. It wasn't the implied accolade that had prompted him to accept: it was the opportunity to talk about a period in his life when, for the first time, he had been truly happy. That, *and loneliness.*

The most popular speakers were those who left an audience wanting more. Knowing this, he planned to talk for forty-five minutes and allow another fifteen for questions. It had taken him half a day to choose the pictures.

While the founder of the club made a short speech of introduction Bryce poured water from a carafe into a glass and drank. There was a burst of polite applause. The lights were turned off. As the first image appeared on the screen he took a deep breath and started talking.

Within moments all shuffling and coughing ceased. Sensing he had their total attention Bryce relaxed. Time flew by as he talked of sights he and his brother had seen and recounted amusing or terrifying events. Among the portraits he had included a Mishmi tribesman, the district officer at Zayul, and a Kampa woman. Though the photograph was black and white, he remembered the bright blue of her cotton skirt and jacket, her brown skin, and plaited dark hair twisted into a coronet that revealed heavy silver ear-rings set with coral and turquoise.

He had allowed himself one photograph of Tarun. Omitting him would have been a denial of invaluable help without which the trip could not have gone ahead. But though that was a legitimate reason it was not the real one. The truth was he could not forego this rare chance to talk about the man who had both saved his life and changed his life. But he chose his words with care and kept a tight rein on his tongue.

After the vote of thanks and more applause people left their seats to gather around the trays of tea and coffee that had been sent up.

Glad it was over Bryce began packing up.

'Congratulations. It was a fascinating talk.'

Glancing up he saw a man he didn't recognize. 'Thank you.'

'It must have been the journey of a lifetime.'

'It was.'

'Marcus Croft.' The left hand was offered, the right remaining out of sight in his trouser pocket. After a moment's confusion Bryce shook it. 'Our esteemed founder spoke very highly of your technique. Now I see why. Those portraits were remarkable. Especially the one of your young assistant.'

Bryce took the compliment at face value, a tribute to his photographic skill. 'Thank you.' He placed the prints he was holding into a folder.

Resting his left arm on the epidiascope, Marcus Croft leaned forward, apparently studying the prints still on the table. 'If you asked people what was the most important requirement on a trip like that the majority would say money, food, porters. But what you really need is total trust in your companions. Especially in extreme conditions when a wrong move might mean the difference between life and death.'

The cold hand of grief squeezed Bryce's heart. 'True.' He kept his gaze on the leather case as he fastened the buckles.

'It's a hell of a wrench, isn't it?' Croft said

quietly. 'Like losing a limb.'

Glancing up involuntarily Bryce met a look of understanding that stopped his breath. *What had he said? Or done? How did Croft know?* Despite the weeks that had passed his sense of loss was still raw, a wound no less painful for being invisible. Clenching his teeth he nodded briefly then lifted his case and turned away.

'It happened to me you see,' Croft continued. 'Similar circumstances, I daresay. Out in the wilds: danger threatening: fell sick. I was on the North-West Frontier.'

Bryce turned back. 'You were a soldier?'

Croft shook his head. 'Combat photographer. Until I stopped a couple of bullets during the Malakand campaign.' He moved his right shoulder. 'Kamal, my guide, bodyguard and interpreter, got me to a field hospital. They saved my arm. Christ knows why for all the use it is. I wanted to stay on. Everything that mattered, everything I cared about was in India. But I was shipped home.' His ironic smile was laced with bitterness. 'They tell me I'm one of the lucky ones.'

Glimpsing a devastation far deeper than that caused by bullets, Bryce held Croft's gaze. 'You survived.'

'For what?'

Bryce understood. He knew that feeling. 'How long have you been back?'

'Four years. I still miss–' He cut himself short. 'Feel like a drink? Not that.' He nodded towards the tea and coffee. 'A proper drink. At the King's Arms.'

Bryce cleared his throat, his heart still racing from shock. 'How did you–? How did I give myself away?'

Croft shook his head. 'You didn't. At least it was nothing they' – he indicated the emptying room – 'would register. Call it intuition.' He leaned forward. 'Recognition perhaps? So,' he straightened. 'How about that drink?'

Bryce shook his head. 'Thanks, but I'd better get home.'

Croft shrugged. 'Another time.' He walked away.

Bryce didn't move as the blissful relief of knowing there were others like him was crushed by panic. Now the secret was no longer his alone. If it ever got out – imagining the impact on his family tied his stomach in painful knots.

Walking beneath the archway that led into the chain garden, Grace inhaled the sweet fragrance of jasmine and honeysuckle. She could see her mother at the far end, resting on her ebony cane as she watched Ben Hooper finish planting some purple pansies. In her high-necked day dress of lilac muslin she looked cool but fragile. A wide-brimmed hat shielded her face.

Realizing they hadn't yet noticed her Grace paused to admire the colours: red, pink, gold, purple, lemon and occasional touches of white all enclosed within a line of circles of dark green box. As an example of summer planting it was beautiful. Why then could she not simply accept it as such?

Her gaze sought the bed intuition told her was hers. At the centre, cream and cerise aquilegia signifying *modesty* were encircled by pink petunias that meant *do not despair*, godetia that said *your secret is safe with me*, marigolds for *grief*, and pansies for *thoughts*.

Her innermost fears and hopes were laid bare to be read by anyone who understood the language of flowers. She had seen the book on a stall at the summer fair years ago. Intrigued by the idea that the Victorians had assigned meanings to flowers and gemstones and under pressure from the stallholder, Mrs Eddyvean, she had bought it. But with recognition had come regret. She would far rather have remained in ignorance.

The planting could not be simple coincidence, chosen merely for colour. Not when it was so accurate, so significant. Yet how did her mother *know* her thoughts and feelings? She never confided in anyone. She had certainly never breathed a word about her attraction to Edwin Philpotts. Nor, she was certain, had her behaviour at the party or the summer fair betrayed anything other than her shyness, and discomfort at being the focus of attention.

Her gaze slid to her father's bed, to vibrant red gladioli tall and proud in the centre: gladioli that stood for *strong character*. Seeing them surrounded by pink and white godetia, Grace flinched. None of the other beds contained godetia; only hers and her father's. *Your secret is safe with me.*

What was her father's secret? A flash of intuition told Grace it must be something he believed his wife unaware of. Otherwise her mother would not have made the floral statement.

Her mother's bed had lupins at the centre. Lupins signified *dejection*. Bryce's and Richard's both contained gladioli and sweet William: for *strong character* and *gallantry*. Flowers that were right for them, and yet... Her gaze lingered and her forehead tightened in a frown. They were twins but they were very different. Odd then that her mother should have made their beds almost identical, with no acknowledgement that despite Bryce's stronger build and sporting prowess he was the more sensitive, the more vulnerable.

She looked at the bed between her mother's and her own, where lemon gladioli were ringed with pink and white pelargoniums signifying *eagerness*. Whose was this link in the chain? She had always assumed it was for Grandfather Chenoweth. But for the first time it occurred to her that perhaps it wasn't. She'd had four grandparents so why would only one be included? Was it possible there had been another child before her? A child who had not survived? A loss too great to be spoken of?

At that moment Louise looked up. 'Hello, darling.' She beckoned Grace forward. 'Do come and see. Aren't the colours beautiful? Doesn't it all look splendid?' Her gaze swept along the linked beds, her smile one of satisfaction.

Grace did not know what to think.

'Don't want it.' Becky Collins turned her head away from the proffered sandwich.

Grace put the plate back on the table. Since her last visit a week ago Becky's flesh seemed to have melted away leaving only transparent skin over bird-like bones.

Crouching beside the chair Grace coaxed, 'Please, Becky. You must eat something.'

The shrivelled woman closed her eyes. 'No.'

'Shall I ask Dr Ainsley to stop by?' There was no response and swelling anxiety compressed Grace's lungs. 'If you're in pain–'

'Please,' Becky whispered, 'just leave me be.'

There must be something she could do. Panic fluttered like dark wings. She had emptied the bucket, made up the fire, fetched clean water and tidied the squalid kitchen as best she could. Becky had refused to be washed. But she needed food. Without it she would die. Yet short of forcing it into her mouth... Jumping to her feet Grace filled the kettle. She made a fresh cup of tea and set it within Becky's reach.

'I'll call again as soon as I can.' There was no response. Grace's chest tightened. Becky was the same age as her mother. That wasn't old. She clamped her lips together to stop the fear, the plea, from spilling out. *Don't die.* 'Try and drink the tea, Becky.' She picked up her basket.

As she pulled the cottage door shut behind her Ernie came out. He must have been watching from his window. He shook his head. 'She 'aven't got long.'

'I'm going to ask the doctor–'

'Begging your pardon, miss, but you'd be wasting your time, and his.'

'You can't say that.' Tension made Grace's voice shrill. 'You don't know–'

'Yes, I do, my 'andsome. I seen it before, see? Mollie went 'xactly the same before she died. They do retreat inside theirselves. 'Tis like they're cutting the ties. 'Tidn no good trying to reach them or call them back. Truth is, 'tis their time to go even if we aren't ready to let them.'

Grace's eyes filled. She gripped her basket

so tightly her knuckles ached.

'C'mon, my bird.' Ernie's tone was gruff and kindly. 'Don't take on. Here, Will and Betty's babby was born last night. A little boy. I went up and seen him this morning. Handsome he is. Got some great thatch of dark hair.'

Choking down panic she didn't understand, Grace forced a smile. 'Congratulations, Ernie. How does it feel to be a grandfather?'

'Bleddy great, begging your pardon, miss. Molly would be some proud, dear of her. I'm going up the cemetery later and tell her all about it. I s'pose I'd better let Minister know, seeing how they'll want he to do the christening when 'tis time. Well, I'd best let you get on. Don't you fret now, miss. You done all you could for Becky, a bleddy sight more than that sister of hers.'

Swallowing the lump in her throat Grace stepped down on to the cobbled street. 'Have they chosen a name for the baby?'

Ernie looked startled. 'Dear life! I never thought to ask. That's a man for you.'

This time Grace smiled without effort. 'Please pass on my congratulations and best wishes to Betty and Will. I've got a little gift at home for the baby. Can I leave it with you next time I'm down?'

'Why don't you take it round yourself? Be glad to see you they would.'

Grace shook her head. 'This is a family time. I wouldn't want to intrude.' She couldn't possibly tell him the truth: that she longed to see the new baby, to hold him and imagine what it would be like if he were hers. The longing was so powerful it was a physical ache. But to hold this tiny bundle of life born of the love Betty and Will felt for each other and face the possibility this was something she would never know... She couldn't.

Drawing level with the manse she remembered Ernie's words. If Becky was – if the doctor could not help, then maybe the minister. *It wasn't her business.* Then whose was it? Becky's only family was a sister too busy with her own problems even to visit. Ernie had done what he could, but he had a new grandson.

Grace leaned her bicycle against the wall. Opening the gate she walked to the front door, her heart thumping furiously as she rehearsed what she would say.

'Yes?' Flora Bowden glared at her.

Grace felt herself flush. 'Good afternoon, Miss Bowden. Could I speak to the minister please?'

The sharp eyes narrowed. 'What do you want to see him about?'

She had no right to ask such a question. But Grace did not want to increase the housekeeper's antipathy by saying so. Her tongue snaked across dry lips. 'It's a private matter.'

Flora sniffed. 'Well, he isn't home.'

'Do you know when he might be back?'

'Couldn't say. Rushed off his feet he is. With three villages in his care he don't have time to waste.'

The implication brought a further rush of heat to Grace's cheeks. 'I see. Thank you.' She turned away.

'Want to leave a message?'

Grace hesitated, wondering how to phrase her anxiety about Becky. Then realized it was too complicated and delicate to be condensed into a sentence or two. She shook her head. 'No, thank you. I'll–' What would be best? To write? Call again? A repetition of the last few moments did not appeal.

'Not important then.' The door was abruptly closed.

Sweating with humiliation, Grace walked down the path. As she closed the gate she looked back at the house and glimpsed movement at one of the upstairs windows. For an instant she thought it was the housekeeper. Then the figure drew closer. There was no mistaking the flash of white collar against the black vest.

If he was at home why had Flora Bowden said he wasn't? *Had he seen her arrive? Had he told his housekeeper to say he wasn't at home?*

Grace's breath caught on a sob. Fumbling the catch on the gate she seized the handlebars and hurriedly pushed her bicycle up the street wanting to get away as quickly as possible. Though her reason for calling had been genuine she had welcomed the opportunity to talk to him again. She wouldn't have delayed him long. She knew how hard he worked, the demands he faced. Her breath rasped as mortification scalded her skin.

'Miss Damerel! Wait!' Edwin Philpotts's voice rang out.

She was tempted to keep going. But he called her name again. This time he was much closer. Screwing up what remained of her pride she stopped and glanced over her shoulder.

'I'm sorry if I disturbed you. Miss Bowden said—'

Tight-lipped and frowning, he made a visible effort to overcome anger. 'Miss Bowden should— You must have had a reason for calling at the manse?'

'Yes. I've just been visiting Becky Collins.' Haltingly, Grace explained her concern. He listened, his eyes never leaving her face. She dropped her own gaze to stare at the dusty road. 'It was just – I thought you might be able to offer her comfort. If she's really– I can't reach her any more. She has no one–' Her voice wobbled and she broke off.

'Of course I'll go and see her.'

'Thank you.' In the silence Grace heard gulls shrieking. The fishing boats must be coming in on the tide.

'I'm sorry–' he began.

'Of course.' She didn't let him finish. 'You must be busy.' She hurried away, desperate to get home.

Mrs Tallack knocked and put her head round the door. ''Scuse me, Doctor. Mrs Moyle is here.'

'Ellie.' John rose to greet her. 'Come in.' His housekeeper closed the door quietly.

Despite the summer sun, Ellie's face was drawn and pale except for the dark smudges under her eyes. Her hair was scraped back into a careless knot. Escaping wisps hung untidily over her face and down her neck. Once as bright as burnished copper it was dull and greasy and threaded with silver. Her sprigged blouse and blue calico skirt, both faded and worn thin, were grubby.

Exhausted and careworn she looked a decade older than her real age. Which was not surprising given what she had been through these past months.

She had caught him in the village this morning and asked to see him. Her voice low and her eyes evasive. He had offered to see her at home to spare her the walk, but she had refused, hurrying away as soon as the appointment had been agreed, as if anxious not to be seen talking to him.

He indicated a chair. 'Sit down, Ellie. I'm so very sorry about Paul.'

Ellie simply nodded, chewing her lower lip, fretting at a fold in her skirt with fingernails bitten down to the quick.

John sat down at his desk and swivelled his chair around so he faced her. 'What can I do for you?'

She took a deep breath. 'Expecting again, aren't I?'

Startled, John nodded slowly. This was something he had not anticipated. 'How far along are you?'

'Four months. Paul was careful like, but...' She bit her lip, shrugging wearily.

'You weren't using birth control?'

Ellie shook her head. 'I know what you said. What with Mark just a few months old an' all. I was willing. But Paul didn't like it. He said it wasn't natural.'

Crushing his irritation, John nodded once more. 'Well, it's sooner than I would have wished but–'

'No, you don't understand. I can't have it. Not now Paul's gone. I don't know how I'm going to feed the four I got. Doctor, you got to help me. I can't – I just can't...' Tears spilled down her pallid cheeks as her face crumpled.

Pulling a pristine handkerchief from his

breast pocket, John leaned forward and pressed it into her trembling hands. He understood Ellie's plight. He saw too many women worn down by continual breeding because their husbands didn't like using contraception.

'Ellie, I understand how you feel.'

'No, you don't. You got no idea. I can't have it. *I can't.*'

If she'd ever had difficulty delivering, or if there was a risk to her health, there would be strong medical reasons to justify terminating the pregnancy. But each time her labour had been relatively short and the births trouble-free.

'Ellie, think what you're saying.'

'What d'you think I been doing?' she cried, raising swollen, bloodshot eyes. 'I haven't done nothing but think about it. I can't eat, can't sleep.'

'I'll give you something that will help.' He wanted to calm her before trying to explain why what she was asking was impossible.

'I don't want *that.*' She leaned forward, her features tight with desperation. 'Help me, Doctor. I'm begging you. I'll never tell. I swear on my babies' lives.'

'It's Paul's child, Ellie. Just like Polly, Meg, Daniel and little Mark. You're asking me to destroy Paul's child.'

Screwing her eyes shut, Ellie shook her head violently. 'It isn't a proper baby. Not

168

yet. I can't have it. I won't. My Paul's lying in his grave and I miss him awful. I got no money. But how can I go out working when Mother's doing two jobs and there isn't no one to mind the children? I can't expect Polly – God love her, she's only six. Don't you tell me to go on the parish neither. I know women who done that and their kids was took away. What am I s'posed to do?' Her voice had risen to a thin shriek.

Rising, John opened the door and called to his housekeeper. 'Fetch a blanket and sit with Mrs Moyle, while I make up a sedative.'

When the draught had taken effect, Ellie agreed to an examination. John knew there was little doubt that the changes she described were symptomatic of anything other than pregnancy. He was trying to buy himself time, and that surprised him.

He could not do what she wanted. He had sworn an oath to *do no harm;* to save and protect life. Despite her strain and grief, and some signs of under-nourishment, Ellie was basically strong. She had already produced four healthy children. There was no reason to suspect a fifth would present any problems.

Completing the examination he drew up the blanket and went to wash his hands. As he soaped, rinsed and dried, he felt an ache begin at the base of his skull. He knew if he refused Ellie's request there was a risk she might go to one of the old women known to *help out* in such situations. He would warn her of the danger to her life and long-term health and promise his support during her pregnancy. He'd ask Grace to make sure Ellie had what she needed for her lying-in and for the new baby.

His profession was governed by rules, a code of ethics. To break them would be a betrayal of everything he believed in. His heart ached for Ellie. He understood her grief. He had lost a wife he loved. But he had no choice. His calling demanded he protect the unborn life she was carrying.

Chapter Ten

Becky Collins lingered for two more weeks. Hot dry weather during which the hay was cut, wheat and oats began changing from green to gold, and mud on the paths and tracks dried in hard ankle-wrenching ruts.

Hedges were dressed with pale pink blackberry blossom and white convolvulus. Bracken unfurled green fronds. Valerian, crane's bill and fragrant meadowsweet flowered along the ditches. Starlings began to flock and rooks strutted in the pastures.

The breeze whipped up whirls of dust from the village streets, and the stench from gutters and privies caught the nose and throat.

Grace sent for Becky's sister Vera, who arrived complaining about the inconvenience.

Grace believed that her own visits every other day bringing food and fresh milk were all that stopped Vera abandoning her sister. She persuaded her uncle to call at the cottage, waiting outside while he made his examination.

'Grace,' he was gentle. 'Mrs Collins is beyond my help.'

'Surely there must be something? If it's a matter of cost.'

'No.' John Ainsley shook his head. 'All the money in the world wouldn't make a scrap of difference. My dear, you have to stop this. You're assuming responsibilities you have no right to. I say this not out of criticism but from concern. You'll make yourself ill.'

'But she'll die.' Grace's throat was so stiff and tight her voice was strangled.

'Yes,' John agreed calmly. 'And there's nothing you or I or anyone else can do to prevent that.' He took her hand. She recognized his compassion but it gave her no comfort. *He didn't understand.* 'Mrs Collins has suffered a great deal. Grace, she's tired. Too tired to want to struggle on any longer. The kindest thing you can do for her, and for yourself, is to accept it. You have to let go.'

Edwin Philpotts had called as promised though Grace hadn't seen him. 'He needn't 'ave bothered for all the notice Becky took of'n,' Vera grumbled. 'But at least he appreciated what it was costing me to be here what with all the trouble I got back 'ome. He might be young but he got a nice way with'n. That's more than you can say for the one we got. All hellfire and damnation he is. Well, you don't want it, do you? Not every bleddy Sunday.'

After fourteen days of heat the air turned

sultry and humid. Towering thunderheads blotted out the sunlight and the darkening sky was split by jagged darts of lightning accompanied by cracks of thunder so loud that windows shook. As the first slow heavy drops of rain burst on the dusty earth Becky Collins sighed softly and slipped away.

The funeral took place the following week. After three days of blustery showers the clouds rolled away and the sun shone in a sky the colour of delphiniums and streaked with mare's tails. The chapel was full. Miners off-shift, remembering Becky's husband and son, accompanied the coffin to the cemetery.

Vera refused Grace's offer to help with refreshments. 'I 'aven't got money to spend like that. I thought Sister might have a bit put away somewhere. But I 'aven't found nothing. I been away too long already. If people do want a cup of tea they'd best make their own when they get 'ome.'

Reminding herself that grief sometimes showed itself in unusual ways, and that she shouldn't criticize, Grace masked her shock with a nod of acceptance. 'What about Becky's clothes and possessions?'

'Dump the lot.'

Grace blinked. 'But – surely you'd like something as a keepsake?'

'I already took what I want. The rest is only fit for the fire.'

As everyone dispersed leaving two men shovelling earth on to the coffin, Ernie and Grace accompanied Vera back to the cottage.

Unlocking the door, Vera handed the key to Grace and picked up two bundles, each tied in a knotted sheet. 'Right, I'm gone.'

Ernie stared after the departing figure. 'Well, bugger me,' he murmured. Then added hastily, 'Begging your pardon, miss.'

Grace pretended not to have heard. She would not have expressed herself quite so bluntly but she shared his reaction. She looked round the dark kitchen. The range was cold and so was the room. She shivered.

'You get on home, my 'andsome,' Ernie urged. 'Ben and me can clear the place out. I'll give you the key back in a day or two.'

'That's kind of you, Ernie.'

'No such thing.' He was gruff. 'Get on with you now. Looking fagged you are.'

Putting her bicycle away, Grace entered the house through the servants' door. Violet was in the kitchen.

'All right, miss? Good turn out, was it?'

Grace nodded. During the service she had clenched her teeth so hard that pain stabbed her temples. Holding in sobs as she kept hearing Becky's grief-stricken *what's the point of it all?* had made her hot and dizzy. She had not disgraced herself, but the effort had cost her dearly. She cleared her throat.

'M-my mother?'

'Not come in yet, miss. She's prob'ly still down the chain garden.'

'I'll go to her as soon as I've changed.' Having lost two children her mother disliked reminders of mourning. Grace sympathized, and could not help thinking it a little unkind of Granny Hester to cling so determinedly to her black.

Twenty minutes later, wearing a simple blouse and skirt, Grace went out through the garden entrance. She paused on the steps but there was no sign of Ben or her mother. Perhaps she had retired to the folly to update the big diary in which she recorded her planting schemes for each of the linked beds.

The sun was still warm but looked watery through the thickening veil of cloud. The breeze had dropped, the air was still, and sounds were unusually sharp and clear. Fledglings with fluttering wings and insistent cries followed weary parents demanding to be fed. Clouds of gnats spiralled beneath tall sycamores on either side of the folly, a sign of more rain to come.

Grace walked up the steps. Her mother considered Ben the perfect assistant. He was quiet, knowledgeable, and took seriously his responsibility to have ready the plants whose names and colours were listed on a plan she worked out each autumn.

What was it that gave her such pleasure? Grace pushed the door open. Was it the

175

sense of continuity in the endless cycle of seasons? The delight of seeing her vision transformed into colourful fragrant reality? Was it that the garden, unlike her health, was something she could control? Or was it something altogether deeper and darker?

In her favourite chair by the window, her straw hat on top of books lying open on the low table, Louise Damerel's head rested against the high back, her face turned towards the view.

'Mama?'

Louise didn't respond, didn't move. A familiar pang of concern and sympathy pierced Grace. The hours in the garden had been too much. Her mother had fallen asleep.

'Oh Mama,' she sighed. Crouching beside the chair she took her mother's thin hand. It lay cold and unresponsive in hers. Grace chafed it lightly. 'Mama? Wake up. It's time to–' Shock tingled unpleasantly from her scalp to her toes as blood roared in her ears. 'Mama?' Her throat was so dry it hurt and her mouth tasted of tin. Fear poured through her veins, ice-cold, white hot. *No.*

'It's all right, Mama.' She could hear her voice. It sounded strange, high-pitched and breathless. 'Don't worry. Everything will be all right. I'll just go and – you'll be fine – we must get you back inside where it's nice and warm.'

Scrambling to her feet she stumbled out of the folly and ran on weak trembling legs towards the house. She burst through the door. Kate was crossing the hall and started violently, one hand flying to the frilled bib of her starched white apron.

'Dear life, miss! You gived me some fright.'

'Patrick!' Grace shrieked, ignoring her.

The butler appeared, still adjusting his coat. 'Miss Grace?'

'My mother—'

'Where, miss?'

'The folly,' Grace gasped through chattering teeth. *Why was she shivering?*

Patrick took charge. 'Kate, go and fetch Thomas Coachman. Tell him to go straight to the folly. Quickly, girl!'

As Kate turned and ran, Grace whirled back towards the open door. Grabbing a handful of skirt she flew down the steps and back along the path to the folly with Patrick close behind her.

'I'm s-sure she'll b-be better once s-she's in b-bed,' she stammered over her shoulder. 'She's so cold you see. It's my fault – the breeze – I should have – a jacket, or a shawl around her shoulders.' She leapt up the steps into the folly, and stopped suddenly on the threshold. The fragile figure hadn't moved.

'By your leave, miss.' Easing past her Patrick rested his fingers on the side of her mother's neck.

Grace wrung her hands and looked back to the path. 'Where is Thomas? Why doesn't he come? My mother shouldn't be out here. It's turning chilly. That's why she's so cold. It's not good for her, Patrick. She should be in the house.' Hearing running footsteps she glanced round. 'Thomas, what took you so long?'

'Sorry, miss. I–' He looked past her to the still figure in the chair. '*Jesus.*'

'All right, Thomas.' The butler was quietly repressive. 'Shall we carry her between us?'

The burly coachman shook his head. 'Easier for me to do it by myself, Mr Patrick.'

'As quickly as you can, Thomas,' Grace begged. 'We must get her to her room before she takes another chill.' She saw the coachman glance in bewilderment at the butler.

'Don't you worry, Miss Grace,' Patrick soothed, nodding at the coachman who bent over the chair and scooped up Louise Damerel as if she weighed no more than a child. 'Come along now.' He propelled her gently along in Thomas's wake. 'You've had a nasty shock.'

'I-I'm all r-right,' she stammered, her teeth clicking like castanets. 'It's not me you need to worry about: it's my mother.'

The butler's hand was warm and steady beneath her elbow. 'No, miss. Not any more.'

Grace looked at him. 'You're wrong.' It

was disbelief, denial and plea. 'She's not – she can't be. Send someone for my uncle. He always knows exactly what to do. He'll make her better.'

In the hall, Grace stood stunned and helpless while Patrick instructed an ashen, hand-wringing Kate to send Jamie for the doctor. As Thomas carried his mistress towards the stairs Violet leaned over the carved balustrade on the landing.

'Mrs Chenoweth want to know–' As she caught sight of Thomas and his burden her hand flew to her mouth. 'Oh God save us. Oh, my dear life. She's never–'

'Violet? What's all the shouting for? What's going on?' The querulous demand from Hester Chenoweth's bedroom made the shocked maid gasp.

Patrick jerked his head, a silent command for Violet to return to the old lady. Her hands pressed to her cheeks, Violet darted away.

A moment later, Grace flinched as her grandmother screamed, the sound cut off by the closing door. The hall began to rock and sway. Patrick caught her and steered her into the library and across to a leather sofa the colour of a ripe chestnut. She sank down among green velvet cushions.

'That's right, miss. You just rest there a minute.' He moved away and she heard the rattle of the decanter, a brief gurgle, and the chink of the crystal stopper being replaced. Leaning over her he pushed the cut-glass tumbler into her trembling hands, gently forcing it towards her lips. 'Come on now. Drink it down. You'll feel better.'

She'd said that to Becky. Becky was dead.

Grace swallowed, coughing as fumes filled her nose and throat. She shuddered and gasped, swallowing convulsively. Her eyes watered and perspiration broke out on her forehead. It dewed her upper lip and prickled her back like a million scurrying ants. But as the brandy hit her stomach warmth radiated along her palsied limbs. The weakness receded, replaced by crushing realization. Overwhelmed by terror she shut her eyes, clutched the glass and gulped down the rest.

'Easy, miss.' Patrick drew the glass away. 'You'll be better directly.'

Grace relinquished it, still unable to speak. Fumbling for her handkerchief she wiped her mouth and forehead. 'I tried so hard, Patrick.' Rasped by the neat brandy her voice was a hoarse whisper. 'All for nothing.'

'Don't you ever think such a thing, miss,' he scolded. 'Mistress would never have lasted as long as she did but for you. You didn't have no easy time of it neither. Mistress was some lovely lady, none better, but she liked her own way. No one could've done more'n you did, miss. Now if you'll write a note to the minister I'll have it taken down the village this minute.'

She looked up blankly. She could hear him speaking but the words didn't mean anything. 'Minister?'

'Yes, miss. With respect, Mr Philpotts might be the best person to break the news to your father, him being familiar with such matters, and you having had such a shock.'

Her father. He would say she shouldn't have left her mother. He would say it was her fault. It was. It always had been.

'Come along now, miss,' Patrick urged.

She was so tired. She didn't have any strength left. She felt a hand under her elbow helping her to her feet and guiding her to the walnut writing-desk by the window. A tapestry chair pressed gently against the backs of her legs. Writing paper and a pen were placed in front of her. She stared at them.

'What do I– I don't know what...'

'Just a few words, miss,' Patrick coaxed. 'Don't have to be much. But 't would be best if minister was here before master gets home.'

Dipping the pen Grace bent over the paper and wrote *Please come. My mother* – but her fingers were trembling and slippery and she could only scrawl *please help*. Signing it *Grace Damerel,* she folded it and

181

addressed the envelope, *Reverend Edwin Philpotts*.

'Now you just sit there a minute. Soon as I've seen to this,' Patrick lifted the envelope, 'I'll send Kate to you.'

As the butler closed the door behind him Grace stared out of the window. From childhood she had clung to the belief that if she accepted responsibility for the household and shielded her mother from any stress nothing bad could happen. But it had. Without warning death had sneaked in. Years of effort, of biting her tongue, doing the right thing, putting everyone else's needs first: in the end none of it enough.

Rage exploded inside her, blinding, searing. She couldn't breathe and pressed clenched fists to her temples as screams too big for her throat threatened to split her skull and shudders wrenched her body.

As suddenly as it had attacked the fury departed, sucked out like a tide. It left her beached, boneless, and utterly exhausted. Stumbling to the sofa she lay down and let darkness take her.

Chapter Eleven

Riding home on the busy main road in the gathering dusk, Henry Damerel ignored carriages, horse-drawn omnibuses and farm carts. Familiar with the route his sturdy cob needed no guidance. There was nothing to distract Henry from his thoughts. Like claws and sharp teeth they nipped and tore, shredding his optimism, gnawing away at his confidence.

Despite fevered efforts by the engineer, the blacksmith, and two carpenters, the worn-out leaky pump had defied all attempts to keep it functioning. By mid-afternoon the level of water in the north shaft had forced the men in the lower levels to abandon the stope. That alone would have been sufficient cause for worry. But soon after the afternoon shift in the south shaft had gone down, boys working bellows in the ends were sent back up to grass as one pare after another found that the lode had suddenly pinched out.

With a new setting day due, when miners bid for the pitches they would work during the coming months, Joe Buller insisted the only solution was to go back on tribute. 'I tell you, sur, 'tis the only way. They'll find'n again, don't you fret. You could put 'em down there blindfold and they'd smell out the tin. But you got to make it worth their while.'

He would not give up. *Yet how much longer could he carry on?* He needed money: a lot of money. That need wasn't simply urgent, it was desperate.

His butler met him in the hall. 'If I may have a word, sir?'

'Later, Patrick.' Henry waved him away. 'It's been a long day and I'm tired.'

'Begging your pardon, sir, but this can't wait. May I suggest the library?'

With a sigh Henry turned as the butler closed the door and crossed to the silver tray. Pouring a generous measure of whisky into one of the cut-glass tumblers, the butler set it on a small tray of polished figured tin and offered it to his employer.

Taking it, Henry rubbed his forehead where a headache throbbed. 'All right. What is it? I daresay I can guess. My wife is unwell again. Has Ainsley been sent for?'

'Sir, it is my unhappy duty to tell you that Mrs Damerel passed away this afternoon. Miss Grace came back from the village and found her in the folly. Sitting in the chair she was, and looked very peaceful.'

'Dead?'

'I'm very sorry, sir.'

Lifting the glass Henry swallowed half its

contents. *Thirty-one years.* She had almost died the night Grace was born. The threat had hovered over their lives like a shadow ever since. But now it had happened he didn't know how to react. Surely he should feel something?

Patrick cleared his throat. 'On behalf of all the staff, sir, I'd like to say how sorry we are.'

'Thank you.' Draining the glass, Henry crossed to the tray and splashed more whisky into the glass, astonished to see his hand shaking.

'Doctor Ainsley is upstairs now, sir. He's with Mrs Chenoweth at the moment. As you can imagine, the shock...'

'Indeed.' Henry raised the glass to his lips. A thought struck him, accompanied by a flash of irritation. 'Where's Grace? Why isn't she–?'

'Miss Grace is in her room, sir. I understand from Kate that Dr Ainsley has given her a sedative. Took it bad she did, sir. The minister should be here directly.'

'The minister?' Henry repeated. 'Whose idea–?'

'Mine, sir. Seemed to me Mrs Chenoweth and Miss Grace might be glad of such comfort at this sad time. I hope I did right?'

'Yes. Of course.' Henry passed his free hand over his face, feeling stubble rasp against his palm. Exhaustion swamped him like a breaking wave. He felt tired to the depth of his soul.

'I expect you'll want to go upstairs, sir?'

'What? Oh, yes. Of course.' Swallowing the last of the whisky Henry set the glass back on the tray. It didn't seem real. Louise *dead?* Over the years there had been so many close calls he had become inured to anxiety. Just for an instant he wondered if there had been a mistake. *Foolish.* He started up the stairs. Patrick followed.

'Madam is laid out in her own room, sir. Violet has attended to all the necessary. Minister shouldn't be long. Mr Bryce has taken the trap and gone to meet him.'

Flora Bowden set the plate down in front of Edwin. 'I 'spect you're ready for that. Been some long day for you. Reverend Peters was good as gold, God rest his soul, but you do twice what he done in a day.' She moved the salt and pepper closer. 'I can't help thinking that people do take advantage. But p'raps it isn't for me to say,' she added quickly.

Edwin suppressed irritation and flashed a brief smile. 'Thank you, Miss Bowden.' As he picked up his knife and fork Flora bustled towards the door.

'You just ring when you're ready for your afters.'

As the door closed behind her he gazed at the lumps of grey meat, mashed potato, and cabbage that had been boiled with bicarbonate of soda to a vivid green stringy mush. He recalled fish and vegetable curries made with coconut and spices, subtly flavoured dishes of dhal, and salads of exotic fruits that he had taken for granted. Though conditions at the mission had been spartan, food was cheap and they had eaten well. He sighed. If not exactly appealing it was adequate as fuel. He opened the book beside his plate, and began to eat.

He was midway through his meal when the sound of raised voices brought his head up. A moment later the door was flung open and Bryce Damerel strode in.

'You got no business–' Flora bleated behind him.

'Be quiet!' He turned on the minister. 'Was the message not clear enough? Or is your dinner more important?'

Startled, Edwin rose, wiping his mouth. 'I'm sorry? What message? I've had no message.'

'Don't give me that.' Bryce glared at him. 'My sister wrote asking you to come to the house as quickly as possible. Patrick sent Jamie Couch down with it. What do you mean, you didn't receive–' At the same instant both men's eyes turned to the housekeeper.

'Would you excuse me, Mr Damerel?' Edwin put one hand on Flora's back and shepherded her towards the door. 'I won't keep you a moment.'

'Listen–'

'Please sit down. I'll be right back,' Edwin said over his shoulder as he closed the door.

Seething, as he pushed the housekeeper ahead of him, he remained silent until they reached the big kitchen. It cost him dearly to keep his tone mild.

'The letter, Miss Bowden?'

Her thin cheeks flushing she smoothed her apron. 'Reverend Peters was always very grateful to me for not bothering him just when he was going to sit down to his dinner or his tea.'

'I appreciate your thoughtfulness, Miss Bowden, but I would prefer to judge for myself the urgency, or otherwise, of any message.'

'But 'tis never right; expecting you to jump when they call, just like you was a servant.'

Biting down the sharp retort Edwin replied carefully, 'But that's exactly what I am, Miss Bowden: a servant of the Lord, and of the people who seek his comfort. Where is the message, if you please?'

'I was going to give'n to you soon as you'd finished your tea.' She pulled the sealed envelope from her apron pocket and thrust it into his outstretched hand. Her lower lip trembled and her eyes filled. 'I didn't mean no harm.'

Edwin clung to his patience. 'I'm not Mr Peters. I do things differently. Not only has your action caused Mr Damerel and his family great anxiety and upset, it reflects badly on me.'

Her eyes widened. 'Oh my dear life, I never meant–'

'I'm sure you didn't. But in future if someone brings a message I want to receive it immediately. If I am not here you may leave it on my desk so I will see it as soon as I return. Should someone come looking for me while I am out, you will kindly write down that person's name and the time that they called. If I am at home you are to come and tell me at once. Is that quite clear?'

He glimpsed resentment before shock rounded her red-rimmed eyes.

'Even if you're in the middle of your dinner?'

'Even then,' he said firmly, tearing open the envelope. Reading the brief plea penned in a shaky scrawl that revealed appalling distress his heart contracted. Turning abruptly he strode back to the dining-room.

'I'll come at once, Mr Damerel. I can only apologize.'

'Hid the note, did she? Someone should have warned you. She's a jealous old biddy.'

'A misunderstanding,' Edwin replied, leading the way across the hall to the front door. 'It won't happen again.'

189

'Don't count on it,' Bryce warned. 'Being the minister's housekeeper has given her a taste for power. Because he was a lazy old man who liked his comfort, Mr Peters allowed her free rein. She won't want to give that up.'

'Miss Bowden understands that remaining here as housekeeper requires she adjust to *my* way of doing things. I intend no criticism of Mr Peters but I believe it's my responsibility to be available to anyone who needs me whenever that might be.'

Bryce seemed about to speak, but instead he clicked his tongue, urging the horse into a faster trot.

Edwin had noted the bruise-like marks of exhaustion beneath his eyes. Bryce Damerel was deeply troubled. But confidences could not be forced. He lifted the note. 'Mr Damerel, your sister started to write something about your mother.'

'My mother's dead,' Bryce said flatly. 'Grace found her this afternoon. She blames herself.'

'But why?' The words were out before Edwin could stop them.

'Grace has always taken care of my mother. Of all of us.'

There was a tightening in Edwin's chest as he pictured her in the village, at the May Fair and in the chapel. Always doing for others, always giving. *Who cared for her?* He cleared his throat.

'Forgive me, but could your grandmother not have helped?'

'You've met my grandmother,' Bryce said. 'Not a warm woman. Except where Zoe is concerned, of course. But my uncle says she's taken Mother's death very badly. It's understandable, I suppose. She only had two daughters and has lost them both. You won't have an easy time with her. As for Grace–' He broke off.

'What about her?' Anxiety made Edwin's voice sharp.

'She's been hurt enough.'

'Mr Damerel, I need no such warning. I admire your sister more than–'

'Do you give poetry to all the women you *admire?*'

'The situation has never arisen. I promise you I would never do anything to hurt her.'

More than anything he yearned to offer Grace the comfort and support of his love. But because of the secret that lay like a dark stain on his soul, he dared not. All he could do was pray for help to find words that might ease her suffering.

As he approached the front door, dropped off by Bryce, John Ainsley was in the hall about to take his leave.

'Ah, Mr Philpotts,' the doctor said offering his hand. 'A sad business. I've done all I can. The rest is your province. Mrs Cheno-

191

weth is refusing to settle until she has seen you.'

'How is Miss Damerel?' Edwin enquired steadily.

The doctor frowned, shaking his head. 'I must admit to some concern. Grace was aware that this could happen at any time. It was touch and go with her mother on several occasions during the winter months. I have to say I didn't expect this reaction, not from Grace. She has always been the one on whom the rest of the family relied.'

To avoid betraying himself Edwin caught the inside of his lower lip between his teeth and tasted the hot saltiness of blood.

John Ainsley drew a gusty breath. 'It might not have hit her so hard had there been some warning. I've given her a sedative so you might find her a little slow. Hopefully she'll buck up in a day or two.' He nodded in farewell. 'Doubtless we'll see each other again soon.'

'Indeed.' Swallowing questions and comments his calling forbade him to voice, Edwin wished him good evening then waited, fighting impatience, for the butler to conduct him upstairs to Grace's room.

After knocking and receiving no reply, Patrick opened the door. 'Miss Grace?'

'Please go away.' Her voice was barely audible and held a flat hopelessness that Edwin found far more moving than tears.

Still fully clothed she lay facing the wall, a tartan rug covering her lower body.

'Miss Damerel?' Edwin said.

She jerked upright. Her face was ashen but her haunted eyes betrayed far more than relief.

'You came. I thought– I was afraid...' Covering her mouth with shaking fingers, she shook her head.

Having just promised her brother he would never hurt her, Edwin knew with terrible certainty that he was going to cause her untold pain. And there was nothing he could do to avoid it.

Grace looked down to free herself from the entangling blanket. The brief respite allowed Edwin to regain control.

'I'm sorry I'm so late.'

Alongside him the butler cleared his throat. 'Beg pardon, miss. Now Minister's here how about I ask Kate to bring you both a nice cup of tea?'

Knowing she needed it despite the nausea that flitted across her face, Edwin spoke quickly. 'How very kind. What an excellent idea.'

Turning to leave, Patrick whispered, 'Try and get her to take something, sir. They'll all be looking to her. She'll never cope if she don't eat proper.'

Grace sat hunched on the edge of the bed, her hands tightly clenched, head bowed.

Edwin's fingers curled into his palms as he remained where he was, his jaw aching from tension as drops of perspiration trickled down his back.

She looked up, her grief stark and raw. 'Help me.' The words were wrenched from her, as if her need were something to be ashamed of.

Crossing the space between them in two swift strides he sat beside her. After an instant's hesitation he took her hand. *Surely it could do no harm? She needed comfort so badly.* Her fingers gripped his. 'I can't make it better, Grace. Grieving for a loved one is a journey each of us must make alone.'

As a minister charged with the care of her soul his use of her name was perfectly acceptable. But it was the man's heart not the minister's that ached for her grief, ached for her.

'You don't understand,' her voice broke.

'That you think it's your fault?' he said gently. 'That if you had done something differently your mother would not have died?'

Her face contorted in pain too deep for the relief of tears.

'Everyone thinks that, Grace. The death of someone close, especially when it's sudden, is attended by all kinds of powerful feelings. Of course there's grief, but there's guilt and anger as well.'

Her gaze was intent, searching.

He looked down, forcing himself to release her hand. 'I'm not going to say I know how you feel. No one can know that, because each person's loss is unique. But I do know that every bereaved person experiences the emotions you are experiencing. They don't mean you are strange or wicked. They are a normal response to a devastating event.'

Clasping her arms across her stomach she began to rock. 'I'm so afraid.' Her voice was little more than a whisper.

'Of what?'

Compressing her lips she shook her head.

He would have tried to draw her out, but footsteps and the clink and rattle of china heralded the arrival of Kate with a tray. A few moments later there was a knock on the door and Violet peered in.

'Beg pardon, Miss Grace, Reverend. I'm some sorry to interrupt, but Mrs Chenoweth want the minister. In some state she is.'

As Grace's face closed and she replaced her half-full cup on the tray, Edwin turned to the maid.

'Tell Mrs Chenoweth I'll be along in a few minutes.'

'No,' Grace said wearily. 'You'd better go. Now she knows you're here you'll get no peace. She'll only send Violet back again.'

Reluctantly he stood and set his cup on the tray. When he turned back Grace had lain down again, curled up like a child, her face to the wall.

Dorcas stood in her cottage doorway, the afternoon sun warm on her upturned face. Louise Damerel had adored her garden and on a glorious day in summer gardens were at their best. So perhaps it was fitting that she should be laid to rest beneath blue skies and sunshine.

Opening her eyes Dorcas replaced her glasses and surveyed the brilliant swathes of colour. A gentle breeze carried the twitter of birds and the lazy drone of bees.

Henry had come to her the morning after Louise's death. Listening as he talked out his disbelief and confusion she had been sucked into painful memories of Zander's death and its aftermath. But she had said nothing. Though long expected, Henry's bereavement was still so new that her experience would seem irrelevant. Besides, he was jealous of her life with Zander and did not like her speaking of it.

Her time with Zander had been short. But he had been her *bright particular star*, the love of her life. Though she loved Henry and had been faithful to him for thirty years, it was a different kind of love.

She looked down at the letter and photographs she still held, the tenuous link across thousands of miles separating her from her son. Since John had confirmed her fears she found herself missing Hal in a way she hadn't done before. She wished it were possible, before her sight failed completely, for her to see him as the man he was now.

When he had left for South America vowing to raise enough capital to develop the pumping engines Henry deemed too advanced and too costly to be commercially viable, she had sent him on his way with her love and her blessing. It had never occurred to her that when eventually he returned, as he promised he would, she might need to rely solely on touch to discern the changes time and experience had wrought on his cherished features.

Inhaling deeply she closed her eyes and tilted her head once more so the sun might dry tears that traced cool tracks beneath the glasses and down her face. Henry still didn't know. When he had come to tell her about Louise she had sensed there was something else. After gentle coaxing he had poured out the disaster of the failed pump. It would have been cruel to add to the burdens he already carried.

While he clung to her, as if she alone were keeping him afloat in his raging sea of troubles, she thought about the future. His wife's ill health had been such an integral part of their lives that she had never imagined Henry being free. Now, suddenly, he was.

And knowing him as she did she was certain that after a decent interval he would bring up the subject of marriage again.

In the past she had laughed it off, saying she was perfectly content with their arrangement. But so much had changed. She had meant what she'd said to John Ainsley about continuing to paint. It would require a complete change of technique. But the challenge would stretch her both as an artist and a woman. Painting was so much a part of who she was that to stop was unthinkable. As long as she could develop a new way of expressing herself through art it would not be quite so hard to forfeit independence in other aspects of her life.

Her face felt tight where salt tears had evaporated. But the sun's warmth was a benediction. What could not be cured must be endured. If change was inevitable she would embrace it, make it work on her terms. The next time Henry talked of marriage she would accept.

Chapter Twelve

Standing by the drawing-room fireplace nursing a crystal tumbler half full of whisky, Henry Damerel watched family and friends talking.

Mary appeared beside him. 'It was a lovely service.' Taking a glass of sherry from Patrick's tray she waited until the butler had moved on then added, 'But I imagine you're glad it's over.'

Henry's brows rose, surprise tinged with relief.

'When my parents died,' she confided softly, 'I was acutely aware of people watching me to see how I was coping. I overheard comments about my bravery in the face of tragic loss. The fact was my parents were old and sick. Death was a merciful release for them both. I actually said this to one person.'

As Henry's brows climbed higher Mary raised a hand to shield her mouth so only he could see her smile. 'You're right. It was a dreadful mistake. Her expression condemned me as an unnatural daughter totally lacking in proper feeling. After that I simply thanked people for their kindness and waited for it all to be over. Grief is a private matter.' She paused. 'Though some appear to derive greater comfort from sharing their feelings with others.'

Henry followed her gaze towards his mother-in-law. In one corner of the rose damask sofa Hester Chenoweth, shrouded in black bombazine, clutched a wisp of lace handkerchief in the bony hand pressed to her flat bosom while with the other she gripped the arm of the woman sitting beside her.

'Poor Mrs Laity,' Mary murmured. 'Should I rescue her?'

Henry saw that though the woman's face wore an expression of sympathy, her posture betrayed her desire to escape. 'No, she'll manage.' As he spoke, Mrs Laity gently detached Hester's hand, patted it, and backed gracefully away out of sight behind another group. 'Told you. You stay here. Then no one else will come and bother me.'

An impish smile flitted across her face. 'Such a comfort to know I'm useful.'

'No, I – that wasn't–'

'It's all right, Henry. I know what you meant.'

He felt himself begin to relax. He knew most would interpret his stony expression as a stiff upper lip. But the truth was he didn't know what he felt *apart from relief*, and guilt because of it. 'More than useful. I couldn't have stood any more fuss. For years – you reach a point where–' He broke off, knowing he'd said more than he should. He cleared his throat. 'You did a good job with all this.' He gestured with his glass.

'There's nothing like charity committees to refine one's organizational skills. I sit on several. It's one of the hazards of being unencumbered by family responsibilities. As a result I've found I'm naturally bossy.'

'I've never found you so.'

'Good heavens! I must be better at it than I thought.' Her quick smile faded and she sighed. 'Besides, Louise was my friend so I consider it a privilege to be useful at a difficult time. I shall miss the chats she and I used to have in the chain garden. I imagine Grace will look after it now.'

Henry grunted. 'She'll have to pull herself together first. At the moment she's no use to man nor beast.' He downed half his drink. 'What in God's name's she at? Taking to her bed. As for leaving all this for you to arrange.' He shook his head and looked towards the dining-room where guests had begun to help themselves from the platters and dishes arrayed on the long table.

'All I did was work out the number expected and discuss a menu. It was Rose Trott who produced the wonderful spread. That woman is a treasure.'

'That's as may be. But Grace has no right to be so selfish. She knows the pressure I'm under.' As his voice rose Mary touched his arm lightly in warning. He drained the glass, feeling the spirit burn his throat then loosen the knot in his belly. 'Sorry. It's just—'

'I know,' Mary soothed. 'Henry, try to be patient with her. Grace has spent most of her life taking care of her mother. The shock of finding her ... she probably feels she has failed in some way.'

'That's ridiculous.'

'Not to her.' Her gentle smile robbed the words of any sting.

He watched her survey the milling people. She was a paradox: unremarkable in her gown of dark-grey silk, her brown hair neatly rather than fashionably dressed. Yet her contained public manner was totally at odds with the quick wit and ironic sense of humour she revealed to her friends.

'Only another hour,' she murmured, 'and they will all be on their way. Perhaps I shouldn't say this, but being an only child with few relatives, all of them delightfully distant, has its compensations.'

Henry's muffled snort of laughter took them both by surprise.

'That's better.' She darted him a swift smile. 'I'm so glad Zoe was able to get home, even if she can't stay long. That was a beautiful solo. She has an exquisite voice. Her presence has certainly mellowed Mrs Chenoweth. I imagine John Ainsley and Edwin Philpotts will both be hoping the improvement is permanent.'

Henry's mouth twitched.

'I know,' she said. 'But surely I can be honest with an old friend?'

As their eyes met, an awareness of something shared warmed Henry. *Honest with an old friend.* She had given him the opening he needed: an opportunity he could not afford to ignore.

'Mary, I – er...' As doubts crowded in he panicked and broke off, clearing his throat.

'Yes, Henry?'

'I-I'd like to talk to you. Not now. In a week or so, perhaps? I just have to–'

'Take all the time you need, Henry.' A faint flush coloured her cheeks but her voice remained perfectly calm.

If only it were that easy. But as he nodded he felt his mood lift and gazed at his younger daughter, a slim, golden-haired beauty striking yet ethereal in black silk and lace.

'She is lovely,' Mary said. 'You must be very proud of her. Indeed you have reason to be proud of all your children.'

Henry didn't reply, absorbed in an idea that initially had shocked him. Yet the more he considered it the more sense it made. Dorcas would understand. After all, nothing had changed for them. Nor would it. Dorcas was part of his life, part of him. But Mary was a wealthy woman.

His plan had been to ask her to join the

adventurers. But her advisers would never countenance more than minimal investment and that was simply not enough. But if he *married* her – he shifted uncomfortably, ashamed of such thoughts at a time like this. Yet what choice did he have? Louise was dead. But for him, for the family and everyone dependent on the mine, life had to go on. Problems had to be overcome by any means available.

If he married Mary he would have access to considerable wealth. With that kind of money he could replace the pumping engine; buy water-cooled drills; perhaps even repay the bank the money he'd borrowed using the house as security. *Would she have him?* They had always got along well. The family liked her. She was intelligent and level-headed. Most important apart from the money – she enjoyed excellent health.

Though she made light of being single and even extolled its advantages, what woman would forego the status and comfort of marriage in favour of lonely old age? *It was far too soon.* Yet waiting a respectable year was a convention he literally could not afford. Even so, he mustn't rush fences. Mary was a woman of breeding and class. He would need to tread very carefully.

'What was that? Oh yes. Colonel Hawkins tells me the boys are making quite a name for themselves in the gardening world.'

Standing unnoticed at one side of the doorway, Grace watched her sister move from group to group accepting with a deprecating smile and downcast eyes the compliments showered on her. Zoe was sophisticated and beautiful and talented and loved. While she – *could not go in*. Swallowing nausea that made her hot and dizzy, Grace fled upstairs to her room.

Henry felt drained yet edgy. It had been an exhausting week. The engineering works at Hayle had supplied the necessary parts for the pump only after he had promised payment – in cash – by the end of the month. The impertinence still rankled. Yet in his heart he couldn't blame them. After working day and night over the weekend his men had got the pump operating once more. Three days later miners had been able to return to the lower levels. Now everything depended on their skill in picking up the lodes again.

They would be drilling horizontally, which made far more dust than stoping. But other than reminding the captains to tell the men to cover their noses and mouths there was nothing he could do about it. The tin was there. The tributers would find it. They had to.

Standing at his study window he saw her drive up. His heart gave a sudden thud and he drew back quickly, irritated and unsettled by his reaction. He went to his desk and sat down then immediately got up again and crossed to the door, opening it as Patrick knocked.

'Miss Prideaux, sir.'

'Mary, do come in.' The fact that she had chosen to wear lavender silk inspired both relief and hope.

'A tray of tea, sir?'

'What? Oh, yes.' As the door closed he turned, rubbing his hands together. 'A pleasant journey?'

'Very pleasant, thank you.' She sat down.

Beneath the brim of her hat her cheeks were pink. This both startled and reassured him. But as she folded her hands and looked up waiting for him to speak, he wondered if he'd made a mistake, misjudged her. This jolted confidence that was already shaky. He paced the room wondering how – where – to start. Telling himself not to be so ridiculous he coughed.

'Mary, I ... er..' He stopped. He hadn't the faintest idea how to continue.

She raised one hand, her colour deepening. 'Would it help if I were to tell you I have an idea of what it is you wish to say?'

'You do?' he blurted. 'Forgive me. It's just–' he shook his head. 'Should I continue? Or would you rather–?'

'No, please go on. But – and please don't take offence – I would appreciate total honesty.' She must have seen the shock he couldn't hide for she added gently, 'I like to think we are friends, Henry. Between friends there should be no misunderstanding.'

'You're right.' He owed her that. Abandoning his planned approach he paused to gather his thoughts. Then just as he drew breath to begin there was a knock. With a snort of irritation he threw open the door.

'Your tea, sir.'

'Thank you. On the desk.' He turned away as Kate set the tray down.

'Shall I–' the housemaid began.

'No. That will be all.'

'Very good, sir.' Bobbing a curtsy Kate scuttled out.

'Would you?' he indicated the tray.

'In a moment. You were about to say?'

Resuming his pacing he told her the unvarnished truth about his desperate need for money if he were to hold on to the house, keep the mine functioning and maintain the family's standard of living.

She listened without interruption. When he'd finished he passed a hand over his cropped head feeling helpless, angry and ashamed.

'Henry, I'm so sorry. I had no idea.'

'I should hope not. It's hardly something to be proud of.'

Turning towards the tray she poured the tea. Then to his astonishment she added a dash of milk and half a teaspoonful of sugar to one. As she held it out to him she dipped her head so her hat hid her face. He thanked her absently. But her awareness of his taste kindled a fresh spark of hope.

After taking a sip of her own tea she replaced the cup and saucer on the desk and folded her hands once more in her lap. Though she appeared calm her whitened knuckles betrayed her.

'Henry, we wouldn't be having this conversation were it not for my considerable wealth. I am willing to invest a substantial amount of money in Wheal Providence. However, there is a condition.' She stopped. 'Henry, do you think you could sit down?' One hand strayed to her throat and she gave a breathless laugh. 'This is not easy for either of us. You pacing like a caged animal doesn't help.'

Setting his cup and saucer down with a clatter he subsided into the chair opposite hers. Relief made him tremble.

'A condition? Only one? Name it. I am already in your debt for the way you dealt with everything after – when Grace took to her bed. Your handling of my mother-in-law has been awesome.'

'Thank you. Such kind remarks make it easier for me.' Rising, she moved towards the window. 'As you know much of my life was devoted to nursing my parents.' She glanced over her shoulder. 'I would not have you think I begrudged one moment. Indeed it was a privilege to be able to return the love and care they lavished on me while I was growing up. But while they needed me marriage was not an option. After they died I was no longer in the first flush of youth and it was not my person but my fortune that attracted suitors.'

She turned to face him. 'However, despite increasing loneliness I found myself unable to consider offers from men I either could not respect, or for whom I did not feel that depth of affection one hopes for with a life partner.'

She stopped again to moisten her lips. Henry was intrigued. He had never seen Mary other than totally in command of herself.

'The welcome I have received in the Damerel household has brought me more happiness than words can express. I was deeply fond of Louise.' She stopped speaking and gazed out of the window.

Henry waited, literally biting his tongue.

'But spending as much time with her as I did, I could not help being aware – for a man such as yourself, strong and active, marriage to someone of such frail constitution cannot have been easy.' She turned to face him, straight-backed, her cheeks stained crimson. But her gaze was unflinching. 'My own health I'm pleased to say has always been exceptionally robust.'

Henry stared at her momentarily dumb-founded. Thrown by her quiet dignity and request for total honesty he had abandoned his planned proposal. He had laid his financial problems before her and hoped for no more than an offer of investment. But she was proposing... Good God, she was *proposing*. Marriage was her condition for giving him the money he needed.

As all the implications of her final remark registered he realized with a jolt that she wanted more than his name and the status of being *Mrs*. She wanted a full marriage with the possibility of children. She wanted *him*. Astonishment gave way to pride and darting excitement. It was years since he had experienced either.

An image of Dorcas flashed across his mind. He pushed it aside. She would understand. The mine was his life just as painting was hers. She knew how long and how hard he had struggled as disaster loomed ever closer. Marriage to Mary meant more than survival. It meant he could build Wheal Providence up to rival the richest mine in Cornwall. He loved Dorcas. Nothing would change between them. What Mary did not know could not hurt her.

'Henry?'

Jerked from his thoughts he saw shadows of uncertainty and mortification cloud her face.

He reached her in two strides and caught her hand holding it between both of his.

'Forgive me, lass. It's just – well, to be blunt, I didn't expect–'

'Why should you? Do you think me shameless?' Her smile was unforced and self-mocking. But he sensed uncertainty.

He squeezed her hand. 'How could I?' Then in affection and gratitude he raised it to his lips. 'We understand one another. Mary, will you do me the very great honour of becoming my wife?'

Her eyes glistened as she smiled up at him. 'Thank you, Henry. I will.' There was a small awkward pause. They both spoke at once.

'Naturally, I wouldn't–'

'When had you–?'

Henry cleared his throat. 'I was thinking if we did not wish to wait too long–'

'Perhaps a month or two?'

His thoughts raced. Would she make him wait for the money until after the ring was on her finger?

'Public opinion does not concern me,' she continued. 'But I am fond of your family and, as our decision inevitably involves them as well, I feel a short delay would be tactful. Don't you think?'

He nodded. He had no choice.

'A quiet ceremony in the chapel with just the family would suit me very well. It is, after all, a very private and personal matter.

Meanwhile I will make appointments with my lawyers and the bank.'

'You won't regret this, Mary.' His voice was thick. As he pressed another kiss on to her knuckles she shyly touched his cheek.

'Henry, about telling the family.'

'Best leave it a while. Not long,' he added quickly, not wanting her to think him reluctant. 'But what you were saying about tact – well, it's only a week since – you do understand?'

'Of course. When the time comes would you rather make the announcement on your own?'

'Good God, no. What I mean is–'

'I know exactly what you mean, Henry.' Her dry tone was belied by an understanding smile. 'We'll do it together.'

'Mary.' He hesitated. 'Would you tell Grace? Privately? She and her mother – you know. I think she'd take it better from you, being another woman. Would you mind?' He could feel himself sweating, and eased his stiff collar with a forefinger.

She pressed his hand. 'Of course not.'

After seeing her out he returned to his study and sat at his desk. He must tell Dorcas. But it wasn't urgent. Right now he had more than enough on his plate. He could wait a week or two. Once the news got out the village gossips would pounce like crows on carrion. But Dorcas would understand.

Chapter Thirteen

Just after ten on the last Sunday in July, Edwin left the manse carrying an overnight bag to make the five-mile walk to Godolphin Wollas where he would preach an afternoon and evening service. Heavy dew still spangled the grass that edged the road, the glittering droplets indicating a fine day. In a bluebell sky small clouds were piling into fleecy billows that trailed shadows in their wake as they sailed high over the landscape.

From the hillside he looked down onto woodland boasting every shade of green from the dark gloss of holly to the pink-tinted jade of sycamore and the burgundy richness of an occasional copper beech.

Cut hayfields looked scalped and pallid against lush pastures where cattle grazed. Scarlet poppies dotted fields of ripening wheat and barley *like splattered blood*. The thought – a dagger thrust between his ribs – stopped his breath. He thrust it away and inhaled deeply. *Not now. Not today. Concentrate on something else*. His gaze caught by two peacock butterflies fluttering above a pale-green field of oats that rippled in the breeze like water, he thought of Grace.

Her portrait lay in the bottom of his bag protected by two sheets of writing paper. She had glowed that day. Her lacy gown a change from her usual skirt and blouse. Even allowing that she had been her mother's principal nurse and companion, closer to her than anyone else, bereavement had affected her more severely than he would have expected.

Now a door had closed on part of her life. What would she do with the rest of it. *How he wished...* Such thoughts were worse than foolish. She deserved so much more than he could offer. But knowing that didn't ease the ache or stop the yearning.

It was almost 11.30 when he reached the farm. A broad carriage drive led up to a heavy front door that on most Cornish farms was only ever used by the undertaker. Edwin walked round to the back.

The house was large and solid, the granite walls softened by a green tangle of ivy and Virginia creeper that reached to the eaves and fringed deep, white-painted sash windows, whose many small panes reflected the sun. Following the flagged path that separated the house from the kitchen garden he arrived at the ever-open back door as his host came out to greet him.

Norman Angove was wearing his black Sunday-best suit, a starched collar, a gold watch chain looped across his waistcoat, and a broad smile.

'How do, Mr Philpotts.' Seizing Edwin's hand he gave it a hearty shake. 'Handsome day, isn't it?'

'It certainly is,' Edwin smiled.

'Surely better'n the last time you was here. Mind you, we needed the rain. C'mon in.' He led the way into an airy kitchen rich with the savoury aroma of cooking. Edwin's stomach gurgled and his mouth watered in anticipation.

'Morning, Mr Philpotts.' Lucy Angove glanced up, her plump face flushed and smiling. On the top of the Cornish range three saucepans bubbled. Gripping one corner of a large roasting tin with a folded cloth, she ladled the juices over the browning meat, her frilled blouse and dark skirt protected by a crisp white apron.

As she replaced the tin in the lower part of the oven, Edwin glimpsed another on the top shelf full of golden roast potatoes. Hunger sent pangs through his stomach. Slamming the oven door shut, Lucy hung the cloth over the brass rail and wiped her hands on her apron.

'Won't be long. I 'spect you're ready for it. 'Tis some way from Trewartha. Norman, haven't you offered Mr Philpotts a drink? The poor man just walked five miles in the sun.'

'Give us a chance, woman. Fancy a gla

of apple juice, Mr Philpotts?'

'Thank you. That would be most welcome.'

'Fetch a fresh flagon, Norm. The boys near enough finished that one in the larder.' She turned to Edwin. 'Sit down a minute and rest your legs.'

Dropping his bag Edwin pulled out one of the hoop-back wooden chairs. Spread with a gleaming white starched cloth the oblong table was set for five. He gazed round and felt the welcoming atmosphere enfold him.

Sunshine streaming in through the window above a stone sink big enough to bathe in illuminated spotless flagstones. Scrubbing had bleached the grooved wooden draining board almost white. Cheerful red-checked curtains were fastened back to allow in as much light as possible. Beneath the sink stood a full bucket of clean water drawn from the pump in the yard.

Cupboards stretched along one wall from waist height to floor. Above them on a wide shelf holding saucepans, baking tins, mixing bowls and serving dishes, a floral-painted tea caddy sat next to wide-topped stone jars labelled *salt, sugar* and *flour.* Colourful crockery was displayed on an enormous oak dresser.

Below the range, inside one end of the polished brass fender, a huge black kettle waited for space on the stove. At the other end stood fire irons and a coal-scuttle. Drawn up to the ceiling on its rope and pulley, a slatted wood clothes airer was today bare of laundry.

Though similar in size and content the manse kitchen bore little resemblance to this room. The difference was one of atmosphere. Edwin had noticed it the first day he came and on every visit since. Here he felt drawn in, welcome. But at the place supposed to be his home he felt like an interloper.

At least he had his study. A place of privacy and quiet in which to read, write, and prepare his sermons, or to talk to villagers who sought comfort or advice. Here, as on most farms, all the paperwork was done at the kitchen table. On the mantelshelf above the range the space behind the clock was stuffed with letters. Between numerous ornaments farm bills, receipts and accounts were speared on to metal spikes with round wooden bases.

Norman returned from the dairy carrying a brown stone flagon. He looked past Edwin who heard a door open behind him.

'Here's Matthew and Oliver.'

Rising, Edwin turned to shake the calloused hands of two stocky young men whose suit jackets strained across shoulders bulky from hard physical work. Beneath hair combed flat their sunburned faces were freshly shaved. Both nodded and murmured a greeting.

Norman removed the flagon's stopper. As he poured the cloudy liquid into glass tankards Edwin smelled the sharp tang of apples. On his first visit to the farm, Edwin had found the apple juice so tasty and refreshing that he had accepted a second glassful. Being Methodists the Angoves were staunchly teetotal. Condemning wines and spirits as the devil's brew they claimed what emerged from their apple press was simply *apple juice*.

Edwin was uncertain if this was genuine naivety. But weighing his responsibility as a guest to accept with thanks whatever he was offered against the risk of slurred speech and a pounding headache, he was careful now to accept only one glass. This he would sip slowly over the course of the meal.

'Right,' Lucy announced. ''Tis nearly ready, so I'll take you up and you can drop your bag.'

The room was furnished with flowered wallpaper, a big brass bed with a feather mattress covered by a blue counterpane, rag rugs on a wooden floor polished with lavender wax that faintly scented the air, and a large oak wardrobe. There was clean water in the tall china jug, a towel next to it, and a small vase of flowers on the bedside table next to the oil lamp.

'Don't be long now. Look like you could

do with a good meal, you do.'

Recognizing concern in her sharp eyes Edwin smiled. 'The walk has certainly given me an appetite. I'll be down again in a few minutes.'

Lucy bustled out, closing the door behind her.

After rinsing his face and hands and combing his hair Edwin returned, much refreshed, to the kitchen table. He said a short prayer of thanks. Then Norman carved thick tender slices from the roast leg of lamb while Lucy passed round dishes of roast potatoes, peas and carrots, and jugs of gravy and mint sauce.

While Matthew and Oliver focused on their heaped plates, Norman, a chapel steward and thus responsible for the fabric of the building, told Edwin of the rot discovered in the windows.

'We can't leave it another year,' he said, between mouthfuls. 'The glass'll fall out. All they windows should be repainted before the bad weather set in, and the woodwork do need to be done before they can start painting. I got a couple of estimates for the carpentry and the painting. I'll give them to you before you go.'

'Thank you.' Edwin was grateful. Norman's forethought meant all he had to do was pass the estimates on to his circuit superintendent. Once financial consent was given work could begin.

'Sad about Mrs Damerel going like that,' Lucy remarked. 'Must 'ave been some awful shock for Grace, dear of her. She's a lovely girl.'

Startled to hear Grace's name mentioned when he was trying so hard to avoid thinking about her, Edwin swallowed convulsively and choked on a piece of potato.

'All right, are you, Reverend?' Lucy enquired, her forehead puckering in anxiety.

He nodded. 'Fine,' he croaked. 'Wrong way...' He patted his chest, his face hot with embarrassment, eyes watering. '...apologize.' Reaching for his tankard he sipped the apple juice.

'You got them muddled, Mother.' Oliver looked up from his plate. ''Tis Zoe got the looks.'

'Looks aren't everything, my lad,' Lucy replied. 'You'd do well to remember that. Zoe might be pretty as a picture, and we all know she got a lovely voice. But she isn't what you'd call a *giving* girl. Grace now, she got a heart as big as a bucket. I just wish she could find a man to love her like she deserve.'

No. Edwin's instant and violent rejection of the very thought of anyone else loving Grace appalled him. He felt shaken and ashamed. His breathing once more under control, his appetite completely gone, he put his knife and fork together, fervently hoping his flushed and sweating face would be attributed to his coughing fit.

'Now, Reverend,' Lucy beamed. 'How about some raspberry tart? Fresh from the garden this morning. Here, Norm, pass Mr Philpotts the cream.'

'Thank you.' Forcing a smile, Edwin accepted the dish and picked up his spoon.

The next few hours were a blend of clarity and confusion. During the walk to the chapel and the opening hymns, his thoughts strayed continually to Grace.

With two services to preside over and aware that many in the congregation would attend both, he had planned his sermon to last only twenty minutes. Afterwards he was wryly amused to find his brevity praised by some but scorned by others who didn't consider a preacher had done a proper job unless they had been harangued for at least an hour. But thundering scolds and dire warnings were not his style. God knew he had more guilt on his soul than any of those present.

As parents and grandparents headed home to enjoy an hour without youngsters under-foot, Edwin joined the children in the Sunday school. Listening to Miss Butteridge, the sour-faced elderly teacher droning on, he sympathized with the children's boredom-induced fidgeting. When Grace taught at

221

Sunday school her audience was rapt and silent. She had a way of telling Bible stories that brought them to vivid life. She also divided the session with short break and, if the weather allowed, sent the children outside. Giving the boys a ball to burn off their excess energy, she chatted to the girls.

His compliments on her insight and understanding had brought a fiery blush to her face. But she had refused the praise, explaining that anyone with younger brothers knew they could not sit still or attend to anything for longer than twenty minutes.

Her rapport with children made a mockery of Miss Butteridge's stern efforts. *She would make a wonderful mother.* Clenching his fists he struggled for objectivity. He had forfeited any right to happiness. He must think only of Grace's wellbeing. But perhaps she could extend her teaching. Maybe join the staff at the village school? He would suggest it when next they met. It would give him a reason to talk to her: to help her find purpose and a new direction for her life.

By the time he got back to the farm, Norman, Matthew and Oliver were doing the afternoon milking while Lucy laid out a spread of bread and butter, cold meat and pickles, saffron cake, scones with home-made strawberry jam and thick clotted cream, and cups of strong tea.

Edwin walked in the garden rehearsing his next sermon while the men washed in the scullery before going upstairs to change once more into their Sunday best. Then after tea everyone returned to chapel for the evening service.

Later that night as Edwin prepared for bed, he wondered what to do about Miss Butteridge. After Sunday School she had complained to him about the children. He had ventured that adding a little fun might make them more attentive. Retorting that Reverend Peters would never have suggested such a thing she stalked away, her mind as tightly shut as her thin mouth.

He wondered if umbrage might keep her from the evening service. But when he entered from the vestry she had been sitting in her usual place and glared at him, radiating disapproval, from the opening hymn until the final prayer.

Rinsing his hands he reached for the towel. As he dried himself, picturing the children's faces, another child's image filled his mind: a brown-skinned child with huge dark eyes and blue-black hair.

He sank on to the bed engulfed by sickening guilt as, yet again, the questions hammered relentlessly. Why hadn't he realized? How could he not have seen? Was there something he could have done? Could he have stopped it? Had others known? But if they had then surely they would have said something. *Unless they believed he was aware and had chosen not to see.*

He buried his face in the towel, lashed by crucifying self-reproach.

Like so many of the mission children, Akhil had been found on the street: a bundle of rags, starving, filthy, and covered in sores. Most children reacted to food and care with a wary greed that gradually evolved into trust. But any attempt to touch Akhil had met with thrashing feet and fists and strange inarticulate grunts. When at last a sobbing but clean Akhil was wrapped in a towel, Edwin and his two helpers were soaked to the skin.

Lewis had left them to it. Overworked and always busy he preferred to deal with more amenable children who showed gratitude for their good fortune. So the task of trying to make Akhil understand he was safe had fallen to Edwin.

Under the mission's regime of wholesome food, regular baths, medical care and days structured around basic schooling and physical exercise, Akhil had gradually revealed an intelligence that in an English 10-year-old would have been praiseworthy. In an abandoned deaf-mute street child it was amazing.

Despite being debilitated by the heat, humidity and intermittent fever, Edwin's work with the orphans and other outcasts cared for at the mission gave him a deep sense of fulfilment. He took particular pleasure in Akhil's remarkable progress.

But after several months Akhil's behaviour changed. He became destructive, breaking toys and defacing work into which he had put hours of effort. One day Edwin found him huddled in a shadowed corner of the compound, keening softly while he deliberately and repeatedly cut the soft skin on the inside of his forearm with an ivory handled dagger. Edwin recognized it immediately. Lewis had picked it up for a few rupees in a street market and used it as a letter-opener.

Applying antiseptic and bandages the harassed doctor had shrugged. 'What do you expect from such a child?'

Edwin quietly returned the dagger to Lewis's office while he was elsewhere, and said nothing. Desperate to help, wondering if the boy's self-mutilation stemmed from frustration at his inability to communicate, Edwin pushed himself even harder to find time to give Akhil additional instruction. Akhil responded by following him around like a shadow, convincing Edwin he had solved the problem. *Such conceit. Such blindness.*

Lewis's warning about pride brought him up short. It had never occurred to him that his pleasure in Akhil's progress might be construed as vanity and thus a sin. Though it was a wrench he forced himself to relinquish some of the boy's lessons to Lewis. Akhil's development was what mattered – not who guided it. Besides, weakened by another bout of fever, he was finding it increasingly difficult to cope with the additional work Lewis had apologetically delegated to him.

One evening after falling asleep over a meal he had little appetite for, he crawled off to bed. Waking with a start several hours later, he lay sweating beneath the mosquito net, listening, and heard a muffled cry.

In the dormitory the boys were quiet. He realized later they had been too quiet for genuine sleep: realized *too late* they had known what was happening but were too frightened to tell. He stood in the passage holding his breath as he strained to hear. It came again. *From Lewis's room?*

That was when the nightmare had begun. Only there was no awakening. He would never be free.

Despite the months that had passed, those horrifying images were still vivid: seared too deep into his memory ever to be forgotten.

Silent on bare feet he had opened Lewis's door. He had stood unable to move, his brain refusing to accept what his eyes were seeing.

Akhil was sprawled face down and naked on a mound of pillows, his eyes huge with fear and pain above the cloth wrapped tightly around the lower half of his tear-streaked face. His bound wrists were stretched above his head and tied to the rail of the bedhead. Kneeling behind the boy, curved over him like some evil bird of prey, Lewis's white skin was oily with sweat and gleamed in the lamplight.

Edwin retched, shuddered and sucked in a gasping breath as terrible realization dawned. Akhil's destructive behaviour and self-mutilation: Lewis's accusation of vanity: the additional work designed to keep him busy *and out of the way:* it all made dreadful sense.

He recalled the silence in the dormitory. How long had this been going on? *How many others?* With a roar of rage he dived forward, slamming his fist into the older man's face with such force that Lewis was thrown off the bed and crashed sideways against a chest of drawers. On top of the chest Edwin saw the dagger. How many times had the child been threatened with it? Or subjected–

Edwin blanked out a thought too horrific to contemplate and reached for the dagger to cut Akhil free. Lewis kicked at his legs and, stumbling backwards, Edwin fell to the floor.

Lewis crawled forward, blood trickling from a swelling cut on his temple, and lunged for the dagger.

Edwin tried to fight him off. 'How could

you?' he choked. 'How *could* you?'

Flinging himself forward, using his body to hold Edwin down, Lewis's mouth twisted in a grotesque smile. 'What can't speak can't lie.'

For a split-second Edwin didn't believe, *couldn't* believe, what he'd heard. As fury roared through him he forgot his calling, forgot his vows and lashed out with feet and fists, driven by loathing, horror, and his own terrible guilt, to punish, to *destroy*.

Lewis gave a sudden jerk, a strangled groan, and fell backwards. Dazed, heaving air into starving lungs, Edwin pushed himself up, wiping the sweat from his eyes with a shaking hand. *His hand was covered in blood.* For a moment he stared at it, not understanding. Then he saw the swathe of bright red spots splattering the wall.

His gaze swivelled to Lewis slumped between the chest and the wall, hands pressed to his belly where the dagger's ivory handle protruded amid slowly welling blood.

'Oh dear God.'

Lewis raised pain-dulled eyes. 'No doctor.'

'But–'

'No.' A spasm of agony tightened Lewis's grey-white features. 'Better this way.' The words rustled like dead leaves.

A muffled whimper from the bed jolted Edwin from his paralysis. Swallowing the

228

nausea that threatened to overwhelm him he grabbed the crumpled nightshirt from the floor and laid it across Lewis's lower body to hide the terrible wound and the worst of the blood. Then on trembling legs he stumbled to the bed. Pulling the gag from Akhil's mouth, he tried to reassure, to soothe, not recognizing his own voice as he fumbled with the knots that tied the boy's arms to the bedhead. His hands shook, his fingers were weak and clumsy. It would have been quicker to cut the cords. But the only knife – he shut off the thought.

Akhil was racked by tremors. Shock had turned his face the colour of tallow and his eyes were glazed. Ripping the sheet from the bed Edwin wrapped it around the shivering child and carried him back into the dormitory. As heads rose from pillows he ran his tongue over paper-dry lips. *Jesus Christ, how often had they watched this happen? How many others had been–?*

'Go back to sleep. You are safe now.' His voice cracked and his throat closed. He swallowed hard. 'You are safe. I promise you.'

Drawing the covers over Akhil's quivering body, Edwin gripped the boy's shoulder for a moment. God alone knew if he would still be there in the morning. But right now there was no time to do more.

Back in Lewis's room the air was thick with the sickly-sweet smell of blood. Edwin's gorge rose as he crouched beside the man he had admired and trusted; the man he had considered a friend. He ought to do something. *But what?* He gazed helplessly at Lewis, head and heart pounding with shock, rage and horror at what he'd done.

Lewis's head rolled against the wall as he looked at Edwin. Once more his face contorted with pain. 'Couldn't stop. No strength, no will.' His grimace of self-loathing shook Edwin to the core. *What was it like to be Lewis?* But his brief sympathy was crushed by a sudden stark vision of Akhil's scarred arms and the gag that had smothered his cries while his eyes screamed silent terror.

Revolted, Edwin drew back, and saw the pale lips twist in recognition. Stiffening suddenly, Lewis tried to straighten, his gaze fastening on Edwin's. 'Remember, it wasn't–' His eyes widened, his mouth opening as if in surprise, then with a long slow rattling exhalation, he slumped back against the wall, his body flaccid, eyes half-closed and empty.

As a wrenching sigh caught in Edwin's throat, jerking him back to the present, he wiped his face with the towel and wished he could as easily wipe away the memories. *Remember.* As if he could ever forget.

Folding the towel, he laid it beside the flowered china basin. Then, swiftly removing the rest of his clothes, he pulled on his nightshirt and slid between Lucy Angove's crisply ironed sheets, inhaling the faint fragrance of lavender that perfumed most Cornish linen chests.

He closed his eyes desperate for sleep. He didn't want to think any more. He felt battered, bruised. But it was hopeless. Once started the nightmare had to run its course. Suddenly he was back in Chowringhee.

Chapter Fourteen

On his arrival at the tall, elegant building Edwin had been led up a wide curving staircase to the room where he was to sleep and told to remain there. Someone would come to him.

The room was simply furnished, functional rather than welcoming, walls and ceiling painted a flat cream. The deep window was hung with dark green curtains. A plain fawn rug covered the polished wood floor between the bed and wardrobe. A white woven coverlet shrouded the bed. Beside it on a cane stool stood an oil lamp and a box of matches. The only other furniture was a plain table that would double as a writing desk, and a straight-backed chair.

After unpacking his soap and razor, hairbrush, nightshirt and towel, Edwin placed the empty bag beside the wardrobe and sat down on the edge of the bed to wait. Some time later a knock on the door roused him from the numb state of non-thinking the doctor had told him was the aftermath of shock. Lacking the will or energy to move he simply called, 'Come in.'

The man who entered was short, plump

and balding. Peering over pince-nez cling-ing halfway down his snub nose, his eyes were as bright and sharp as a bird's. He wore a black suit, a stiff white collar, a black tie, and a warm smile that released some-thing in Edwin's chest.

'Good afternoon, Mr Philpotts. My name is Drew. I will be speaking on your behalf at the forthcoming enquiry.'

Edwin watched dumbly as he crossed to the table, opened his leather case, took out a pen and several sheets of paper, then pulled the chair forward and sat down.

'I'd like you, if you will, to describe exactly what happened the night Mr Preston died.'

Edwin noticed he said *died*. Not *was killed*. Or worse, *was murdered*. He swallowed and took a shaky breath. He wished he didn't have to go through it again. A tide of shame engulfed him. He should not complain. It could all have been so very much worse. He had expected the police to be involved. But the doctor had said it was an internal matter that did not concern the Indian authorities and would be dealt with by the Mission Board. Weak from shock and fever Edwin had accepted this.

He forced himself to think back, to relive scenes and events he would have given everything he possessed to be free of. After a halting start he was once again caught up in the horror of that night. Words poured from him. Drew made notes, interrupting occasionally to ask a question.

Eventually Edwin stopped, his head in his hands.

'Thank you, Mr Philpotts. That is most satisfactory.'

It took a moment to penetrate. Then Edwin's head jerked up.

Drew had recapped his pen, gathered up his notes and was on his feet, hand extended. Edwin rose and shook it.

Reaching the door, Drew looked over his shoulder. 'The hearing will take place tomorrow morning at eleven. Naturally you will attend but you will not be required to speak. Indeed should you find yourself moved to do so I strongly urge you to resist.' He flashed a brief smile. 'That is *my* job.'

Edwin stared at the closed door. *Most satisfactory.* What had he meant?

Following a night of very little sleep Edwin bathed, dressed, forced down half a cup of tea, and followed an Indian servant down the sweeping staircase and across the wide hallway into a lofty room.

They were seated behind a mahogany table: five black-suited sombre-faced men who would determine his future.

Drew repeated in broad outline what he had been told the previous afternoon. There was nothing Edwin could argue with, certainly nothing untrue. And yet...

The Board asked no questions. They did not even retire. Their deliberations consisted of low-voiced murmurs and nodding heads. Edwin realized then that discussions had already taken place: that the purpose of the hearing was simply to observe proper procedure. He should have been shocked, or at least surprised. He was beyond either.

A few moments later he heard the soul-shattering events neatly disposed of as *a tragic accident.* Then he was asked to stand as the most senior member of the Board had addressed him.

'Mr Philpotts, we do not hold you responsible in any way for the unfortunate happenings that have been disclosed at this hearing. Nor is there any question mark over *your* standards of work or behaviour.'

Relief at the chairman's exoneration made Edwin's heart lurch. His eyes burned and he swallowed repeatedly. He had been terrified they would think he had been aware of what Lewis was doing. That he had deliberately kept silent. He could not have borne it if they thought that. Yet how would he ever have convinced them otherwise?

'However...'

Of course. He should have expected it. There was bound to be a 'however'.

'However, we have a duty and responsibility to look beyond the immediate. We have to consider and circumvent any potential repercussions. You will appreciate that it has taken years of work by a large number of very dedicated people for the mission and its work to be accepted by the Indian authorities. You will also understand how vital it is that nothing should undermine our good name. We cannot afford even a whisper of scandal.'

Edwin's relief turned to uncertainty, and uncertainty to dread.

'So I'm afraid it will not be possible for you to remain at the mission.'

He flinched as if he'd been struck. He should have foreseen this. They could not possibly afford to have him around, a constant reminder of something best forgotten.

'Having read the doctor's report on your recent health problems, the Board believes it would be best if you returned to England and a less physically demanding ministry.'

At least they weren't forcing him to leave the church. Relief swung to resentment. *How could they? He had done nothing wrong*. Then realization stopped his breath: *he had killed a man*.

Unpleasant duty done, the chairman smiled and rubbed his hands. 'I daresay you'll be glad to go home again, eh?'

Edwin had stared at him, beyond speech. *Home?* His home was here. Apart from his schooling, he had lived in India all his life. He opened his mouth. And closed it again.

The decision had been made. No amount of pleading would change it. He was an embarrassment. His efforts counted for nothing against the past, present and future work of the mission. Of course he had to go. But he wanted – *needed* – to go to somewhere familiar.

'S-s-sir? M-m-ay I ask one f-favour?'

The chairman's smile grew wary. 'What is it?'

'Could a place be found for me in Cornwall? It's where my family came from and where I went to school.'

He sensed their relief. He wasn't going to make a fuss.

After more shared glances and nods the chairman said, 'I don't see why not. I'm sure the fresh air and milder climate will soon restore you to good health. I will ask Mr Drew to draft the relevant letters.'

Edwin was not permitted to return to the mission. He never found out what happened to Akhil. Within days, stunned at the speed with which everything had been arranged, he was on a ship back to England.

Grace lifted an apricot négligé from the drift of silks, gauze, and lace piled on the white satin counterpane. She recalled her mother wearing it the morning the letter arrived announcing the twins' homecoming. It seemed such a short time ago.

Folding the frilled chiffon she laid it gently in the tissue-lined trunk standing on the floor beside the bed. Grace wiped her eyes and nose, tucked the damp handkerchief into the waistband of her skirt and picked up another bedgown. This one was white gauze trimmed with pink ribbons. She could hear her mother saying that knowing she looked attractive speeded her recovery and she owed it to her visitors to make an effort.

Grace fumbled for the handkerchief again. She wasn't ready for this erasure of her mother's presence. It was too soon. She didn't understand her father's urgency.

They had met in the hall the previous evening. She had been on her way to bed, he to his study.

'Grace, I want you to sort out your mother's bedroom; her clothes and so on. As soon as possible. Start tomorrow.'

Her shock must have shown on her face for his expression immediately hardened. 'Look, nothing will bring her back. So it can't make any difference whether you do it now or in six months' time.'

Except to her, whose grief *and guilt* were still agonizingly raw.

'I've neither the time, nor the...' He gestured helplessly. 'It's a woman's job. You're her eldest daughter so....'

It's your duty. Automatically Grace completed the sentence. Heard first in child-

238

hood when she was too young to understand fully what it meant, that phrase had
formed her character, shaped her life. Now,
bereft as she was of love or comfort, it kept
her functioning.

'You were close to her. You'll know what to
do with everything, how best to dispose of...
I want it all gone, Grace. No reminders.' He
took a breath as if he were about to add
something. Instead he turned away. She saw
a muscle twitch in his rigid jaw as he ran a
hand over his cropped head.

Their paths had rarely crossed since the
funeral. She had been – she recoiled from
the shameful memory of her uncharacter-
istic behaviour – best to call it *unwell*. He had
spent his days away from home visiting various engineering works. Overhearing Thomas
Coachman tell Violet that Master had been
all over Cornwall looking at new equipment
for the mine Grace had been surprised. She
had understood the mine to be in financial
difficulty. But either she'd misunderstood or
the problems had been resolved.

She gazed at her father. She had often
wished his tongue might be less quick, less
scathing. It was rare to see him lost for
words. He had never been an easy man to
know.

But not showing his feelings didn't mean
he had none. Or that they weren't as painful
as hers. Perhaps even more so, for he had

239

lost his life-partner, the mother of his children. How would she feel in such circumstances? She couldn't even begin to imagine. So though what he was asking appalled her, how could she refuse?

Blinking back ever-present tears she had tentatively touched his arm. 'Of course I'll do it, Papa.'

The faint fragrance of lavender swelled the lump in her throat. So many clothes. So many memories. She wished Violet were with her. Violet's practical common sense would have made the task more bearable and two of them could have done it in half the time. But her grandmother had been adamant.

'No. You can't have Violet. If you're so anxious to turn out your dear mother's closets, and her hardly cold in her grave, you must do it alone. I'm not well. I need Violet here with me. Now go away. I can't bear the sight of you. Heartless, you are. Cruel and heartless. Oh, I wish Zoe was here. She would understand. She's such a comfort to me. Not like some.' Closing her eyes, she had turned her head away.

Each bitter recrimination another hammer-blow on her bruised spirit and too tired to explain, Grace had gone.

Folding the last of the frothy garments she laid it gently on top of the others. Her mother's jewellery had been taken care of by

240

the will. She and Zoe had each inherited various pieces. Some were family heirlooms, some gifts from her father. The twins had received other items for when they married.

She straightened up. Her swollen eyes were gritty and sore. Her head throbbed. She felt utterly wretched. Crossing to the wardrobe she hesitated for an instant then opened the double doors. Her mother's perfume wafted out, piercing her like a blade. Tears welled, blurring her vision then spilling down her cheeks as she drew a trembling hand across a rainbow of silk or satin-lined lace gowns, finely embroidered cotton blouses, skirts and jackets of taffeta and velvet.

Clutching handfuls of the rich materials she buried her face in them, convulsed with grief. *She was so lonely.* Suddenly a wave of anger engulfed her, so powerful, so violent, she almost blacked out.

Bathed in perspiration she staggered backwards, sank on to the bed and gripped the carved post, her hands slippery on the polished wood. She must not faint. *Breathe.* As the roaring in her head receded she was aware of someone knocking. She forced her head up. The door opened and Mary's head appeared.

'Ah, Grace, Kate said I'd find you – my dear, are you all right?' Quickly closing the door, she hurried forward. 'Of course you're not. How could you be? Oh, my sweet girl, this must be dreadfully hard for you. I had hoped – but no, this isn't the time. I'll come back another–'

'No, please don't go.' Fumbling for her handkerchief, Grace pressed it to her temples and upper lip. 'I'd rather you stayed, honestly. I'd be glad of your company.'

'Well, if you're sure.'

'I'm fine now. It was just...'

Mary nodded. 'I know. I remember after my parents died. I had to deal with all their personal effects. They were ill and tired and death was a release. But it was still difficult. In fact it was terrible. And they were far older than your mother.' She paused. 'Grace, all this' – she gestured – 'her clothes, her personal bits and pieces, they're only *things*. You don't need those to remember her. You have a lifetime of memories to enjoy whenever and wherever you choose.'

What memories? Her frequent illnesses? Constant anxiety? Trying to keep the twins occupied and quiet? Zoe complaining, or running to Granny Hester and winning comfort and treats by telling tales?

She caught her breath, shocked and horrified at the thoughts cannoning around the inside of her head.

'Grace? Is something wrong?'

'No. I'm – it's...' With enormous effort, Grace pulled herself together. 'Would you like some tea?'

Mary's frown of concern softened into a shy smile. 'Later perhaps. I'm glad to find you alone. There's something– I have some news. I – that is, we – wanted you to be the first to know' She stopped. Then seating herself beside Grace on the bed she folded her hands in her lap. 'Your father has asked me to marry him.'

It seemed to Grace that time slowed. She was aware of turning, seeing Mary's brows pucker in her anxiety to explain, to be understood, Mary's voice coming from a long way off.

'I know it seems very ... hasty. I would have preferred– But there are reasons – financial reasons – why for your father to wait would be neither wise nor desirable.' She swallowed.

Grace had always considered Mary to be a confident woman, self-contained rather than diffident.

'I will be honest with you, Grace. I was very fond of your mother. Through her I was privileged to get to know you all. Being accepted – welcomed – as a family friend has meant more to me than you will ever know. Had your mother lived that is what I would have remained, a loyal friend. However' – she paused. 'Grace, your father has proposed to me and I have accepted. I know I am asking a great deal of you, but I would like – it would mean so much to me if you could–'

243

'Give you my blessing?' *Was that what she was asking?* Grace felt disoriented. This on top of everything else was too much.

The anxiety that had tightened Mary's features dissolved into a radiant smile than made her look ten years younger. Seizing Grace's hand, she pressed it between both of hers. 'Oh, I hoped so much that you would understand. I do not expect to be so fortunate with Mrs Chenoweth.'

Grace's stomach clenched painfully as she pictured Granny Hester's reaction.

'But you are not to worry,' Mary said. 'I'll tell her. And should it come to a battle of wills I shall win. As to the house, I want it to remain a welcoming home for all the family.'

Doubt wormed through Grace's mind. Was Mary speaking for her father as well? Grace didn't think so.

'Of course, the chain garden must stay just as it is. It was Louise's pride and joy and a beautiful memorial. I know you will want to continue her work.'

No. I don't. I hate it. As denial and rejection swelled her chest and climbed her throat, she fastened her teeth on her lower lip and bent her head, gripping the bedpost so hard that pain cramped her fingers.

While Mary's relief and happiness bubbled over in a request for help with her bride clothes, Grace gazed unseeing at the floor. Duty and responsibility settled their crushing weight on her shoulders.

'In fact, I would be very surprised if you do not receive a proposal yourself very shortly.'

Grace looked up. 'What?' She felt slow and stupid.

Mary raised her brows, her smile fond. 'From Edwin Philpotts, of course.'

Pins and needles pierced every nerve in Grace's body. 'No, you're wrong. He doesn't – do you really think? But surely he would have–' Soaring from disbelief to hope she plunged into despair. 'No.'

'My dear, believe me it's only a matter of time.' Mary's tone carried total conviction. 'The way he looks at you, it's as plain as a pikestaff.'

Grace shook her head. 'He's never *said*.'

'No, and do you know why? It's simple. Someone in Mr Philpotts' position has to consider most carefully before proposing marriage. His job requires his wife to be a very special person. Not only must she support him in his ministry; she will also be expected, while raising her family, to involve herself in many of the chapel activities. Then every three years she must be prepared to move and start all over again on a new circuit. Your devotion to your mother and the rest of the family, and their dependence on you, might have made him wary. Especially as he has been in the village

245

only a few months.'

'But...'

'But now much has changed.'

'Everything,' Grace whispered.

Mary pressed her hand. 'Indeed. Who will be more aware of this than he? So being a thoughtful man he's probably allowing you time to come to terms with all that's happened before he declares himself.'

Grace searched Mary's face. 'Do you really think so?'

Mary nodded. 'I do.'

Grace lowered her eyes, desperate to believe but terrified Mary might be wrong.

Dorcas rinsed the brush in the jar of murky water and wiped it on a rag. Her glasses lay on the grass by her chair. On her right stood the low table holding her paints, palette, rags, and pot of brushes. A broad-brimmed hat of soft straw shaded her eyes from the sun.

She had spent two days at her easel painting a memory: walking with Zander in the craggy hills between St Ives and Zennor on a fine October day.

It surprised her how often during recent weeks Zander had appeared in her thoughts.

On that particular autumn afternoon she had been in the middle of saying something to him as they rounded a curve in the steep hillside. Halting in mid-stride and mid-sentence she had gazed at the view below then at Zander who smiled.

Drinking in the scene, automatically noting colours and perspective, angles and quality of light, the shapes and textures of the landscape, she had felt intense joy that they shared so much, that he *knew* and understood.

From harbour and bay's edge the town surrounded the church and spread up valley and hillside. Beyond the town the rugged coast was edged with miles of golden sand all the way to the Godrevy light. The sinking sun had laid a glittering path across the water's surface. It lightened from indigo and sapphire to turquoise and aquamarine before breaking in fine white frills against sharp black rock and ochre sand.

Before starting, Dorcas had removed her glasses. For the first time the image she painted would not be a faithful represent-ation of what she could see. Because soon – a few months, a year or two if she was lucky – her failing eyes would no longer allow her to see what she had painted.

She had sat for some time mentally projecting the picture on to the thick paper pinned to the backing board and gathering her courage. Zander's voice had echoed in her head. *If you do your best then no matter what the result you have not failed. The only failure is not to try.* Heart pounding, scared sick, she had selected a large sable brush and begun.

Forced to abandon a lifetime's technique she plunged into the unknown. She worked purely on instinct, on hope, and the need to know finally, one way or the other.

The painting had evolved as she darkened the landscape with a glaze of thin washes to enhance the luminosity of the sky. Taking it into the cottage last evening she had brought it out again this morning and had worked all day in air fragrant with summer flowers.

The hours had flown. When at last she stopped, knowing the painting was complete, that anything she did now was simply tinkering, she was stiff and aching. Focusing on her inner vision, rather than the blurred patches of colour had demanded fierce concentration. The effort had cost her dearly.

As she rinsed the last brush she waited for the deep sense of satisfaction that usually accompanied the completion of a painting. Despite the lingering warmth of late afternoon a shiver tightened her skin. In painting a sinking sun and gathering clouds she had aimed to capture a joyous fragment of her past. Why then this premonition that it was also a glimpse of her future?

She was tired that was all. She had not worked so intensively for years. Attempting techniques she had never used before was exacting in itself. She was fifty-six years old. At this moment she felt the weight of every one of them.

Picking up her spectacles she polished them with the hem of her cotton skirt, aware she was putting off the moment. Mocking herself she put them on, settled them comfortably, then turned to her easel.

It started as a hollow feeling behind her breastbone and expanded into an aching void. In her mind's eye the scene had been so clear. Though she had envisioned the detail she had not attempted to paint it. What she had tried to do was use shape and colour to convey an *impression*. So that anyone looking at it would see what she had seen, feel what she had felt.

What lay on the paper was unrecognizable.

Her mouth tasted of ashes. How glib, how foolish had been her promise to John Ainsley. She would never stop painting. *She would simply change her style.*

Anyone familiar with her previous work would turn from this in pity or embarrassment. Those who had never heard of her would frown and ask each other what on earth it was supposed to be.

What now? Panic flared. She fought it down. Where was Henry? Why hadn't he come? In the past his had always been the greater need. She had understood that.

Louise's frequent illnesses would have put strain on any man. In recent years problems at the mine had added to his worries.

Henry had always liked to talk to her. Often he had talked *at* her. But she had been happy to listen. She never offered advice. It was neither sought nor wanted. She knew that putting a problem into words cleared his mind, enabling him to see for himself the best solution.

But she had not seen him since the night of Louise's death when he had seemed unable to believe that it was finally over. Whether his reaction stemmed from shock or relief, even she – who had known him almost thirty years – could not have said.

Days had lengthened into weeks. Obviously he would have had things to do. But she wished he would come. She wanted – *needed* – the warmth and comfort of his physical presence, his arms around her. She needed to hear his voice, needed to hear him say she was strong, that she *would* cope, *would* survive. That being unable to paint was *not* the end of the world. Because right now that was what it felt like.

Her joints stiff and aching, she got slowly to her feet and walked into her cottage, leaving table, easel, and painting outside in the gathering dusk.

Chapter Fifteen

It was 5.30 in the afternoon. Held in the Polytechnic Building the camera club meeting had begun at two and finished at four. After the official business of the day ended most members said their goodbyes and headed for home. Others – the club-within-the-club – made their way discreetly and by different routes to the hotel just behind the waterfront where once more they unpacked cameras and set up tripods and reflectors.

Aware of being merely an observer, an outsider unable to participate in what for most people was normal life, Bryce had still been dubious about accompanying Marcus a second time. The repercussions should he be discovered were too dreadful to contemplate. But loneliness, curiosity and the desire to find somewhere he might fit in had pushed fear aside. His visits had quickly become a habit, a need.

He had heard that in the pubs and squalid hotels down by the waterfront prostitutes would, for the right sum, do anything a man wanted. The police knew. The local authorities knew. But everyone ignored it provided business was conducted away from respect-

251

able areas.

Yet a man seeking that same service from another man was not only a target for blackmail, he risked two years in prison with hard labour. And should his preferences become public knowledge he would be ostracized: an object of disgust and derision to those same people who viewed female prostitution as regrettable but a fact of life.

Bryce had given no thought to any of this while he was with Tarun. He had been happy in the jungle and the mountains. Each day had posed a new challenge, another difficulty to be overcome as they pushed themselves further and harder to find new shrub species and photograph them before gathering seeds and other samples.

The nights he and Tarun had spent out in the vastness of the mountains, away from Richard, Pinzo and the hut at Zayul, had been voyages of discovery. On those nights he had plunged into a world of intense, exquisite, breath-stopping sensation that set every nerve-end on fire. He had stepped from the safety of his known world into another dimension; a stranger to himself as he surrendered to emotions that stirred his deepest soul.

By comparison his life now was a desert. He filled his days with work at Polwellan, immersing himself in the painstaking work of aerial and ground layering, and trying different techniques to germinate the seeds he and Richard had brought back. But it wasn't enough. *Inside he was shrivelling up, dying by degrees.*

During the meetings he photographed poses that in his eyes conveyed the strength and beauty of the male form. The other tableaux he simply watched. Remembering, yearning, but still not ready to break out of the cage of self-imposed abstinence. Conscious of being very much a newcomer and wanting to remain inconspicuous, he spoke little other than responding to greetings. Marcus was good company and immensely knowledgeable. But he was subject to erratic moods Bryce found unsettling.

His own increasing nervous strain was beginning to show. Each morning as he shaved it was difficult to avoid, harder to ignore, the sharpening planes of his face, the deepening grooves on either side of his mouth, the shadows that darkened his eyes. Fortunately all in the family were currently preoccupied with their own concerns. But it could be only a matter of time before someone noticed. Then the questions would start.

How could he answer? Tell the truth? Say he was heartsick? Pining for his lost love? They would ask her name. Richard would look bewildered. They had met few women during their travels. Apart from the Kampas most had been the wives of officials. If he said he was unwell Grace would want him to consult Uncle John. Maybe he should. He knew he wouldn't. He couldn't take the risk. If his father ever found out... Reflex made him swallow. Thrusting dread aside Bryce made a minor and completely unnecessary adjustment to the backboard of his camera and noted grimly the faint tremor in his fingers.

Light poured in through three north facing windows: diffuse light that caused no strong shadows: light perfect for the necessarily long exposures. But despite the heat of late summer, the staleness of air tainted with the smell of pomade, sweet-scented oil, male sweat and the musk of excitement, the windows remained tightly closed. Though the room was on the second floor making it impossible for casual passers-by to look in, none of the gentlemen present wanted to risk his voice being overheard and possibly recognized.

Bryce's initial anxiety had amused Marcus.

'Do you think any of us would be here if we weren't sure it was safe? I'm willing to bet the original inspiration for the three wise monkeys was a hotel owner. This one certainly knows which side his bread's buttered. Compared to him clams are chatty.'

So it had proved. Their host had made only one request: that furniture be moved *quietly* and restored to its previous position before the room was vacated. What happened in the meantime was not his concern. The additional security of allowing Nat and Spencer to enter from an adjoining room via an interconnecting door was considered by club members to be well worth the extra cost.

Bryce stood a short distance behind the intense and silent group peering through focusing screens at the two men: one fair, one dark; one smooth, the other hairy; limbs entwined, oiled skin gleaming. After exposing a single plate he moved his camera back. Processing even one such shot was a risk. But that particular pose had rekindled memories too powerful and erotic to resist.

With the skill of experience gained in very different circumstances he had judged the strength and quality of light and the length of exposure. When he replaced the lens cap he instinctively knew he had obtained a negative he would be able to translate into different kinds of print: varying clarity and tone, and thus the impact of the image.

'Here.' Bryce looked up as Marcus handed him a small leather-covered box. 'What do you think of this?'

Turning it over Bryce's brows rose in surprise. 'It's a camera?'

Marcus rocked his splayed hand conveying his own opinion. 'It has its supporters.'

Though his own camera was set up on its stand Marcus had not joined the group. He seemed uninterested in the activity presently taking place under the focused light.

Bryce turned the little box in his hands amazed at the developments during his three years abroad. 'It looks like a toy.'

'Probably because it was originally developed for children. It has fixed focus, fixed exposure and uses roll film.'

'What about developing and printing?'

'Ah, that's the clever bit. When all the film has been exposed you send the entire camera back to the manufacturers. They develop and print the film, fit a new one into your camera then return it with your prints.'

Bryce handed it back with a shrug. 'I suppose it's ideal for children who can't be trusted with chemicals. Or for people who don't like the mess. But it's my belief that if you want a high quality result you have to do your own processing.'

Marcus indicated Bryce's camera mounted on a scarred wooden tripod. 'Like the Hare, do you?'

Bryce nodded. 'I bought it ten years ago when it was the first folding camera. As far as I'm concerned it's still the best. I've grown so used to it I don't even have to think about lens field, film scale, quality of light or paper emulsions. But what I like most is that it can be adapted to take small plates, sheet films or film packs. And it has ground glass focusing as well as focusing scales.'

Marcus's burst of laughter won him irritated glares over hunched shoulders. 'You'd make a great salesman. But as it happens I agree with you. I used one in India.'

Bryce handed back the little box camera. 'Have you ever exhibited? The photographs you took in India, I mean?'

Marcus's mouth twisted. 'God knows I tried hard enough. My photographs should be compulsory viewing for governments and for army commanders who direct wars from comfortable offices and never actually visit the front line. Galleries were prepared to show the pretty *life in India* shots.' His tone dripped bitterness. 'But they refused my best stuff. The scenes I captured during battles and those showing the aftermath.'

Bryce frowned, astonished. 'Why? Shots like that are unique. They're a frozen moment of reality.'

'Exactly. And that's the problem,' said Marcus. 'The war artists and sketchers blur the horror. They *compose* their pictures. They imply heroism. They play down the reality in order to create whatever emotional effect will sell the most newspapers for their paymasters. They make scenes of battle palatable. Photographs don't do that. Photographs show the naked truth. Every gallery owner who saw my photographs said the same thing. Too graphic. Too sensational. Too horrifying. Jesus Christ, what did they expect? War *is* horrifying. It's ugly, violent, brutal and bloody.' He breathed hard down his nose as memory fanned remembered anger into fresh hot flames.

Not knowing what to say Bryce remained silent. After a long moment Marcus shrugged.

'Combat photographers are useful insofar as we provide the images from which illustrators produce their copy for newspapers and magazines. Artists can paint pictures that show war in all its glorious obscenity and have them hung in the National Gallery. But to quote some fossilized idiot from the Royal Academy – *despite a certain technical expertise and emotional impact, photography will never be accepted as art.*' Marcus glowered, visibly trembling with barely contained rage. Then with one of his lightning changes of mood he sucked in a breath and raised his head.

'Have you heard of a periodical called *Camera Notes?*'

'No. Is it–'

Marcus snapped his fingers. 'Of course you wouldn't have. It was only launched last year. It's American, and devoted exclusively to pictorial photography. Alfred Stieglitz started it. Emerson's protégé?' When Bryce nodded, acknowledging he knew the name, Marcus continued. 'Stieglitz used to edit *American Amateur Photographer* but he left there to set up this new venture. A pal of mine who's in New York sent me a copy. The quality of the illustrations is amazing.'

Bryce's interest stirred. 'Do you think I might–?'

'Certainly. I'll bring it with me next time.'

'Thanks.'

The tension that had permeated the room suddenly relaxed into laughter at Nat's groan and Spencer's exaggerated shriek as they disentangled then stretched to ease stiffened limbs and aching joints. Two men who had been avidly watching began to pack up their equipment. Four others stood in low voiced conversation.

Marcus touched Bryce's shoulder lightly. 'I'll see you next week then.'

Reaching for his camera, Bryce glanced over his shoulder. 'Aren't you coming?'

'Not for a minute.'

Bryce looked around. As two made their way towards the door the others started reloading with fresh plates or film packs. 'What are they doing? I thought we'd finished.'

'You have. Best be on your way.'

'So why are you staying?'

'I have another commission. It's specialist

market stuff. Not for you.'

Intrigued and unwilling to return to the unhappy atmosphere at home, Bryce countered, 'How do you know? Anyway what do you mean? What kind of–'

'Look, go or stay. I don't care. But' – Marcus thrust his face close; his eyes glittered – 'if you stay you keep quiet. Understand?' He smiled with all the warmth and humour of a shark. 'It'll broaden your education. Who knows, you might enjoy it.'

As Bryce hesitated, intuition warning him to leave, curiosity and the prospect of a long lonely evening urging him to stay, Spencer returned from the adjoining-room with a towel wrapped sarong-style around his waist. A small boy of nine or ten held his hand. Looking down at him Spencer murmured a few words. The boy grinned. He had fair curls and big brown eyes. A sprinkling of freckles dusted his snub nose and rounded cheeks. He was dressed in a frilled shirt of some gauzy material that fell just below his knees. As Spencer pulled him forward into the light it was clear this was his only garment.

Bryce swallowed a sudden dryness in his throat as unease flared. Spencer bent toward the boy. Scolding? Warning?

'Not a word,' Marcus warned quietly.

Unfastening the towel, Spencer tossed it aside and reclined on the *chaise-longue*, pulling the boy forward.

From where Bryce was standing the boy's face was clearly visible. A nervous smile flitted across the small features. The men began to call out instructions. Spencer and the boy altered their position and remained still while the seconds were counted. Then grasping the boy's head between his hands Spencer drew it down and threw his own head back.

Bryce stopped breathing. In the brief silence the sound of the sharp hiss though other teeth was loud. Suddenly he saw the boy's eyes fill with tears. They gathered in huge drops that trembled on the blond lashes then spilled down the freckled cheeks leaving a silver trail.

Shocked to his senses, appalled by what he was watching and at himself, Bryce tensed. He felt Marcus's hand on his arm.

'Don't interfere. It's not–'

Bryce wrenched free, guilt and shame fuelling his anger. He barged through the group heedless of the angry cries as cameras wobbled precariously.

'Stop!' His throat was dry, his voice hoarse. His face burned. 'This is wrong. You can't ask a *child* to–' His protest was lost under the storm of rage.

'For God's sake! You nearly knocked my camera over.'

'Bloody amateurs!'

'Who asked you?'

As the men roared their fury, the boy hurled himself forward. Bryce automatically opened his arms, his only desire to protect.

The boy's small face was scarlet. He attacked Bryce, kicking and punching with clenched fists.

'What d'you do that for?' he shrilled, his snub nose wrinkled, mouth contorted in a snarl.

Startled, wincing as the blows landed, Bryce grabbed the boy's hands then crouched to address him face to face. 'Hey! Stop that. I want to help you.'

'Piss off, then,' the boy shouted, wriggling like an eel as he struggled to free himself. 'If I don't do what they want I won't get paid and me da'll kill me.'

'Of course your father won't kill you.' Bryce's reply was automatic. But even as the words left his lips doubt tightened his stomach. For what kind of a man would allow his child to be used like this.

'Ha! Don't know nothing, you don't.'

Bryce held him fast. 'Look, you don't have to do this.'

'You bleddy daft?' The boy glared at Bryce. 'It's me job innit? I do what they say and I gets paid. Now you gone and made trouble. But it's me who'll get the blame.' Though his tone was angry, fear had drained the boy's colour so his freckles stood out like tiny flecks of gold. Tears welled up and spilled over once more. 'Me da'll be mad as 'ell. He'll take his belt to me.'

'Don't cry,' Bryce begged. He had acted on impulse thinking he was preventing the defilement of an innocent child. Only this child was no innocent. Unsure what to do next he glanced up and saw anger and condemnation on every face except one. But Marcus's cynical amusement offered little comfort.

Bryce turned back to the boy. Fumbling in his pocket he extracted a gold sovereign. 'Now your father won't beat you.'

The boy's eyes widened as he reached for the coin. Bryce heard Marcus sigh wearily, '*No,* you fool.'

He looked up startled, saw the cameras focused on him, uncapped lenses recording the moment. Snatching the coin the boy pulled free and scampered over to Spencer waving it, his tear-stained face grinning in delight.

'Look what I got!'

'Aren't you lucky?' Turning to Bryce, Spencer winked and blew a silent kiss. 'Got one of those for me?' His voice simpered but his eyes held only cold contempt.

Bryce felt himself flush. Then Marcus grabbed his arm.

'Pick up your stuff and get out of here.'

'Just a minute!' One of the men snapped.

'Don't worry.' Marcus placated the muttering group as Bryce swiftly dismantled camera and tripod and grabbed his case. 'He knows the rules.'

'He'd better not forget them,' another warned. 'Not unless he wants everyone in his family seeing a copy of that photograph.'

Bryce's head swam. *What had he done?*

'You understand?' a third demanded.

Bryce gave a brief nod. He couldn't look at them.

'Speak up!'

Bryce cleared his throat. He wondered if he was going to vomit. Cold sweat beaded his forehead and upper lip. His underwear clung to clammy skin. 'I won't say anything.' *What a fool.* But he'd never expected – how could he have known?

Out in the passage, Marcus turned on him, low-voiced but livid with anger. 'What in the name of hellfire d'you think you were doing? Didn't I warn you to keep quiet?'

'I know, but–' Bryce rubbed the pounding ache in his forehead. 'The boy was crying, for God's sake. I couldn't just–'

'Of *course* he was crying.' Marcus hissed in exasperation. 'He's been coached. Clients are always willing to pay extra for real tears. He can turn them on like a tap. With some of the others we have to use onions or glycerine. But it's never as good. Albie can be a sulky little so-and-so but he's very popular with the clients.' Marcus's thin mouth twisted. 'His father's a damn nuisance. Always demanding more money. Though considering the number of boys he and his brother are running they must be raking in a fortune.'

Bryce's stomach heaved. He swallowed convulsively.

Marcus studied him. 'You really didn't know?'

Beyond speech Bryce shook his head.

One corner of Marcus's mouth lifted in a cynical smile. 'You'd be amazed how many pillars of local society are willing to pay substantial amounts of money for photographs like the one you so clumsily interrupted. Some of their collections must be worth a fortune.' He gave a satisfied sigh. 'I do like working for connoisseurs.'

Bryce ran his tongue over paper-dry lips. But as he opened his mouth Marcus spoke first, cool and mocking.

'You're going to ask why, aren't you? Why do I do it? Well, when you've seen what I've seen, believe me, this isn't so bad.' Suddenly his mood changed and his mouth curled in bitter resentment.

'If my work had received the recognition it deserved–' He snorted in disgust. 'I risked my life. I came back a cripple. I lost – I lost everything.' His expression revealed despair and self-loathing. 'All for this?'

Bryce shivered. Now, far too late, he saw that this man was more complex and more damaged than he had realized. Sensing it would take very little to push Marcus over the edge Bryce stayed silent.

Marcus shrugged. 'I need money like everyone else. I need it for rent and food. I need it to buy film, chemicals and printing papers for my camera. I particularly need it' – his mouth twitched in a bitter smile – 'for some of life's little luxuries.' He gestured towards the closed door. 'That is my bank. I'm good. I'm one of the best. And I have a list of private clients who pay me well to supply their particular preferences. It's business. Everybody gains. Nobody dies. What are you waiting for?' The sudden barked question made Bryce jump. 'Go home. If you've got any sense you'll forget everything you've seen this afternoon.'

As he hurried toward the livery stable to collect the trap, Bryce's thoughts stung like angry bees. *What had he done? What if his family found out?* What if the photograph–? Even if he tried to explain, who would believe him? He had sought escape from loneliness but had slid into corruption and depravity. Forget what he had seen? If only he could.

Chapter Sixteen

At last the number of fever cases was beginning to fall. The source of the contamination had been traced to a decomposing badger in the stream that fed the well. As soon as the corpse had been removed the well was drained and disinfected.

'Yes?' He glanced up from signing the report as his housekeeper knocked then put her head round the door.

'Miss Prideaux to see you, Doctor.'

'Thank you, Mrs Tallack. Show her in, will you?'

He rose from his chair, straightening his jacket as the door opened wider.

'Mary, this is a surprise.'

'Good afternoon, John.' She hesitated. 'You were expecting me?'

'Yes, yes. Forgive me. Of course I knew you were coming. What I meant was that I rarely see you as a patient.'

Her expression cleared. 'Isn't it a lovely day?'

'It is indeed.' He gestured towards the faded rose velvet. 'Take a seat.' He returned to his own chair and swivelled it to face her. He smiled. 'I don't understand.'

'What don't you understand?' Removing fine kid gloves that perfectly matched her gown of lilac gauze over silk she laid them on her lap. From a deep frill of lace over her bosom fluted gauze rose to a high collar. A hat of fine straw was trimmed with pink flowers and lilac ribbon was set at a slightly rakish angle on her upswept hair.

'Why you have made an appointment for a consultation when it is perfectly obvious you are in extraordinarily good health and spirits. You really are looking remarkably well.'

Laughing, Mary inclined her head. 'Thank you, John. Indeed I'm feeling remarkably well. Happiness, I am discovering, has the delightful effect of fine wine.'

'Am I permitted to know the source of such wellbeing?'

'You are. In fact, it's the reason I'm here.' Colour bloomed in her cheeks. John had always liked Mary Prideaux. He enjoyed her dry wit. Asked to describe her he would willingly have called her pleasant, even mildly attractive in a quiet, understated way. But this afternoon she looked positively *pretty*.

'Indeed?'

'I'm to be married.'

Expert at hiding his feelings he masked the leap of surprise with a broader smile and leaned forward to grasp her hands. 'My dear Mary. What wonderful news. I wish you every happiness.' Settling back he crossed one pinstriped trouser leg over the other. 'How have you managed to keep it so quiet? More importantly, who is the lucky fellow? Might I know him?'

Her lashes flickered briefly as she moistened her lips. 'You know him well. It's Henry. Henry Damerel.'

Totally unprepared, John felt his mouth drop as he stared at her. He recovered quickly and was about to make light of his reaction but Mary spoke first.

'I know what you're thinking.'

You know about Dorcas? Mary's next words showed her thoughts were running on a totally different track.

'You're shocked that he – that we – should even be thinking of such things so soon after Louise. In all honesty I would have preferred–' Mary gazed at her hands for a moment then raised her head again. Her cheeks were flushed, but she met his gaze squarely. 'It is not as yet a love match. Though we are very good friends and have been so for several years.'

'Then why?' The words were out before he could stop them. He raised one hand. 'Forgive me. It's none of my business and I have absolutely no right to–'

'It's all right, John.' A wry smile flickered at the corners of her mouth. 'You would have to be superhuman not to ask. Why such urgency? The truth is, there are important financial reasons why the wedding should not be delayed.'

In her gaze John saw defiance and a plea for understanding. She sat straight-backed, her hands gripping each other.

'You are Henry's brother-in-law, John, part of the family. So you must be aware of the situation at the mine. Henry needs money urgently. I am in a position to supply that. But in case you should think the arrangement entirely one-sided, I want to reassure you. I have as much to gain as Henry. I shall no longer be an old maid, pitied because no one ever thought me desirable enough to marry. In fact, Henry–' Her blush deepened and she shook her head, darting him a swift shy smile. 'Well, never mind that. I'm here because although I enjoy excellent health I am not a young woman. I want your reassurance that I can – that a child – should we be blessed–'

'Of course,' John came smoothly to her rescue. 'I commend your good sense.'

'Am I being sensible? I wonder.' She drew a deep shaky breath. 'But I do care for him. And I know he's fond of me. That's not a bad basis for marriage would you say?'

'I've seen some very happy unions grow from far less hopeful beginnings.' John's reply seemed to comfort her.

An hour later, having asked a number of

questions and made a brief examination, he left Mary behind the screen while he returned to his desk to write notes on her card.

She emerged a few moments later, immaculate. Her colour was still high, but a little of the tension surrounding her had evaporated, as if she had survived an ordeal. Which, he realized with sudden sympathy, is exactly what it must have been.

'So everything is – as it should be?'

Meeting her anxious gaze he smiled. 'Everything is absolutely fine. I see no reason why you should not bear strong healthy children.'

The last of her tension dropped away like a discarded coat. 'Thank you.' Her smile was radiant.

He accompanied her to the front door and watched her walk away to make her promised call on Hester Chenoweth. He did not envy her the visit. Yet there was new determination in the tilt of her chin.

Returning to his office he went into the tiny dispensary. As he selected items to take with him on his afternoon calls his thoughts returned once more to Dorcas. How had she reacted to this bombshell?

He had always assumed that when Louise died Henry would make an honest woman of Dorcas. And considering her approaching blindness... But maybe he'd got it wrong.

Dorcas had been independent for a very long time. Too long perhaps? Had Henry proposed only to be turned down? In which case having refused him she could hardly object to his marrying someone else.

But as John rode down towards the village, unease rode with him. Something didn't feel right.

'Ah, Mrs Renowden, do come in.' The bank manager closed his office door and ushered her to a comfortable chair. 'How nice to see you again. Is it really a whole month since your last visit?'

'Time seems to pass more quickly as we get older, Mr Williams.'

He returned to his seat behind the desk and selected a document from among the neat piles. 'You're aware Mr Hal's instructions to me were that I should invest in property the money he sends back to Cornwall. Well, I have some excellent news. When a small parcel of land attached to the Damerel estate was recently offered for sale by private treaty I was able to purchase it. The parcel comprised your cottage and the surrounding land.'

Mr Williams beamed, convinced his news was giving her unalloyed pleasure. Dorcas stared at him.

'As you have lived in the cottage for almost thirty years it is most unlikely that

272

Mr Damerel would ever have ended your tenancy. But the fact that your son now owns the property which he has requested me to register in your name must surely give you a far greater sense of security.'

She pulled herself together. 'Oh. Yes. Indeed. Thank you, Mr Williams.' What if the bank manager had not learned of the sale? What if he had not acted swiftly enough? What if someone other than Hal had bought it? *What if the new owner had wanted her to leave?* She shivered, suddenly cold. How could Henry have done this without even mentioning it to her?

After spending the morning at the village school helping the younger children with their reading and writing, Grace returned home for lunch. But she was too nervous to do more than pick at her food. That afternoon it was her turn to clean the chapel.

Dismounting from her bicycle she rested it against the wall. Her heart beat painfully hard against her ribs as she opened one of the big double doors and walked round the frosted glass screen. Mrs Nancholas paused on her way down the aisle. Under her arm she carried an ancient scuffed leather music case crammed with sheet music, some pages dog-eared and yellow with age.

'I thought I heard the door. All right, my bird?' Her thick brows puckered into a

273

single line. 'Dear life, girl, what you been doing? Red as boiled beetroot you are.'

'I rode down on my bicycle.' Setting down her basket on the back pew Grace removed her straw boater and self-consciously tucked stray wisps of hair behind her ears. Her face radiated heat as she took an apron from the basket.

'You'd never get me on one of they contraptions. 'Tis all right going *down*hill. But you got to go back up again. Too much like hard work that is. Anyhow, the seat's too small. 'Tis all right for you. Built like a whippet, you are.' Patting her broad bottom she gave a theatrical shudder. 'You won't catch me sitting on no knife-blade. I like me comfort.' Grace felt a smile curve her mouth and realized it was the first for days. 'Well,' Mrs Nancholas announced. 'We'd best get on.'

Grace picked up her duster. *Please, please let him come.*

Up on the balcony Mrs Nancholas lifted the lid of the organ keyboard. A few moments later she filled the chapel with the joyous sound of harvest hymns, her body swaying as her fingers moved from keys to stops and her feet danced over the pedals.

An hour later she closed the organ and thumped heavily down the stairs. 'I'll be off then. I got to go uplong to visit me sister. In bed with her leg again she is. She got ointment from the doctor but it don't seem to be doing much good. See you dreckly, my bird. Mind you look after yourself now.'

Grace worked on. Completing the right-hand block of pews she started on the centre, dusting the seats, the arms, and the narrow shelf on which to rest hymnbooks. The door opened. Her heart leapt and heat rushed to her face.

'Ah, Grace. I hoped I'd find you here.'

The disappointment was so acute she could have wept. Her face felt stiff as she forced herself to smile. 'Good afternoon, Mrs Williams.'

'All on your own?'

Grace folded and refolded the duster. 'Mrs Nancholas was here for an hour. But her sister's not well again.'

Mrs Williams snorted. 'Between you and me, that leg would be a lot better if she put it to the ground more often instead of lying in the bed expecting people to wait on her.' Mrs Williams snorted again. 'Bone idle she is. Maggie Nancholas got a heart of gold and that sister of hers do lead her some awful dance. Anyhow,' her tone changed and she smiled. 'Never mind that. I want to ask you a favour. You know 'tis the regatta next week. Well, we thought along with the stalls it would be nice to have Mrs Renowden doing her drawings again.' She touched her hat. 'I'm some pleased with that one she done of

275

me. Jimmy had it framed with glass and all. Hanging in the parlour it is. So I was thinking, seeing how you got her to come down for the May Fair, you'd be the best one to ask if she'd be willing to do it again. 'Tis all in a good cause.' She beamed and checked the angle of her hat. 'If you could see her in the next day or two I'd be some grateful. You can tell me Sunday. If she say yes I'll get the boys to put up a little tent. Let's hope it do stay dry. Right, I'll leave you to get on then.' She bustled away.

The mention of portraits sent a sharp pang through Grace. Did Edwin still have the sketch Dorcas had made of her? Did he ever look at it? Perhaps it was lying forgotten at the bottom of a drawer. Perhaps he had thrown it away. *Surely he wouldn't have?* He had pressed her to have it drawn, paying far more than the agreed charge. And he had insisted on keeping it. He wouldn't have done that unless it meant something to him. Would he? Maybe he had done it simply to encourage those watching. Maybe everything else existed only in her imagination.

Opening the duster she bent to the next row of pews. After another hour she had finished. She changed the water in the flower vases, dusted the plain pulpit and the lectern. Then there was nothing left to do. He hadn't come.

Her disappointment was crushing. Chewing the inside of her lip she took off her apron, put on her hat, picked up her basket and let herself out. Locking the door behind her she put the key under the flowerpot. Mr Rogers, the steward, would collect it later. Turning her bicycle she started pushing it up the hill.

Why hadn't he come? In the past he had often dropped in when she was there. Of course he'd always had a reason: something to collect or leave in the vestry, or a message for one of the ladies.

It was over a fortnight since he had called at the house. But perhaps he had been needed at one of the other villages on his circuit.

Mary had sounded so sure that Edwin's interest was deeper than mere friendship. Because of Mary's certainty, she had allowed herself to hope.

Yet though he only slept away from the manse on alternate weekends he had not come to call on her. Nor had she seen him around the village. She would have expected their paths to cross *somewhere*.

She had picked up the threads of her life: in the classroom, the chapel, at Sunday school, visiting the sick and elderly. She craved a sense of worth. She yearned for just a fraction of the admiration, warmth and smiles that Zoe's name evoked. But as each day passed she started to feel oddly detached. She seemed somehow set apart from everyone else and the distance was increasing.

Each night she climbed into bed trembling with fatigue but unable to settle, tormented by a vivid and ever-changing kaleidoscope of images that tangled distant and recent past. When at last sleep claimed her it was not peaceful or restoring, but full of fractured dreams from which she would wake with a wet face and tear-soaked pillow.

Each day it took more and more effort to get out of bed. But the twins greeted her with smiles and exclamations of relief at seeing her *back to normal*. One morning her father even patted her shoulder and nodded his approval. So she had to carry on. She felt as brittle as glass. Her strength was leaking away. She spoke less and less. But busy with their own concerns no one seemed to notice. Inside her head she was screaming.

One warm sunny afternoon she mounted her bicycle and set off down the drive to honour Mrs Williams' request. Blowsy white clouds rode the fresh breeze across a forget-me-not blue sky. Yet again her throat was dry and her heart thudded against her ribs. But this time the cause was not hope or anticipation. It was the aftermath of another unpleasant scene with her grandmother who had called her cold-hearted and selfish, a wicked girl who cared nothing for the sufferings of others.

Waking late after a disturbed night caused by two helpings of curried lobster at dinner, Hester Chenoweth had demanded a plain lunch of coddled egg and a slice of plum tart. Within an hour she had returned to bed complaining of severe pain and sent Violet for Grace.

''Tis heartburn.' Violet rolled her eyes. 'I warned her 'bout having plum tart but she wouldn't listen.'

Hester lay on her bed clutching a lace handkerchief, her free hand pressed to her thin chest.

'I'm ill. I need a doctor. Send for John at once. You'd better fetch the minister as well. Hurry up, girl. Don't just stand there.' She closed her eyes moaning softly.

Grace had longed for a reason to call at the manse. But despite her yearning to see Edwin again she would not call him out on a fool's errand. Her gentle suggestion of carbonate of soda with ginger and camomile to ease the discomfort met with shrieked invective from spittle-flecked lips. She stood rigid and silent until, running out of breath, Hester collapsed against the mound of pillows wailing. Violet's arrival with a soothing draft of magnesia, cinnamon-water and spirits of lavender had permitted escape.

Outside in the passage, overcome by dizziness, Grace had leaned against the wall fighting for breath. She would not weep.

279

Granny Hester hadn't really meant all she'd said. She was old, she felt ill and she was grieving.

In her room, though all she wanted to do was lie down and sleep, Grace bathed her face, tidied her hair, then went downstairs to fetch her bicycle.

The hayfields had already been cut by rows of men wielding scythes. After turning and drying, the clover and sweet grass had been raked up and stacked in bulky ricks. Now it was the turn of this year's wheat. She could see the mechanical reaper drawn by two heavy horses working its way down the field, cutting and tying the heavy-headed golden stalks into bundles. Men followed behind, wading through the pale stubble to prop the bundles into shocks. The reaper was halfway across the field and everyone would work on into the evening until it reached the far side and harvested the remaining crop.

In the past Grace had always enjoyed harvest time. Apples were ripe in the orchards. Cherries and plums already picked had been made into preserves, or bottled to provide a taste of summer during the cold winter months. Blackcurrants, gooseberries, raspberries and strawberries were still fruiting on bushes and in beds, with the promise of blackberries to come. All had sprung from tiny seeds.

Was it the same in life? Were joy and tragedy just random events striking purely by chance? Or were they reward or retribution for past actions: the fruits of some long-buried seed. If that was so was she still being punished for causing her mother a lifetime's ill health? Why else would she feel so isolated, so lonely? Now her mother was dead. So how could she ever make amends?

Dismounting she rested her bicycle against the hedge. Opening the squeaking gate she walked into Dorcas's garden. As she rounded the corner she spotted the easel and alongside it a low table cluttered with tubes, rags, and a pot of brushes. She stopped, reluctant to interrupt. But there was no sign of Dorcas.

Unusually the cottage door was closed. Grace hesitated. But having made the effort to come she might as well find out if Dorcas was at home. Following the path up to the door she knocked lightly.

Chapter Seventeen

She heard movement, the soft thud of something dropped, the scrape of a chair leg against wooden floorboards. Then the door flew open to reveal Dorcas beaming with pleasure and relief. 'I thought you had–' She stopped, her face losing all expression. 'Oh.' Then with visible effort she smiled again. 'Grace.'

'Good afternoon, Mrs Renowden. I hope I haven't – is this an inconvenient time?' Her anxious glance took in the thick glasses that made Dorcas's face look older, more tired somehow, and definitely thinner. She couldn't help noticing that the older woman looked slightly unkempt. Her upswept hair was untidy and there were food spots on the front of her blouse.

'Not at all. It's always a pleasure to see you.' As Dorcas stepped back and gestured for her to enter Grace's spirits rose fractionally. *She sounded as though she really meant it.* 'Come in. Sit down. Would you like some lemonade?'

'I don't want to put you to any trouble–'

'It's no trouble. I made some fresh this morning.'

'Thank you. That would be lovely.'

'I was sorry to hear about your mother,' Dorcas called from the kitchen. 'You must miss her.'

Yes, and no. Yes, because she was my mother, because I cannot remember a time without her, because my life was inextricably bound up with hers. No, because I had grown so tired. Now I'm even more tired. Grace said nothing, listening to cupboard doors open and close. She heard the rattle and clink of glass then Dorcas reappeared carrying a jug and two tumblers on a tray spread with a small square of finely embroidered linen. 'These past weeks will have been very hard for you.'

'Mmm.' Grace swallowed the sudden stiffness in her throat.

As Dorcas bent to set the tray on a side table her face was momentarily hidden. 'How is your father?'

An image of her father's face filled Grace's vision, frowning and discomfited as he instructed her to dispose of her mother's clothes. This merged into one of Mary blushing radiantly as, half-joyful, half-anxious she confided to Grace her father's proposal of marriage.

She swallowed. 'He's well. Though I've seen very little of him lately. He's been terribly busy travelling all over the county on business.'

'Ah.' Dorcas straightened. Grace glimpsed

relief, which seemed so unlikely and out of place she knew she must be mistaken. 'Men have always used work to distance themselves from emotions they find hard to deal with.'

Grace's experience of men was restricted to her father, her brothers and Uncle John. Even that was confined to their behaviour within the family circle. What the rest of their lives were like she had no idea. Not knowing how to respond she simply nodded.

Then her heart tripped on a beat. *Was Edwin burying himself in work as an escape? But from what? Was Mary right after all? Did he care for her but thought it too soon to speak? Or was the opposite true? Was he avoiding her to spare both of them embarrassment?* Shutting out a thought too painful to contemplate she moistened dry lips with the tip of her tongue.

Sitting down Dorcas reached for the jug. 'I hope you'll forgive a personal remark, my dear. But you don't look at all your usual self. Though that's hardly surprising. Your father's absence must have meant even more responsibility for you.' As she poured the sharp scent of lemons filled the air.

Suddenly thirsty Grace took the proffered glass. She shook her head. 'Actually I've done very little. After – after my mother died I – I wasn't well. If it hadn't been for

Mama's close friend, Mary Prideaux, I-I don't know how – she was so kind. She took care of everything. She even managed to calm Granny Hester. I couldn't. I still can't,' she added quietly. Vivid memories of her grandmother's rage rasped across her raw nerves. The glass clattered against her teeth and cool tangy lemonade soothed her parched throat. 'So really it makes perfect sense. I'm sure everyone else will see it that way too, once they've got used to the idea. I must admit I found it difficult at first. But not,' she added quickly, 'because of anything against Mary.'

'Grace, my dear,' Dorcas broke in gently. 'You've lost me. What are you talking about?' She reached for the second glass.

'I'm so sorry. My head's in such a muddle.' Grace watched Dorcas half-fill the tumbler. 'I'm talking about my father and Mary. He's proposed to her.'

The jug crashed down on to the tray and the tumbler slid from Dorcas's fingers. Grace stared, frozen, as the tumbler rolled and lemonade soaked into the embroidered cloth.

'Your father is going to marry Mary Prideaux?' Dorcas's voice and expression were stunned, disbelieving.

Grace nodded. 'I have to say I was shocked when Mary told me. It seemed wrong – too soon.' She clasped both hands around the tumbler. 'But as Mary pointed out, all the grieving in the world can't change what's happened. It won't bring Mama back. Life hangs by a thread that's so easily snapped.' Her voice broke and she cleared her throat. Now she had started talking the words just kept coming. 'I can see what she means. I suppose when you're older you're more aware of time and how quickly it passes. The thing is, Mary is wealthy and Papa desperately needs money. Though I'm sure that isn't the only reason for the marriage. I mean Mary wouldn't have accepted unless she was gaining something from it too, would she?'

'No.' Dorcas's face was the colour of ashes and she sounded as if she were in pain. 'She'll gain the status of being Mrs Henry Damerel. She will be mistress of a large house and estate, stepmother to a grown-up family. Perhaps she hopes for children of her own.' Righting the fallen tumbler, Dorcas poured more lemonade, a violent tremor rattling the lip of the jug against the glass.

Pretending not to notice, for no doubt Dorcas was already embarrassed by the state of the tray, Grace took another sip of her own drink. 'So much has changed. When I was a child the mine was prosperous. Even though Mama was often unwell Papa always managed to stay cheerful. He seemed so strong no matter how bad things were, like when Charlotte and Michael died. He owned property in Falmouth then: a row of four cottages in Quay Hill near the waterfront. But he was so proud because they weren't inherited like the estate. It was property he had bought himself.'

Dorcas gulped, almost choking on the tart liquid. On top of the shattering news of Henry's remarriage, Grace's innocent remark was a stinging blow. *A row of cottages in Quay Hill.* She cleared her throat.

'Are they still in his possession?'

Grace shook her head, her face sad. 'No. When the price of tin collapsed he sold them and invested the money in the mine.'

Her fingers numb and unable to feel the tumbler, Dorcas set it down unsteadily. She felt a pain deep in her chest. There was only one row of four cottages in Quay Hill. After Zander's death she had moved to Falmouth and rented one of them.

Henry had owned her cottage? But that meant that Henry had been her landlord. Henry had personally arranged her eviction to force her to move here. He had never told her. He had kept it a secret. From her: who, for almost thirty years, had shared her life and her bed with him, who had borne him a son. His eldest son. The son he had educated but never acknowledged.

Now he planned to marry Mary Prideaux. He had proposed marriage to another woman. Yet he had not bothered to come and tell her. The enormity of his betrayal was almost too great to comprehend. She felt sick and cold perspiration bathed her body. Shock tingled along her nerves and the room spun. *This room where they had spent so many hours together: this room he had always said was his true home.* She heard a long low moan of agony and realized it had come from her own throat.

'Mrs Renowden?' Grace's voice, thin with anxiety, hauled her back from the brink of unconsciousness. 'What's wrong? Are you ill? What can I do?'

With enormous effort Dorcas raised her head. 'Was this your father's idea?' Her voice was raw with grief and pain. 'Could he not at least have found the courage to come and tell me himself?'

'I don't understand. Tell you what? About his marriage?' Grace's face betrayed her bewilderment. 'But why should he tell you at all?'

Dorcas drew a shuddering breath. 'Because' – her chin lifted – 'because for thirty years I have been your father's mistress.'

All colour drained from Grace's face leaving it grey-white. 'M-m–' She couldn't form the word. Couldn't get it past blood-less lips. *'Thirty years? He and you? But–'*

Dorcas's laugh was brief and bitter. 'You never guessed.' It was a flat statement. 'No one did. I was very discreet. I discouraged casual callers. And because I earned my living as a painter my desire for solitude was accepted as an artist's eccentricity.'

'But how – when–?'

It was painfully clear to Dorcas that Grace didn't want to believe what she was hearing. Yet recognized it as the truth.

'I met your father when I was living in one of those cottages in Quay Hill. I didn't know he owned them. He never told me. Not then. Not ever. I had discovered I was pregnant when a fire at the gallery that sold my work destroyed most of my paintings. Soon afterwards I received a solicitor's letter informing me my cottage had been sold and I would have to leave. I had no money and no home and I was expecting a child.' She paused. 'Your father's child.'

Trembling uncontrollably Grace hugged herself. 'Hal?'

'Is your father's eldest son. Your half-brother. Hal doesn't know. He believes his father died before he was born. He believes that because I lied to him, to my own son, in order to protect your father, and you, and the rest of your family. And now...' She pressed shaking fingers to quivering lips and shook her head, choked with grief and rage and loss. 'It was your father's idea that I moved here. I didn't want to but he insisted. He said it was for my safety. I have loved him and been faithful to him for thirty years. He sometimes talked of marriage, of what we would do if he were free. But he wasn't. And I never expected or asked for what he could not give. But when your mother died, that changed everything. He was free. Free to marry me. But not only has he chosen someone else' – her voice thinned, cracked– 'He didn't even have the courage or the decency to come and tell me himself.'

'I-I don't know what to say,' Grace whispered. 'I'm so sorry.'

'*You're* sorry?' Dorcas was suddenly weary to the marrow of her bones. 'Why should you be sorry? Grace, you've done nothing wrong. Nor are you responsible for your father. I have told you things you need never have known. My dear, it's I who should apologize. I hope some day you'll find it in your heart to forgive me.' She drew another deep shuddering sigh and pushed herself out of her chair. She felt weak and shaky, as if she had been – was – deathly ill. 'I'll make some tea. I think we both need–'

'No.' Grace rose. 'No, thank you. It's very kind, but – you cannot want me here.'

Too tired to argue Dorcas gestured acceptance. 'As you wish.' She followed Grace to the door. 'Why *did* you come here this afternoon?'

Grace turned. 'Because Mrs Williams asked me to. It's the regatta next week and she was hoping you might be willing to draw portraits again.'

'Portraits?' Removing her glasses Dorcas passed a shaking hand across her forehead as hysteria bubbled and swelled in her chest. 'No, Grace. Please convey my regrets to Mrs Williams.'

'Of course. You won't want – won't feel like–'

'You don't understand,' Dorcas broke in. 'It's not that I don't *want* to. God knows I would give *anything.*' She swallowed. If she said the words aloud, brought them out into the world, shared them with another person, she had to accept them as truth. Once she did that she could no longer pretend, no longer cling to the stupid, stubborn, *desperate* hope that somehow the clock might be stopped, the deterioration reversed: that it wasn't going to happen.

She replaced her spectacles, feeling their weight press into the groove on the bridge of her nose. But it *was* going to happen.

'Not *won't,* Grace. Can't. No drawing, no painting. Not ever again. I'm–' She stopped. She wouldn't say the word. She wasn't blind. Not yet. Tilting her chin, seeking to salvage a few shreds of dignity, she said quietly, 'I am losing my sight.'

'Oh *no.*'

'I want your word of honour you will not tell anyone.'

'But–'

'Anyone, Grace. John Ainsley knows, but no one else. I particularly do not want your father told.'

'But surely, if he was aware—'

'He would change his mind?' Grace shrank under Dorcas's bitter smile. 'No. He has made his choice. Let's leave it at that. The very last thing I want is pity.'

After Grace had given her promise and gone, Dorcas stood in the doorway, her eyes closed, her face lifted to the afternoon sunshine. The heat on her skin could not reach the chill in her soul. Why go on? What was left?

Shivering she went back inside. As the sun sank lower and the light faded she huddled in the armchair sifting through the wreckage for some shred of comfort. Not only had the shattering news abruptly altered her perception of her future, it forced her to re-evaluate the past, to look again at everything she had believed solid and secure, everything she had assumed would last until either Henry died or she did. *Why had he not come and told her himself?*

She looked again at her own attitudes: her independence, her lack of involvement in village life. Had they been her choice? Or had her isolation been dictated by her involvement with Henry and the necessity of protecting his family.

It was too late now for regrets. Her life had

not been easy, but whose was? She had much to be grateful for. She had known one great love. She and Henry had adapted to each other's needs. She had been blessed with a fine son who was making his mark in his chosen world. Hers had not been a conventional life, but it had been a productive one. Though she did not consider herself wicked, perhaps she too had been guilty of selfishness.

She could never tell Henry about her sight. Not now. It would smack too much of emotional blackmail. Thanks to Hal she was financially independent and her home was safe. But painting had given her life meaning, and a purpose beyond her role of mistress and confidante. *Now – what?*

Eventually she lit the lamps, rekindled the fire in the range, boiled the kettle and made herself some tea.

But as days passed and he still didn't come, her grief and hurt hardened into a protective scab of anger.

Bryce stood slightly aside from the three men studying one of the cold frames. Some of the seedlings inside it were the first attempts to grow species never before seen in this country. Others were hybrids so new that their characteristics would not be revealed until they flowered. All were unique, sought-after by other enthusiasts, and cause for delight and celebration.

But while Richard and head gardener Percy Tresidder responded to Colonel Hawkins's desire to hear every detail concerning the development of different varieties, Bryce found it impossible to concentrate. As an aching tooth attracted a probing tongue so his thoughts kept returning to the hotel in Falmouth and sickening realization that his naive attempt to placate the child would look anything but innocent when the plates were developed.

The all-too-possible threat of blackmail dried his mouth so that swallowing was painful. Flooding anxiety made the blood roar in his ears and his head swim. *What if the family found out?*

Richard's nudge made him start and he realized the colonel was looking at him, brows raised, his short hair and bushy beard gleaming silver-grey in the sunshine. There was no point in pretending. The colonel was no fool.

'I beg your pardon, sir. I didn't catch that.'

The blue eyes were amused. 'Been burning the candle at both ends, young man?'

'No, sir.' Bryce knew his tone and expression were wooden. He had to make more effort if he was to avoid arousing curiosity that would lead to questions he could not possibly answer.

'It's an *auriculatum* hybrid.' Richard indicated the row of tiny young plants. 'These are the first that Percy has managed to propagate from the seed we sent back during our second year.'

The colonel's eyes crinkled as he beamed. 'Well done, Percy.'

'Thank you, sir. We're hoping for a dwarf habit but with good-sized flowers, white flushing to rose pink, and a sweet fragrance.'

'When will it flower?'

'Ah,' Percy grinned. 'That's the best bit. All being well it should be June and July.'

'So we'll have species in bloom from January to mid-summer. Capital!' Colonel Hawkins sighed with pleasure. 'What of the repotting programme?'

'Coming on fine. Keeping these two busy any rate.' Percy tipped his cap back, scratched his head and resettled his cap all in a single movement. 'Colonel, about that letter from Kew. I picked out five trees. If you got a moment to choose which you want to send, I'll mark 'em.'

'Of course. I'll be with you in just a moment.' As Percy touched his cap and stumped away, Colonel Hawkins turned to the twins. 'I have strict instructions from my wife, who is convinced I am working you too hard, to invite you both to stay to dinner. Your acceptance would not only delight my daughters, who also consider me a slave driver, it would afford me an opportunity to express my gratitude for the sterling work you've been doing since your return.'

'Thank you, sir.' Bryce saw Richard's face flush with pleasure at both the invitation and the unexpected opportunity of spending an evening with Sophie. 'That's most kind. I'd be delighted to stay.'

Bryce shook his head. 'I'm terribly sorry, sir. It's very kind of you, but I' – as Richard caught his eye he deliberately averted his gaze – 'I already have an engagement.'

Colonel Hawkins inclined his head. 'Then you must join us some other time. I wish you a good afternoon, Bryce. Richard, I'll see you later at the house.'

After he had gone Richard turned to his brother. 'What engagement? You never mentioned it.'

'No, well, we've both been busy.'

'Do you have to go? I mean is it important?'

'Yes, it is. Besides–' He broke off, pushing a hand through his hair. 'I'm not very good company. Feeling a bit off.'

'I guessed there was something. You've hardly said a word all day. Oh well, your loss. Mrs Hawkins keeps a wonderful table.' He half-turned then added as an afterthought, 'Alice will be disappointed.'

Bryce swung round, tension exploding into anger. But he managed to keep his voice low. 'For God's sake, Richard. I'm not interested in Alice. I never was and never will be. If you and Sophie really care about Alice take her out and introduce her to other men. But keep her away from me.'

'I've already said as much to Sophie,' Richard replied calmly. 'I wasn't teasing, just stating a fact.'

'Yes, well, there's nothing I can do about it.' Bryce's rage evaporated as fast as it had erupted. Drained, guilt-ridden, he wanted to make amends. 'Rich, I haven't got another engagement. It's just – I couldn't stand her making sheep's eyes at me all evening, wanting something I can't give.' He shrugged helplessly, wanting to say more, to share the dreadful burden. But how could he? He turned away. 'I'll go and carry on with the potting. Several of the tender varieties really ought to–'

Richard caught his arm. 'If they've survived four years they'll manage a few more minutes.' His normally cheerful features were taut with concern. 'Bryce, what's wrong? It's obvious something is. Don't tell me it's Mother's death: I know it's more than that. You haven't been yourself since we came home.'

Seeing his brother's anxiety, his desire to understand, to help, to comfort, Bryce looked away. *He was closer to his twin than anyone – except Tarun. But tell Richard what he was, what he had done? The very thought made his gut contract.*

'What's wrong is too many people interfering in my life. Why won't you all just leave me alone?'

Richard gazed at him for a long moment. 'All right, if that's what you want.' Then he turned and started down the path between the cold frames.

Fists clenched, Bryce watched him go clamping his lips tight to stop himself calling his brother back to apologize, confess, and beg for help. The urge was almost irresistible. But he didn't dare give in. Because once Richard knew the truth...

He turned away, eyes burning, throat stiff, imagining the changing expressions on his twin's face. First there would be disbelief. Then shock would be followed by disgust that would finally, inevitably, harden into rejection. He couldn't bear it. Shuddering, he stumbled blindly along the gravelled path towards the nursery. What was he to do?

Chapter Eighteen

As the train puffed and rocked down the main Truro to Penzance line towards Hayle, Henry Damerel realized he was smiling. Gazing out through the carriage window at the passing scenery: small villages surrounded by a patchwork of farm fields, weathered granite hills shrouded in gorse and bracken, tree-lined valleys, old mine chimneys, and barren red-stained soil strewn with abandoned rusting machinery, he was happy. He relished the sensation. He had forgotten how it felt.

After all the pressures and difficulties of the last few years at last things were starting to look up. Of course there were still a few problems. One in particular was Mary's lawyer who seemed to be dragging his heels.

He had not intended seeing her before the weekend when she would be joining him and the rest of the family for dinner and they would announce their forthcoming marriage. But a refusal by Mr Williams at the bank to advance any further money had forced him to alter his plans and call on her. Thank God she had been at home. Rising from her chair at the walnut bureau she had come swiftly towards him, hands out-stretched in welcome.

'Henry, what a delightful surprise! Can you stay to lunch?'

'Regrettably, no. I have to–'

'A drink then.' Dismissing the maid who had shown him in she moved towards the sideboard. A polished silver tray held three crystal decanters the contents of which were identified by an engraved silver label on a fine chain. Opening one of the doors she took out a crystal tumbler. Pouring a generous measure of whisky she took it to him. 'There you are.' Indicating the bureau she pulled a face. 'I was making another list. I seem to have done little else lately. Henry, there are one or two pieces of furniture I would really like to bring with me. Do you think–'

'Of course.' He curbed his impatience. 'Naturally you will want some of your own things around you. You must make whatever changes you wish.'

'And not bother you with domestic matters,' she smiled. 'A man after my father's heart.' Crossing to a large comfortable sofa upholstered in faded chintz she sat down at one end, folded her hands in her lap, and gazed around her. 'I've been thinking about selling this place.'

Wondering how to raise the subject he had come to discuss Henry was instantly diverted.

'Of course it's not as big or imposing as Damerel House,' Mary said. 'Very few houses in this area are. But it's an attractive property and doesn't require an army of staff.'

He nodded, making rapid mental calculations. 'If you're sure that's what you want to do.' Considering its size, location, and delightful gardens Mary that had designed herself, it would probably realize a handsome sum.

'It's what I'd *like* to do.' She sighed. 'However, after making enquiries I've learned I can't.'

Damn. Forcing a smile Henry shrugged. 'Don't tell me: it's entailed to some distant male cousin who has never even seen it?'

'Not exactly.' Mary's cheeks turned pink. 'It would only go to another branch of the family if I don't have children.'

This time Henry was able to smile far more naturally. 'Then I'm afraid the distant cousin is going to be disappointed.' He watched, astonished and amused, as she dropped her gaze and her face grew pinker. This woman whose shrewd and ironic comments on the activities of their mutual acquaintance enlivened any dinner table, who had always appeared cool, calm, and totally in command of herself, was blushing like a 16-year-old schoolgirl.

Pressing one hand to her flushed cheek

301

and darting him a wry look she indicated the sofa beside her. 'Sit down and tell me why you've come. Considering all the things you told me you planned to do this week it must be important.'

Henry sat down, angling himself towards her as he cradled his drink. 'What could be more important than seeing you?'

A smile flickered across her mouth as she shook her head. 'Henry, we've known each other a long time. I'm aware of your priorities.' She raised her brows encouragingly. 'So?'

Admiration evolved into a renewed tug of attraction. Henry lifted his glass in acknowledgement as the corners of his mouth tilted upward. 'You're no fool.'

'Why thank you,' she murmured drily.

'You know what I mean.' He grimaced. 'I've got cash difficulties. No, difficulty is not the word: *disaster* is the only way to describe it. It *is* always a pleasure to see you. And I wish that was my only reason for coming, but the truth is I need to know what's happening with the financial arrangements.'

Mary's gaze flicked heavenward. 'You know what lawyers are.'

'You did impress upon them the importance of releasing at least some of the funding as quickly as possible?'

'Indeed I did. Mr Bartlett promised to give the matter his personal attention. But apparently it takes time to liquidate assets and sell shares. He wasn't at all happy about making the transfer before the wedding. In fact he did his best to persuade me to wait until *after* the ceremony.'

'Did he indeed?' Instantly defensive Henry felt his hackles rise. 'Correct me if I'm wrong, my dear, but I understood that Bartlett, Mabey and Pearce are paid by you to carry out your instructions. Mr Bartlett's personal opinions are–'

'Of no consequence.' Mary's calm deflected his aggression and soothed his anger. 'Nor was he voicing them. His reluctance is for purely professional reasons. Whatever legal arrangements he makes now will be negated the day we marry. As a matter of courtesy Mr Bartlett wished me to be aware that doing everything twice would double the costs.'

'Ah. I see. Well, that's different.' Henry hesitated. But it was no good. The wedding was still weeks away. To wait until afterwards was out of the question. 'The thing is–'

'You need money now. I understand that, Henry. I told Mr Bartlett that while I appreciated his concern my instructions were unchanged. He is to go ahead and complete the transfers as quickly as possible.'

Draining his glass Henry set it down too heavily on a gleaming rosewood side table. He turned to her his voice thick with relief.

'Mary, you're a gem. You just wait. I'm going to make Wheal Providence a force to be reckoned with. The lodes are rich and with proper investment I can make Providence the most profitable mine in Cornwall. You'll see.' Visions of all the improvements he wanted to make tumbled through his mind. Moved by a sudden surge of gratitude he took one of her hands between his. 'I know we haven't seen much of each other lately.'

Mary waved his apology aside. 'Grace told me that you've been travelling the length and breadth of Cornwall. Did you find what you were looking for?'

Her complexion was rosy, her eyes bright with interest. She was past the first flush of youth but then so was he. Seeing his own enthusiasm reflected in her smile, he realized he always felt better in her company. Not only was she surprisingly intelligent for a woman, she didn't waste time on small talk but went straight to the point. Though it had taken a bit of getting used to, he liked it. Nor had she changed since their agreement to marry. He had been afraid she might. Women did. They became obsessed with domestic trivia.

Louise's world – when she wasn't confined to her bed – had centred on her children and her garden. She had never shown the slightest interest in the mine, despite it being the foundation of their comfortable lifestyle. It was the mine that had paid for her wardrobes full of expensive clothes, servants to run the house, manage the grounds, tend the gardens, and look after the horses.

If it hadn't been for Dorcas – at least she had been prepared to listen when he wanted to talk. Sometimes she had seemed more absorbed in her painting than in his problems. But on balance it was better that she had an interest. Without it things could have been difficult, especially after Hal went. Women needed something to keep them occupied. She was probably out in the garden right now, sitting at her easel in her favourite spot. God knew when he would find time to get round to see her. But she would understand. The mine had to come first. Thanks to Mary's money he had a future. One he could look forward to.

'Have my trips been successful? They have indeed.' He caught her hand. 'I owe it all to you, Mary. You've changed my life.'

'As you have changed mine.' Gently she pulled free. 'I-I have something for you.' Crossing to the small walnut bureau standing against the papered wall she picked up a drawstring bag of embroidered blue velvet trimmed with cream lace. As she came towards him he saw her fingers were shaking as she loosened the braided silk cords. 'Hold out your hand.'

Intrigued, he did so and she laid a roll of paper money on his palm.

He stared at it for a moment, speechless as he realized the thick roll was made up of £100 notes. Shock tingled along his nerves. He had to clear his throat before any sound would come out.

'How...? Where...?'

'My account at the bank.' She moved her shoulders. 'It seemed more sensible to put the money to good use than have it simply sit there. Obviously it won't be enough to buy all the machinery you need. But if you can put a deposit–'

'The compressor. I'll get the compressor. And a new pump.' Seizing her shoulders Henry kissed her startled mouth with such enthusiasm that their teeth clashed. 'Mary you really are – God, this is just–' Releasing her he brandished the money like a talisman. 'Look, I hate to – but if I go now I can probably catch the two o'clock train. I can be down at Harvey's by four.'

Rosy and breathless she waved him away, the empty velvet bag crushed in her free hand. 'Go on, then. Hurry. I'll see you on Saturday.'

He reached the station just in time.

Roused from his thoughts by the whistle's shrill blast Henry glanced at his watch. Returning it to his waistcoat pocket, he straightened in his seat. *Had he thanked her?* He couldn't remember actually saying the words. Not that it mattered. His reaction must have shown her how much the money meant to him. Fancy her doing that. He shook his head. They would make a good partnership. Giving her a child would fulfil his end of the bargain. Reliving the quick kiss he tried to imagine her hair tumbling around her rosy face, her body naked under something long and silky. Desire throbbed and he shifted on the padded seat. All things considered he had done even better for himself than he'd hoped.

To pass the time on the journey home he would write to Dorcas and tell her about all the changes he was planning. No need to mention where the money was coming from. Not yet anyway. He *could* say he had raised it from the sale of her cottage and the other small parcels of land he had quietly disposed of. But she might ask questions. He couldn't be doing with that now. Besides, that money had long gone. When she received the letter she would realize how busy he had been, and still was.

Another shrill blast announced their arrival at Hayle station.

Reluctantly, Grace pulled the small wheel-barrow out of the whitewashed outhouse near the back door. Lifting down a hoe, a pair of shears and a small fork, she laid them in the barrow and relatched the door. Tall leafy limes provided dappled shade as she wheeled the barrow round the side of the house. But once she left their protection the sun's heat scorched through her cotton shirt-blouse. Beneath her wide-brimmed straw hat her hair was sticking to her temples and scalp. As she pushed the barrow along the path towards the chain garden her head began to ache.

She didn't want to be here. It was her Uncle John's idea.

'Just an hour a day,' he had coaxed. 'You'll be out in the sunshine and fresh air. It will give you an interest and help rebuild your strength.'

What about cycling to the village? Playing games with the children at school? Cleaning the chapel? How much more fresh air and exercise did one person need? She had plenty of interests. She certainly didn't need anyone else telling her how she should occupy herself. But he was a doctor and had her wellbeing at heart. Brought up never to argue, she didn't feel strong enough to start now. So trying to ignore the conflict that knotted her stomach and tightened the band around her skull she complied.

Setting down the barrow she looked along the linked beds, vivid with summer colour. She loathed this garden. Its surface beauty was deceiving. It flaunted its secrets, mocking those who couldn't read them.

Today was the first time she had come here since calling on Dorcas. A visit begun as a favour to Mrs Williams had ended by irrevocably destroying her image of her mother and father. It had finally crushed her desperate hope that the circles of colourful flowers had been chosen simply for their beauty: that despite illness and financial problems her parents' marriage had been based on love and trust and strength in adversity.

Dorcas's outburst had blown that hope apart and confirmed her worst fears. It had all been illusion, a façade. The *reality* was thirty years of secrecy, lies and deceit.

She hated Dorcas for showing her the truth. Her gaze flew to the bed between her mother's and her own, the one that had always puzzled her. Now she knew. It was Hal's.

But what she found hardest to accept was that the choice of plants and flowers meant her mother *had known about Hal.* And knowing about him she must also have known about Dorcas. Which explained why her father's link had been planted with flowers that proclaimed his infidelity, his betrayal.

Yet Grace could not recall even a hint of bitterness or blame. *How could her mother have achieved that?* Had she derived sufficient satisfaction, sufficient revenge from this silent declaration to enable her to carry on as if everything was as it should be? *Had her father been aware that her mother knew the truth?*

The chain garden laid bare facets of her mother's character Grace could not understand. And now it was too late. It would never be explained. Fury seethed. She felt cheated, terrified. What was real? What was true? What could she trust? *Who else knew?*

Her whirling thoughts were echoed in her churning stomach as she looked down the beds, each one enclosed within and linked by the low narrow box hedge. Ever since reading that book listing the meanings of flowers the chain garden had made her uneasy. Now she *hated* it. She didn't want to look after it any more.

Guilt filled her. *If she didn't, who would?* Busy with preparations for the wedding Mary didn't have time. Nor with the fruit and vegetable gardens in full production did Jack or Ben or Arthur. Everyone in the family saw it as her mother's memorial. But they didn't know its true significance.

It looked beautiful. In reality it was poisonous. The links were supposed to indicate continuity. But chains imprisoned people, denied them freedom, weighed them down so that they drowned. She shifted from foot to foot wiping her palms down the sides of her skirt.

For as long as she could remember she had shouldered responsibility, put everyone else's needs before her own. It had been expected of her because she was the eldest daughter. She had writhed with guilt at feeling trapped and unhappy. Yet after her collapse Mary had stepped in and everyone's lives had carried on just the same.

All those years of believing it was her duty to see to, organize, manage, take care of. All those years of anxiety and fear, of self-denial, of standing on the fringes watching everyone else enjoying themselves. Never joining in because within hours, days or weeks her mother would be ill again, and it would be her job to take over as nurse while keeping the household running smoothly.

All those years. Yet her absence had made no difference at all. If she wasn't missed then what had it all been for? She had no value: *that* was the truth.

Her agitation increasing, Grace walked the length of the chain and back again. The heat was oppressive, searing through her clothes, burning through her hat, heavy on her skull. Her heart thudded loud and painful against her ribs. She gasped, sucking heat into her straining lungs.

Her father and mother: her father and Dorcas: her father and Mary. Where did *she* fit in? Everything she had believed in was a lie. How could she pretend everything was normal? How could she blot out what she now knew? But if she couldn't, how could she stay here? Yet where else could she go?

Perspiration pricked her forehead and upper lip. It beaded her skin so that her blouse clung. Her petticoat was hot and uncomfortable. Everyone expected her to continue tending this floral display of anguish and bitterness. This proclamation that her father was an adulterer and had sired a bastard son. Hal was her half-brother and she had never known.

As she stared at the linked beds she felt the weight of the chain dragging her down, pressing her into the soft earth until she suffocated.

Seizing the shears she began chopping at the red, gold and purple blooms. Nurture her dead mother's secrets? Her father's lies and deceit? *No!* Not now, not ever again.

After laying waste to her father's bed, she ran panting to her mother's. She loved them and hated them. How *could* they? She had sympathized, admired. It had all been lies. They had betrayed her. The *shame* that she had been so blind, so ignorant and naïve, so *stupid* – was annihilating. She snapped the blades together, slashing what she couldn't cut, racked by sobs that hurt her chest. Blinded by scalding tears she jerked her head so they spilled and fell. The muscles in her arms and shoulders screamed. But the flowers had to be destroyed. They knew. They stood there so bright and proud. They were laughing at her. She could hear their mockery, see their sneers.

The garden was a furnace: the sun a relentless hammer. Her breath burned in her throat and her head swam. She mustn't stop. The pain in her arms was almost unbearable. But she could not – must not – stop. Her slippery hands were so weak and shook so badly it was hard even to hold the shears. She staggered on, flailing at the flowers with the closed blades, trampling the bruised petals and broken stems, jarring her heels and back as she stamped the pulpy mess into the earth.

Trembling violently, her head pounding, she stumbled through box on to gravel. She swayed, bewildered. Then saw the folly looming in front of her. It was done, finished. The shears slid from her agonizingly cramped hands and clattered on to the gravel. Every muscle in her body was on fire. But it was the pain inside she couldn't bear. Unable to straighten up she folded her aching arms across her body, convulsed by sobs that stabbed her chest and tore at her throat. She heard shouts. Black spots danced in front of her eyes. The shouting was closer. A soft rushing sound filled her head. Darkness rolled forward and enveloped her.

Chapter Nineteen

Voices: distant: a woman's and a man's.

'But *why?*' The tone was hushed, shocked and anxious. 'I don't understand. Grace was devoted to her mother. And Louise adored that garden.'

'An emotional breakdown can have all kinds of causes. Louise's ill health placed the entire family under considerable strain. As her mother's devoted carer Grace bore the brunt of it. Grief is often accompanied by guilt at having been unable to prevent the death. This can show itself as anger directed against the loved one for leaving.'

'I understand. But I never expected, never imagined – not Grace. Such *violence...*'

Though both were speaking softly, she knew who they were. She tried to open her eyes. They were so swollen that the lids barely cracked apart. She was in her room lying on her bed. Someone had removed her shoes. But the dampness and the smell told her she was still wearing her sweat-soaked, earth-stained clothes.

She drew a deep breath and felt it catch in her chest. Her hands were burning and stinging. She lifted one to find out why.

Every muscle in her arm protested. Burst blisters had left her palm raw and bloody. That explained it. She felt quite detached. Her body was a mass of different hurts but it didn't seem to matter.

'Feeling better now?' Her uncle's face appeared, his expression reflecting sympathy and concern. She was aware of her eyes filling and hot tears slid down her temples and into her hair. Mary's face swam into view. Grace felt her temples gently mopped with a cambric handkerchief.

'Violet is running you a nice warm bath.' Mary's smile was calm and reassuring.

Grace swallowed, moistened dry lips. 'Thank you.' She wanted to tell them that what she had done was necessary. But she hadn't the strength to make such an effort. She heard her uncle's voice.

'Send someone up to the lodge in half an hour. I'll prepare arnica ointment for the strained muscles and a balm for her hands. Make sure she keeps them bandaged for at least three days.'

'Is there anything else I can do?'

'After she's had a bath give her hot sweet tea and something to eat. Then let her sleep.'

As they moved towards the door Mary spoke too softly for Grace to catch the words. But her uncle's reply was clear.

'No, leave it to me. I'll tell Henry.'

Grace closed her eyes.

Edwin turned his pen between his fingers, staring blindly at the half-written page, his thoughts with Grace. He knew exactly how many hours had passed since he had last seen her. He knew she would have expected him to call in at the chapel as he had done in the past when she was working there. He knew she would have been disappointed that he hadn't, and was probably wondering why. She would never know what it had cost him to stay away.

But after that night at Angwin's farm reliving the horror that had brought him here he'd had to face the truth. Marriage to Grace was an impossible dream. She was gentle, kind-hearted, hard-working; every-thing he could ask for in a wife. He was totally unworthy of her. Trying to put her out of his mind he had altered his routine; avoiding places their paths might cross.

As days passed without a glimpse of her he desperately hoped his memories would lessen and fade. Instead they became stronger, more insistent. He would start some task and moments later was forced to wrench his attention back to whatever he was doing because he had remembered something she said. Not simply remem-bered the words but heard her voice saying them, saw the expression on her face, the way she lowered her head, her cheeks flushed and glowing because she was self-conscious. The images as clear and real as if she were in front of him. It was exquisite torture.

Where was she? What was she doing at this moment?

A rap on the door made him start. Without waiting for a response his housekeeper opened it and poked her head around.

'Doctor's here,' Flora hissed. 'I've put'n in the front parlour. You never said you was feeling bad,' she accused.

'I'm not.' Suppressing impatience Edwin forced a smile. 'I'm perfectly well, thank you, Miss Bowden. Would you show him in here please?'

Flora's head withdrew and he heard her footsteps cross the tiled passage. Putting down his pen, Edwin pushed back his chair and rose to greet his visitor.

'Doctor Ainsley, good afternoon.'

'Good afternoon, Mr Philpotts. This isn't an inconvenient time is it? Only as I was in the village anyway—'

'Not at all,' Edwin interrupted, aware of Flora's curiosity as her gaze swivelled between them. He nodded to the house-keeper. 'Thank you, Flora.' Closing the door gently he turned and gestured towards the comfortable armchair at one side of the fireplace where his housekeeper had placed an embroidered screen in front of the empty grate. 'Do sit down. Is it old Mr Doble? When I called in to see him earlier in the week he seemed to have rallied.'

'To the best of my knowledge he's still hanging on. I saw him two days ago and I've heard nothing further from the family. He's determined to live long enough to see young Kate married. No, I wanted to talk to you about Grace.'

Hearing her name Edwin flinched, disguising his reaction by returning to his chair in front of the desk. Biting his tongue hard he resumed his seat. If he spoke he would betray himself. *What about Grace?* He waited.

Since his arrival in the village he had begun to understand what made a good minister. Strangely, it had little to do with finding the right words of spiritual consolation. When he visited the sick or dying, after he had greeted them he rarely needed to say anything else. They didn't want him to talk. They wanted someone to listen: someone to whom they could pour out all their fears, anger and regrets. Someone who wasn't family so wouldn't be hurt. Someone they could trust, knowing that what they said would never be repeated.

Drawing a chair up close to the bed he would let them talk. Occasionally, if there was great distress, he might briefly touch an arm or hold a hand. Having purged their anger or grief or guilt they would tell him how much better they felt, and how grateful they were. Then he would leave, having done for someone else what he craved for himself.

Edwin watched John Ainsley rub the back of his neck in a gesture that betrayed both concern and uncertainty.

'Two days ago Grace had some kind of' – he gestured helplessly – 'I don't know what to call it: breakdown, brainstorm. You've visited the house. Have you seen the chain garden?' Edwin nodded. 'When Louise – Grace's mother – was well she spent every moment she possibly could out there. In winter, or if the weather turned cold or wet, she would go to the folly instead. Violet or Grace would make sure a fire was lit for her and she'd spend hours planning her planting schemes for the following year.' He paused.

Seething with impatience Edwin stayed silent. Questions clamoured: damming up behind his clenched teeth. His jaw ached.

John shook his head, clearly bemused. 'That garden was Louise's passion. Grace ... Grace attacked it with a pair of shears. She destroyed it all. She didn't just cut down every plant and flower, she stamped on them, ground them into the soil.'

Edwin's in-drawn breath hissed between his teeth. *Grace?* Gentle, caring Grace? What

319

could have driven her to such behaviour? He realized John was still talking.

'Such devastation – I've never seen anything like it. Grace, of all people.' He shook his head again.

Edwin ran his tongue over dry lips. Now he could ask. 'How is she?'

'I imagine she's in severe discomfort from muscle strain.'

'You imagine?'

'She hasn't complained. In fact that's one of the reasons I'm here. She won't talk. One can see she's in pain. She can hardly move. Her hands are a mess with burst blisters and so on. But apart from that there doesn't appear to be anything else physically wrong with her. She's aware of her surroundings. She'll accept drinks. She allows Violet to bathe her, apply arnica salve to her back and arms, and change the dressings on her hands. But she won't eat. Rose Trott has tried to tempt her with light and tasty dishes. Violet and Mary Prideaux have both done their best. Grace simply closes her eyes. I've rarely seen such complete withdrawal.' He sighed. 'At first I assumed it was delayed reaction to losing her mother. Now I wonder if there might be more to it than that.'

Edwin stood up so quickly he almost knocked his chair over and quickly caught the back as it tipped. 'I'll go at once.'

'No.' The doctor rose to his feet. 'I

appreciate the thought. Indeed I'm reasonably sure that whatever's wrong falls within your sphere of expertise rather than mine. But from a medical point of view she needs a few more days' complete rest before she'll be strong enough to face and deal with whatever precipitated her action.'

Wait a few more days? While his beloved Grace lay suffering, trapped in some hell? How could he wait? Because he must. To rush round there now might answer *his* need. But if it harmed her...

'I see. But if she's not eating how can she regain–'

'As long as she's accepting fluids her refusal to eat is not, as yet, a major problem. Also I've prescribed a mild sedative to ensure she sleeps as much as possible. Violet is very experienced with such doses. You may be aware she is also personal maid to Mrs Chenoweth?'

'Ah,' said Edwin.

'Exactly,' John said. 'Mrs Chenoweth is also benefiting from mild sedation. Anyway I'm much obliged to you.'

As Edwin followed him out into the hall there was a knock on the front door.

'It's all right, Miss Bowden,' Edwin called, as Flora bustled out from the kitchen. 'I'll answer it.'

Muttering that it was 'never right nor proper', Flora retreated again.

321

Reading surprise and amusement in the doctor's raised brows Edwin gave a wry shrug. 'Miss Bowden and I have different ideas about a minister's role. I think she misses Mr Peters.'

'The village certainly saw a lot less of him than it does of you.'

'So I've been told.' Edwin opened the door. Martha Tamblin was standing on the step, hand raised to grasp the knocker again and clearly in the grip of powerful emotion. She blinked as the doctor appeared. But after a brief nod and a murmured, 'Aft'noon, Doctor,' she ignored him.

'Listen, Reverend, I'm sorry to come bothering you but you did say–'

'I did, Mrs Tamblin. I'm glad you took me at my word. How can I help?' Feeling the doctor pat his shoulder as he passed Edwin raised a hand in acknowledgement. But he didn't shift his gaze from Martha's anxious face.

'Polly's home in my kitchen sobbing her heart out. Took me ages to find out what was wrong.' Martha's chest swelled and she reddened with anger. 'Little buggers! Telling the child her mother didn't slip on the path and fall in to the river, she jumped because she wasn't right in the head. Yet everyone knows the bank is steep as a cliff along there. I tell you there's some spiteful people in this village and that's the truth. No youngster would think up something like that by theirselves.' She glared up at Edwin, her eyes full of tears. 'Then she asked me if it's *her* fault her ma drowned.' Martha pressed a hand to her face, her mouth trembling. 'I tell you, Reverend, if my heart wasn't broke already – that little maid have been looking after her sister and brothers since she could walk. Good as gold she is. I told her and told her it wasn't nothing she done or didn't do. I said her ma had gone to heaven to be with her da. I meant it for the best. Only I shouldn't have said it because Poll think that means her ma didn't love her and Meg and the boys, else she wouldn't have gone away and left them.' Wiping her wet eyes she sniffed. 'Poor little mite. I dunno what to do, Reverend. Will you come and–?'

'Of course I will.' Pity wrenched Edwin's heart. Conducting Ellie's funeral service so soon after her husband's had shaken him. Six-year-old Polly had not cried in chapel or at the graveside. Chalk-white apart from the dark circles round her eyes, she had held her toddler brother on her skinny hip while Martha carried the baby on one arm and held little Meg's hand with the other.

The coroner had called Ellie's drowning a tragic accident. But that hadn't stopped the whispers. His housekeeper considered it her duty to keep him abreast of all the village gossip. When he tried to tell her he wasn't interested she had startled him by demanding how he could do his job properly if he didn't know what was going on.

Later, thinking it over in his study, he saw that she had a point. He did not have to believe the rumours. He certainly never repeated them. But being aware enabled him to call on someone – always offering a legitimate and totally unrelated reason – when spirits were lowest and comfort most needed. Occasionally he was turned away. But when he went back, as he always did, he was usually invited in. Sometimes the invitation was grudging, sometimes defiant. He didn't mind.

'Step inside a moment,' he opened the door wider. 'I just have to tell my house-keeper I shall be out for a while.'

Martha shook her head firmly. 'I'll wait here if it's all the same to you.'

Edwin sighed inwardly. He wanted the manse to be a welcoming haven to all those seeking his help. But while people like Mrs Williams, Mrs Nancholas, or the stewards and elders were happy to sit and drink coffee or tea while they discussed chapel business, few of the villagers would step over the threshold. They wouldn't say why. But he knew.

Flora Bowden was an efficient housekeeper who had clearly suited Mr Peters very well, but as Edwin didn't share his predecessor's ideas or methods, his relationship with the housekeeper was not comfortable. In any case he didn't want a housekeeper he wanted a wife. He wanted Grace. *Grace who was suffering God knew what agony of mind.* Slamming a mental door on that thought Edwin smiled at Martha Tamblin. 'I won't be a moment.'

Polly's incoherent grief brought back painfully vivid memories of Akhil. Sitting opposite the little girl at the kitchen table he repeated softly and gently that her mother had loved her – loved all of them – very much and would never willingly have left them. Then while Martha fed the baby and Meg played with her brother on the floor, he asked Polly to tell him some of the things her mother had said or done that made her feel warm and happy.

Later, when Polly rubbed her eyes with her knuckles and said she was sorry for making her nan cry, he ached with compassion. She was six years old. She had lost both parents within a few months of each other. She had spent her childhood taking care of her siblings. Now she was apologizing because her grief had upset her grandmother.

He supposed he ought to tell her to be brave, that her mother wouldn't want her to weep. But the words stuck in his throat. Instead he told her that sometimes, if she felt very sad, it was all right to cry. Her nan wouldn't mind because she understood.

'Even though your mother was a grown-up she was still your nan's little girl. So your nan misses her too, just like you do.'

Polly peered at her grandmother whose face was wet with tears. After an instant's startled glance in his direction Martha nodded. Edwin watched comprehension *and relief* fill the little girl's red swollen eyes.

'So I don't have to be brave *all* the time?'

Catching Martha's eye Edwin waited, saying nothing.

Swallowing audibly Martha smiled through her tears. 'Of course you don't, my bird. But shall us try not to cry in front of the little ones? I tell you what, when we've had tea and got these three up to bed, you and me'll have a cuddle and I'll tell you some of the things your ma got up to when she was your age. Like that would you?'

'Oh yes,' Polly breathed nodding vigorously. 'Did she do naughty things sometimes?'

Martha nodded. 'A little terror she was, and got her bottom smacked for it. But I loved her just the same. Like I love you.' Her voice breaking she cleared her throat loudly.

Scrambling down from the chair Polly picked up the empty water pitcher.

'C'mon, Meg, coming up the pump with me?'

As the two children went out hand in hand Edwin followed them to the door.

Martha put down the bottle and tilted the baby forward over her splayed hand. As she rubbed and patted his back his head wobbled like a flower too heavy for its fragile stalk. 'You're a good man, Reverend.'

The words cut deep. Edwin raised a finger to his lips to silence her. 'You know where I am if you need me, Mrs Tamblin.'

As he reached the junction between Miner's Row and the main street the clock in the tower struck six. It had been a long and busy day. This last hour had resurrected memories he wished might have remained undisturbed. Bitterness snaked through him. God certainly moved in mysterious ways. In seeking to bring comfort to a child and her grandmother he had been brutally reminded of the reason his yearning for Grace could never be fulfilled.

He loved her but could never tell her so. He had deliberately avoided her. Now Dr Ainsley's request for his help meant he had to see her again. Rejoicing at the prospect he was horrified at the reason and anguished as he tried to imagine her suffering. He must never forget even for a moment that for him nothing would change. Though the opportunity to help her through this crisis was a precious gift, keeping his own feelings hidden would demand the kind of strength he wasn't sure he possessed.

He started across the road taking little notice as a horse trotted up from the smithy.

'Mr Philpotts?'

Glancing up he saw Bryce Damerel rein in.

'Could I – do you have a moment?'

Edwin hesitated. 'Is it important?' Bryce's expression blanked like shutters closing and Edwin realized he had been misled by the smile. This had not been a casual enquiry. Swiftly he tried to retrieve the situation. 'Of course it is, or you wouldn't have asked.'

'No, it doesn't matter. Really.' Bryce shortened the reins and his horse moved forward. To delay him Edwin said the first thing that came into his head.

'Doctor Ainsley called to see me earlier.'

'Doctor Ainsley?' The colour drained from Bryce's face.

'Yes. About Gr– About your sister. Was that what–?'

'No, yes – I – excuse me, I have to go.'

As the horse broke into a trot Edwin stared at Bryce's back. He had an unpleasant feeling he had missed something important. No one could force a person to talk if they didn't want to. But his initial response had hardly been encouraging. When he visited Damerel House in a few days' time he would try to catch Bryce and apologize.

Dorcas's garden gate squealed as Henry opened it then closed it again behind him, buoyant after his successful trip to Hayle. He was back where he belonged, on top and in control.

Expecting her to be in the garden his mouth had already shaped itself into a smile of greeting as he walked round the corner. The familiar sight of her easel with the chair behind it and the low table to one side warmed him. A backing board still rested on the pegs.

Now he was here he realized how much he had missed her. But there were only so many hours in a day. It was a matter of priorities. The cottage door was wide open.

As he approached it Dorcas appeared on the threshold, warned of a visitor by the squeaky hinge. But instead of coming out to greet him as she usually did, she remained where she was and folded her arms.

Guilt turned to irritation. He wasn't in the mood for a scene. He raised his hands. 'I'm sorry. I know it's been weeks but I've–'

'Been busy? Indeed you have.'

Her tone made him think of a cliff-edge on a stormy night. *Something was wrong.* In all the years he had known her he had never seen that expression on her face. It stripped the flesh from his bones, exposed every nerve. Though distorted by the thick spectacle lenses her gaze was hard enough to bore through rock. He opened his mouth but she didn't allow him time to speak.

'I understand congratulations are in order.'

How had she found out? Who could have told her? 'Dorcas–'

'You're not going to deny it then? Tell me it's all a mistake?'

'No.' He was determined to regain control of the situation. 'I think it would be better if we discussed this inside.'

'Still worried about your reputation?' Her tone was a corrosive mixture of bitterness and pain.

'No. But I am concerned about yours.'

'Liar!' As her face crumpled she whirled round and vanished inside. He followed, closing the door from force of habit. It was going to be far more difficult than he'd imagined. He stood looking out of the window on to the garden. He heard her moving about in the small kitchen. There was a splash of water. A few moments later she came back to the cosy living-room. He watched her cross to the only armchair.

In the past they had always sat together on the old sofa she had reupholstered in holly-green velvet and brightened with gold and crimson cushions. Now he sat alone.

'Dorcas, nothing will change. Nothing has changed. I was married before.'

'To an invalid.'

'I need no reminder.'

'But Mary Prideaux is by all accounts a very healthy active woman. So' – Dorcas's spurious brightness set his teeth on edge – 'is this to be a marriage in name only? I thought not,' she murmured as he looked away. 'She'll want a child while she's still able.'

'What's wrong with that?' Angry at feeling guilty, Henry was sharp. 'Surely it's a perfectly natural desire?'

'Oh yes. And if she is blessed, her child, unlike mine, will be fortunate enough to grow up knowing who its father is.'

Sliding from the sofa Henry knelt in front of her. He reached out to put his arms around her. But when she fended him off he sat back on his heels resting his hands on his thighs.

'Dorcas, try to understand. Mary is my only hope. Without her money Wheal Providence is finished. Thirty years of my life will be wiped out. Can't you, just for a moment, think beyond your own hurt pride? Everything I possess is tied up in that mine. I've mortgaged the house. Over the years I've sold off every disposable asset–'

'I know,' she interrupted bitterly. 'When I was living in Falmouth you had me evicted from my cottage so you could sell that.'

How in God's name did she know? Shaken, he rallied every argument he could think of.

331

'You couldn't have stayed there. Not after you fell pregnant. Isn't this cottage better in every way? Doesn't it have the garden you said you always wanted? Haven't you told me countless times how happy you've been here?'

'Yes. But that's not the point.'

He pushed himself up on to the sofa, deliberately putting distance between them. 'Then I don't know what your point is. I brought you to a place where you were safe, where you could paint in peace, where you had privacy to come and go as you pleased–'

'That was for your benefit, not mine.'

Ignoring this inconvenient truth he carried on. 'You have lived here for thirty years and it hasn't cost you–'

'I've paid rent,' she flared.

'Which barely covered the repairs and maintenance.' He tried to get a grip on his temper. 'I did it with the best of intentions. Because I loved – love – you. I wanted our son to grow up in safe surroundings.'

'*Our* son? Suddenly Hal is *our* son? So why have you never acknowledged him?'

This was too much. 'For God's sake, Dorcas!' Henry exploded. 'Why are you bringing all this up now? Haven't I got enough on my plate? Without Mary's money it will all be over. Everyone who invested in the mine and remained loyal during the hard times will be wiped out. I don't mean just the adventurers, the major investors; I'm talking about the dozens of small business owners and the miners themselves. More than half the men in the village will lose their jobs. I didn't have any choice. Can't you see that?'

'So what happened to the money you raised from selling this cottage?'

He swallowed. 'How–?'

'It doesn't matter how I found out. This is the second time you have sold my home over my head. Why didn't you tell me, Henry? Didn't you think I'd be interested?'

'It was a simple business move. A means of raising capital I desperately needed. Besides, it hasn't made any difference. For heaven's sake, you haven't been put out on the street. You're a sitting tenant. You're safe. If this is your reaction I'm glad I didn't tell you. You might at least *try* to understand my position.'

Taking off her glasses Dorcas rubbed her face. 'Henry, I have spent the last thirty years understanding your position. Couldn't you have talked to me first?'

He shrugged uncomfortably. 'Everything happened so fast. Besides you're so much a part of my life it never occurred to me it would make any difference. I still don't see why it should.'

She stood up so quickly her glasses slid off the arm of the chair on to the floor. 'It already has. You had better go.'

'Dorcas, wait–'

333

'No, Henry. Just go.' As she went to open the door she tripped over the edge of the rug and staggered forward, banging her shoulder against the doorframe.

'Are you all right?'

No, she wasn't.

'Here.' He thrust the spectacles into her hand. 'There's no point having them if you don't wear them.' He saw her bite her lip as she put them on. 'Did you hurt yourself?'

'What do you care?' Her voice was flat and cold as she held the door open.

'You're being ridiculous.' There was no reasoning with her in this mood. With a shrug he walked past her and out into the evening sunshine. 'I'll come and see you again, when you've had time to–'

'I don't think so. There's nothing more to be said. It really is a pity you couldn't have found time to talk to me first: I'd have told you my good news.'

'Well, tell me now. What good news?' It was probably something to do with her painting and he wasn't really interested. But for old times' sake he didn't want to part on bad terms. He'd leave her alone for a month or two, give her time to start missing him.

'Mr Williams at the bank tells me that Hal has been sending money back to Cornwall. He wanted it invested in property. So guess who bought this cottage when you put it up for sale?' She raised a hand not giving him

334

the chance to interrupt. 'He has also been putting money into shares for me. I didn't know anything about this until a few weeks ago when I received a letter from a stockbroker in London. I'm a wealthy woman, Henry.' Her mouth twisted briefly. 'I've been waiting for you to come and see me so I could tell you.'

While he stood on the step, stunned and speechless, she quietly closed the door in his face.

Chapter Twenty

Edwin waited five interminable days. To get through the long hours he kept himself busy. It wasn't difficult. For a minister who took his work seriously there was always more to do than time available. He made his usual visits to the sick and elderly housebound. He spent twenty minutes each day at the school. He wrote letters, presided over meetings and put in an appearance at numerous village activities.

This morning he had woken knowing he could wait no longer. Today he must – would – go and see Grace. But by the time he had dealt with a succession of unexpected callers it was almost one and Flora was complaining about his lunch getting cold.

Telling her he would be out for the remainder of the afternoon and reminding her to write down any messages, he closed the door before she could ask where he was going and set off up the village. After the previous week's violent storm, sultry heat had given way to gentle sunshine and invigorating fresh air. Dandelion clock clouds were driven by a cool north-westerly breeze across a clear blue sky.

Edwin walked fast hoping that brisk exercise would dissolve the tension making his heart race and his hands shake. He was oblivious to the sights and sounds of an almost completed harvest, the honeysuckle and fat blackberries entangled in the hedge-rows, the branches of elder bowed under the weight of glossy black clusters the size of tea plates. While he walked he prayed for guidance and help in alleviating her distress. Then he prayed for the strength to resist his own yearning.

As he approached the house along the avenue of lime trees he saw her on the portico that sheltered the front door behind massive columns rising to roof height. She was dressed and lying on a tartan blanket that covered the slats of a folding wooden chair. Propped up on cushions, her head tipped to one side, she appeared to be asleep. But as his shoes crunched on the gravel he saw her look up. Her hands flew to her mouth.

His heartbeat was loud in his ears, painful against his ribs. He kept walking. Pleasure at seeing her again made him smile. As he reached the steps she sat up. She was visibly thinner and her cheeks were wet with tears. She fumbled for a handkerchief. Finding a square of lace-edged cambric she pressed it to her face as she struggled for control.

Watching her try to swallow sobs as her shoulders heaved he sensed her isolation, her belief that what she had done disgusted him. He couldn't allow her to think that was why he'd stayed away.

'I wanted to come sooner.'

At his words her gaze flicked up to meet his. In her tear-washed eyes he read hope and a desperate wish to believe him. He felt his resolve slipping.

'Your uncle – Dr Ainsley – came to see me five days ago. He told me what had happened. I wanted to come immediately, but he asked me not to. In fact he forbade me. He said you needed complete rest.'

She watched him, still silent.

Fighting the overwhelming urge to take her in his arms and hold her close he glanced around, looking for another seat. But the porch was empty. To remain standing would be intimidating and convince her he was poised to leave at any moment. Her chair, made of teak, was sturdy and wide.

'May I?' he smiled, indicating the area near her feet. 'That is if you feel up to having company for a while?'

Shyly she moved her legs to one side and he perched on the lower corner of the chair, resting his weight on one hand.

'I thought...' Her voice sounded strained and husky, as if speech was an enormous effort. 'I didn't want– I was hoping–' Words tumbled incoherently as she fretted with the damp crushed cambric. His heart was wrenched by her effort to smile. 'Would you like some lemonade? Or tea? I can ring.'

'No, please don't.'

Her gaze slid away. 'They think I'm mad.'

'Do you think you're mad?'

She sank back against the cushions. 'I think I was. For a while. You see I'd found out, and I couldn't tell anyone.' Her breath caught on a sob. 'But what I did was so wicked. Those flowers – it wasn't their fault. I can't believe I–' She covered her trembling mouth with her fingers, her eyes huge and haunted.

Pulling a clean handkerchief from his pocket he shook the folds from the crisply ironed cotton and pressed it gently into her fingers.

''nk you,' she mumbled, wiping her eyes and nose again. Then she shuddered violently. 'My head *aches* with all... I can't stop thinking. I didn't want to believe – but I know it's true.' She looked up at him, beseeching. 'I don't know what to do.'

'Talk to me,' he coaxed quietly. 'There's no one here but us. As a minister I am bound never to reveal a confidence. As a friend I give you my solemn oath that I will never, as long as I live, repeat anything you tell me.'

Her eyes filled again and he sensed the battle raging inside her. He leaned forward, linking his fingers, elbows propped on his parted knees.

'Trust me, Grace. Please. I want to help.'

Her face crumpled like a child's. As she covered it with the handkerchief, her body shaking with sobs she was trying valiantly to suppress, he gripped his clasped hands painfully tight to stop himself reaching for her.

She took a deep jerky breath. 'I never liked it – the chain garden.' Her voice was almost a whisper. Leaning forward so as not to miss anything he caught a faint waft of her fragrant soap. He flinched, tried to disguise it with an encouraging nod, and looked down at his hands, swallowing hard. *God help him.*

'Could you tell me why?'

She shrugged helplessly. 'It was just a feeling. Then I bought a book at one of the chapel sales. I didn't realize– If I'd known–' She rubbed her forehead. 'I'm sorry, I'm not making much sense, am I?'

'It's all right,' he said gently. 'Take as long as you need.'

Slowly she began to explain about her mother's planting schemes, about the flowers and their meanings, her mother, her father, Mary, Dorcas, and Hal. Now the dam of silence had been breached words poured from her in a torrent.

As he listened Edwin struggled with

complex emotions, the strongest of which was compassion. Who knew better than he that under intense emotional stress people did things or behaved in ways of which they would not have believed themselves capable. *Not me, I would never... I'm not that kind of person.* But everyone was, given the right circumstances.

Eventually the flood slowed to a trickle then stopped. Grace lay with her eyes closed. Her confession had taken a visible toll. But it had also freed her from quivering tension. Though she was pale and looked exhausted she seemed calmer.

He didn't rush into speech. He sat quietly thinking about what she had said, allowing her time to recover. After a few minutes she opened her eyes, watching him, waiting and growing anxious.

'It seems to me,' he said, 'that the chain garden may have been your mother's way of dealing with a situation she could not fight and over which she had no power. When she died everyone's life changed. Yours most of all. It was right for you to cut the ties that bound you to the past. Especially if they were not of your choosing. Though you were driven by impulse, I think what you did took great courage.'

Grace stared at him, her eyes wide with shock. He could see the effort it was costing her to adjust. Because she would have been

341

expecting censure, disapproval, and condemnation. *Even from him.*

'Courage?' She tested the word but could not accept it. 'Oh no.' Her head moved against the dark-green velvet cushion. 'I wasn't brave; I was angry. I've never – such *rage*. It was terrifying.'

Edwin nodded. 'Perhaps your mother had similar feelings and used the chain garden to express her anger and pain. But in doing so she also created something that was superficially very beautiful.'

Grace's eyes filled again. 'I destroyed it.'

'I said superficially,' he reminded her gently. 'What you destroyed were reflections of unhappiness. No one else in the family would have dared suggest changing the chain garden. It was too closely associated with your mother. But now it's like – like a blank canvas. The beds can be planted with' – he spread his hands – 'what about pink roses? They will fill the garden with beauty and perfume. And *their* only significance is love.'

It was only when he saw soft colour creep into her pale cheeks that he realized the deeper, more personal implication of what he had said. Glimpsing sudden leaping hope in her eyes he looked down at his hands. He had to tell her. If he did it could mean the end. She might never want to see or speak to him again. But she had trusted him and bared her soul. Integrity demanded he return that trust. He loved her. Instinct and her reaction told him that she felt the same about him. He wanted to marry her, have children with her and spend the rest of his life with her.

But he could not propose, not until she knew the full truth. Only then would she be in a position to decide whether she could commit her life and future into his care. He had to tell her.

Something of his agony must have shown in his face. For when he looked up she caught her breath.

'What is it? What's wrong?'

He gripped his hands more tightly, deliberately digging his thumbnails into his palms. 'Grace, we've talked about what you did, about your reasons, and how guilty you felt afterwards. I hope I've helped you to see it differently now?'

She nodded. 'Yes.'

His mouth was so dry he had to swallow before he could speak. 'I must tell you that I have a stain on my soul far greater than any you could aspire to, or even imagine.'

Then without once allowing his gaze to drop from hers he described the nightmare events that had resulted in his departure from India.

As he talked her expression vividly reflected her horror at Lewis's betrayal of all that the mission stood for, and her grief for Akhil's suffering. When at last he stopped, her mouth was trembling. Leaning forward she laid a tentative hand over his white knuckles.

'What Mr Preston did was a terrible, *terrible* thing. All the worse because he was in a position of trust. I'm sure there must be a special place in Hell for people who harm children.'

Edwin steeled himself. 'The thing is... Grace, I will never know for certain if Lewis's death was truly an accident.'

Bewilderment deepened her frown. 'I don't understand. I thought – didn't you say Mr Preston grabbed the dagger? That you were fighting him off when ... when he ... was stabbed?'

Nodding, Edwin moistened his lips. 'Yes. But for an instant, in my heart, I *wanted* to kill him. I didn't think he deserved to live after the dreadful damage he had done, to Akhil, and all the other children I never knew about. As a minister of God I preach forgiveness and redemption. Yet I wanted to take the life of another human being.'

Seeing that she didn't know how to respond he stood up. 'I'll leave you now. You must be very tired.' The sound of hoofs made him look over his shoulder. 'You have another visitor. I think it's the doctor.'

John Ainsley had dismounted and was

walking briskly towards the steps.

'Thank you.' Grace spoke quickly in a low tone. 'For everything.'

Teeth clenched, Edwin nodded. He wished they had longer. But he knew she would need days rather than hours to absorb fully what he had told her and all its implications.

'Good afternoon to you both.' John Ainsley's smile held relief as his gaze slid past Edwin to Grace. 'How are you feeling, my dear?'

Watching Grace's wan face, Edwin's emotions were in turmoil. *He shouldn't have told her. She had been through enough. Yet having asked for and been given her total trust, how could he have remained silent? But now she knew, what would happen?* Her tear-swollen gaze caught his, the contact too brief for him to read. Then she looked at her uncle and tried to smile.

'Better, thank you.'

As Edwin turned to leave, John patted his arm and murmured, 'Well done.'

Edwin nodded grimly and walked away. She needed time: time to recover and time to think. All he could do was wait. Purgatory could not be worse than this.

Bryce turned so that the lowering sun was at his back and raised his camera. Beyond the moored schooners and brigs, quay punts and fishing boats, two six-oar gigs knifed through the dancing water, their muscular crews practising tactics. Treworthal regatta, the last of the season, would take place the following week, and competition between the boats was fierce.

Golden light and lengthening shadows warned him he was unlikely to get optimum results from his new purchase. But he didn't want to leave the quay just yet. There was a camera club meeting at the Polytechnic Gallery. He wouldn't attend.

He had tried to picture himself turning up as usual. But when he thought about the effort of pretending everything was fine, that he hadn't a care in the world, he knew he couldn't do it. Though half the members had no idea about what had happened, the others – those who knew only too well – would be watching him. He had not breathed a word. Surely they realized that he wouldn't? He could only expose them by admitting his own involvement. The repercussions for his family were too appalling for him even to consider such a move.

But nor had he been able to face staying at home. Though Grace was showing signs of recovery she was vague and self-absorbed, not hearing when spoken to, going off for short walks by herself. He had asked if anything was bothering her, hoping for a chance to re-establish their former closeness. But she had shaken her head, claiming she was still tired. He couldn't blame her for not wanting to talk to him. In recent weeks when she had tried, he had almost bitten her head off. Now he wanted to build bridges and needed a confidante he could trust, she was preoccupied.

Granny Hester seemed to be in a permanent state of nervous collapse. But at least she was keeping to her room so they were spared her constant carping and self-pity.

As for his father, though bereavement and problems at the mine offered some excuse, his unpredictable swings from jocular to irascible made him difficult company. Not that he was around much. The business trips he was making almost daily demanded an early start whether he was travelling by train, on horseback, or in his light carriage. He rarely returned before dark.

For Bryce his father's absence was a relief. Often there were only Richard, Grace and himself at dinner. Conversation was usually about their work at Polwellan. When Grace asked where they had first found a particular species of rhododendron Richard would tell her stories about the people they had met in the borderlands and Tibet. These tales provoked agony and delight as Bryce thought of Tarun and dared not trust his voice.

The soft breeze ruffling his hair carried the scents of tarred rope and fish, coal-dust, smoke and seaweed, wet wood and frying onions. In Calcutta those familiar smells had been laced with exotic spices, incense and cow dung. Hot, humid, colourful, noisy, dirty Calcutta.

Shutting off memory before it could overwhelm him, he lowered the camera. Winding on the film he pressed the button to retract the bellows, raised the front plate that would protect the lens and snapped it shut. In the shop he had looked at a Sanderson folding camera that had offered a symmetrical lens and three double slides. But this Thornton Pickard used daylight-loading spool film. The moment he picked it up it had felt right in his hands. The fact that it had been four shillings cheaper was an additional bonus. But had it been the more expensive he would still have bought it.

The setting sun turned the water to liquid bronze and flamed windows of the houses lining the waterfront across the river at Flushing. Then it sank behind the hill. He remained where he was watching the light change and the clouds turn from pink and gold to lilac and purple.

The sky grew pale then began to darken as dusk crept across the water. Warm day had given way to cool evening. Turning from a view of which he never tired, Bryce walked along the quay and up the slope to the street that ran parallel to the wharfs fronting the river. He looked at his watch then back along the street. Had tempers cooled? Should he wait and offer to buy Marcus a drink?

It was beginning to get dark and he had a four-mile ride home. He set off along the street. He should have started back after buying the camera. Why had he stayed? There was nothing for him here. But he wasn't comfortable at home either. He didn't belong anywhere any more.

Most of the shops had closed but the street was still busy. The lamp-lighter and his boy were lighting the gas lamps. Seamen from ships moored in the harbour or docked for repairs strolled in pairs and groups looking for a favourite inn or ale house. Whores with painted smiles, hennaed hair and low-cut dresses beckoned from shadowed doorways.

The light was almost gone, shut out by tall buildings on both sides of the road. As he approached the steeply sloping side street that offered a shortcut up to the livery stable, Bryce saw, but took little notice of, the two men and a small boy coming towards him. The men were talking in low voices and laughing.

'Hey, Da! That's 'im. That's the man.'

Bryce glanced up at the boy's excited

349

shout. His breath caught and his stomach clenched as he recognized the angelic-looking child from the camera club. The boy Marcus had called Albie.

Should he keep walking? Turn back?

The men didn't pause. They moved in close, one either side. Gripping his arms just above the elbow they hustled him into the side street. It had taken no more than seconds. In the glow from the gas lamp by the entrance, Bryce saw the cobbled gutters were shiny wet and smeared with filth. The sour stench caught in his throat.

'You wait by the lamp,' Albie's father growled at the boy. Skipping past Bryce, Albie stuck out his tongue.

'Wait,' Bryce began then his breath exploded in a grunt as Albie's father punched him just below the breastbone. He doubled over, winded and wheezing as the men dragged him up the alley deeper into the shadows.

'You broke the rules,' Albie's father hissed. The other man punched him low on the right side of his back.

Bryce staggered, gasping as pain knifed through him. The camera flew from his hand and bounced on the cobbles. 'No–'

'We don't like troublemakers.' Another vicious punch sent Bryce crashing to the ground, every nerve end screaming. He hunched forward, arms across his stomach, bringing his knees up to protect himself. A boot made vicious contact with his shoulder and agony radiated outward. Through red-hot waves of pain Bryce heard scampering feet then Albie's urgent whisper.

'Da, someone's coming.'

He tried to shout for help, but could only manage a hoarse groan. He heard a crunch as a heavy boot stamped on something. There was another crunch and a sharp crack. *His new camera.*

Warm beer-tainted breath against his face, a grating voice warning, 'Keep your mouth shut or else,' then they were gone.

He tried to summon the energy to shout. He ought to move. But the effort was beyond him. He felt horribly sick and his insides quivered like jelly. The side of his head was throbbing. Lifting a bruised aching arm he touched it carefully and felt sticky warmth. The bleeding worried him less than the sharp stabbing in his ribs each time he breathed. The beating had been brutal and merciless. What if they had not been interrupted? *Would they have killed him?*

Footsteps approached, stopped. Bryce felt supporting hands under his arms. 'I thought it might be you.'

He squinted up at the shadowy figure. 'Marcus? What–?'

'Come on, up you get.'

The ground rose and fell, his head

throbbed and spun, blackness threatened and his legs shook as Marcus helped him to his unsteady feet.

'How–'

'I followed you along the street. I thought about trying to catch you up, maybe suggest a drink, but you disappeared. Then I saw Albie hanging about on the corner. His father and uncle never let him out by himself: he's far too valuable. He didn't look at all happy to see me. So when he took off I followed.'

Bryce clung to Marcus's arm, swaying, his head bent. 'He said I'd broken the rules, but I haven't talked.'

'Someone has. I hear the law has been asking questions. I'm not surprised.' Marcus snorted. 'The man's a fool. I warned him. The money he demands for the use of those boys is sheer extortion. Sooner or later someone was bound to want him taken down a peg.'

Wincing and moving with great care Bryce straightened up. 'Will he stop now?'

'What an innocent you are. Of course he won't. There's a vast amount of money involved here. Besides, it will never come to court. Quite apart from the fact that no one would be willing to give evidence, half the local judiciary would have to declare an interest.'

Bryce stopped gingerly flexing bruised

limbs to stare at him. 'You can't mean–'

'Can't I? You don't know the half of it.'

'No, and I don't want to.' Carefully bending down, Bryce picked his broken camera out of the gutter. *'Bastards!* I only bought it today. One of them stamped on it.'

'Which should tell you two things: that's what you can expect if you talk out of turn. And if they can afford to smash your camera rather than steal it to sell later they're not short of money. Come on, I'll take you back to my place, get you cleaned up. You could probably do with a drink.'

'Thanks, but I'd rather go home.'

'How are you going to get there?'

'My horse is at the livery stable.'

'You're mad. You'll never make it.'

'I'll be all right.' Though he was shivering with shock and ached all over, nothing would have induced Bryce to remain in town overnight.

'Well, if you're determined to go I won't try to stop you. But if you've any sense you'll hire a cab. You can tie your horse on behind.'

The cab driver wasn't keen. But when Marcus explained that Bryce had been injured trying to stop his camera being stolen, the driver had leaned forward, sniffed suspiciously, then agreed for double the normal fare.

During the ride home Bryce realized he

couldn't spend the rest of his life in constant fear of discovery, blackmail, betrayal or further beatings. Reaching the outskirts of the village he paid the remainder of the fare and unhitched his horse. Too stiff to climb into the saddle he led the animal down the hill over the bridge and into the shoeing shed beside the forge. Knotting the reins through the iron ring he left the horse and walked up through the moonlit street.

The glow through the glass at the top of the door told him it wasn't too late. He knocked. A few moments later he heard approaching footsteps. A bolt was drawn and a key turned. The door opened. They looked at one another.

Bryce swallowed. 'Sorry. I shouldn't have...' He began to turn away.

'Yes, you should.' Edwin pulled the door wider and stood back. 'I'm so glad you did. Come in.'

Chapter Twenty-one

Stepping hesitantly over the threshold, still not sure what he was doing there, Bryce's nerves tightened as he saw Flora Bowden hurrying down the stairs refastening the buttons on her cuffs.

'My dear life! Whatever have you done? Accident was it? Fall off your horse? Your clothes is in some mess. You got blood all down the side of your face.' She frowned and her breath hissed between her teeth. 'If you been fighting you got no business coming–'

'That will do, Miss Bowden,' Edwin interrupted. 'Please go on back to bed. Come with me, Mr Damerel. We need to clean up that cut on your forehead.'

''Tisn't your place to go doing things like that, Reverend!' Flora scolded. Bryce caught Edwin's eye and started to turn away as she continued with audible reluctance, 'I s'pose I could–'

'I wouldn't hear of it.' Again Edwin cut her short. 'Thank you for offering, Miss Bowden, but I'm perfectly capable. I dealt with far worse than this during my time in India. Besides, weren't you telling me earlier what

355

a busy day you've had and how tired you are?' Closing the door he turned the key. Then, lightly touching Bryce's arm, he gestured towards the far end of the tiled hall.

As Bryce followed, he heard Flora Bowden thump heavily up the stairs muttering, "Tis never right nor proper.' Annoyed that he had been invited in, she was clearly furious at being dismissed with her curiosity unsatisfied.

As they entered the big kitchen Edwin went at once to the range and stirred the embers into a blaze with fresh coal before pulling the big black kettle over the flames.

A few minutes later, Bryce was seated at the scrubbed kitchen table not sure he should be there but too weary to leave. He watched the minister make a pot of tea then pour the remainder of the hot water into a large basin to which he added several spoonfuls of salt.

'An excellent antiseptic,' Edwin explained. 'Don't move.' He left the kitchen, returning with two clean towels and a bottle of brandy. 'Being Methodist and a minister I'm teetotal. But I'd be foolish indeed to deny the medicinal powers of brandy.' After pouring the tea he added milk then liberally laced one of the cups before pushing it towards Bryce. 'Drink; it will do you good.'

Taking a mouthful of his own tea he began

tearing a piece of soft clean rag into strips. 'That's a nasty head wound.'

Bryce's trembling made the cup rattle against its saucer as he tried to pick it up. Gripping it in both hands he raised it to his lips inhaling the brandy fumes as he swallowed. It burned its way down spreading instant comforting warmth and soothing ragged nerves. He cleared his throat.

'It was just a stupid accident. But I didn't want the family to see me looking like this.' He bit back a wince as Edwin gently bathed the caked and crusted blood from his face. The water in the basin turned pink then red. He closed his eyes. Why had he said that? *Because he couldn't sit here indefinitely without speaking.* He waited for Edwin to ask why he hadn't simply ridden to his uncle's house? After all John Ainsley was a doctor. More importantly he lived at the lodge which was only a few hundred yards from Damerel House.

'Of course not.' Dropping the now crimson rag into the cooling water Edwin carefully dried around the wound. 'That's quite a swelling. It's not actually bleeding. But to keep it clean a bandage would–'

'No. No, I'll let the air get to it. It will heal more quickly.'

'And a bandage might excite unwelcome attention. I should have thought of that. Nor do I blame you for wanting to avoid such an event. Mrs Chenoweth would immediately assume you had deliberately acquired this injury for the express purpose of diverting attention away from her.'

Surprised, Bryce looked up and met Edwin's rueful grin.

'It is not always easy to be as charitable as one might wish.' Sitting down, Edwin picked up his cup. 'I'm truly glad you came. I've been hoping for an opportunity to apologize for my behaviour the last time we met. You were looking for help—'

'No—' Bryce began in automatic denial, but Edwin carried on as if he hadn't spoken.

'...but because I was tired I knew I wasn't at my best and wouldn't be able to give you the attention you needed.' His grimace was both wry and shame-faced. 'Only I didn't explain myself very well, did I?'

Bryce tried to shrug and gritted his teeth to stifle a groan as his ribs and shoulder protested. Sweat broke out on his forehead. Raising the cup once more he swallowed deeply.

'Are you bleeding anywhere else?'

Bryce shook his head.

'Anything broken?'

He pressed one hand to his ribs. 'Just bruises and strains I think.'

'Arnica ointment is good.'

Bryce gave a brief nod. 'Grace has got some.'

358

'How is she?'

'Better, I think. But very quiet. You know, thoughtful?'

Edwin reached for the pot. 'Another?'

'It's late. I should go.' But he didn't want to move. It was quiet here, and sanctuary of a sort.

'Have some more tea,' Edwin urged. Without waiting for an answer he filled both cups and added another dollop of brandy to Bryce's. Lifting his own cup he rested his elbows on the table and sipped.

The silence stretched. Within Bryce tension built, bubbling up like molten lava inside a volcano. Eventually it reached the surface.

'It wasn't an accident,' he murmured. Something shifted inside him as the admission triggered a wonderful sense of release. 'It was a beating.'

Edwin nodded and continued sipping his tea.

'Aren't you going to say anything?'

'Such as?'

'Well, I don't know. Ask why, for a start.'

'If you want me to know you'll tell me.'

Bryce swallowed. Bending his head he passed a hand over his face then rubbed the back of his neck. 'I – it's not ... easy.'

'Perhaps not. But will telling me be worse than what you've already suffered? What you are still suffering?'

Raising his head Bryce saw on the minister's features the same lines of strain his shaving mirror reflected back at him each morning. Meeting Edwin's gaze he glimpsed torment but there was no sense of identification. Edwin was troubled but he was *normal.* Not like him.

Slowly, painfully, he related the whole miserable story: his awareness of being *different,* an outsider; his loneliness and the embarrassing attempts at matchmaking by friends and family. He spoke briefly of Tarun. Shyness and remembered wonder made him stumble over disjointed phrases as he tried to describe recognition, attraction, gratitude, love. By the time he reached the events of earlier that evening the teapot was cold, his voice hoarse.

'I didn't *choose* to be like this,' he said bitterly. 'No one in his right mind would deliberately *choose* a life that would label him evil, perverted, a criminal. I swear I didn't know they were using children. When I saw – when I realized – I tried to stop them. The child was crying. I thought he was an innocent victim.' He gave a bitter laugh. 'He attacked me, accused me of interfering and causing trouble for him with his father. Tonight his father beat me for *breaking the rules.*'

'The child is a victim,' Edwin said quietly. 'Though he may never recognize it. Do you regret what you did? Trying to protect the boy?'

'No. How could I? I may be a misfit' – his mouth twisted bitterly – 'a pervert. But a child...' He shook his head flinching at the pain. 'That's wrong, wicked. No, I don't regret it. But I can't stay here.'

'In the village?'

'In Cornwall. I shall go back to India. Not just for the family's sake. Though obviously if I'm living abroad people here are far less likely to hear anything that might cause gossip or a scandal. When Richard gets married he won't want to travel any more. Someone will have to find new species to increase the Hawkins rhododendron collection. Who better than me?' He paused. 'But the real reason I'm going is because in India I was truly happy for the first time in my life.'

A smile flickered across Edwin's mouth. 'You were fortunate. Some people never achieve that.'

Bryce was deathly tired. His bruises were stiffening and he ached all over. Yet for the first time in months he felt a spark of anticipation, a glimmer of hope. He had made his decision and the relief was incredible. 'Thanks for listening. For not condemning me.'

'What right have I to condemn anyone?' Edwin glanced away his features tightening in a spasm of anguish. Bryce wondered if the minister was ill. He looked exhausted. But before he could enquire, Edwin straightened in his chair. 'Have you not heard the saying: do not judge a man until you have walked a mile in his shoes? When do you plan to tell your family? About returning to India, I mean?'

'As soon as possible.'

'And your injuries?'

Bryce shrugged, and winced. 'My horse shied, threw me off.'

They both stood up.

Edwin extended his hand. 'Good luck. I hope you find happiness.'

Bryce gripped the outstretched hand. 'Thanks. You too.' He hesitated, then blurted, 'Are you and Grace–' He stopped short as a spasm tightened Edwin's features. 'Sorry, none of my business.'

Reaching for the doorknob Edwin smiled with effort. 'I've known despair. I learned how to deal with it. But hope – hope is far more difficult.'

Wickram Pearce, the senior partner and grandson of the original founder of Pearce, Grylls and Curgenven, laid several documents on the broad oak desk. 'Please read each of them carefully, Mrs Renowden.' He hesitated.

Sensing concern, she glanced up at the portly, balding figure, formal in black coat,

362

pinstriped trousers and stiff collar. Behind his wire-rimmed spectacles his pale eyes held concern.

'You are quite sure?'

'Yes, Mr Pearce. I'm quite sure. I'm also very grateful to you for the speed and efficiency with which you have managed everything.' They both knew he'd had little choice. Without actually saying so she had made it abundantly clear that if he wasn't able – or willing – to do as she asked, and quickly, she would take her business elsewhere.

Dorcas had little interest in money for its own sake. Its use lay in what it could do. In this instance it had ensured completion within a few days of arrangements that under normal circumstances might have taken weeks. But these were not normal circumstances. Without money neither her plans, nor their achievement, would have been possible.

'It is always a pleasure to assist a valued client like yourself, Mrs Renowden. While you read through the papers I shall fetch two of my clerks.'

Dorcas focused on the neat copperplate. She glanced up as the two clerks attired in black suits and stiff collars entered the book-lined office.

Mr Pearce cleared his throat. 'Mrs Renowden, are you entirely satisfied that the documents accurately represent your wishes?'

'I am.'

'Then will you kindly append your signature to each one.' Uncapping his gold-nibbed pen he offered it to her.

She signed, then watched as each clerk added his name as a witness. When they had finished, retreating as silently as they had come, the attorney picked up the documents and scrutinized them to ensure the ink was dry.

She knew he did not understand or agree with what she had done. But it was her money, her decision. Though she would not see the effect, this act was reward enough.

A few minutes later she took her leave. Climbing into a cab she gave the driver directions.

Almost an hour later she alighted.

'Please wait for me. I won't be long.'

She crossed to the front door and dropped the polished brass knocker twice. A liveried manservant led her into a large room furnished with valuable antiques and pieces obviously kept for sentimental reasons. Though unusual the overall effect was comforting.

A few moments later Mary Prideaux entered, greeting her visitor with a smile that did not entirely hide her puzzlement.

'Good afternoon, Mrs Renowden. Please sit down. May I offer you some refreshment?'

'No, thank you. I won't keep you long.

There is something you should know. What you do with this information is up to you. You will not see me again.'

A few minutes later as her hostess sat stiff and blank-eyed on a faded sofa Dorcas quietly left the room. She had not come out of malice or jealousy. But after so many lies and so much deceit it was time for truth.

Back at the cottage she changed into old clothes and cleaned every room from top to bottom. As the evening approached she built a bonfire of her unsold canvases including her final disastrous effort. As they crackled and burned she threw into the leaping flames everything that might conceivably link her with Henry. Then she bathed. Tying a robe over her nightgown she made herself a cup of tea, lit the oil lamps, sat down at the table and wrote to Grace. After that she packed.

Soon after dawn the following morning, dressed in a travelling costume of holly-green skirt and jacket over a cream high-necked blouse, her hair piled up beneath a smart hat trimmed with pheasant feathers, Dorcas walked through the cottage, checking that everything was clean and tidy.

She opened the cottage door to the cab-driver's knock.

He glanced at the two suitcases standing side by side. 'That all?'

'Yes, that's all.' They had been Zander's.

She was glad she had kept them.

'Holiday, is it?'

'No. A longer journey.'

Shrugging, he carried the cases out. Dorcas locked the door and put the key under the flowerpot at one side of the path. The gate squealed as she closed it.

'Need a drop of oil on they hinges,' the driver said. Helping her in, he swung himself up on to the driving seat, picked up the reins and clicked his tongue. The horse broke into a brisk trot. The clop of hoofs and grinding rumble of wheels was loud in the sharp morning air.

Dorcas removed her spectacles and polished them with her handkerchief. She did not look back.

An hour later she was sitting in the stern of a small boat as it pulled across the river. She smelled the first hint of autumn in a cool breeze that carried the sweet pungency of wood smoke.

Swifts and swallows wheeled low over the water, feeding on insects to build up their stamina for the long flight back to the warmth of North Africa. When they returned next spring she would not be here to see them. She looked seaward. Though her vision was blurred, in her mind she could see with crystal clarity the view out into the estuary, the lighthouse on the headland and the open sea beyond. She had painted them countless times, in different seasons and at different times of day.

The shrieking gulls and the rhythmic creak and splash of the oars sounded loud. The weather was changing. Soon the wind would spring to life, ruffling the water then whipping it into choppy waves. Curtains of rain would hide a departing ship. When they parted and the sun came out once more the ship would be long gone. So would she.

For a while she had thought about giving up. Oblivion had seemed infinitely tempting after the loss of everything that had given her life shape and purpose. What had stopped her was Hal: her memories of him as a baby, a child, and a young man. What would it do to him if she were to kill herself? He would feel that it was his fault for taking a job so far away. He would be hurt and angry and suffused with guilt. How could she, who loved him so much, deliberately inflict such unwarranted punishment?

Gradually she had realized that though the life she had known was over, there could be another life. A door had two sides. One faced the past the other the future. She was losing her sight but there was nothing wrong with her other senses and she was in good physical health. Recent arrangements had substantially reduced her wealth, but she still had more than enough to take her in comfort wherever she wanted to go. At the moment she could manage alone. When a time came that she needed permanent assistance she would be able to afford it.

The decision to leave Cornwall had been a difficult one evoking mixed feelings. But if she wanted to see Hal and add to her treasured memories visual images of the man he had become, it was the only way. And wherever she went – starting with South America – the village, Cornwall and Zander would be with her in spirit. Perhaps in time when the wounds had healed, as all wounds eventually did, she would be able to remember happier times with Henry.

'I'm feeling a lot better, truly,' Grace said.

John Ainsley's expression was dubious. 'You're still pale. And I'd like to see a little more flesh on those bones. Are you eating properly?'

Grace groaned. 'I'm doing my best, Uncle John. Rose and Kate bully me unmercifully. I know how it must feel to be a goose being fattened up for Christmas.' She looked round as the morning-room door opened and Kate entered carrying a tray. A crisp white apron covered her black dress and a frilled white cap perched on her fair hair.

'Hot chocolate for you, Miss Grace. Coffee for the doctor.' She set the tray down on a side table.

Grace sighed. 'Kate, I didn't ask for

whipped cream. In fact–'

'Didn't you, miss?' Kate's face was open and innocent. 'Want me to take it back, do you? Rose said it would build you up a bit. She've been some worried. Still, if you don't want it...'

'No, that's all right. I wouldn't want to upset Rose.' Grace shot a meaningful look at her uncle, who turned to the maid with a smile.

'How's your grandfather, Kate?'

'Not too bad, thank you, Doctor. He said that there stuff you gave him taste so horrible it must be doing him good. He do feel a bit down sometimes. But I've told him I won't walk down the aisle without I got his arm to hold. Now the date is fixed and the hall booked for the reception, if he's going to keep to his bed he'll have to tell Ben hisself, 'cos I aren't going to.'

John Ainsley's brows rose towards his hairline. 'Will that threat work?'

Kate nodded briskly. 'It have so far. Ben's a lovely quiet man most of the time. But if this wedding have to be put off he's going to be awful mad. Granfer won't want that.'

Grace compressed her lips to hide a grin as she caught her uncle's eye.

'No, I shouldn't think he would.'

'I'm trying to get him to go down to the quay on Saturday. He haven't missed the regatta in sixty years. Ron who live next door

369

said if Granfer couldn't walk he'd push him down in the wheelbarrow.' She rolled her eyes. 'Hell to go there was. Begging your pardon, miss. Now, want anything else do you? Could you fancy a bit of saffron cake? Or–'

'No, Kate. Thank you.'

As the maid closed the door Grace picked up her hot chocolate.

'Why don't you go down to the regatta?' John suggested. 'It would do you good to get away from here for an hour or two.'

Grace's fingers tightened around the cup. Edwin would be there. But would he want to see her? He hadn't been back since – since they had each bared their souls. He had shown her such kindness, such sympathy. Had she done as much for him? She had tried. But after telling her of his shame for wanting, just for a moment, to kill Lewis Preston, he had left too quickly. Before she'd had time to take it in properly, much less frame a response. Did he regret telling her? Was that why he hadn't come back?

'Grace?' her uncle prompted.

'I'm not sure.'

'Will you at least think about it?'

'Yes.'

The door opened and Hester Chenoweth entered leaning heavily on Violet's supporting arm. 'There you are, John. I've been an hour waiting for you to come and see how I am.'

Noting the pinched and bitter line of her grandmother's mouth Grace steeled herself.

'Really, Grace,' Hester snapped. 'I'm surprised at you keeping John talking when you knew I wanted to see him.'

'I didn't–'

'No, now I think about it I'm not surprised at all. You're getting some very mistaken ideas about your own importance. Putting everyone to so much trouble.' Saliva gathered at the corners of her mouth. Her eyes were narrowed, her tone venomous. 'In case you've forgotten, Louise was my daughter. You have no idea what I've been through.'

'Granny, I–'

'It's all right, Grace.' Setting his cup down and rising to his feet in one smooth movement John put his hand under his mother-in-law's elbow. 'Come along, ma'am. Let's go back upstairs where we can chat without any interruptions. How did you sleep last night? Are those drops I prescribed helping at all?'

As her grandmother's complaining tone and her uncle's soothing responses faded, Grace took deep breaths to try and slow her racing heart. Her grandmother's attacks still unnerved her. She turned to the maid.

'She's finding it very difficult.'

'She isn't the only one.' Violet folded her hands under her bosom. 'With respect, miss,

371

I can't take no more. I never heard nothing like it in all my born days.'

Grace tried to catch up. 'I'm sorry, Violet, what?'

'Her spite, miss. That's what it is, plain spite. I know she's grieving, but so's all of us. 'Tis never right she should be saying such things to you. Or that I should be hearing them. Over twenty years I been here, Miss Grace. Your mother was a dear soul, always grateful for anything we done for her. I do miss her awful. You know I aren't one to complain, Miss Grace, but–'

'I know you aren't, Violet.' Jumping up from her seat, Grace seized the maid's workworn hands. 'You've been strong and brave and – and absolutely marvellous. I'll ask my uncle to speak to granny. She may not realize–'

Violet snorted. 'She realize all right.'

'Yes, well,' Grace admitted. 'I'd try talking to her myself but' – she grimaced – 'I don't think it would do any good. She'll listen to him because he's a man as well as being her physician. Please, Violet, give me a chance to speak to him.'

'All right, Miss Grace. If that's what you want. But I got to tell you, if she don't stop her carrying on, then I'm going.'

Chapter Twenty-two

Rain drummed on the glass roof of the greenhouse and trickled like tears down the panes. Standing in front of a deep bench that held trays of propagated cuttings he was supposed to be examining for any sign of disease or infestation, Bryce stared out through the rain-streaked glass. He gazed blindly past the rows of cold frames to the elms and beeches thrashing the tips of their leafy branches in the wind.

In the past two days the sharp pain in his ribs and shoulder had dulled to an ache, a scab had formed over the cut on his head, and though large areas of his skin were purple and crimson the bruises were hidden beneath his clothes. His claim that his horse had shied and thrown him had been accepted. Though he had brushed aside Grace's sympathy he appreciated her concern.

He hated lying to her. But that was preferable to burdening her with information she was bound to find deeply upsetting. If he were honest, he could not bear the thought of watching as she tried to hide shock and disgust. He loved her and had felt closer to her than their mother. He was leaving anyway and wanted her memories of him to remain untarnished.

The first twenty-four hours had been the worst as shock and his body's physical response to the beating took their toll in sweats, bouts of trembling and an overall feeling of sick weakness. But now, provided he was careful, he could move without wincing.

Last night after everyone had gone to bed and the house was silent he had written to Tarun.

The greenhouse door opened and Richard burst in, turning to shake the rain off his umbrella before shutting the door.

'Percy wants me to give him a hand digging out the first of the specimen trees for Kew.'

'Rich, it's bucketing down.'

'I know, but at least the rain will have given the tree a good soaking as well as loosening the earth around the roots. Besides, Percy is sure the sky is lightening and the rain will have stopped within half an hour.' Richard's shrug and grin signalled long familiarity with the head gardener's reading of weather signs. 'Anyway I just stopped by to let you know where I'll be. And to see if you were all right.'

'I'm fine.'

'You look like a corpse.'

'Thanks.'

'Look, why don't you leave that. It can wait. Go back home and soak your bruises in a hot bath. Let Grace fuss over you a bit.'

'I might in a minute. Rich' – he might as well get it over with – 'this probably isn't the best time or even the best place – though perhaps it is in a way. The thing is I've decided to go back to India.'

Richard stared at him. 'Oh.'

Bryce wiped his hands on the brown workman's apron covering his waistcoat, shirt and trousers. 'That's it? Just *oh?*'

'No, of course it isn't. But you caught me on the hop. Why?'

'Why am I going? Because all this' – Bryce indicated the seedlings – 'and that' – he pointed to the cold frames – 'it's you, Rich. You're happy here. I'm not. I don't feel I belong here any more. It's– I want to go back to... I want to go back.'

Reactions crossed Richard's face like cloud shadows on a breezy day. Eventually he spoke. 'I'll miss you.'

Bryce aimed for the mockery that characterized their relationship and masked the deep bond between them.

'Of course you won't. You're going to marry Sophie and raise a family. Colonel Hawkins will be grooming you to take over the nursery. And with Percy talking about retirement you'll be far too busy to miss me.'

375

The silence stretched. Then Richard asked the question Bryce had guessed would come. 'Will you be contacting Tarun? You and he made a good team.'

Trying to decide how best to answer had kept him awake for much of the night. 'I've written to him. I hope he'll join me.' Bryce was proud that his voice remained rock-steady. 'I shall go anyway.'

Richard nodded. 'I will miss you. But I can see you have to go. You've not been yourself since we got on the boat at Calcutta.'

'I miss the mountains, Rich. There's so much contrast. Jungle in the river valleys, densely forested slopes, and wild windswept plateaux and peaks. The sky is bigger and the air is so clear. It's wild and dangerous and beautiful and ... and I can breathe there.'

Richard grinned. 'My brother, the adventurer.' Taking a couple of quick steps forward he hugged his brother. 'Look after yourself, all right?'

Bryce caught his breath and immediately Richard tried to draw back.

'Sorry, sorry, I forgot.'

'It's all right. It doesn't matter.' Bryce held him close, blinded by tears.

Richard lightly patted his brother's broad back. 'Five years should get the wanderlust out of your system. Then you'll be desperate to come home, settle down, and live a quiet life like me.'

'You could be right,' Bryce croaked, playing the game. When he boarded the train he would be making a one-way journey. He would not see his twin, or Cornwall, again.

At the sound of hoofs on the drive Grace leapt up from the velvet-covered stool in front of her dressing-table and hurried to the window. Looking out across the lawn to the wooded skyline she waited for her heartbeat to return to normal. This was foolish. Who else but the postman would call at 8.45 in the morning?

The previous day's rain had washed dust from trees and shrubs so that the colours had a jewel-like depth and brilliance: emerald grass, sapphire sky.

She watched the postman ride away. Then came the distant thud of the front door closing and a moment later her brothers appeared at the bottom of the porch steps, talking together as they walked briskly along the drive towards the stables, bound for Polwellan.

Her thoughts returned to the problem that for days had occupied her every waking moment and denied her sleep. She understood Edwin's reasons for telling her the circumstances that had brought him back to Cornwall. But what had compelled him to confess his brief urge to kill Lewis Preston? That was not something she could ever have discovered by accident. Had his intention been to drive her away?

A memory of his face filled her vision as clearly as if he were standing before her. She heard the torment in his voice, the anguish as he laid bare his shame sparing himself nothing. She recalled the tension cording his neck, the rigidity in his shoulders. She remembered the look in his eyes.

Grace covered her mouth with quivering fingers. What courage it must have taken. For if she rejected him he could not hide. Inevitably their paths would cross: in the village, in school, or at chapel. Each time they met they would both remember his confession and his shame.

Suddenly she realized. He had told her because he knew from her experience and his own how dangerous secrets were. Sooner or later they seeped out, stealing beneath the surface of relationships to erode trust and spread suspicion.

He could not have missed her enormous relief after confiding her shock and confusion about the chain garden; the reality of her parents' relationship, Dorcas's revelations and the discovery that Hal was her half-brother. Had he felt that same sense of release after confiding in her? She hoped so. But he had hurried away so quickly she couldn't be sure.

Hearing the man she knew as gentle and

compassionate admitting a violent urge to destroy another human being had shocked her. This shock had deepened as, looking into her own heart, painful honesty forced her to recognize fragments of similar feelings.

This realization inspired aching sympathy for Edwin. He had admired Lewis Preston: believed him a trusted friend. The little boy had already suffered so dreadfully in his short life. To be abused and terrorized by someone supposedly caring for him, someone he could not escape, unable to speak so unable to tell. Grace's eyes burned and she caught her lower lip between her teeth. What if she had made such a discovery? How would she have reacted? *Exactly as Edwin did.*

Resting her forehead against the folds of the curtain she felt the hard window frame beneath. More than anything else she wanted to be Edwin's wife. To share his life, support him in his work and, if it pleased God, to bear his children. Did she want this in spite of, or because of, his confession? She wasn't sure.

Uncertain of how she would react or what she would decide, he had told her because he believed she should know. He had trusted her to honour his confidence, as he would honour hers. What happened next was up to her.

Did Edwin want to marry her, but felt

unable to ask until she knew the worst and had time to discover her true feelings?

Her heart fluttered, making her catch her breath. She turned from the window. Today she would go to the folly and collect up all her mother's gardening books. It was time to let go of the past.

As she started down the stairs it occurred to her that she hadn't seen Mary for several days. But there was probably a lot for Mary to catch up on at home besides preparing for her wedding.

Grace's steps faltered. Did Mary know about Dorcas? If she did then presumably she had accepted the situation. But what if she didn't know? Should she be told? *By whom?* Perhaps her father considered his past actions were not Mary's business.

But by that standard she need not have told Edwin what had driven her to destroy the chain garden. And Edwin need not have confessed his desire to kill Lewis Preston. Yet in doing so each had shown that their trust in each other was deeper and of far greater significance than their relationships with other people.

Grace was utterly still as she recognized what her train of thought had revealed. *She and Edwin trusted each other more than they trusted anyone else.* But the decision to confide had been hers and Edwin's. No one could impose such action on others. Her father's relationship with Mary was their private business. She had no right to interfere.

Swallowing the last mouthful of scrambled egg and bacon Henry set down his knife and fork, pushed aside his plate, and reached for his cup. The coffee was strong, steaming and richly fragrant, exactly the way he liked it. He sighed, infused with a sense of well-being and scooped up his mail from the proffered salver with a grunt of thanks. Patrick laid the two remaining letters beside Grace's plate then withdrew.

As Henry glanced through the envelopes one caught his attention. Slitting it open he extracted the thick sheet, picked up his cup, and settled back to read.

His violent start slopped coffee over his hand and on to the polished table. He clattered the bone-china cup clumsily on to its saucer, scalded fingers clutching his napkin as he stared at the copperplate script. His heartbeat thudded loudly in his ears. His skin tingled. Shock drained the blood from his face and everything went black. He gasped, shaking his head to clear it.

His gaze flew back to the top of the page and he read the short paragraphs again, shock eclipsed by galvanizing terror. Hurling his napkin on to the table he hurried from the room, the letter crushed in his fist.

'Patrick!'

The butler appeared in the doorway leading to the servants' quarters and kitchen. 'Sir?'

'My horse, at once.'

'Not the gig, Sir?'

Henry tried to think. Which was more important this morning? Speed, or maintaining the façade of wealth and success? Speed won. 'No. My horse. Immediately.'

With a brief nod, Patrick vanished again.

'Good morning, Papa.'

Glancing up Henry saw Grace's smile fade.

'Is everything–'

'Not now.' Cutting her short he strode towards the front door, stuffing the letter into his jacket pocket as Patrick hurried forward with his hat.

He took every possible shortcut through the back lanes. The forced pace thoroughly unsettled his normally placid mount. Soon Henry's wrists and shoulders ached from trying to control the tossing head as the cob fought the metal bit.

Where there was no alternative to the main roads, common sense forced him down to a steady trot on stretches busy with other traffic. The last thing he wanted was to excite gossip. But even as it occurred, the thought provoked a harsh, desperate laugh. For if the letter were not the result of some foolish misunderstanding, the gossips would soon be feasting like carrion crows on the corpse of his life's work.

Sweating as much from fear as from exertion he was racked by convulsive shivers. He would not accept that. It *must* be a mistake. It had to be. He couldn't even consider the alternative.

As the door opened he held his breath, only releasing it as the manservant took a step back inviting him to enter. So intense was his relief that nausea rose in his throat and he had to swallow repeatedly. His legs felt weak and shaky. He removed his hat with trembling fingers.

He would find out what had happened and ensure that the person responsible received a reprimand of such severity it would never, ever be forgotten.

He was shown into the drawing-room. The manservant withdrew without offering to take his hat. Henry barely noticed this omission. Too tense and anxious to relax he remained standing. Vases of roses and sweet peas scented the air. Polished wood gleamed, rugs and carpet had been freshly brushed.

The room looked exactly as it had on his last visit. He knew Mary to be methodical and organized but he would have expected some small sign of disruption as she set aside the items she would be bringing with her to Damerel House.

The door opened, jerking him from that

train of thought and back to his reason for coming.

As Mary closed the door and turned towards him, neat and elegant in dove-grey, he started forward. But she lifted her hand to stop him. There was no smile of greeting. Her face was alabaster pale except for her eyes. These were pink-rimmed and slightly swollen.

'I know why you're here, Henry,' she said, before he could speak. 'If you need confirmation from my own lips, then yes, it's true.' Her gaze flicked to the crumpled letter he had extracted from his pocket. 'I have instructed Mr Bartlett not to proceed with the transfer. I will not fund you. Nor will I marry you. Please don't insult my intelligence any further by asking why.'

'Mary, listen, I don't know what's happened, but whatever it is we can–'

'I'll tell you what happened, shall I, Henry? Three days ago I received a visit from a close – no, let us not be coy – an *intimate* friend of yours, Mrs Dorcas Renowden. Need I go on?'

This wasn't happening. Henry knew he should stay calm, defuse the situation with cool detachment. But his voice emerged ragged with fear and desperation. 'Please, I can explain–'

She continued as if he had not spoken. 'The day you proposed to me, Henry, I told you that all I asked of you was honesty. Do you remember?'

Stunned, he stared at her. *He could hear her saying it.* But he thought she had meant honesty about his financial troubles. It had never occurred to him – in any case it hadn't seemed important, not in the greater scheme of things, not with so much else to consider and plan and arrange. He hadn't given it another thought. 'Yes, I remember.' He did now. 'But, Mary, I haven't *lied* to you.' The look in her eyes made him shrivel inside. Suddenly anger surged through him. She had no right to do this.

'Not only did you omit even to mention your long-standing relationship with Mrs Renowden, it appears you intended to continue that relationship after we were married.' She shook her head slowly. 'You really believed you could get away with it. I find such monstrous arrogance almost impossible to comprehend.'

Guilt fuelled his rage against her. 'You were getting what you wanted, weren't you? It was a fair bargain.'

'It was. But you broke the agreement, Henry.' A spasm tightened her face, and she raised one hand, pressing her fingers to her forehead. It was the first crack in the facade, the first sign of weakness she had shown. Though she immediately regained control and lifted her chin he felt a rush of hope.

'Mary, please, I'll never see Dorcas again. I give you my solemn promise.'

'You are willing to abandon the woman who bore your first son and was loyal to you for thirty years? The woman who clearly believed that after your wife died you would propose marriage to her?'

Too anxious, too reckless, he clutched at the perceived straw. 'Yes, yes. Whatever you want.' Immediately he realized he'd made a terrible mistake. Her expression made him feel small and ashamed. He hated her for that.

'Do as you choose, Henry. It is no longer any concern of mine.'

This wasn't the way it was supposed to be. Fear welled up again. It dried his throat and filled his mouth with the hot taste of tin. 'Maybe you would prefer not to be reminded, but *you* were the one who wanted this marriage.'

A painful flush stained her face as she recognized in his tone the implication that she had blackmailed him. The colour drained away almost at once, leaving her ashen. She had aged visibly since their last meeting. Yet as she met his challenging gaze her back was straight, her dignity impregnable. 'True. But that was when I trusted you and considered you a friend.' She crossed the room and tugged the bell cord beside the fireplace.

He started towards her. 'Mary, please, I

shouldn't have said– I've done so many things wrong. I know I have. But you cannot imagine the strain.'

Neatly avoiding him she returned to the door. 'We have nothing further to say to each other.'

He rubbed sweating palms together. *She didn't mean it.* 'No, not now. You're upset. I can understand that. But in a week or so, when you've had time–'

'Not ever. I'm going away for a while.'

'How long?'

'Indefinitely.' The door opened. She inclined her head with the perfectly judged politeness her breeding demanded, now and forever a stranger. 'Goodbye, Henry.' She turned to the manservant who stood waiting. 'Mr Damerel is leaving.'

Henry watched, helpless, as she walked out of his life.

Grace's breakfast grew cold as she read then reread the two letters. By chance she opened Mary's first. Brief, formal, it stated that she would not now be marrying Grace's father and would be away from home for the foreseeable future. The hurt embodied in those few lines was almost palpable. Even as Grace wondered why, the answer came instant and appalling: Dorcas.

Sadness welled up as she recalled Mary's pleasure, the glow of happiness that had

387

brought colour to her cheeks, brightened her eyes and imbued her manner with new warmth. Grace had ignored Granny Hester's spiteful warnings, sensing that Mary's transformation had nothing whatever to do with arrogance or a desire to take over the household. Despite her undoubted intelligence, charm and kind nature Mary had needed a proposal of marriage to validate her as a woman.

The second letter was from Dorcas and hoped Grace would understand why she had told Mary. She wished Grace richly deserved happiness, and ended by saying that by the time the letter was delivered she would have left the village for good.

Grace turned towards the window without seeing the blue sky. Despite confusion and unease about Dorcas's relationship with her father she had liked Dorcas as a person: finding her company both relaxing and stimulating. She had always left the cottage feeling better than when she arrived. Did that make her disloyal to her mother? She rubbed her forehead. Relationships were more complicated and emotionally confusing than she had ever imagined.

The dining-room door opened and Kate came in with a tray.

'All right if I clear away, miss?'

'Yes. Yes, of course.'

'Lovely day for it,' Kate beamed.

'What?' Grace looked blank.

'The regatta. Going are you, miss?'

'I hadn't– I'm not quite...'

Rising from the table Grace picked up her letters, her thoughts racing. Her parents had regularly attended chapel while hiding secrets that eventually poisoned both their lives. Richard was blissfully happy with Sophie and had quickly settled back into work at Polwellan. But Bryce had changed during his years away. Returning with eyes full of shadows he had retreated behind an impenetrable wall. Only in the last few days since his announcement that he was returning to India had his air of strain begun to dissolve.

Then there was Zoe. Beautiful, talented, fêted and admired, yet restless and dissatisfied. What of herself: striving to win approval by fulfilling other people's wishes but lonely and unhappy with her enforced role.

She thought about what might have happened if Lewis's activities had not been discovered, if he had not died. Edwin would still be in India. She would not have met the first man she had ever loved. A man she admired above all others for his courage and honesty. A man who had confessed to her his darkest secret, had laid his heart at her feet. All her self-doubt suddenly evaporated. If Edwin loved her she must be worth loving. *And Edwin loved her.*

'Yes, I'm going.' She felt warm and quivery with excitement. 'There's someone I want to see.'

Henry remounted his horse. Chilling fear gripped his bowels. Mary had cut off his lifeline, his future. What now? *Dorcas.* Slamming his heels into his horse's sides, he retraced his route. But this time he kept up a breakneck speed all the way. So what if he was seen? People could think what they liked. He stood to lose everything he cared about. Compared to that, other people's opinions counted for nothing.

By the time he reached Dorcas's cottage his horse was lathered with sweat. Sliding off, his legs trembling from unaccustomed effort, he looped the reins over the gatepost. The hinges squealed as he opened the gate and stumbled down the path.

As he rounded the corner he saw the charred and sodden remains of a bonfire on a patch of grass between the flowerbeds. Too intent on his purpose to wonder at its unusual siting he hurried on towards the closed door. Normally she only closed it when he was there, or when she went out. He turned the knob. The door was locked. She probably she didn't want to see any callers. But she had to be in there. She had to. He rapped briskly then hammered with his fist, rehearsing apologies and promises.

After a minute he pressed his ear to the wood listening for a sound, any sound, to indicate a presence. There was nothing. If she wasn't inside, where in God's name was she? He ran towards the orchard then searched the rest of the garden, peering into the shed and the wood store. He couldn't leave without seeing her. He would have to wait until she got back.

The key. He knew she never took it with her; she was afraid of mislaying it. He looked for the flowerpot. Tipping it, he snatched up the key and fumbled it into the lock.

As he stepped over the threshold he paused. The cottage was different. There was no smell of bread baking, no tang of apple wood burning on the fire. The living-room was tidier than he'd ever seen it. The usual clutter of books and papers, the vases of flowers, bits of painting paraphernalia, the faded emerald and crimson paisley shawl she sometimes wore against the morning and evening chill were all gone.

He walked quickly through to the kitchen. It was equally tidy and spotless. He raced up the narrow staircase and into the bedroom that was as familiar to him as his own. The bed had been stripped. Blankets and quilt lay neatly folded below the pillows on the bare mattress. The dressing-table was bare. In dread he wrenched open the doors of the old oak wardrobe. It was empty. The room spun, blackness yawning in front of him. He staggered backwards and sank on to the bed clutching the brass rail at its foot.

He sucked in breaths, willing the faintness away. Icy perspiration soaked his clothing, beaded his forehead and dampened his palms. He pulled himself up and walked unsteadily down the stairs. A letter: there had to be a letter. He searched: scanning every surface, opening every drawer and cupboard. All right so she was angry. But she wouldn't have gone without a word. Thirty years had to count for something. For God's sake it was almost a lifetime. She wouldn't just leave. Not after all this time. Not after all they had meant to each other. Not *Dorcas*.

But she had.

Chapter Twenty-three

After another restless night Edwin forced down some breakfast and left the manse at 7.30. Sleep would have been impossible anyway because of the noise. On regatta day preparations started early.

In the village's main street he held ladders while men tacked up red, white and blue bunting that zig-zagged all the way from the top to the bottom of the road. On the open ground in front of the carpenters' workshop he helped lay boards over the saw pit, then carried trestles and planks to form a make-shift stage for part of the afternoon's entertainment.

At midmorning he returned to the manse, dragged a folding table out to the front gate, filled every cup and glass he could find with lemonade, and called the sweating thirsty men to help themselves. They gulped down the tart liquid with more mockery and banter than thanks as they wiped their mouths on brawny hands. He grinned, recognizing approval and acceptance as they stomped away to the next task.

Down on Williams's field where stalls were being set up he carried benches into the tea tent. Along one side of the field wagons of different sizes were being decorated with flowers and greenery ready for the carnival procession later in the afternoon. He pinned swags of dark blue cloth around the platform where the band would play and unloaded wooden chairs from the schoolroom off a cart.

At one o'clock, having worked off some of the physical tension generated by increasing anxiety, he returned to the manse to wash and eat cold ham and fried potatoes. It was he who had told Grace she needed to rest and recover. It had been his idea she took time to think about what he had told her. He hadn't realized how hard the waiting would be.

By two he was out in the street again. People were pouring in from all parts of the village. Most came on foot. But the occasional farm trailer creaked past drawn by a huge carthorse with fringed hoofs the size of dinner plates and crammed with laughing youngsters perched on straw bales.

Edwin remained near the manse gate, making himself available to those who attended village functions seeking comfort and company. Most were regulars at chapel and he had come to know them well. As usual he learned more than he wished to about various ailments, and nodded sympathetically at the latest developments in family feuds and fallings out with neighbours. While he listened, responding to the cheerful greetings of passers-by with a nod, a smile or a wave, he could not resist glancing up the street. That was the direction from which she would come. If she came. Please let her come. Then for a moment he was alone.

'All right, Reverend?'

He turned. Pushing an elderly perambulator, Martha Tamblin was crossing the road from Miner's Row. She had changed her normal working clothes for a full-sleeved, cream pintucked blouse and dark-green skirt. A straw boater with a faded red band shaded her eyes from the sun.

'Good afternoon, Mrs Tamblin.' As she drew level he looked into the pram. Baby Mark was asleep at the top end; Daniel sat at the bottom, his chubby legs dangling from the calf-length trousers of an over-large sailor suit. Walking beside Martha, Polly held her younger sister's hand. Both girls wore frilled white pinafores over pink cotton dresses and had ribbons in their hair.

'Hello,' Edwin smiled. 'You're both looking very pretty this afternoon.'

'We're going to see the 'gatta,' Meg beamed.

'I hope you have a lovely time.' Digging a hand into his pocket and swiftly sorting the coins by touch, he withdrew a shilling. Looking to Martha for permission – granted with a nod and a grateful smile – he handed it to Polly. Her eyes widened and her pale cheeks turned rosy with pleasure.

'Can I have one?' Meg demanded.

'Sshhh.' Polly tugged her sister's hand, darting a shy glance at Edwin. 'It's for all of us.'

'There's a sweet stall down on the quay,' Edwin said. 'And Mr Benny is there with his barrow selling paper windmills.'

'Dan'l want a windmill,' Meg announced.

'What do you say, Pol?' Martha prompted gently.

'Thank you, Mr Philpotts.' Polly's cheeks dimpled briefly. It was the first time Edwin had seen her smile.

'It's a pleasure, Polly.'

'Bless you, Reverend,' Martha murmured.

'Can we go now, Nan?' Meg was edging backwards, dragging her sister away.

'The children are looking well, Mrs Tamblin. So are you.'

Martha rolled her eyes. ''Tis some job, Reverend. But Poll's good as gold. We're doing all right. Going down the quay are you?'

'I expect I will later.'

'May see you down there then.' With a nod Martha shepherded her grandchildren away.

Edwin looked up the road again. *Please, Grace. Please come.* He walked slowly down towards the carpenters' workshop. Standing at the back he watched an appreciative

396

crowd tap their feet and join in the chorus of popular songs from the music hall sung by Edie Banks and Stanley Bird. Stan and Edie were popular entertainers at chapel and village functions, tailoring their repertoire to suit the occasion and the venue. This afternoon they were accompanied on an ancient accordion by Zeb Rollins who, having abandoned his crab pots for the day, mouthed 'Af'noon, Rev'rend' across the heads of the audience; and on the violin by farmer Donald Keverne.

Edwin had only been in the village a week when he learned about Donald's legendary gift from Mrs Nancholas, the chapel organist. Donald had inherited the violin from his grandfather who had also taught him to play. After the old man died Donald married the only child of a neighbouring farmer. This happy union had united two farms and produced three strapping sons. But Donald's well-meaning attempts to soothe their teething or tantrums by playing his violin had the opposite effect. Eventually his harassed wife banished him to the cow byre to practise.

Donald's discovery that the cows responded to his playing by increasing their milk yield had been met with hoots of derision from other farmers. Until a test conducted under strict conditions vindicated his claim. His status had soared. Any farmer with a decreasing yield, a nervous

397

heifer giving birth for the first time, even a bad-tempered bull, sent for Donald and his violin.

The song ended to an enthusiastic burst of applause. As Zeb and Donald struck up a new tune Edwin turned away, looking up and down the road. Was it possible that with so many people around he might have missed her? Had she seen him talking to someone or listening to the music and been reluctant to interrupt? He would try the quay.

It was crowded. So was the water. Boats of varying sizes milled around the start and finish lines of a course marked by buoys and flags. In tiny craft little bigger than a clam-shell eight-year-olds plied the short oars like veterans. Teenagers in clinker-built randans traded insults as they rowed round each other. Further down the river a slender gig sliced through the water like a knife blade, powered by six burly men who bent and stretched in perfect unison over the sweeps.

At the back of the quay he saw Polly and Megan among the clamouring throng surrounding the confectionery stall. Another group of children gazed fascinated at the brightly coloured paper windmills. Standing upright in jars and buckets on a flat-topped wheelbarrow they hummed as they spun in the breeze.

In the water a few feet from the quay a dozen boys, supple as eels, were diving for a china plate. The watching crowd in their Sunday-best clothes laughed and clapped as the victor shot to the surface, spurting a fountain of water through his pursed lips. A grin split his face as he held the blue and white patterned plate high above his head. Then splashing his way to the quay he clambered out dripping, to claim his prize. A scolding mother wrapped a ragged towel around the hunched shoulders of another shivering urchin.

Scanning the faces, not seeing the one he sought, Edwin tried to keep his disappointment hidden as he turned away. More from habit than hope he glanced up the road towards the village. His heart leaped violently. Wearing a pale-blue dress of some finely pleated material trimmed with white lace, and a matching hat, Grace was walking down towards him, apparently alone.

Immediately he started towards her. His heart gave another lurch as she gave a little wave, only to hesitate as if wondering whether she should have. The days and nights of agony seesawing between hope and dread were forgotten. As they drew closer her lashes dropped to veil her eyes and a fiery blush flooded her face.

'You surely didn't walk all the way?' he blurted, concern overriding his normal good manners.

She looked up, shaking her head. 'Uncle

John dropped me off by the school.'

As a roar of approval went up they both looked towards the quay.

'That will be the shovel race,' Grace said. At his blank expression she explained. 'Each boat has a team of four. Only instead of oars they have to use shovels. It's really hard work and always hugely popular.'

'Would you like to watch it?' Edwin offered instantly. 'I'd be happy to escort you.'

Grace glanced away for an instant, clearly reluctant. 'It's very kind of you but I'd rather not.'

Something cold and slippery flopped over inside him. Terrified, dreading her rejection, he didn't know what to say, what to do. Her colour deepened and she twisted the silk cords of her pale-blue velvet drawstring bag.

'Would' – swallowing, she moistened her lips – 'would you mind if we walked round to the field instead?'

Relief engulfed him like a tidal wave. 'Of course not. It's quite a crush.' The corners of his mouth turned down briefly then he smiled. 'Noisy as well.' He offered her his arm and felt his heart swell with delight and pride when she slipped her hand under his elbow. They started walking. 'It's such a pleasure to see you ... looking so much recovered,' he added hastily. *Slowly. Slowly. Don't rush. Give her time.*

She tilted her head shyly. 'Thank you. I'm

feeling very much better.'

At the junction they turned down the hill towards the bridge. Behind them, music-hall singers and musicians were sitting in the sun laughing and chatting as they enjoyed a well-earned cup of tea. The audience had dispersed. For a moment the street was empty. Edwin felt Grace's fingers tighten briefly on his arm, heard her soft intake of breath.

'I wanted to say,' she began. Glancing down he could see her cheeks flaming beneath the edge of her hat. 'I can only imagine what – what it cost you to tell me. Not just what had happened, but your thoughts and feelings. That must have taken great courage. It seems to me those events have given you far greater understanding of – of your congregation. Surely such understanding and – and compassion must make you a better minister? Your superiors think so. I mean, they could have asked you to leave the church... It would have been wrong and unfair, but no doubt they could have found a way to justify their decision. Yet they didn't. Instead they moved you from missionary work to pastoral care.' She swallowed again. 'I'm so very glad they did. And that you came here, to Treworthal. For if you had not, then I – we...' She faltered, breathless with effort.

While she was talking they had crossed the bridge and reached the open gateway into the field. Stopping abruptly under the leafy canopy of the huge oak that formed part of the hedge, Edwin turned to her, his own fingers covering hers where they rested on his forearm. His hand trembled.

'This may be too soon,' he blurted, encouraged by her confession and unable any longer to contain his desperate need. 'If I have mistaken your kindness for something else then I most humbly beg your pardon. But if I have not, if you do care for me.' His voice cracked and he cleared his throat. 'Grace, the first day I saw you I *knew*. You were the woman I wanted to spend my life with. Since then everything I have learned about you has only made me love you more.' He watched her face change as every muscle that had been held taut by nervousness relaxed. Her flush of anxiety softened into glowing happiness.

'You do? Oh, Edwin. I wasn't sure. I've waited – hoped– I have loved you for weeks. But I thought– I was afraid–'

'You do?' His voice jumped an octave. 'Then would you be willing to consider– Grace, it would make me the happiest man on earth if you would marry me. Will you, please?'

Her eyes sparkled. Her smile was radiant. 'Oh yes, Edwin. I will. I will.'

Clasping her fingers he raised them to his lips. She stepped closer and rested her cheek against his hand. He could not resist. Bending to avoid her hat he pressed his lips gently to hers. Her mouth was warm and soft and shyly responsive. Profoundly moved he drew back and looked into her widening eyes.

'Oh,' she whispered. 'I never dreamed...' She touched her lips. Her fingers were trembling.

He coughed to clear the lump from his throat. 'I think perhaps a cup of tea?'

She nodded gratefully.

As he drew her hand through his arm she glanced up at him. 'E-Edwin, if we cross the field like this—'

'Exactly. The entire village will know before nightfall.' His grin faded. 'Or would you prefer to wait until I've spoken to your father?'

Grace smiled up at him, her fingers tightening on his arm. 'No. I just wanted you to be aware.'

'I am.' Covering her hand with his own he glanced towards the women grouped round the nearest stall, all staring in their direction. 'In any case, it looks as if my concern is far too late.'

Grace darted him a joyous smile. 'Oh well.'

As he gazed at her his mind flashed back to the day the Elders told him he had to leave India. It had seemed like the end of the world. Yet if none of that had happened he wouldn't be here now. God did indeed move in mysterious ways. 'Ready?'

Beside him Grace drew a breath and nodded. 'Ready.'

An hour later, while they watched a man dressed up in a nightshirt and nightcap expertly manoeuvring a small punt to try and evade the six-oar gig chasing him, he listened as Grace told him about her letter from Mary.

'Apparently Dorcas went to see her.'

'Ah. Then the wedding?'

'Will not now take place,' Grace said. 'I had a letter from Dorcas as well. She wanted me to understand that she meant Mary no ill, but believed it only right that Mary know the truth. Anyway, Dorcas has left the village.'

'Permanently?'

Grace nodded. 'The thing is – Edwin, she's given her cottage to me.'

His brows rose. 'What a remarkably generous gesture.'

'You're wondering why. So did I. I've never– I meant I simply couldn't imagine why she would.' Grace's cheeks grew rosy and she broke off, shaking her head.

'She did give you a reason?' Edwin enquired gently, already suspecting what it was and moved by the loneliness implicit in the gift.

Grace's colour deepened as she nodded.

'She said I was the only genuine member of the entire Damerel family. But I don't think she meant to include the twins, do you?'

'I'm sure she didn't.'

'Anyway, she had always enjoyed my visits and the gift was a small token of her esteem. She said that though I will live in other places–' Grace broke off. 'How could she possibly know that?'

'Mrs Renowden was an artist. Artists are acutely sensitive observers. In all honesty, I don't think there are many people to whom our engagement will come as a complete surprise.'

Grace darted him a shy glance. 'Mary guessed weeks ago.'

Edwin smiled. 'A lady of exceptional good sense. What else did Mrs Renowden say?'

'That the cottage meant I would always have a home in Cornwall to come back to. Then she wished us every happiness.'

Cold February rain driven by a gusty wind lashed against the office windows. Henry Damerel slumped against the button-back brown leather, his hands hanging loosely over the arms. Flames danced in the small grate but made little impact on the chilly draught creeping in under the panelled door.

Wearing expressions that matched the sombre formality of their black coats and striped trousers, his solicitor and bank manager sat on the far side of a table covered with neat piles of documents.

Sunk in bitterness he barely listened as procedures relating to his bankruptcy and the closure of Wheal Providence were explained.

A lifetime's work: decades of juggling, of strain, of effort, and for what? He had lost everything. All saleable machinery had been auctioned off to raise money to pay some of his creditors. Everyone blamed him. But of all of them he had lost the most. What more did they think he could have done?

The house and estate were being bought by some industrialist from the Midlands who wanted to retire to Cornwall. The damned upstart had even wanted to retain the servants. Not one, God rot them, had refused. Bitterness burned, hot and acid in Henry's gut. So much for loyalty.

At least he was free of his mother-in-law. John Ainsley had found her a small town house in Truro and dealt with everything from legal arrangements to transferring her furniture. Resentment curled Henry's hands into fists. John was safe, untouched. His life was continuing just as it always had. He was even staying on at the lodge: the industrialist only too delighted at the convenience of having a doctor at the top of the drive.

Henry rubbed his aching forehead. Six months ago he had been a man of property and substance. The situation had been difficult, even precarious. But with Mary's money he could have turned it all around. He could have made Wheal Providence profitable again. He'd been willing to give her what she had wanted. But just because he'd forgotten to tell her about something that was none of her damn business anyway, now all he owned were his clothes. Even the roof over his head belonged to his daughter.

If Dorcas had told him she had come into money he would never have taken up with Mary. He had been doing his utmost to save the mine, and they had both deserted him.

How had Dorcas found out he had mortgaged the cottage to the bank then been unable to keep up the payments? To learn that she had bought the cottage had been shock enough, but that she should have given it to Grace – that news had stunned him.

Why Grace? He longed to know. But he wouldn't ask. He had his pride. Besides, he wasn't sure how much Grace knew about his relationship with Dorcas. Not that it was any of her business.

All Grace had said was that the gift had been unexpected and a great shock. Then she had told him he could, if he wished, live with her. After the wedding, when she moved into the manse with Edwin, he could stay on at the cottage and Rose would come in three times a week to cook for him. He'd agreed. Where else could he have gone?

Grace had changed. It wasn't just her marriage. Ever since Louise's death she had been different. He couldn't imagine what Edwin Philpotts saw in her. She had none of Zoe's sparkle or beauty. Her only talent was taking care of the village's lame ducks.

In the past when he had reminded her of her responsibility to the family she had always apologized and made additional efforts to please.

Now when he complained of her neglect, or pointed out her shortcomings, she simply waited until he'd finished then asked him to excuse her and left.

What really infuriated – *unnerved* – him was the expression in her eyes. She tried to hide it. But he wasn't blind nor was he stupid. How dare she look at him like that? With *pity*.

'Mr Damerel?'

He looked up. Both men were observing him over half-moon spectacles, clearly waiting for his response to a question he hadn't even heard.

He flapped a hand. 'Do what you like. I don't care.'

Chapter Twenty-four

Freshly bathed, wearing a loose light robe of pale pink double-layered muslin with ribbon ties and trimming, Grace sat at the breakfast-table enjoying a second cup of tea while she ran through in her head all she hoped to do that day. She glanced up as the door opened.

'Fetch some more toast, shall I?' Violet enquired, as she set down a small pile of mail by her mistress's empty plate. 'Eating for two now, you are.'

'Honestly, Violet, if you and Rose had your way I would look like a bolster.' She smiled up into the maid's concerned face. 'I'm fine, really.'

'Ben Hooper have sent down a great basket of fruit and veg.'

'That was kind of him. He really shouldn't though. All the produce belongs to the new owner now.'

Violet snorted. 'He got more'n enough. Anyway, I reck'n Ben want to say thanks for all you done for Kate while she was mourning her granfer. She still miss him something awful. Shame he never seen the babby.'

'At least he lived long enough to see Kate

409

married. He promised he would. He even walked her down the aisle.'

Violet's normally dour features softened. 'Get on, Kate near enough carried him. Still, he didn't weigh no more'n a handful of feathers. I tell you, miss – madam, I should say – Rose and me stopped breathing. We was both afraid he'd never get so far as the front pew' She looked round as the door opened again.

'Here's Master. If you're sure you don't want nothing else I'll go and get on.'

'Thank you, Violet. I'll see you later.'

Grace felt her heart swell with love as her husband passed the maid with a nod and a smile. She raised her face as he dropped a kiss on her forehead then bent to lay a gentle hand over the curve of her stomach.

'How are you both?'

'Blooming. Is Mrs Endean...?'

'She died an hour ago. It was very peaceful. But her sister was rather upset so I stayed while her daughter went for the undertaker. George Penrose has had a busy time since Christmas.'

Grace laid her hand over his in silent sympathy. 'Sit with me for a moment. Would you like a cup of tea?'

Shaking his head he pulled out a chair and sat close enough to hold her hand. His open affection for her was something she treasured and gave thanks for every day.

'No, I'm awash with tea.' He glanced at the mail beside her plate. 'Anything interesting?'

'Lots.' Grace sifted the pile. 'Bryce and Tarun are off to Tibet again. In fact as the letter was written a month ago they are probably there by now. There's a postcard from Mary.'

'Where is she?'

'Scotland. She says the scenery is absolutely glorious.' Grace touched his face with loving fingers. 'I am so very grateful for you.'

Catching her hand he pressed his lips to her palm.

'There's also a summons from Granny Hester.' She pulled a wry face. 'She says she's had a letter from Zoe but complains no one ever goes to visit her.'

'You went to see her the week before last.'

Grace nodded. 'I expect she's forgotten. Her memory isn't what it was.'

'It's selective, certainly,' Edwin said. 'Tell me when you plan to go and I'll come too.'

Grace felt a rush a gratitude and relief. 'Would you? I'd really appreciate it. But you're already so busy.'

'Hush,' he scolded. 'I know if you don't go you will only worry. But I'm not having you bullied or upset, especially now.'

'You're so kind to me.'

'I love you,' he said simply.

'I'm worried about Zoe.'

'Why? Your grandmother's descriptions paint a picture of a young woman at the top of her profession enjoying all the lavish trappings of stardom.'

'I know. I truly wish I could believe Zoe's life is as perfect as she says it is. But' – she shrugged – 'haven't you noticed? Everything is always wonderful. Nothing ever goes wrong. Perhaps it really is like that. I do hope it is. Only...'

'You don't think so.'

She shook her head. 'Granny Hester might know more. But even if she does she's unlikely to tell me.'

'She might tell me though, especially if she's worried. Besides, after her behaviour last time she knows I won't let you visit her on your own.'

Grace gazed at him in dawning comprehension. 'So this letter is a ploy to get you to visit her?'

'Possibly. We'll find out when we go. Perhaps we'll call in on your father on our way home. I know he's made it clear he doesn't want to see anyone, but John's worried about the amount he's drinking.'

Grace sighed. 'I wish there was something–'

'There isn't, Grace,' Edwin interrupted gently. 'One of the many things I love about you is your generous heart. But when people choose how they live their lives they must also take responsibility for the results of their choices.'

Twining her fingers in his she smiled at him. 'I am the happiest, most blessed woman I know.' She sighed. 'I am also wasting time when there is so much waiting to be done.'

'It will wait a little longer.' He kissed her hand then helped her to her feet. 'I've been down to the hall. Edna and her ladies have already made a small mountain of cheese sandwiches to go with the soup. Mrs Laity had set up three long tables to display the clothes, one each for men women and children. Judging by the piles on each, people have been incredibly generous.'

'I hoped they would be. Since Wheal Providence shut down the miners and their families have had a desperate time. Helping with food and clothes is all very well, but what the men really need is work. I saw a piece in the paper about a place that opened in London recently. It's called a Labour Exchange. Employers who need workers send in information about vacant positions. While men looking for work go there to find jobs. I was just wondering if we might be able to do something similar here in the village.'

The adoration on her husband's face warmed her heart and her cheeks. 'What?' she laughed, as he slowly shook his head.

'You,' he said simply. 'You are a constant

413

joy to me. It's an excellent idea.'

Hearing the heavy thud of the front-door knocker they exchanged a wry smile.

'Go on,' she said, releasing him.

'We'll talk about it later,' he promised.

Tapping briefly, Violet popped her head around the door. 'Mr Angove to see you, Reverend. Put'n in your study, shall I?'

'Thank you, Violet.' He smiled over his shoulder and followed the maid as she clumped out.

Grace stood for a moment, her hand on her belly, thinking of how far she had come. Though the journey had been hard, it had been infinitely worthwhile. The baby kicked against her palm. Her smile widened. It was time she dressed. There was work to do.

The publishers hope that this book has given you enjoyable reading. Large Print Books are especially designed to be as easy to see and hold as possible. If you wish a complete list of our books please ask at your local library or write directly to:

Magna Large Print Books
Magna House, Long Preston,
Skipton, North Yorkshire.
BD23 4ND